THE OTHER SIDE OF SUMMER

ELYSE DOUGLAS

COPYRIGHT

ISBN-13: 978-1512024302
ISBN-10: 1512024309

Summer opens its wide lemony
sky and blesses all true lovers with
its good hot sun.

—*Allison Fields*

For Constance, who roams the beach and looks at stars.

THE OTHER SIDE OF SUMMER

Part 1

The Chance Lover

Chapter 1

25 Years Ago

Thirty-one-year-old Joanna Halloran stared uncertainly out the open bedroom window of her beach house, perched on a rocky bluff facing the Atlantic Ocean. The storm crawled toward her from across the sea, like a dark eerie fog. Erratic bursts of wet wind punched at the curtains, scattering her long ash blond hair, and bullying the gulls as they strained against it, losing strength and altitude.

Restless, Joanna lit a cigarette. She raked strands of hair from her clear almond eyes, as she watched the waves roll in and pound the beach. What was once a sizzling July afternoon was suddenly plunged into an astonishing gray and purple darkness, reminding her of a bruise, as if the world had received a violent punch from Mother Nature.

When the first sound of thunder rattled heaven and earth, she wondered if soldiers heard such sounds in battle. Lightning flashed from cloud to cloud in jagged veins, startling her. She stepped back from the window, mesmerized, recalling that for the Vikings, lightning was produced by Thor, as he rode his chariot across the clouds, striking an anvil with his hammer.

As the first drops of slashing rain struck the window, she paced, feeling a stiffness in her right foot that often came after she walked too much or stood for too long. It had been a birth defect, a deformity that many childhood operations had failed to correct, and so she had a slight limp.

She drifted back to the window, preoccupied. Everything had a sharpened edge to it: the wind, the sea, her thoughts and emotions. She felt a strange kind of agitation, as if the end and the beginning of a cycle of life were about to collide.

As a professional astrologer, she knew that change was coming and that it would probably come from the sea. Neptune, the ruler of the sea—the ruler of confusion and deception—was in aspect. Uranus, the ruler of unexpected events and erratic change, was aspecting her Sun and Moon. Mars, the ruler of force and impulsiveness, and Venus, representing love and pleasure, were dynamically aspected. Some "thing," some event, was poised to strike.

She leaned toward the beaded up window, touching its cool glass with the tips of her fingers, as if to reach out and initiate an act of change. She wanted it—and she feared it.

Although most people think that astrology is about fortune telling, Joanna knew that it is not. It's a science and, like any science, you can't always accurately predict the outcome of a situation: there are too many variables. All she could do was forecast the trends—and this trend shouted of change.

In the distance she heard the drone of an airplane engine. It chilled her. Frightened her. Who would be flying in this storm?

Thirty three-year-old Robert Zachary Harrison should have waited out the storm in Connecticut, before flying to Block Island. But his fiancée, Connie, was waiting. They had been planning this weekend for over two months, to iron out the final details of their wedding, which was only a month away.

He took off at a little after 2pm, certain he'd beat the storm. He pointed his blue and white single-engine plane east, toward the sea. Once airborne, he encountered gray stringy clouds and bumpy skies. He stared uneasily as he drifted over a red lighthouse, heading out to sea. He adjusted the throttle and eased back on the controls. The plane ascended, gliding high above white caps. A burst of wind jolted it and it jerked and veered.

He flew into the darkening afternoon feeling that he had total control of the airplane—until he was about 70 miles from Block Island. Then the sky turned ugly. Muscular gusts rammed him, shuttering the craft. He fought the turbulence, humming an improvised tune to help calm his nerves, a technique he'd learned as a fighter pilot in Vietnam.

His throat went dry, his neck and forehead dampened. As a driving rain beat against the windows, his hands tightened on the controls. His air speed became erratic. The altimeter, which measured height, showed a steady loss of altitude. Robert felt that pit-of-the stomach sensation of freefall as the plane plunged and rose, straining against the updrafts and downdrafts.

A wall of wind punched him so hard that it jarred his eyeballs. The engine sputtered and coughed, teetering on the edge of a stall—and if it stalled—the plane would drop from the sky. Robert frantically reached for his radio to call out his position and request the location of the nearest airport to land. He issued a mayday call just as a gut wrenching gust slapped him. It tossed the plane, like a toy, toward the raging sea.

Robert slammed the throttle forward, fighting for control, teeth clinched, temples pounding. At the last feverish moment, he yanked back hard on the yoke. The plane caught an updraft and the engine growled to life, rising, struggling for height. Robert had just caught a grateful breath, when, to his horror, another wind shear pitched him into a sharp dive. His teeth clamped down on his bottom lip. In terror, he struggled for altitude, bracing for impact. As the hard angry sea rushed up at him, he cursed it, refusing defeat. He wrestled the controls.

The airplane skipped across the top of the water, like a flat stone across a lake. Robert braced for impact. A towering wave licked at him like the angry tongue of a sea monster. It caught him.

Robert covered his face with his arms, as a powerful jolt pitched him forward, shattering glass, punching the air from his lungs in a desperate scream. A shock spray of cold water exploded across his body as the plane unraveled angrily around him.

Miraculously, he was tossed into the hostile, churning sea, struggling for breath, hands slapping at dark choppy water. He yelled, reaching for any debris to cling to, and sank beneath a huge curling wave.

As the storm was sliding off to the west, Joanna approached the face of the cliff and gingerly descended the steep wooden stairs to the broad damp beach below. She wandered toward the edge of the water, binoculars about her neck. She wore brown khakis, rolled up above her ankles, and a loose fitting yellow polo shirt. Her hair was tied in a ponytail. A white canvas beach bag, swung over her left shoulder, held flip-flops and a towel, just in case she decided to go for a swim.

She roamed the beach in the windy, unstable afternoon, shading her eyes as she viewed the expanse of sea. It was after 4 o'clock and the beach was deserted. The waves were breaking heavy on the shore. It was one of her favorite times to walk the beach—just after a storm. She drifted to the edge of the tide as waves splashed and foamed around her ankles. The water was cool and refreshing and helped to ease some of the aching in her right foot. She strolled with her hands locked behind her back, squinting into the gray moving sky. She watched the raw surf curve and break across the beach, observing sandpipers skitter along the edge of the foam, pecking for food.

She lifted the binoculars to her eyes and scanned the horizon, looking at white caps and distant sails. Smoky white and purple wisps of clouds hugged the horizon. She picked at the shells and toed the sand, exploring the stringy seaweed, driftwood and plastic trash, all pushed to shore by the storm. Again she pointed her binoculars toward the sea. She spotted something bobbing in the waves.

She jolted erect, adjusting the focus. At first she thought it was a kayak. She moved toward the water, straining her eyes. Was it some kind of raft? The current was drawing it toward the shore.

Her eyes shifted, and then focused. She saw a body—a person—clinging to a piece of something, floating in toward the beach. It drifted toward a large swell, was seized by the current and then tossed helplessly, bobbing and twisting in a surging wave. It was a man! He was desperately holding on.

Joanna dropped her bag and binoculars, darted into the water, plunged into the cold surf and swam toward him. Coming up for air, she saw him clinging to a piece of debris, wearing an orange life preserver.

As she closed in, another wave struck, smashing down on top of them, spinning him away from her. She dropped under the wave, came up, recovered and relaxed, feeling her shirt swimming around her. She allowed the current to do the work; to carry her in the same direction as the man. Drawing near, she kicked and swam, using all her strength to reach him, before the next charging waves impacted. One threatened, gathering rolling strength, rumbling toward them like thunder. The man reached for her weakly, arms flailing, his pallid face stretched in agony.

"Help me…," he called.

With her outstretched hand, she reached and snagged him by the collar of his shirt. She yanked him toward her.

The wave struck. Joanna wrapped him with her arms as it pounded them, shoving them carelessly toward the beach.

Together, they thrashed toward shore, gasping. Catching her breath, Joanna struggled to her feet, stumbling for balance across the rocky bottom. Anchoring herself, she helped the man to find his footing. She wrapped an arm around his waist and led him up the beach to safety.

Drained, he wavered, and then dropped to his knees, exhausted. Joanna helped him shed the life preserver. She stood over him, chest heaving, flinging stringy wet hair and water from her eyes. She stared down at a strongly built man, in his 30s, wearing a ripped blue shirt and torn khakis. His pale warrior face showed nicks and cuts. The determined chin had a swollen white gash. His short black hair was caked with grease, and he shivered.

She anxiously searched the long expanse of beach, but no one was close.

"I'll go get help," Joanna said, still panting.

He struggled to speak. "Wait…"

She paused in mid stride. "I'll be right back."

The man coughed and spit water. "No…No…don't leave…"

She hurried to her bag, yanked out her beach towel and returned to him, wrapping it around his trembling shoulders.

"Can you stand?" she asked.

"No…look… I need to lie here… just for…a …minute."

He toppled over and rolled onto his back, his eyes pinched shut.

"Are you in pain?" Joanna asked.

He shook his head. "I'll be okay…okay…." He lay still.

Conflict and hesitation came over her face. Her damp clothes clung to her and she trembled. The sun reappeared and flecked the sea golden. It bathed and warmed them just enough to briefly revive him. His eyes opened.

"My house is just up those stairs," Joanna said, pointing to the wooden stairs that climbed the cliff. "Can you make it?"

"I…I think… so."

"Is anything broken?"

"No…I don't think so. Let's…try….for it."

She crouched, took his left arm and helped lift him to his feet. He groaned and winced as they staggered across the sand to the foot of the stairs. He paused, winded. "Damn! My left leg's giving out on me."

"Put your left arm around my shoulder. I'll help you up," Joanna said.

They ascended the first flight—about 10 stairs—and then rested on the level platform before continuing up the final 20. Joanna's own foot throbbed and she took the opportunity to arch and stretch it.

They progressed in slow, agonizing steps. At the crest, Robert paused again. "You're strong," he said, grimacing.

Joanna shouldered him on until they reached the house and mounted the few stairs to the wraparound deck. She eased him down into a cushioned white wicker chair. He slackened and let out a long sibilant sigh.

"I'll call a doctor," Joanna said, starting for the door.

He shook his head. "No… I'm okay…" he said, weakly. "I'll be alright…"

Joanna stood concerned and anxious, seeking answers. "You should go to the hospital…"

"No! Hell, no. I'll be fine…" He softened. "Really…"

Joanna swallowed hard. "Were there others?"

"No…no… just me. Can you get me to a bed or couch? And…water…please."

Joanna rushed inside, poured a glass of spring water and took it to him. He drank half, slowly. His chaotic eyes stared ahead, at nothing. He trembled. His hands began to shake. The glass fell from his grasp and shattered. He looked up at her pitifully.

Chapter 2

Fifteen minutes later, Robert Harrison was asleep in the guest bedroom, wearing one of Joanna's old baggy T-shirts and a pair of swimming trunks her brother had left during his last visit.

Joanna spent the next hour out on the deck, striding back and forth, arguing with herself. She should call for help, but the last thing she wanted were people crawling through her house: emergency workers, reporters, TV cameramen, barking out questions, snapping pictures. She could just see the local headlines. *Mermaid Occultist saves Man from Sea.*

She poured herself a glass of white wine. Selfish? Yes. Self preservation? Yes. She tilted her head slightly to the left as she sipped. Would it help her book sales? Yes. Would it be worth it? No. Definitely not. It had taken years to build respect and a good reputation as a consultant and author in a field where most people thought she was an eccentric nut.

She turned toward the house. But what if he was seriously injured? She knew a doctor—only a half hour away in Amagansett. Dr. Ned Palmer. He liked her. They had dated once over a year ago. He'd asked her out twice since but she'd always made an excuse.

Could she trust him not to blab the story all over Long Island? She circled the space, struggling for a way out, finally stepping inside and picking up the phone.

She found the doctor's number in her address book and dialed it. It was Friday afternoon and she hoped he'd already left the office for the weekend. When his secretary answered, Joanna paused before asking to speak with him.

Joanna sat in a wicker chair on the porch, her knees pulled up to her chest. She'd showered and washed her hair and changed into white cotton pants and a royal blue sweat shirt. The storm had left behind chilly easterly winds and a damp briny odor that she loved. She watched the dramatic sunset, staring out of focus at the blush of the clouds, following the birds as they drifted lazily over the cliffs, feeling the pace of the day diminish and soften. Off in the gentle throb of evening, she heard insects scratch and sing; heard the gentle whisper of the sea below. A jeering restlessness arose. As she reviewed the events of the afternoon, she grew increasingly agitated.

She nibbled cheese and was on her third glass of wine, irritated that her life was disrupted by such an absurd event: a man washing up on her shore. She toyed with her long left earring—a glittering little crab—representing her astrological birth sign Cancer.

Dr. Palmer had left only an hour ago. He had arrived, tentative and concerned. He also seemed flattered that she'd called him. Joanna strongly repeated her need for secrecy and privacy. "Please, don't tell anyone about this," she pleaded.

"That depends on the patient's condition, Joanna," he'd said, authoritatively. "Now tell me who he is and where he came from."

"I don't know."

Ned Palmer was a stocky man of 38, with a square face, clipped black hair and no nonsense dark eyes. He eyed Joanna doubtfully. "Where did you find him?"

"In the sea."

Dr. Palmer's eyebrows lifted. "The people in this town never cease to amaze me. How's your foot? It looks swollen. Everything okay?"

"Yes…"

Nervous, Joanna led him into Robert's room and left them alone.

Five minutes later, Dr. Palmer joined her in the living room. "He threw me out… From what I could see, which wasn't much, he's pretty banged up. He has some superficial cuts and bruises and he twisted his left leg but he wouldn't say how. He also wouldn't say who he was or what happened to him. I offered him a sleeping pill but he refused it."

Dr. Palmer gave her a brief glance. "You sure you don't want me to call the police?"

"No…at least not yet."

"You want me to hang around for awhile?"

Joanna shifted her wary eyes toward Robert's room. "No, I'll be fine."

"Well… I didn't smell alcohol and he seems pretty normal. He should go get some tests, but he's not going to, so that's his choice."

Joanna didn't meet his eyes.

"Are you sure you're gonna be okay, Joanna?"

"Yes… fine. Thanks for coming."

The doctor pulled a breath and sighed it out. "That's one helluva catch of the day, Joanna. You be careful and call me if you need anything."

After Dr. Palmer left, Joanna had checked on Robert several times throughout the evening. He breathed uneasily, but had hardly stirred. He seemed comfortable. The doctor had placed a Band-Aid over the wound on his chin. He'd wake up soon, call his family or friends and they would come and fetch him. That would be the end of it.

When darkness descended, she lit a candle and poured another glass of wine. Having him there made her uncomfortable. She pushed up, feeling hazy and lightheaded from the wine, and looked in on him again. He had rolled over on his side, and was sleeping soundly. There was some perspiration on his forehead and upper lip. She dampened a washcloth and gently blotted his face and neck.

Standing there, she felt an unexpected pleasure. There was something sexy about having a man you've just rescued sleeping in the 4-poster bed you'd slept in as a teenager, when silly daydreams about a man drifting in from the sea in dire need of a rescuer were somewhat common. Her father and brother had toted that bed all the way up from Cincinnati two years ago.

Robert groaned, and mumbled something inaudible. He spoke again in his restless sleep. "Will…you help me…"

An indescribable emotion caused her to shift her weight from left to right; something wistful and yearning. She felt a slow burn in the center of her chest. In the dim glow of the nightlight, she admired his appealing face. She recalled his searching eyes. They'd looked up at her gratefully. She'd forgotten that. They were honest eyes. Blue?

She'd felt the firmness of his body as they'd struggled toward the house, and it was impossible not to notice his trim waist and powerful shoulders, as she had helped him into bed. He was in good physical shape. Maybe that's what had saved him. He couldn't be more than 35.

With reluctance, she left the room and returned to the deck, grabbing a blue cotton jacket and floppy beach hat on the way.

She sat quietly in the fresh night air. Her breath was shallow for a time—then it came in a jerky inhalation. How long had it been since she had been with a man? Almost two years? Yes, two years and, of course, she'd thought about it—sex. She'd even considered it a couple of times. Men had approached her. She wasn't a beauty, she knew that, but she wasn't ugly either. Often if men saw her limp, they asked if she'd twisted her ankle.

She'd always said the same thing. "No, it's a defect."

Many cooled on her after that. When she was younger, she'd had lovers: one was a social worker who wanted to save her. She often saw pity in his eyes whenever she was having a bad foot day and her limp was more pronounced. She grew to hate him.

Another lover—a struggling poet and playwright from England—told her how lucky she was. "You, Joanna, are so lucky to have that slightest of limps," he'd said, dramatically. "You are stronger because of it. Wise because of it. Blessed because of it. I have grown a better man because of it."

His intensity and constant self-indulgent bantering finally drove her crazy. She threw him out of her apartment for good after she'd read his newest play. He said that he had crafted his main character after her: a vengeful woman who was angry, pitiful and weak.

But it was after her marriage had failed some years later that Joanna decided to write about love and relationships from an astrological point of view. The book was entitled: *Astrology Looking for Love*, and it became a success in the occult world. After the second printing, it achieved moderate success within the women's movement and the growing genre of pop psychology.

Joanna poured another glass of wine and drank generously. The man in her house had also brought bitter memories of her ex-husband: a man with the face of an impractical adventurer. His eyes were always wide and restless, his promises always hollow and their bed, as she learned later, nearly always occupied with some young girl. He taught freshman psychology at Hunter College (which she thought ironic). He didn't need a wife. He needed a good psychologist to help stabilize his erratic fixation on young blonds, marijuana and cognac.

Minutes later, after the wine had softened her and dissolved the bitter creatures of her mind—the bad memories—she changed positions, sitting up cross-legged in the chair. She felt a little drunk and she liked it. It loosened her, made her sleepy. She turned back toward the house and giggled.

"Hey, Joanna, there's a strange good looking man sleeping in my bed. I rescued him. Will he rescue me?"

Chapter 3

The fragment of a terrifying dream awakened Robert with a start. He jerked up to his elbows. Even with his eyes open and bulging, the sounds and images clung to them: the shattering of glass, water gushing in, choking and trapping him. He wiped his eyes, caught a breath and pushed out of bed on wobbly legs. Dizziness overtook him and he fell backwards on the mattress in a bounce. A sharp stabbing pain in his left leg made him wince. He massaged it. Panic arose. Where was he!? What had happened!? He wiped perspiration from his face with the back of his forearm. The faint sound of raspy waves drifted in from the window.

He blinked around, taking in his surroundings. The walls were blue. The curtains were a canary yellow. They billowed like sails, catching the ocean breeze. The shiny hardwood floors beneath his bare feet felt cool. Above his head, a white ceiling fan twirled lazily, making a little clicking sound. It cooled his damp neck and chest. The furniture: a desk, a chest of drawers and a double bed, all white, seemed to glow in the sunlight, bringing peacefulness.

His full memory returned in a rush: the plane crash, the raging sea, his rescue—his rescue by the woman! He flopped backwards, trembling, gazing up at the ceiling uncomprehendingly. His eyes were quick and searching. His head pounded. His ribs were sore. His entire body felt bruised. The quiet seemed a threat.

He was terrified—irrationally terrified! How could he have survived a crash like that? How was it possible? He turned his head left, noticing a peach floral vase filled with fresh wild flowers lying next to the bed. Next to that was a pitcher of water, a washcloth and a glass. Did she bring them? How much time had passed?

He rose, stiffly, grimacing. What about Connie?!

A searing heat spread across his face and down his body. He felt oddly suspended, disconnected from his own thoughts, as if someone else were thinking them and he was observing.

Robert lifted the T-shirt and examined himself; his legs and muscular arms. There were dark bruises on his chest, arms and shoulders, but nothing seemed broken. He had been remarkably lucky. He remembered the doctor and frowned.

He shivered and perspired. "Calm down," he said at a whisper. "You're fine... You made it."

He stumbled forward, and then stopped abruptly. He felt a sudden stir of weariness. His body seemed heavy and sinking. "Connie!..." he said, with alarm. He closed his eyes and wandered back to the bed. He dropped down, flopped backwards and fell into a deep sleep.

He awoke, startled. His stomach growled; his mouth was stale and sticky. He was ravenous. Robert stood, steadied himself against the bedpost, and then shuffled over to the window. Parting the curtains and shading his eyes from the glaring afternoon sun, he peered through slitted eyes. The panoramic scene startled him. He saw an endless dazzling sea, flowing dune grass and white rolling sand. Birds soared and sang, and on the hot line of the horizon, sailboats leaned. Robert lifted the window, felt the warm intoxicating breeze and he took a deep breath. It revitalized him.

He ripped off the T-shirt and found a shabby blue cotton bathrobe in the closet—it came up short in the chest and high at the knees—but he shrugged off his ridiculous appearance and left the room, on unsteady legs.

He padded across the cool glossy wood floors, holding his sore ribs and limping slightly on his left leg. He viewed the floor-to-ceiling windows, with unobstructed views of the ocean, dune fences and distant secluded beach houses. He stepped across lavish throw rugs, glancing at seascape paintings on the white walls, as sunlight poured through skylights. He felt the high ceiling fans stir the air.

He wandered about, stiffly, like an old man, until he found the kitchen. Hunger was beating in his stomach like little fists. In the refrigerator he found milk, vegetables, orange juice, whole grain bread, cheese, yogurt and fruit juices. In the wall cabinets he found Special K. He poured a large bowl full, doused on some milk and filled a glass with orange juice. Dropping down slowly onto a wooden stool, he spooned a bite and shoved it into his mouth. His body lifted gratefully to the flavors and smell. He downed the orange juice, trembling. Ignoring his shaking hands, he ate aggressively, finishing one bowl, pouring more and finishing that. It was after he'd eaten a piece of cheese, that he began looking for her—the woman. He continued eating, stuffing his mouth full of whole grain bread, and reaching for another glass of orange juice. He looked around, listening for human sounds, feeling the pure sea air pass through the screen door that led out to the porch and wraparound deck. The day sparkled with magnificence.

He stopped chewing, closed his eyes and tried to bring the woman's face forward from the depths of his mind. Young? Old? Attractive? His usually sharp memory was blunted by fatigue and a deep sense of loss. Loss? His eyes opened. Loss? He felt his rough beard. What loss?

He chewed on that thought for a moment, and then pushed to his feet. Through the kitchen window, he saw the deck with a broad view of the ocean. He grabbed the half drunk glass of juice, and had one foot on the deck when the phone rang. He paused. It stopped on the third ring.

"Connie…?" he asked, aloud.

He stepped outside onto the deck. It was furnished with a cafe table, padded wicker furniture, potted plants and low hanging wind chimes. He stood for a time in the full glow of morning sunlight, still feeling shaky. The wind stirred the chimes, and the sound softened his ragged edges of fatigue. He tugged a wicker chair into a patch of shade, and losing the battle with an assertive weariness, he sat, sighing heavily and falling asleep.

As Joanna approached the house in her long, unhurried strides, she saw him. He was slumped in the chair, head back and turned aside. The sun was warm on her bare shoulders, and the cool afternoon wind scattered her hair, exciting her skin. She had just had a glorious swim, diving gleefully into waves, wallowing in the surf, and executing an easy 4-beat crawl out beyond the breaking waves. To complete her relaxation ritual, she lay on her orange towel under her pink beach umbrella and dozed, only vaguely aware of the pulse of sun and sea; the piling up of soft clouds on the eastern edge of the sky; a chunky gull standing stoically on one foot.

The pleasure of it all had left her tranquil and easy. The height of sensation—the intoxication—often lingered for hours. She felt like the Goddess of something. The sea. The sky. The cliffs. She felt fertile and daring, hovering delicately on the edge of desire; of wanting to merge and be absorbed. And so, she would open a bottle of wine. She would eat. She would smoke. She would work.

She approached Robert quietly. Her bikini was orange, skimpy and revealing. She knew this. She did not put on her robe. She wanted him—this man from the sea—to see her long tanned legs, her tight stomach, her round breasts. If he was to leave within hours, she wanted the hopeful pleasure of his approving eyes. The gift of the day had offered her this—this possible pleasure.

Joanna paused at the edge of the porch and with half-hooded eyes, she studied him: the housecoat lay open and askew, revealing the tight bathing suit, his broad chest and muscular legs. His face was surprisingly boyish, for the man's body, and she saw a softness there or, at least, the potential for it. His eyelashes were long, his mouth full. He did not stir or snore—not a flicker of the eyes. He slept tranquilly.

Joanna suddenly felt willful. She felt a sense of urgency. Fantasies arose. Ridiculous and prurient fantasies. She recognized the symptoms. She'd counseled them—exposed them in herself and others, using her clinical and astrological skill and training. These were the starved emotions—eccentric emotions born from loneliness, desire, guilt and fear. These were the suppressed emotions—demons rattling the cages, demanding expression—demanding to be set free.

Joanna lowered her beach bag, turning away. "A lost and pathetic woman," she thought, with a little shake of her head.

Robert made a sound—frightened. He sat up and his eyes opened, bold and wild. They fixed on Joanna, seeking answers and recognition.

She didn't speak. She couldn't.

"Where…?"

She was silent. She forced herself to focus on his face. His wan face. His painful expression.

"Where am I?" he asked.

Joanna lifted from the torso, defensively, as if he could read her thoughts. "Montauk."

He blinked fast. "Montauk?"

He still didn't seem to see her. It was as though he were in a deep well, looking up into glaring sunlight. "Montauk…Oh…Yes… Long Island…"

"Do you remember what happened?" Joanna asked, because the words rushed into her mind.

He swallowed, sitting stiffly. "Yeah…Yeah, I remember."

"The storm…"

"Yes."

"A boat?" she asked.

"Boat?"

"Yes…you must have been caught in the storm," Joanna said, now feeling his eyes on her. Perhaps appraising her.

"Boat… No…Plane…"

She stared. "What?"

"I crashed into the sea."

Stunned, Joanna stumbled over words. "…You…You crashed… How?"

"The storm."

Joanna suddenly felt naked and foolish. She pulled the robe from her beach bag and slipped it on, folding her arms.

He, too, recognized his near nakedness. He pulled the housecoat snugly about him, gripping it tightly at the collar.

"I had no idea… I mean, I thought you'd fallen from a boat. You're lucky to be alive."

"…I'm okay."

"The doctor thought you should be in a hospital."

"I told you I didn't want a doctor," he said testily.

Joanna stiffened. "You're in my house."

He turned from her, wincing a little. "Oh…is that how it is."

"Yes…"

The phone rang. Joanna went to answer it. Robert noticed her limp for the first time.

In the kitchen, Joanna reached for the telephone. "Hello."

"Joanna. It's Ned Palmer."

"Yes…"

"They're looking all over the damned ocean for that guy. Have you seen the papers or watched TV?"

"No…"

"He's Robert Harrison of *the* Harrison family. His father's a senator."

Joanna twirled the phone cord into a knot. "Oh…"

"Have you called the police?"

"No."

"Joanna…This is big stuff. Call them. Let them know he's with you."

"But…"

"Do it, Joanna! What the hell are you waiting for?!"

After she hung up, Joanna loitered in the kitchen working on several thoughts. Finally, she returned to the deck, scrutinizing him with new eyes.

He squirmed. "What is it?"

"The doctor… checking up on you."

He grinned. It was almost a smile. "Look, I have a thing about hospitals and doctors I don't know. They almost killed me once—and the doctor was an uncle. Believe me, I'm okay. I was incredibly lucky. When the plane hit the water, I was somehow thrown clear." Then, as an after thought, he continued. "Besides, I don't want the whole world knowing what an idiot I was getting caught in a storm and crashing my plane. I have too many friends and enemies who'd never let me forget it."

"They're going to find out eventually," she said.

"Eventually, yes, but not today."

Joanna moved closer. "You're Robert Harrison."

He lifted his eyes, blinking fast. "Yes. The doctor tell you?"

"Yes. They're looking everywhere for you."

He nodded. "Doesn't matter. I'll call them…I'll call them all in a little while." He sank a little lower in the chair. "In a minute…Right now I feel like I weigh 500 pounds."

"Do you want me to call for…"

He cut her off sharply. "No!"

"The Coast Guard's looking and …"

"…Yeah and the FAA and the Air Force Rescue Co-ordination Center are probably out there, too," Robert added. "They've probably given me up for dead."

"They're still looking…" Joanna said.

"Well, the truth is I feel like I'm dead, or close to it. I feel like I've been kicked by a couple of horses…and beaten with a hammer."

"That's why you should…."

He interrupted again. "…I'm not going to a hospital!"

He looked at her deeply, as if seeing her for the first time. His dull, swollen eyes pried and examined. "What's your name?"

She hesitated, feeling the pleasure of his attentiveness. His day old shadow of a beard attracted her. "Joanna."

"…Joanna. Joanna," he repeated, with a little nod. "Nice name. Thank you, Joanna, for saving my life."

"I didn't. You would have made it to the beach."

"I didn't even know I was close to the beach. I was about to drown. I don't know how I found the life preserver. I'd forgotten I kept it in the plane. It just kind of floated over to me some time after I hit the water. Makes you think, doesn't it?"

Joanna was silent.

He continued to stare at her.

She receded a little, feeling awkward.

"I must have released my seatbelt when I hit the water. But I don't remember…"

Joanna turned to the house. "Have you eaten?"

"Some cereal."

Joanna looked for some place to put her hands. She ran them through her hair. "I can fix you something hot."

He smiled. "Sounds good."

It was a lovely smile that warmed her.

"Do you live here alone?"

"…Yes. Alone." She hoped she didn't sound defensive.

Robert examined the brown two story house, with its generous upper deck, and blue shutters. "Built in the 1960's?"

"Yes. 1967."

"I like it," Robert said.

"I have pasta and chicken. I can put them together with a sauce."

His eyes lingered on her. The sea seemed close. "Good…"

She disappeared inside.

Robert massaged his eyes. Yes…they were looking for him. Connie would be frantic. His family frantic. He should get up and call. Get up and make a simple phone call to let them know he was alive and well. Have them call off the damn search.

But he didn't move. He felt made of stone. He felt a little scared. He felt damaged in some strange way. He felt removed from them all. Connie, his family, his friends were so far away. They were off on another planet in some distant galaxy and he was an astronaut who had crashed somewhere in another time and place. He was marooned. What a nice word that was, "marooned."

His thoughts seemed foreign to him, uncharacteristically soft and chaotic. He didn't have the damn strength or the inclination to push himself up and walk to the phone. "Make the call, Robert," he said, aloud.

He settled lower in the chair, as if to escape any detection. He'd make the call later, after dinner. Just another couple of hours. As he leaned his head back, he closed his eyes. An old song entered his thoughts. A little "lullaby" his grandfather Big John Harrison used to sing to him as he rocked him on his knee.

Fly with the bees and make honey, honey, honey

Work with the bees and make money, money, money
So buzz, buzz, buzz, while there's light in the day
And you'll sleep tight, tight, tight and be happy
and gay.

Robert grinned at the thought. He had been buzzing for years. Making honey and money for years, just like all the men in the Harrison family did. Old Big John Harrison, the stiff neck attorney—the steely eyed rampart who had fathered three sons—all little ramparts. He would be proud of his grandson. Surely he had risen from the dead to bless Robert's curly head and his inevitable political career.

"Yes sir," he would say, matter-of-factly. "Yes, Robert, you are the product of steel, hard work and determination. Yes, sir, Robert, you will become the President of the United States within 25 years! I know that. I sanction that! I bless that!"

The cycles of life had turned, like a well oiled machine. The relentless march toward the best grades, the best schools, the best life had pitched him through the vicissitudes of life like a javelin, never wavering toward the bull's-eye. No rain, sleet or snow had ever halted its sure sharp flight. No obstacle had ever dared to rise up and stop him or his family as they pursued their noble visions.

But Robert felt tired. So damned tired inside. He felt like an egg falling from its nest, about to shatter on the hard ground.

His eyes opened. What the hell was happening to him? These weren't the familiar thoughts of Robert Harrison, the respected, confident man. They were thorny, unmeasured thoughts—desperate thoughts. Chaotic thoughts that he'd always managed to hold in check. He shook his head, struggling for control and clarity.

The sound of the sea comforted him. Kitchen sounds, drifting from the window, comforted him. The thought of this alien woman—attractive—from another planet, calmed him. Her voice was lilting, low and pleasurable. Her liquid brown eyes held secrets. This woman who had saved his life. Saved him!? It was an astonishing thought. But saved him for what?

He should call them. Get up and make the phone call! But he didn't move. He sat rigid and obstinate, feeling the rise of some of the darkest thoughts of his life: Let his family wait and worry and believe that he was killed so that their tight grip and squeezing pressure at his throat would cease—at least for awhile. In the past, as he pursued his family's goals, he'd been tempted but had never stepped from the narrow path—he'd walked the razor's edge, even when every cell in his body had rebelled and he felt the tyranny of family obligation, heavy and burdensome.

He looked skyward. Maybe it was time he left the path. The false path. The family path, not his own. Maybe at 33 years old, it was time he went his own way—walked his own path. Perhaps it was the gods or fate or Joanna who saved him just for this singular propitious moment, giving him the opportunity of a lifetime. Perhaps it was his last opportunity.

Here, away from the world, he wasn't shackled at the ankles by the chains of his family name or by their constant expectations of him. The unremitting patter of ancestral voices, encouraging achievement and power, had already fallen into low murmurs. Robert lay dead still, mentally detaching himself from them, feeling an eerie excitement. He felt a boy's inestimable skipping-prep-school glee. He felt like a fighter pilot again—the only time in his life when he'd felt in control and free to live the life of his dreams.

As his thoughts escalated, an avalanche of emotions overwhelmed him. Fatigue struck and he became spooked. He closed his eyes. He saw the egg again. He was falling and he would shatter.

His face was slick with sweat.

Terrified, he yelled. "Help me. Help!"

Chapter 4

Robert slept fitfully. Concerned, Joanna sat next to the bed in a chair, staring into the night. She stumbled through tangled emotions, old memories and silly fantasies. She had been sitting there for at least two hours and the amber clock on the night stand said it was almost one in the morning.

Robert had called to her, his voice frantic. It had scared her. When she'd rushed out of the kitchen to the deck, he stood reaching for her, his face tight with fear, his eyes set in hope and recognition. It was stark and unmistakable. There was a catch in her heart and a release of startled truth: they knew each other well! In those few seconds—long wonderful and agonizing seconds—she saw in his eyes an irresistible invitation. In those seconds she knew she'd have him, and nothing would stop her from having him.

Now, in the bleak, sterile darkness, she retracted everything she'd felt. She had allowed herself to fall under the spell of Neptune—the planet of illusion. It can produce the ultimate deception.

Joanna left the room quietly, pulling the door shut behind her. She needed a distraction. Down the hallway, she entered her office, flipped on the light and sat down in her padded leather chair behind her oak desk. She reached into the file cabinet and drew out two folders that contained the astrological charts and data of two of her clients. Both would be calling the following morning for counseling, and Joanna felt she needed to explore their charts more deeply: the transits and progressions; the planetary movements and aspects.

The first chart involved a woman who wanted to know if she should marry "the man of her dreams." She had included the date, time and birth location of her "dream man" so Joanna had created his chart as well and laid them side by side.

Each had a steamy Mars-Pluto conjunction: high sexual energy. Their Venuses, the planetary ruler of love and romance, were also well aspected. That had been the attraction. But his Saturn—ruler of restriction and obstacles—opposed her Mars-Pluto and squared her Venus. These were difficult aspects. There were additional stresses in the chart and Joanna weighed and measured the strengths and stresses of each aspect, systematically, the way that her father had taught her many years before.

Finally, in Joanna's opinion, this was not her client's "dream man" at all. Neptune was also involved. He would deceive her, as he often deceived himself. He was probably lying to her in any number of small ways. Since Gemini, "the twin" ruled his house of relationships, he would undoubtedly have more than one marriage and probably many relationships. Ultimately, her client's relationship would prove to be an unhappy failure. It was as clear to Joanna as a blue sky on a bright sunny day. It was Astrology 101.

She closed the file, fatigued, and closed her eyes. The impulse to reach for her own chart beckoned, but she denied it. No need to look again. She'd memorized every aspect and nuance long ago. She knew every square, trine, opposition and inconjunct. She knew the degree of her planets; the Ascendant, Decendant and Midheaven. She knew the Arabian points and the midpoints. She knew the strengths of the chart and she certainly knew the weaknesses.

Her father used to say that "Astrology is nothing but a broad two-lane road with signs posted along the way. Turn off here! Slow down, pull over and stop! Wait awhile. It's raining, turn on the wipers. Full speed ahead. Don't stop in that town! Pick up that hitchhiker! That one will change your life forever!"

"Sometimes I don't want to know what's coming, Dad," she'd say. "I don't want to look ahead. It's too hard! I just want to deal with whatever comes—trust my instincts and go for it."

"Oh, bullshit! It just means you grow up, read the signs, and take responsibility for your life."

At 2:30 in the morning, Joanna stepped into the shower. She soaped up and lifted her tired face into the warm streams of water. What sign was Robert? He looked like a Taurus: good strong neck and shoulders; a sensual mouth. He's a pilot—maybe some Aquarius there. It rules airplanes. Flying.

In bed, Joanna set her strong resolve to the process of relaxing every muscle. But every muscle resisted. This man had brought a crisis from the sea, Joanna thought, and her body was gnarly with tension. She quickly went to work uncovering the source—to expose it—to understand and release it.

What was the feeling—the emotion—darkly roaming in her gut, that was searching for expression and satisfaction? Give it a name, Joanna thought. She'd often counseled others to use that technique. Give that quiet, frightened and demanding quality a name. Make it alive and incarnate.

Leopold! Why, Leopold? Leo the lion, pacing, hunting, prowling. Yes! Prowling! Be honest. Don't edit the feeling. Okay, she would love to prowl the house, like a predator, enter Robert's room, slip under the covers and reach for him. Yes. Prowl.

She got up and went softly into the kitchen to pour a glass of wine. She stood by the back door, sipping, listening to the sea. Sometimes things are just simple. An attraction. A basic attraction to a man. The needs of a body. Simple. To want to be held. To be close to another human being.

"It's been two years, for God's sake!" Joanna blurted out. And that had been a one night stand in a small town in Kansas, during one of her infrequent astrology seminars. He was younger than she, but virile and persistent. He had been handsome, but not a particularly good lover. He was forceful and fast. He was gone before dawn and she never saw him again.

"You think too goddamn much," her father had often said. "Why in the hell did you get a degree in psychology!? That's the last damn thing you should have majored in. Your friggin' thoughts have always beaten on you like a jockey's whip. Whip you down the track, thinking this, thinking that. Think, think, think! Joanna! Analyze it. Zoom in on it until it makes you sick. Go ahead, keep thinking until you fall down exhausted and depressed. That will protect you from feeling! That will stop you from diving into life."

Joanna angrily shoved the screen door open and stepped down onto the deck. "Shut up, Dad, Okay!" Joanna shouted. "Just shut up!"

She dropped down into a chair, taking a deep breath. Her voice softened a little. "Just…leave me alone for awhile…please, Dad. You always did talk too damn much."

The cool night seemed to press in on her and she covered herself with a sweater she kept close by. It was as though the nails that held down the structure of her life were loosening. She felt a little light-headed and weak. This man—this man from the sea—had injected her with a strange virus that was attacking mind and body.

She drained the glass of wine and poured another. She rolled her shoulders and massaged the back of her neck. As she drank, she heard the far-off drone of an airplane engine. Were they still looking for him? She had not turned on the TV all day nor looked at a newspaper, and she wouldn't.

She should of course call the police and tell them about Robert. But why should she? This was her world. Her life. Her little haven and she wanted no intrusions. Her neck stiffened in resolve. It was nobody's business. Not even Ned Palmer's. Maybe Robert hadn't called because he had something to hide. Maybe there was something he was running away from. Anyway, it was his responsibility to call, not hers.

At a little after 3am, Joanna had grown cold and drowsy. She wandered off to bed, wine glass still in hand, sleepily stopping by Robert's room for a final check. She stared at him as he quietly slept, contemplating the riddle of her feelings. When she smiled, quite by surprise, it felt inadequate and sad.

Comfortable in her own bed, she closed her eyes, hearing the distant swell of the sea, certain that by this time tomorrow, she'd be alone again. In the past, the thought had often brought contentment, lulling her to sleep. Now, it totally disabled her. The only escape from the ache was for her to imagine leaping from a high cliff, drifting down, down and plunging into the sea, into a deep sleep.

Chapter 5

Joanna awoke on Sunday morning, startled and alert. She threw off the sheet, and fingered wild hair into place while she checked her eyes in the mirror. She reached for her robe. Barefoot, she went downstairs to Robert's room. She crept in. To her surprise, he was awake—propped up against the pillows, bare-chested, staring numbly out the window into the abundant sunshine.

"Oh…you're awake."

He rolled his head toward her. "What day is this?"

"Sunday…"

"How long have I been here?"

"Since Friday afternoon."

He blinked slowly, processing the information. "…I don't even know your name," he said.

Her smile was shaky. "I told you my name yesterday…It's Joanna."

He shut his eyes, nodding. "Oh, yes…of course. Joanna." When his eyes opened, she saw that they were blue.

"How do you feel?" she asked.

"I feel a little bizarre. Lucky to be alive. Lucky you found me."

Joanna was silent.

"I'll be leaving today. I'll be out of your hair."

"You don't have to leave. You can stay." Joanna was surprised by her response and then embarrassed.

His eyes held her for a time. But he said nothing.

"Are you hungry?" she asked, recovering.

"Yes."

"I'll fix some pancakes. Do you like pancakes?"

"Yes."

"I'll bring them to you."

"No, I'll get up."

"Should you?"

"Yes…I'm feeling stronger. I walked around a little last night."

Joanna ran her hand along her lower neck. "Really? I didn't hear you."

"I was quiet."

There was an intimate pause as Joanna pursued the thought, wondering if he had stopped by her room during his wanderings and looked in on her.

She pointed toward the bathroom. "If you want to shower, I put out a towel for you. I found some shaving cream and a razor from when my brother was here. There's also soap and shampoo. In the drawer are a few more of my brother's T-shirts and clothes. He's smaller than you but maybe you can find something that fits."

"Thanks…"

"I'll go into town this morning and buy you some clothes if you want."

Her words seemed to echo with personal sexual overtones. Robert was silent, but his eyes roamed her and she welcomed him in.

The moment cracked opened in a surprise of desire that amplified the private silence. It brought a near misstep into passion. Their expressions sought affirmation and clarity. They were defined by the triumph of morning light; by the sound of the sea and the far-off sound of a train whistle; by a burst of wind through the window that puffed the diaphanous curtains and stirred a fresh quiver of excitement.

"Did you sleep soundly?" Robert asked, almost at a whisper.

Joanna turned her face toward the window.

"I hope you don't mind that I watched you sleep."

Joanna was still, her heart racing. "No…"

The room settled into a cooling silence.

Joanna withdrew.

In the shower, she stood unmoving, ice-eyed, hoping the water would wash away those "heated bedroom emotions."

She stepped out of the shower, turbaned her hair, wrapped herself in a robe and, in bare feet, padded into her bedroom. She grabbed a cigarette and Zippo lighter, slid open the glass doors to her private deck, stepped out into the glorious morning and lit the cigarette. She smoked pensively, staring out into wide sea. The agitation of attraction filled her, engulfed her.

"You know how self-indulgent you can be, Joni," her father used to say. "Don't forget you've got those Pisces planets, and Saturn is in opposition to your Venus. And if that wasn't enough, Venus is squaring your Uranus. That's why your first marriage didn't work. It's an unstable aspect. Not known to support successful relationships. On- again-off-again emotions. You push things down that don't fit into the image you have of yourself and then—pop goes the ugly old weasel, and you go shooting off in the opposite direction, like an arrow shot wild. And you know you have that tendency to want to escape from things: from the world and from yourself. That's the

12th house influence. Use the strength of Mars in Scorpio, Joni. That will keep you focused and strong, as long as you don't let it overwhelm you."

Joanna glanced down at her watch. Her client would be calling in a little over an hour. Joanna had already cancelled her once.

Joanna sat before the mirror smoothing on light makeup and pink lipstick. She plucked her lashes and fussed with her damp hair, gone frizzy from the ocean wind. She approved of it. As she studied her reflection—the careful almond eyes, the elegant features, the sharp nose, she tested a little tight smile. It pleased her. It said nothing. Nothing at all.

She wore tight jeans. She wore a tight-fitting peach floral cotton blouse. She slipped into sandals. As she started downstairs for the kitchen, she heard the downstairs shower. She paused on the last step, burning with a hopeful pleasure. It was the first time a man, other than family, had occupied her house. Her house. Her teenage bed. Her territory.

She started the coffee and prepared breakfast quietly. No radio. No music. The warm breeze helped dry her hair and stir up old memories.

"When are you going to get married and give me a grandchild?" her father persistently asked.

"I was married once, Dad. That was enough."

"Don't you feel your biological clock ticking away?" he asked. "I hear so many women talking about it."

"What would I do with a child? I've never felt old enough to have a child."

"It would be the best thing that ever happened to you. It would mature you."

"You know my chart better than I," she said. "You know there's no promise for children there."

"Oh, no, no, no, daughter dear. The ruler of your 5th house of children makes very interesting aspects to Venus, the Moon and Jupiter. I suspect, Joni, that you will have a child and that child will have a powerful influence on your life."

On his way to the kitchen, Robert smelled coffee. It energized him and then stopped him: the aroma reminded him of Connie. She'd spilled coffee on her pink and white dinner dress last month.

It was at a dinner party in Southhampton on a warm June night. They were seated at an elegantly decorated dinner table, with a creamy tablecloth, crystal glasses and napkins that stood up like little skyscrapers. Under glistening chandeliers and a domed ceiling, with floor-to-ceiling murals of figures in puffy clouds, they dined. The stalwart and important men wore white dinner jackets and talked of energy, oil and politics. The women fluttered and glittered with diamonds and bestowed looks of support and adoration on their powerful husbands.

Connie lifted the golden demi tasse. Coffee dripped from the elegant little saucer. She cursed under her breath at the four drops of coffee, like black tears, that fell on the purest of white ruffles, near the waist, a stain that would never be cleansed. She excused herself, gave Robert a knowing glance and then, with charm and style, they left the party of 30 for the grandeur of the plush, scented gardens on that wealthiest of early summer nights.

"I really despise this," Connie said, stopping to examine the damaged flowing gown. "Just really hate it. I feel so defiled."

"You're over-reacting. It's just a dress, Connie."

"But it fits me perfectly. Do you know how difficult it is to get a designer dress that fits perfectly?"

"No, I don't. I get all my dresses at Macy's."

"It's not funny, Robert. I'm really upset. And it cost a fortune."

"Your father can afford it."

"That's not the point. I can't go back in there looking like this."

"They won't care. They won't even notice."

"They will notice, Robert. These women notice everything. The image of four drops of coffee staining my dress could wind up in a gossip column, or at a Washington dinner party."

Robert shoved his hands into his pockets and rolled his eyes skyward, wishing himself at 30,000 feet. "Okay, fine, so we'll leave."

"We will not leave."

"So we'll stay."

Connie bristled. "You're really making me angry, Robert. You've been flippant and irritating the entire night."

Robert turned toward the four column mansion, bathed in blue and golden light. "You call it irritating and I call it entertaining."

"Those men in there don't think so. They didn't find your jokes very funny at all and they told me so."

"Screw um'. They're the old guard, Connie. I connect to the new guys. The new powerful and connected."

"They're the men who can get us to the next step, if you'll let them. Step by step, Robert. Step by step. You're too impatient and arrogant for your own good. We have to play the game their way, not yours. How do you think your father got to be Senator?"

"My grandfather, Mr. Power himself."

"You'd better listen to me, Robert. You come off as too bold and arrogant."

"Here, here," Robert said. "That's why I was a good fighter pilot."

"You're not a fighter pilot anymore. And don't have any more Scotch. Charles Kenindorfer doesn't drink and he was watching you the whole night; counting every sip you took."

"Ah, the hell with him! Who needs him?"

"We do, Robert! We need him. We need all of them! What is the matter with you lately!? You're acting like a child."

Robert stiffened with anger. "Don't do that! Don't talk to me like that!"

"Then grow up, Robert! Grow up and be the man you're supposed to be!"

"And who is it that I'm supposed to be, Constance Dowd?"

She whirled away from him, patting her hair. "Thank God they all like me in there. Kenindorfer eats out of my hand, so we've got nothing to worry about with him, but you've got to stop drinking so much at these dinners. Word gets around fast."

Robert pulled his hands and turned away. "Yeah, whatever."

Robert returned to the party and improvised a forced charm. He told the concerned and disappointed men that Connie had a headache and was resting quietly upstairs. The women had first masqueraded concern, all hand patting and pinched expressions. The truth was gradually revealed by flirtatious eyes and covert whispers about how pleased they were to have such a formidable competitor removed.

On the way home that evening, Robert half listened to Connie banter on about the ways and means to impress the high and mighty.

"They're basically old-fashioned, Robert, and they like old-fashioned attitudes and values. But you know all this. Your father and mother have so much class and good manners."

"And you're saying that I don't?" Robert said, flippantly.

Connie shot him a hot glance. "It's those kinds of remarks that people find offensive, Robert. They think you don't really care. You come off as a smart ass."

"I am a smart ass."

"You're a little boy."

"Oh bullshit! I am sick and tired of hearing that."

"It's true!"

"Just because I don't kiss asses from Southhampton to Washington D. C. doesn't mean I'm a little boy. It means I'm not going to kiss ass!"

Connie's tone deepened with a tone of authority and wisdom. "Darling, all I'm saying is, there is a time and a place for everything. When we're alone, be as fun and playful as you like. When we're with power…show your own maturity and cater to their ideas and political philosophies. Build solid foundations. Meet and impress the influential and powerful. It's okay to show your passionate side about things, but just don't get carried away. That's all I'm saying."

Robert felt despair and enervation.

Robert had known Connie for three years and they had dated on and off for a little over two. Constance Marion Dowd had been polishing her social skills since the age of five. She was the daughter of a banker, Arthur

Proctor Dowd, who had strong political ties to Washington, and a socialite mother, whose glib superficiality was regarded, far and wide, as a high art.

Connie was statuesque and ambitious. She was generous, intelligent and fond of the powerful, or those fiercely committed souls who marched resolutely toward power. She was not interested in possessing the power directly; she wanted to reflect it, like a startling full moon. She spoke fluent French and Spanish, and she was the epitome of style and grace. Her round gentle face, steady dark eyes and jet-black hair concealed the strength and assurance of a predator. She was bred and educated to be a First Lady, and she had often told Robert that it was clear to her, that if any couple had the potential and conviction to be "White House bound," surely they were at the top of the list.

Before Robert went to bed that night, he stopped by his father's study to bare his soul. It was not an easy decision, in light of the fact that his father, for all his gifts of political compromise on the Senate floor, possessed little of that same compromise in his own home.

"I don't think Connie's the one, Dad," Robert said. "Frankly, she bores me."

The Senator sat behind his reverent oak desk. Robert sat before him, feeling like a bad kid sent before the Head Master.

Senator Raymond Harrison had firm blue eyes, thick frosty hair and a smooth command of everything worldly and practical. He was dressed impeccably in a crisp white shirt, maroon and gray sweater vest and dark slacks. His forehead wrinkled.

"Constance is just what you need, Robert, and you and I know it. She has style, grace, intelligence and a good family."

"I want something more."

The Senator lifted his eyebrows. "Something more? What does that mean?"

Robert lifted his chin. "Something else then. Someone else."

"Who?"

"I don't know."

"Exactly."

"What does that mean?" Robert asked, leaning forward and folding his hands.

"It means you're two months from your wedding. You want another woman? Fine, go out and get one for a night or two. Hell, keep her for a month or two, then go get married to Constance."

"Dad, I'm 33 years old, I flew over 80 missions in Vietnam. I'm a respected attorney."

"…And?" the Senator asked, coldly, unimpressed.

"And, I think I'm old enough and experienced enough to…"

His father cut him off. "To do what? Make intelligent decisions that will not only affect you but this entire family, our reputation and our political status in this country and the world? I wonder about that."

"Are we really that important?"

Senator Harrison wasn't amused. "Yes, Robert, we are; and I'm not sure you have ever grasped the true reality of what it means to be a part of this family. Look, all the plans for the wedding are made. Dignitaries from around the world are invited. The Vice President and perhaps even the President will attend. Do you understand?"

Robert stared blankly.

"Thirty-three years old or not, Robert, I've never been fully convinced that you're old enough or mature enough to understand what you've been given and what you must give back, not only to this family but also to your country.

"Constance Dowd is the best thing that has ever happened to you. Your mother thinks the world of her. She considers her to be a daughter. You know that."

"With all respect, Dad, Mom is not the one who's marrying her."

Raymond Harrison's stern eyes bulged with anger. "Don't you ever get flippant with me or insult your mother! Every goddamn thing has been handed to you. You've lived the good life for so long that you don't know what it means to sacrifice a little for the good of others. Well, you listen to me, son. Constance Dowd will help us toward our goal of achieving the White House. That is our goal. It is defined. It is clear. She knows it and I know it—whether you know it or not!

"Do you think a goal like this is achieved by pure happenchance? Do you think there are no strategies? Do you honestly believe that everything you do now will not be examined and scrutinized in 15 or 20 years? Do you believe that the people you meet now will not be important then?"

The Senator shot to his feet. "Constance has drive, intelligence and connections and she is committed to making sure you have the same. Frankly, sometimes I wish she was the one we were grooming for public office. She has more drive and maturity than you do, son, and I only hope that some of her rubs off on you. Now go to bed before I lose my temper!"

Robert entered Joanna's kitchen. The round table had white paper napkins, blue and white china and two glasses of orange juice. In the center was a leaning stack of smooth, brown pancakes.

He'd changed into a black T-shirt and a snug pair of Bermuda shorts.

Joanna poured coffee and handed him a mug, avoiding his gaze. He eased down into the chair, while she untied her apron, took a mug and joined him at the table. They stared from opposite ends.

"How are the clothes?"

"Tight. But fine for now. Smells good," he said.

Joanna watched him fork four pancakes and shake them onto his plate. He spread butter and poured the maple syrup. He stopped and waited for her.

"Go ahead. Eat," she said.

"I'll wait."

She served herself and they ate.

Minutes passed in silence. There was only the sound of the ticking kitchen clock and the sea.

"How long have you been here?" Robert asked.

Joanna reached for the orange juice. "Almost two years."

The call of the sea became dominant, suppressing conversation, insinuating warning, vitality and possibility. The close and the far sounds of the waves merged with their own breathing.

Robert reached for his coffee mug and his hand began to tremble. He stared down at it, uneasily. "Damn…there it goes again. I keep getting the shakes."

Joanna looked on solemnly. "Have you heard of Post Traumatic Stress Syndrome?"

"Of course I have. I saw a lot of it in the war."

"You were almost killed."

Robert was silent, staring at his hands.

Joanna studied him. "It can last for hours or days."

Robert swallowed some coffee. "I'm very resilient."

She lifted her eyes from the plate, meeting his. "Resilient or not, you'll need to rest. You'll need lots of rest."

"How do you know so much about it?"

"I used to counsel battered women…abused women, for a year or so. I saw a lot of it. More than I wanted to see."

"Abused women?"

"Yes. Domestic violence. Spousal abuse. Boyfriend abuse. Parental abuse."

"At a hospital?"

"No, at a free clinic."

"Admirable."

"Not really." She shrugged her left shoulder. "I was naïve. I wanted to make a difference. I wanted to help."

"And did you?"

She scratched her forehead. "No, I don't think so. Two women wound up dead. One was beaten to death, the other shot. Some of the others…well, let's just say I didn't help them all that much."

"Things get complicated," Robert said. "Life gets complicated."

"People make them complicated."

He paused, mid-bite. Syrup dripped off the pancake. "Okay, people."

The silence returned.

It was just before his last bite that he looked at her again. "These are good, by the way. I was very hungry."

"An old recipe."

Robert nodded. "How did you hurt your foot? I noticed you were limping."

Joanna felt a gathering tension. "It's a defect."

"Defect?"

"From birth."

He looked at her soberly. He didn't comment.

They finished the pancakes and coffee.

Joanna got up and began clearing the table. Robert made the effort to rise and help.

"I'll do it," she said.

He eased back down, watching her. "It's beautiful here. So quiet. It seems far away from everything."

Joanna placed the dishes in the dishwasher.

"Is this an escape for you?" he asked.

"I don't mind being alone."

"Must get cold in winter?"

"Yes…But the sea is gorgeous… and the sky."

"I envy you."

She looked at him. "Envy?"

"Your freedom. Your peace."

"And you have no freedom of choice?"

He gave her the coyest of grins.

There was another long gap of quiet, while he studied her body: her long elegant neck, and her face that was hard but lovely. Her bottomless hazel eyes darted away from him, toward the walls, toward the spinning columns of light pouring in from the window.

She turned to him and crossed her arms tightly across her chest. "While I make some calls and shop for clothes, I thought maybe you'd want to go down to the beach and rest."

He gave her a nervous smile. "Yes… I'd like that."

Joanna let the moment stretch out until the throb in her chest abated and she found the courage to speak her thoughts. "So, you're staying for awhile?"

Robert cleared his throat. "Yes…"

Chapter 6

The town of Montauk had no stop lights, no chain stores and no brand name hotels. It was a private town, rugged and eccentric; the owners and caretakers intended to keep it that way. It was known for its spectacular fishing, and fishermen came from around the world to fish its waters, their boats drifting in and out of the docks from morning until night.

On her first trip to the extreme southern end of Long Island, Joanna had stood on the high cliffs, transfixed, staring out at the gray restless sea as it threw itself against the jagged rocks and weathered cliffs. She'd inhaled the pure raw breath of the place and felt right at home. She'd felt its pulse and its independent energy. She'd felt its quiet, authentic religion.

Joanna parked near the center of town and hurried across the busy street on her way to a phone booth near the casual clothing store. The bluish sky deepened and there was a gentle sound of wind. People roamed the sidewalks in shorts, T-shirts and tank tops, adjusting their sunglasses, sampling the shops in a lazy interest. Some wandered to the gazebo on the village green for shade, or to read the morning paper. Outside the local diners, lines had formed. The sleepy, the aloof from the Hamptons, the parents inventing distractions for their fussy children, all stood chatting and looking skyward with a growing impatience. A full day at the beach awaited and time was slipping away.

Joanna dropped in the coins and dialed Dr. Ned Palmer.

"It's Joanna Halloran."

"Yes, I know. You haven't called anybody about that guy, have you?" he asked brusquely. "You haven't told the police or his family where he is, have you?"

"…No. He doesn't want me to."

He sighed loudly into the phone. "Alright, then I'll do it."

"No!" she said, loudly. Then she softened. "I mean, I'll do it. It's just that… he wants more time."

"Joanna, they're frantic. If they find out where he is and that you haven't called them…"

"I'll call. I will. In a few hours."

"Alright, Joanna, you do whatever the hell you want. But I don't want any part of this, okay?! It's already too late for me to call. If they find out that I had any part of this and that I didn't call right away, they'll destroy me. Don't ever call me again, do you hear me?!"

"Yes," Joanna said, meekly.

"And don't ever, ever mention that I was at your house. I want no part of this!"

He slammed down the phone.

Inside the shop, Joanna removed her sunglasses, allowing her eyes to adjust to the dim light of the room. She moved among the piles and racks of clothing slowly, in a covert inspiration of touch, allowing her fingers to savor the fabrics and imagine them against Robert's body.

Would he approve of the styles and colors she chose? How many pants and shirts should she buy? How long would he stay with her? Would he take the clothes if he left? If so, would he return?

The encouraging eyes of the portly salesman halted her straining questions. She shut her eyes and turned away. After stilling her heart, she began gathering cotton pants and shorts, polo shirts, sunglasses, socks and underwear. She found sandals and deck shoes. She grabbed them. She piled everything on the counter, presented her credit card, and waited for the receipt with the eyes of the bored and preoccupied. The jovial salesman wanted to talk, and he scrutinized her as he handed her a pen. She ignored his question. Something like, "Haven't I seen you around before?"

Outside she exhaled in a gush, feeling a sharp pang of anxiety. She'd seen a newspaper lying on the counter and in the lower left hand corner, she'd seen a photograph of Robert. She'd scanned the caption: "Missing, Presumed Dead."

In the drugstore nearby, Joanna ignored the stacks of newspapers lying next to the cashiers. She purchased men's bathroom essentials, ignoring the memories of her husband's preferences for shaving cream, shampoo and cologne. She'd purposefully ignored those brands, grabbing whatever was nearby. She had the absurd feeling of being watched with disapproving eyes. At the last minute, she grabbed a newspaper.

At the market up the street, she shopped swiftly, feeling invaded by giddy, gabbing tourists, and by their mannerless children, who seemed to be ricocheting off the walls.

She loaded the trunk with her purchases and shut it with a dramatic slam. Inside the car, she reached for the newspaper, found the article on Robert, snapped out the page and began to read:

Robert Harrison, the 33 year-old son of Senator Raymond Harrison and an Assistant District Attorney in Manhattan, has still not been found after his mayday call on Friday afternoon during a violent storm. Rescuers now believe that he was most likely killed when his airplane, a blue and white single-engine Mooney, crashed into the sea off the coast of Montauk, Long Island.

Off the record, some Coast Guard personnel have said that, even if Robert did survive the crash, it is unlikely that he could have survived longer than 12 hours in the 68 degree water.

Some wreckage has been found, and the focus is now being shifted away from rescue to recovery of wreckage. A Navy salvage ship has been called in to help with the recovery operations, in the hope that the main body of the plane, along with the engine, propeller and cockpit instrument panel, can be found. This information will help experts ascertain what may have caused the plane to crash.

Coast Guard Rear Adm. Carthal Lang stressed that "You never give up hope, and I've told the Harrison family that, but we are moving away from rescue and proceeding on to recovery of the wreckage at this time. It's not an easy thing to communicate to a family."

Robert Harrison was engaged to marry Constance Marion Dowd in September in Newport, Rhode Island. The couple had planned to honeymoon in Italy and the Greek islands and then to live in Manhattan.

Constance Dowd is the daughter of Arthur Proctor Dowd, a banker and close friend to the President. She is known in social and political circles as a woman of wit and intelligence, and her Smith College friends have dubbed her "One of the Beautiful People."

Senator Raymond Harrison and his wife, Carolyn, flew from Connecticut aboard a Coast Guard helicopter to Block Island. They completed their journey to the approximate crash site aboard a Coast Guard vessel. They have made no statements or comments other than to thank the Coast Guard for their "generous and persistent efforts in searching for our son."

Joanna folded the newspaper and set it aside. She stared blankly into the middle distance.

Distracted by a never-ending parade of traffic, she finally swung the blue Ford stationwagon out into the swift current and wedged herself between two stubborn sports cars, whose drivers blasted her with their horns. Hunching her tense shoulders, she ignored them, finding enough space to whip out into a free lane and shoot ahead. She drove aggressively, bringing her foot down hard on the brake pedal several times, before leaving the main highway and lunging away down a quiet road toward home.

As she turned into the driveway of her house, and stopped, a new desperation arose. She shut off the engine and escaped into the motion of racing thoughts. She heard the soft buzz of an airplane pass overhead and she poked her head out the window to search for it.

She grabbed the bags from the trunk, closed it, and walked heavily toward the house. Entering through the front door, she closed it with a little kick of her foot. It closed with a metallic catch that echoed into silence. Her eyes were watchful, her throat dry. Her mind leaped ahead to what might happen as the day progressed.

Robert sat on the beach, staring out at the sun-flecked tremulous sea in a wonder, in a sudden surprise of a thought. Blue curling waves rushed the shore, delivering sand, shells and bits of seaweed. He was not normally an emotional man, but he filled up with emotional fireworks whenever Joanna drew near. She exhilarated him. Troubled him. She lived in a mysterious silence; seemed wedded to it. She was the kind of woman one saw at an outdoor cocktail party, on a warm summer evening, lingering on the periphery of familiar groups, not belonging to any particular one; not readily known by anyone and yet so alluring and fascinating that all the men's eyes sharpened on her when their wives turned away. Joanna was a secret to be discovered. Joanna was a new idea.

And here, on this island in the sea, he felt primordial desires, delicious fantasies and the longing to shatter 33 years of "shoulds" and "should nots." He twisted his body a little, feeling less pain, and ventured a look up toward the house. Was she back from town?

The sun aroused him, and he felt an impulsive pleasure as he pondered her tall legs and long wild hair. He admired her independence and self-sufficiency; her quiet sense of authority. She didn't need gossip, designer dresses or shiny jewelry to feel exalted or superior, or to be sexy. She lived simply and honestly—qualities he'd seldom seen in his world. A friction of longing for her pulsed through his veins as he watched a seagull drift over, squealing. It landed a few feet away.

With some effort, he slowly rose to his feet and started for the stairs. Perhaps it was time for him to show Joanna how he felt. As he started across the sand, his eyes held a question and an appeal.

Joanna started toward the kitchen. She dropped her shopping bags filled with his clothes on the living room couch. "Robert?" she called, in a feeble voice. She thought it was the first time she had called his name.

No response. He was probably still on the beach.

She went to the kitchen and dropped the groceries on the center island. She called for him again, her voice stronger. No response.

She searched the deck but it was empty. Heat shimmered beyond it, along the white gravel walkway. The sea was calm. There was the sound of a barking dog, probably down on the beach.

She returned to the kitchen and began stocking the groceries in the cabinets and the refrigerator. She felt a storm gathering in her gut. Would this be the last day with him? She stood silent, in an exhausting sense of dread. She'd be alone again—trapped in a new agony of silence. Lost in a longing for him, regretting that she hadn't offered herself; angry that she hadn't gone to him in the night and made love to him.

"You wanted the silence, didn't you, Joni girl? You wanted to be all alone. That's why you moved here," the voice said, growing in familiarity, as a face gradually formed, rising up from the depths of her anger; that husky baritone voice with a lilting cadence. Her father's voice! Her father's damned critical voice!

"You wanted that silly beach house on a cliff, far 'from the madding crowd', Joni girl, didn't you? You wanted to retreat like a damned hermit and play the wise saint to a lot of lonely women, just like yourself, who are looking for the perfect man and lover. The dream lover that doesn't exist and never will. Well, my daughter, you've got it. You're all alone. Now, enjoy it."

Joanna was placid, but inwardly blazing with desire. She opened the refrigerator door and reached for an open bottle of Sauvignon Blanc. She poured half a glass and drank liberally, to cool her parched throat and heated emotions.

Moments later, she was outside on the deck, glancing about. She finished the glass of wine and inhaled. With an intensity she'd accumulated since entering the house, she left the glass on the table and started off across the walkway, toward the staircase that led down to the beach.

Robert suddenly appeared, cresting the stairs, slightly winded. He stopped abruptly when he saw her. She stood breathless. Their eyes met. They heard the sea surging and loud.

Joanna's sun-glazed appeal captured him.

Joanna saw his eyes light up on her as he approached. It was the expression she'd hoped for.

He lifted his arms toward the sky. "What a fantastic day. A day for gods and goddesses."

She removed her sunglasses, looking at him with the flashing eyes of a new love. "So it is."

She looked down at his blue swimming trunks, his bare hairy chest. His body was trim and firm, anchored with assertion into the earth. "Does the suit fit?"

He tugged at the elastic band. "Well enough."

His blue eyes widened. "Crashed into the sea—the source of all life—reborn from the sea, a better man."

She smiled a little. "So poetic."

"Not bad for an old fighter pilot."

"I got the clothes."

He looked at her with clear, expectant eyes. "Shall I model them for you?"

She held the smile. Her expression was of someone who has just discovered a brand new passion.

There was a conspiratorial aspect to the moment, as they shifted positions and realized their growing commitment to the illegal yearnings of the heart.

"... Of course..."

Back at the house, Joanna removed the pants and shirts from the bags and handed them to Robert. They didn't speak. When Robert left the living room to try on the clothes, Joanna sat, stood and paced with the adolescent body language of desire and nerves.

Robert emerged, feigning a playful, rakish charm, and their eyes danced and their faces grew flush. He stood in olive green Khakis and a yellow polo shirt, and for a moment, Joanna allowed herself to think that she and Robert would fall in love and grow old together. It was a thought she'd never had before; not this exceptional and private thought—not even with her first husband.

When Robert approached and leaned toward her, intimately, she grew in height. "Joanna…I don't want to go just yet. I don't want to call them…They're out there—way out there—somewhere. I don't want to go back. Not now."

Joanna's lips parted, as their private passion expanded. "Then don't go back. Don't ever go back."

Joanna's muscles softened. She leaned against the door of her heart and it opened, releasing the blazing light of desire that she'd tried to smother. She could already feel Robert's breath on her. She could hear his voice in her ear, calling her name in the night. She could feel his hands exploring her, finding her, delighting her.

It was clear, in that little doorway of light, that she'd always wanted him. She would reach for him and close the door behind them.

His face moved close to hers. She felt his warm breath. She felt the raw sexual power of him, silently reaching for her. His lips lightly brushed hers. She shivered. She ached for him. Her eyes went vague and unfocused and she closed them, feeling the sting of tears when his tongue slipped between her lips and probed her mouth.

She traced his cheekbones with her hand, touched his hair and ears, fading from consciousness to a rising ecstasy. He broke the kiss gently, and reached for her hand.

They touched, kissed and scattered clothes through the house as they fumbled their way toward his room—toward the teenage bed. By the time Joanna had released her bra, and stood proudly naked, she was stammering with passion, kissing him and running her hands through his wiry chest, caressing his shoulders, pressing him into her.

The curtains fluttered into the room, and the sudden wind cooled their hot skin, bringing the smell of the sea. When she found his hardness and he moistened her lips, she leaned back against the end of the bed, wanting the fullness of him inside her, pulsing. She called for him, low and tender, as her body awakened to love after two barren years. He took her to bed, eager and impatient.

It was she who held and guided his entry, feeling ripples of pleasure that drove her to movement; to meet him as he arched and found a long easy rhythm. Her body was open and pliant, almost desperate, as the oven of passion dampened her face and chest and desire beat through her veins. She fingered the muscles of his arms and shoulders and wrapped her legs around his back, drawing him back into her with slow madness and power.

Thoughts tried to intrude. Thoughts of right and wrong. Thoughts of old loves, old words and faces, but their energy dissipated into sensation and action, as Robert's persistence caught her, trapped her into taking him deeper, driving her close to the panic of rapture.

He seemed to sense the currents and tides of her passion and he sailed her, his passion lengthening and firm, crescendoing. She fought the end of thrill. She wanted more. She wanted the forever of them. The forever of their union. She struggled against the heat of abandon as she swelled with pleasure, feeling hunted, caught and loved.

She held on, wet with fever. As a light wind puffed the curtains, Joanna stumbled. She fell, plummeting from a high cliff, plunging into searing waters of ecstasy. She sank deeper, fighting tears, reaching for him, as he drove toward climax.

Robert's body tensed and shuddered. In a spasm of bliss, he plunged deep into her soul, exploding the seeds of generations into Joanna's hungry body: seeds of hope and desire, pain and pleasure, love and hate; all met the maturing nature of her flowering season.

Possessed by sensation and timelessness, the two capsized lovers spiraled off in joy and surprise, worshipping the scattering sperm within her, feeling hot skin and lips, sealed in a harmony of sensation and confession.

Chapter 7

Joanna lay beside Robert in the fading afternoon light, watching his eyes twitch, wondering if she was in his dreams. His face was serene, his full mouth relaxed, his hair mussed and damp. Even asleep, there was an animal vigor about him that suggested strength and an earthy wisdom. He did not seem the type of person who'd run away from life—like she had done. He seemed a player in the world; a man who loved to joust and jab at obstacles, fully committed and confident of victory.

But then she also had the impression that Robert had been protected from the harsher aspects of life. There was the sheen of privilege about him, suggesting that perhaps he had not been fully tested by the inevitable vicissitudes of life. The unpredictable thorny trails had surely been scouted and cleared by others, who had been paid handsomely to ensure that Robert's journey was a little more navigable than those people of lesser means with fewer opportunities. He glowed with an assumption of acceptance and appeal and, although Joanna found these traits attractive, she wondered if Robert's accident had intuitively awakened in him the glimmer of a possible alternative lifestyle: one where he wished to traverse those thorny paths, unassisted, and clear them on his own.

As she watched him, dominated by him, she felt like a teenager in love: naïve, silly and adoring. Teenagers feel wild and uninhibited things. They don't think about consequences. It's all about feeling and discovery and "No one has ever felt like this before" and "People don't really understand how I feel."

Robert didn't stir when she lightly kissed him. He slept soundly, deeply. She was sure he'd sleep through the night.

She got up, went to her room and took a shower.

She had plenty of work to catch up on. She grabbed a snack of cheese, bread and fruit, and then held two scheduled phone consultations. Afterwards, she constructed the horoscopes of two other clients. Typically, clients called her requesting an astrological reading. Joanna explained her fee and instructed them to send her a check or money order, along with their date of birth, exact birth time and location. She always stressed that if the birth time was off—even two-to-three minutes—the entire horoscope could be wrong.

Once the check had cleared, Joanna would call the client, set up a telephone consultation date and time and begin working on the chart. Contrary to what most people believed, delineating an astrological chart was an arduous, time-consuming task that took schooling, skill and talent. It was a science, and Joanna saw herself as a scientist.

She stared down at the two newly-created charts: two wheels, little pies, separated by 12 slices, each representing an astrological house: Aries, Taurus, Gemini, Cancer, etc. Inside those slices were the planetary symbols that represented Mars, Jupiter, Saturn, Mercury and so on.

When interpreting an astrological chart, Joanna saw herself as a kind of archeologist unearthing a buried city. She discovered artifacts, entered caves, pieced together small bits of information until, gradually, an accurate portrait of time, place and culture became revealed.

Some astrological digs were easier than others, as they easily gave up their treasures and secrets. Others required the relentless manual labor of pick, shovel and sieve and, even with patience and persistence, the mysteries and complexities came stubbornly. But Joanna liked the difficult ones—often feeling a birth of vitality whenever the recalcitrant chart evaded her. Finding the secrets thrilled her: secrets exposed the ego—the shadows—and their search, discovery and revelation helped to erase the dull moments of her own life.

At a little after eight o'clock, Joanna realized that her mind was divided. With every planetary aspect, degree and house position she'd analyzed, she wondered if Robert had a similar aspect. She wondered whether his Moon was in his 10th or the 7th house. Perhaps he had Virgo rising on the 1st house cusp. She'd constructed an imaginary chart for him in her head, adding or subtracting planets, adjusting house placement and degree, revising it repeatedly until she was exhausted.

She rose from her desk, massaged her tired eyes and stopped by Robert's room to check on him. He was still asleep. She decided to watch the sunset, and then cook dinner.

Robert awoke in the darkness with a jolt. When he heard the quiet static of the sea, he relaxed, recalling where he was and the afternoon of lovemaking with Joanna. He lifted up, stiff and sore, blinking away sleep.

He pushed out of bed, wiped his eyes and wandered into the bathroom. He took a quick shower.

He found his new clothes on hangers and on the chest of drawers: underwear, a pair of white cotton slacks and a blue polo shirt. He put them on, and then slipped on the new sandals. He felt completely refreshed.

He passed through the living room on his way to the kitchen, seeing the glowing yellow light spilling in from the back deck. He heard jazz playing softly in the background. It was Billy Holiday singing "Oh, What a Little Moonlight Can Do." He stepped quietly through the kitchen, past the screen door and out onto the deck.

Joanna was standing at the far end of the railing, gazing out at the ocean. A near full moon hung in the sky, sliding through low purple clouds, dropping golden petals upon the sea. The sight of her pleased him. In the moonlight, her hair played in the wind, her long white dress rippled fetchingly, and she stood statuesque and magnificent like something holy and rare.

The world seemed new to him—unblemished and fine. His chest felt full of his tender heart—a surprise to the man who had known passion and affection—yet who suddenly recognized them as having been only the broken fragments of a youthful love. He stood perplexed and wanting, feeling mature. He'd never felt the unspeakable balance of bliss and desire that touched him so ardently under the light of the lovely moon and the cool draft of wind. And so, in that startled moment of discovery, he waited in silence, watching her.

"...Hello," Robert said, softly.

Joanna turned sharply. Robert noticed the low neck line and the rise and fall of her breasts. "Robert...you scared me."

He opened his hands. "You have nothing to fear from me."

Joanna looked him over, timidly, folding her nervous hands. "Well, look at you all dressed. I barely recognize you."

"I bet you rehearsed that line."

"Yes…for hours… How do you like the clothes?"

"Good. I like them. You have good taste. I miss the housecoat and the undershorts," Robert said, jokingly. "I'm losing the inclination to beat my chest and holler several times a day."

"Please don't stifle yourself," Joanna said, with a little grin.

Robert looked skyward. "A beautiful night."

"Yes… I never get tired of this place: the sky, sea, the beach."

"Why do you live alone?" Robert asked.

"Why not?" Joanna tossed back.

"You're evading my question."

"Yes, I am. Are you hungry? You must be. I thought you'd sleep through the night, so I already ate."

"I am hungry. It seems like I'm always hungry. I've never been so hungry."

"How do baked chicken, broccoli and mashed potatoes sound?"

"Never been a big broccoli fan, but the rest sounds wonderful."

Joanna started for the door. "I'll melt butter over it. You'll love it."

They sat on the deck across from each other, in padded chairs at a wrought-iron café table. The little glass lantern between them flickered yellow light, the wind chimes tickled music and frenzied insects buzzed the porch light. Robert ate voraciously, while Joanna watched in pleasure, sipping wine, skimming through the emotions of expectation and hesitation, keenly aware that their relationship had shifted into something more complex and intimate.

They had spoken of the weather, the town of Montauk, the new clothes that Robert wore, but the words, broken phrases and sentences were straining for the freedom of speech: to say the private unspoken things that lovers say when they're alone and aching for illumination. Each gap of silence brought a lift of the eyes, vulnerable and hopeful, as if, finally, their new relationship was best left to the wisdom and longing of the eyes.

Robert had nearly finished the chicken. He took a last bite and chewed thoughtfully. "I see there's a little cottage down a little way from the house. Is it yours?"

"Yes, it came with the place. It's pretty run down. I've never bothered to have it fixed up. Maybe I will in the fall."

"I could do some work on it. I'm pretty handy with a hammer and saw."

"It needs lots of work. I think the roof may have fallen in."

"I've put on a few roofs in my day. Might be fun."

Joanna crossed her arms. "I don't see you as the handyman type."

"My grandfather loved to build things. When I was a kid, I helped build a summer home for him and my grandmother. He was 75 or 76 years old then and he was right out there helping us, crawling all over that thing like a man of 40. He was one tough old guy."

"Are you like him?"

Robert sat back and dabbed his lips with the paper napkin. "Good question. Well, I suppose I'm a little like him. I'm a bit rebellious and opinionated. But he was a simple man in a way. He just wanted to be the best and toughest attorney around. And he was."

"And what do you want?"

"Oh, I don't know. I go back and forth on that one. I suppose, like everyone, I want to make some kind of difference in the world."

"How?"

Robert took a drink of wine. "How? Politics..."

"Politics?"

Robert saw that the word was distasteful to her. "Yes...at least that's what I'd thought...until recently."

"Local politics? National?"

"My father is Senator Raymond Harrison, from Connecticut," Robert said with a lift of an eyebrow.

Joanna nodded her head. "Yes, I read that in the paper."

Robert grew pensive, staring into the fire.

"Is son like father?"

"Good question. My father's a fiercely competitive man. Very strong-willed and self-assured. He loves power and he's never been a gracious loser. I hope that doesn't sound too unkind."

"It doesn't sound flattering."

"He's very ambitious and he wants me to be."

"And you have your own opinions about that?" Joanna asked.

He paused, thoughtfully. "Let's just say that I'm not totally convinced that I want to follow in his footsteps, or my grandfather's, for that matter."

"Did your grandfather push your father toward politics?"

Robert laughed a little. "You are the psychologist, aren't you?"

Joanna smiled, warmly. "I find the subject, and the person, fascinating."

Robert picked up his glass and toasted her. "Ditto…My grandfather was a strong-willed, no-holes-barred kind of guy and he pulled strings, raised money and drove my father from local city councilman to Mayor to Senator. A week after my father won the Senate race, my grandfather, who was 82 years old, dropped dead from a heart attack."

"You admire your grandfather, don't you?"

Robert picked up his fork, and then replaced it, thoughtfully. "Oh, I don't know. Yes and no. I mean…he knew what he wanted and how to get it. As I look back on him now, it seems like he was programmed like a robot to be what he was. Maybe we're all programmed—pre-wired to be what we are."

Robert sighed. "It just seems so easy to create patterns in our lives and, after a while, we seem to get stuck in those patterns—good and bad. After a time, it's almost as if those patterns control us, because we're afraid to try something new or go down a less traveled path."

He scratched his nose and met her engrossed eyes. "You know what I mean?"

She looked at him calmly and seriously. "Yeah, I think so."

"Since the accident, I just feel like I want to break some of those patterns. I feel like I've been all tied up or something and I just want to break out."

"Maybe the plane crash shook something loose," Joanna said.

Robert screwed up his lips in thought. "Maybe…"

Joanna stared, unguarded, her lovely eyes studying his generous mouth. "How long will you stay, Robert?"

The question surprised him. He looked at her for a long moment and then pushed his plate aside.

The mood turned somber and private. Joanna saw an odd expression on his face. He stood up and wandered to the railing, staring out at the sea. Joanna reached for a cigarette, sorry she'd asked the question. She placed it between her lips and lit it with her lighter.

He shoved his hands deep into his pockets. "I feel strange, Joanna. I don't know how else to describe it. Strange and kind of lost. For the first time in my life, I'm questioning myself. I'm questioning everything. Everything I am and everything I've done. I close my eyes and I see this egg…"

"Egg?" Joanna, asked leaning toward him.

"Yes…it's silly. I keep seeing this tall tree and an egg falling from a nest. Falling toward the cement below and I know, without a doubt, that I am that egg and that I'm going to splatter all over the sidewalk."

"And has it hit the cement and shattered?"

"No. I shake the damned image away before it hits the ground."

"And what do you think will happen if it shatters?"

He pushed away from the railing, agitated. "I don't know." He threw up his hands. "I mean, how and why did I survive that plane crash? Why haven't I called my family? What's the matter with me?"

Joanna allowed an interval of silence while she smoked, excited by his energy, the sound of his voice, by the physical size of him. "Maybe it's because you almost died."

"I've been dreaming about Vietnam lately—even before the crash. I flew more than 100 missions over there. I saw guys die. Hell, I was scared, too, but somehow I believed I was never going to die. My plane got shot up a few times, but I never got shot down. I was lucky. But I think about those times, Joanna, and those guys, especially the guys who died and I keep thinking that surely they didn't die for nothing. Right after the war, I used to wake up, wet and scared, thinking about the dead. That's when I first started thinking that I could have done it better."

Joanna adjusted her chair so that she faced him. "What do you mean, done it better?"

He kept his back to her. "I could have been a better leader. A better President. Made better decisions. On those nights when I can't sleep for thinking about it, when I see the country the way it is today, I truly believe that I could be a good President. I believe that I could lead this country and make it a better country. I could make better decisions. And then I think, yes, I want to play the political game. I want to do whatever it takes to lead this country…and it would take years of preparation and hard work."

"And so, maybe you will, Robert."

He responded to the sound of his name by turning gently toward her and leaning back against the railing. He gazed at her, smiling.

She saw something pass across his eyes, as if he'd just made a discovery. "You are beautiful, Joanna…"

She averted his attractive eyes.

When an airplane drew near, flying low over the sea, they both jerked looks of alarm. Long after it had faded from sight and sound, they tried to recover the romantic mood, but it had slipped away. Lightning flashed in the distant night sky and the smell of rain rode the currents of a growing wind.

They gathered up the dishes in silence, took them into the kitchen and then returned to the deck. Joanna sat, concentrating on him, uncomfortable in the protracted silence. He stood facing away from her toward the sea.

"I wonder if they're still looking." Robert said.

Joanna felt a slow creeping sickness. Was he going to leave? Was this the end before they'd had a beginning? After a breathless interval, she found some well-chosen words. It took two attempts before she forced them out. "Are you going to leave soon?"

He looked at her wearily and fretfully. "No…"

Robert went to her, crouched down and peered deeply into her eyes, as if she were a beautiful apparition who'd just emerged from a hazy mist. Her head was bent a little in surprise, as she waited, her eyes uneasy.

He reached for her shoeless right foot. Joanna retracted it, in reflex, an act of embarrassment and protection of an old wound. Gently taking it in his hand, he leaned forward and kissed it.

Joanna flinched, trembled. She felt the start of tears.

Robert gave her a slow, warm, unhurried gaze of affection. "I don't want to be defined anymore, Joanna. I don't want to live in a box. I'm out of the box and I like it. Can we live outside the box and be undefined?"

Her long eyelashes fluttered. "For awhile, Robert. We can for awhile."

Chapter 8

Joanna awoke and reached, snaking a hand toward the cool empty space beside her on the bed. She slowly surfaced from a dream, becoming vaguely aware of the distant pounding of a hammer. Her heavy eyes struggled to open fully against the bright light of morning. She squinted, scowled and turned from it, burying her head in the soft warm pillow. The hammer persisted, bouncing and echoing, falling away into the flat moan of a train whistle. And then she remembered.

She lifted her head. Her eyes popped open. The habit of awakening to routine and familiarity disintegrated into one startling memory: She and Robert were lovers. Her pulse accelerated. Her body ached for more of him.

She propped up on elbows and glanced left. On the pillow next to her lay three small glowing wild flowers, with a note that read:

> *Dear Joanna:*
>
> *Found these out by the cottage at first light. I've never picked flowers before and delivered them myself—called the florist (or had my secretary do it). Thanks*

for yesterday. I have fallen in love, my darling, and I'm afraid I'll never be the same again.

Forgive my early rising, (habits die hard) and come to me when you wake up. I'm at the cottage.

—Love, Robert

Joanna kicked off the sheet and leaped out of bed, rushing from the room, naked, flying up the stairs to her room. After showering and applying makeup, she dressed in white khakis, a striped blue and white cotton top and white sneakers. On the way out of her room, she grabbed a white cap and tortoise sunglasses, completing a face and body check in the mirror before exiting the room. She descended the stairs in rapid steps, skipped through the kitchen, feeling like a teenager, and burst out the back door into the sunshine. She left the porch in a jump and strode briskly toward the cottage and the sound of the hammer.

Joanna followed a narrow, weed-covered path, past rosehip bushes splattered with white and pink flowers; past scrub pine. She side-stepped gullies that held glistening water from last night's rain. Two red-winged blackbirds scattered, wings whistling over her head, as she tiptoed through oozing mud. She breached the low brush, her breathing rapid in anticipation, the sharp flat sound of the quickening hammer dominating the day. She entered a tranquil enclosed space, where the rickety, gray-shingled cottage lay in old seclusion. She saw Robert.

He was crouched on the slanted roof, hammering in new tiles, with a fine, hard swing of his arm. He wore a new pair of shorts and a yellow T-shirt. He was hatless.

She came up silently, observing, waiting for the new pleasure of his eyes to lift and find her; waiting for the approval of her lover. To rush anything under the cloudless brilliant sky, in her brand new body of easy breaths and high emotion, would be a sin. She crept nearer, folded her arms and watched.

Robert paused to wipe his brow, and he saw her. "Joanna!" he exclaimed, his face alive with joy. "Good morning!"

"Up so early with so much energy after last night?" she asked, slanting a naughty expression.

He grinned, lowering his eyes on her. "Joanna, you inspire me. Not tire me."

She laughed and it was the first time he'd heard it. It started low and lifted an octave. It was effortless and honest, with a little hint of embarrassment.

"You should laugh more often," he said.

"And you *should* be a politician, with slogans like that, President Harrison."

"I'll pepper my speeches with sexual innuendo."

"And all of the girls will swoon."

"As long as you swoon, I'll be happy."

She cocked her head, playfully skeptic. "And a charmer too?"

"Of course."

"You should be wearing a hat in this sun, Robert."

"Well, it's still early and the sun feels so good."

"Are you sure you're strong enough for all of this?"

"I'm feeling better every minute."

"Just don't over-do it."

"Yes, nurse."

"Where did you find the tools and shingles?"

"In the shed over there. There was a whole box unopened. You've got all kinds of tools in there. Somebody had planned to fix this place up. Oh, forgive me; I busted the lock so I could get into the shed."

She shrugged. "I had no idea any of that stuff was there."

"And you've lived here for two years?"

"Almost."

"This would make a great little home office for you."

"I saw a snake out here once and that was it. I figured the place was filled with them—and ticks."

Robert scrabbled across the roof, dodging wet and rotten patches and edged toward the rickety ladder. "Sounds like you're really a city girl."

Joanna went to the ladder to steady it. "Except that I love the ocean."

Robert positioned himself to descend. "The ladder's a hazard, mostly rotten, but it's all I could find."

"Be careful!" Joanna said, as she watched him place his first cautious foot on the top rung.

"Don't worry. I'm a ladder guy from way back."

Once on the ground, he took Joanna's wrist and drew her to him. He kissed her deeply, and there was an endlessness to it, a true marrying of sunlight, desire and sensuous wind.

"What should we do today?" Robert asked.

Joanna kissed him again. "The beach is private, if you know what I mean."

They ate breakfast on the deck under an umbrella. After coffee, Joanna called her clients to reschedule consultations, while Robert made a list of supplies he'd need to complete the renovations on the cottage: a ladder, paint, wood, nails, screws, a ceiling fan.

Joanna placed the order with the local hardware store and agreed to the exorbitant delivery charge. She and Robert had gently argued about it. He was willing to pick up the supplies, but Joanna was afraid he'd be recognized in town.

The rest of the day was spent at the beach. They napped, swam and played. Toward sunset, as the beach cooled and the sky softened to a pastel pink and blue, they found a secluded spot and made love.

For dinner they watched the sunset, eating Montauk mussels and drinking a French Muscadet that Joanna had purchased in New York. With the wild striped bass she sautéed, they opened a bottle of California Chardonnay.

In a chilly plush darkness, wearing long pants and jackets, they carried a flashlight, two cups, and a bottle of French Pinot Noir back to the beach. They piled logs they'd gathered earlier in the day, dug a little pit and lit a fire. The full moon rose at around 10 o'clock and they opened the wine. They sat huddled on a log tasting the wine, poking at the fire and watching the sparks rise toward the stars.

Joanna stared out into the darkness, fighting melancholy. She saw the unknown as a kind of predator, waiting on the periphery of the darkness, stalking back and forth, too frightened to attack because of the fire. But the fire would go out—eventually. The unknown—the relentless tick of time—the predator would attack and everything would change. She beat back the thought that Ned Palmer might have already placed an anonymous call to the Harrison family. She'd been half-expecting a visit from the police the entire day.

"What's the matter?" Robert asked. "You're shivering."

"Oh nothing…just a little chilled."

"Let's move closer to the fire."

They did.

Robert looked at her curiously. "I don't even know what it is you do."

"I'm an astrologer."

"An astrologer?" he exclaimed.

"Yes..."

He turned puzzled. "Really?"

"Yes."

"Interesting. I always thought astrologers were sort of weird looking people—you know—old crones with long noses, wild hair and rotting teeth."

"You mean witches," Joanna said, flatly.

"I suppose. You sort of shatter that image."

Her eyes held mischief. "I have my witchy moments."

Robert grinned as he sipped the wine. "What exactly is an astrologer? I mean, people have read me my horoscope now and then from the paper—but I can't really say I know what an astrologer actually does."

"How an astrologer makes a living, you mean?"

"Yeah, I suppose so. I mean, I know what my sign is but..."

She interrupted. "...Taurus," Joanna said, confidently.

His eyes lifted in surprise. "Yeah...I'm a Taurus. How did you know?"

"Your looks. The way you move."

He seemed to take pleasure in the thought, but Joanna saw that he didn't take it seriously. "Whenever I read about what I'm supposed to be like, half the time it doesn't fit."

"That's because the sign you were born under, your Sun sign, is just one small part of what you are. One small part of the puzzle."

"But the sign you're born under is supposed to be what you're like, isn't it?"

"Well, it's like saying that Denver is the United States. Denver is an important part of the United States, but it isn't the entire country."

Joanna began playing with her hair, twisting it into curls with her left hand. "An astrologer counsels; tries to guide clients to better understand themselves by interpreting the planets and their mathematical aspects to each other. You measure the strengths and weaknesses, the talents, the fears, so that people can take charge of their lives—so that they can make clear, intelligent choices."

Robert cradled the cup of wine, thinking over her explanation. "You won't be offended, I hope, if I say that I don't believe in any of it." Then he smiled broadly to help dissolve any offense she might have taken. "It just seems like fortune-telling to me."

She looked away. "I stopped trying to convince people about astrology a long time ago. If they don't believe in it, fine."

"Not offended?" Robert asked.

"No...," she said, softly, but she was.

"Where did you go to school—college I mean?" Robert asked.

"University of Cincinnati. Cincinnati's where I grew up."

He brightened with renewed interest. "Nice town. I've been there a couple of times. Good baseball town. I love baseball. " He shifted his position, working on a question. "How does one get into astrology? I mean did you just wake up one morning and say 'Today I'm going to be an astrologer'?"

"My father's an astrologer." With a gentle challenge, Joanna faced him. "What do you do?"

"I'm an attorney. I'm an assistant DA in Manhattan. We're known as the 'Crimebusters'. We go after organized crime and white collar guys."

"Did you wake up one morning and decide you wanted to be an attorney?"

"No. My father's an attorney, my uncle's an attorney and my grandfather was an attorney, so I woke up one morning after I returned from Vietnam and found myself in law school."

"Do you like it?"

"Sometimes. Sometimes the politics drive me crazy."

"You who want to go into politics?"

"I'm learning how to fence and jab, bob and weave. What about you? How did you learn all about the planets and the stars?"

"My brother and I grew up with it. It was our second language. At dinner, we didn't talk about politics or sports or what anybody did that day, we talked about astrology."

The wind picked up and scattered her hair. She dropped down and sat cross-legged in the sand, looking up at Robert. "I bet your family talked about law."

"Yep. Law and politics."

"And you went to a private school, no doubt."

"Oh yes. Breakfast was at dawn, then compulsory chapel at 8:15. Classes went from 8:45 to 1:30 p.m. Then there was afternoon athletics—for me baseball. Then there were more classes from," he shut his eyes, straining to remember. "Oh yes," he said, opening his eyes. "3:45 to 6:15. Then there was dinner and hours of homework."

Joanna made an ugly face. "Ugh! I'm glad I went to public school."

"You find ways to rebel."

"And did you get demerits or whatever they call them?"

"I got into big trouble with my father and grandfather. My father used to say 'You've embarrassed our family name.' Of course, I could have cared less about our family name. It just made me want to rebel even more."

"Your poor father."

Robert turned reflective. "Yeah… maybe I haven't changed so much."

Joanna let the comment fall flat, without a response.

Robert quickly changed the subject. "And does your father make a living at astrology?" Robert asked.

"Oh yes. A very good one. He's somewhat of an elder statesman in astrology circles. He went to Stanford and got a degree in economics. He taught high school for awhile, before he started practicing astrology full time. He wrote a whole series of books—sort of astrological text books—a few years ago. They've made him rather famous in the occult world. He gives lectures and classes all over the country and in Europe."

"Your mother?"

"She was a secretary. She was very religious and thought that astrology was of the devil."

Robert lifted an eyebrow. "Of the devil?"

"Yeah, devil's work. So naturally, astrology was a forbidden fruit that was so enticing that I, being the rebellious daughter that I was, began to study it. My mother became somewhat despondent and isolated from the rest of us. And then she expanded her church and charity work and we didn't see much of her. One Sunday morning, while she was shoveling snow off the church walk, she had a massive heart attack and died. I'm sure you get the irony."

Robert flashed her a remote smile. "Yes…I was just thinking about my own mother a little while ago."

The silence lengthened. "Joanna?" He spoke her name softly, almost painfully.

"Yes, Robert."

"What does your astrology say about us?"

Joanna turned aside. "I don't know. I haven't looked."

She warmed her hands near the fire, turning them gently.

Robert stared into the darkness. "The doctor…who came by. Have you talked with him lately?"

"Yes…"

"He knows who I am?"

"Yes, he knows."

"He'll call the police, won't he?"

"I don't know. Maybe. Yes, I'm sure he will. Maybe he already has."

"Then we don't have a lot of time."

Joanna sat still. The wind blew and agitated the flames.

Robert lightened his voice, forcing brightness. "Have you done my astrological chart?"

"You said that you don't believe in astrology."

"Who knows, maybe you'll convince me."

Joanna frowned. "I don't think I'll do it."

"Why? You could explain it all to me. I'm a very good student."

Joanna retreated a little. "I don't want to. I don't want to know about the future."

Robert chuckled, nervously. "I can't believe you take it all so seriously."

His tone irritated her. She turned her face upward and stared into the mass of stars. "It never ceases to amaze me how people can totally dismiss something as trivial and phony, when they've never even studied it and know nothing about it!"

He held up his hand to placate her. "Well, it's just that…"

She cut him off. "…Did you know that Pythagoras and Isaac Newton were astrologers, as were most of the 16th century scientists? Did you know that astrology was taught in the universities until about 1600? These were not stupid people. They obviously had studied it because they realized, through practice, that it worked and was valid."

Robert opened his mouth to speak, but Joanna charged ahead, her voice growing in strength and intensity. "Did you know that Carl Jung studied astrology and that our calendar is based on astrology? A month is roughly the amount of time between New Moons, about 29 days. Did you know that J.P. Morgan used astrology for business and that he said 'Millionaires don't use astrology, billionaires do'?"

"Okay, okay!"

"You're a Taurus, Robert, and Taureans are stubborn bulls. Practical and factual, constantly saying 'show me.' If you can't show a Taurus something—prove it—they'll never believe it!"

"What's wrong with that?"

"Nothing, but I doubt whether it is in your nature to ever study astrology and I'm certainly not going to be able to prove it to you by just talking about it. You are much too practical and skeptical."

"Yes, I don't believe it."

"And you're much too stubborn to ever consider studying it."

He saluted her. "Yes, Ma'am! But, I have to admit that I have heard, through the grapevine, that Ronald Reagan and his wife, Nancy, go to an astrologer for advice. Now, that scares me a little, since he's the President of the United States, but, hey, if it works for them, then that's fine. If it works for you, hey, that's fine with me."

Joanna set her eyes on him, meeting him with a challenge. "Do you know that I could tell you—with a lot of hard work—whether or not there is any potential for you to become president, or, at the very least, whether you could hold some high political office?"

His first look was doubtful, but as he considered her words, a spark of interest gleamed in the firelight of his eyes. "Really?"

"I could match your astrological chart with the chart of the United States of America. That would reveal a lot."

She waited for him while he poked at the fire with a long stick. Confusion came over his half-averted face. "Here I am in paradise, Joanna. I'm happier than I've ever been in my entire life. I'm at peace and I love being here with you. What is it? What in the hell is in us that drives us toward the very things that we don't really want? Or at least, don't want as much as we want other things?" He looked at her. "What is it?"

She looked at him tenderly. "I think it's called ambition, Robert. I don't think you can ignore it. It's part of what makes you who you are."

Robert lowered his head, pinching the bridge of his nose. "I wish you'd never called that damned doctor, Joanna."

Joanna sighed and drained her cup.

Chapter 9

A week passed, without either of them watching television or reading a newspaper. With every phone call or airplane buzzing overhead, they knotted up and exchanged worried glances.

Layers of denial formed around them like strong rings, protecting them from any unpleasant intrusion from the outside world.

Joanna spoke to her father and brother on the phone and, each time, the conversations were short and cryptic. It had always been her style, so nothing out of the ordinary was suspected. Except once, during her last conversation with her father.

"You've got a lot going on in your chart right now, Joni girl. How is it manifesting?"

"It isn't," Joanna said.

"I smell Neptune, Joanna. You're not telling me everything, are you?"

"Nothing is going on, Dad. Nothing."

"Venus and Mars are in there too, along with the 12th house of secrets and your good friend Uranus. Have you captured yourself a lover?"

"No! Of course not. Don't be ridiculous."

"Oh, daughter of mine that I know so well, methinks you protest too much."

Joanna lowered her voice to a calm pitch. "Nothing is going on, Dad. I'm just working on another book."

"What's the subject?"

"Oh, you know…love and relationships."

"Sounds purposively vague."

"It's going to be more commercial. An easy-to-understand kind of book."

"I'm going to England for some lectures in early September. I thought I'd stop by and see you in late August."

She swallowed. "Well…a…not right now, Dad, I've just got a lot of things to catch up on."

"I won't stay long. You know me. I never wear out my welcome."

"September might be good," Joanna said, nervously.

"Well, we'll see. You're too much alone out there in the middle of the sea. We'll talk."

"Okay, Daddy. Fine."

"You be careful, Joni. You've got some heavy transits coming. Some dark clouds ahead."

Work on the cottage progressed quickly under the sparkling sun. Robert wanted to surprise Joanna, so he refused to let her see it, even though she wanted to help. It became an obsession, helping to keep his mind and body occupied, deflecting thoughts of the family, achievement and friends. At night, he was obsessed by Joanna and their love-making intensified, as time became precious and intrusive.

With each high tide, they developed evasive maneuvers to avoid conversations about the world they'd put on hold, although they knew that the cleverly disguised words were nothing more than sand for a sandcastle that would someday be obliterated by that relentless high tide.

Joanna was raised to love in degrees, by daily nourishment from Robert's affection; from his frequent touch; from the sharing of food and sleep; from the sight of him roaming the low tide. Her body blossomed like a rare sexy flower and ripened like an exotic fruit that Robert peeled, squeezed and opened. Her skin softened and bronzed; her hair lightened and blew reckless.

Robert's spirit rose up in indignation to indict and prosecute the devils of his guilt. He struggled to purge them with the argument that God must be a lover of the flesh. After all, we are all made in his image—made of flesh—conceived in flesh, clothed in flesh and trapped within it. In order to experience love we must love and be loved by flesh. His love for Joanna was a good and true love; a love surely sanctioned by the angels. His summation was simple: he had never loved Connie. It had been an engagement of convenience and opportunity.

By the second week of August, the lack of rain had dried the earth into dust and cracks. The afternoon sun was the color of mustard.

Robert worked on, frantically, as if the completion of the cottage was symbolic of their burgeoning love, growing toward a completion and strength that no person or act of God could destroy.

Joanna was in town gathering groceries, when she ran into Dr. Palmer, dressed in shorts and a T-shirt. She was about to duck into the market on Main Street, when their eyes met. His face darkened in stark disapproval. Startled, Joanna froze, presenting a nervous, obstinate face.

"Joanna…" Ned said, pausing beside her.

She nodded.

He shook his head, like a doctor castigating a school girl. "You never called, did you?"

She was silent.

"I thought you were smarter than that. More mature."

Her eyes fell on him with contempt; and then she batted them, uncertainly, and then she looked away from him.

"When it ends, it won't be pretty. Have you thought of that?"

Her breathing quickened.

Frustrated by her silence, he tried another approach. "It doesn't make sense, don't you see that? When all this gets out, the whole world is going to descend on you like a pack of hungry locusts and eat you alive."

Joanna's mouth tightened.

"Don't you understand what you're doing?"

Joanna finally faced him. She cleared her throat. "Have you called them?"

He shook his head again, staring with pity. "I told you I wasn't going to call. What the hell would I say? Your son's shacking up with an attractive reclusive astrologer and doesn't want to come home? Maybe I should blackmail them? Threaten to go to the press with all the juicy gossip, if they don't agree to give me some astronomical amount of money? Hell, maybe I should blackmail you. Maybe I could squeeze you for a few thousand to keep my mouth shut."

Joanna's foot ached and she shifted her weight. Her face was constrained, her emotions unstable.

After a fractional pause, and a doubtful look, he shook his head again. "Frankly, Joanna, I have too much integrity to let anybody know that I was involved with this. If you're worried about me shooting my mouth off, I can assure you, I have no such desires. But let me tell you this. When this gets out—and it will get out—it's going to ruin you. Hell, they'll destroy you. The press will have a field day. You'll be the next bimbo with her 5 minute tell-all sensational story that nobody will take seriously except the sickos, the crackpots and the greedy. You'll be the hot joke, the cheap mistress, the name people will try to remember in a few years when they're playing Trivial Pursuit."

Joanna struggled to project defiance, but his words struck like a knife.

He stuffed his hands into his baggy Bermuda shorts pockets. "Hell, Joanna, I'm just disappointed in you, that's all. Just damned disappointed."

He started off across the street.

She stood awkward, searching.

The following days fell into an easy routine. They rose early, had breakfast and went to work, Joanna to her home office and Robert to the cottage. At 12:30 they met on the deck for lunch. They ate leisurely, dozed, and went back to work around 2:30. At 4:30 they went to the beach and swam and, if no one was around, they made love.

Often, as they lay in bed, with fear and confusion lengthening the shadows, Robert reached for her and she opened to him. Afterwards, they lay awake, talking of the past, of their secrets and dreams. With brave hearts, they tried to extend the night with words, with love and with wine. As daylight leaked into the windows, they arose, searching for infinity in their work and the tides of the sea.

As one day looped into the next, Joanna began to see the gathering worry on Robert's face. Her own volatile emotions vacillated between fear and exhilaration, as if she were a little girl in a schoolyard, swinging on a rickety swing, much too high and much too fast.

At dinner on a Friday night in August, they sat on the deck. Robert was silent and recessive. Joanna talked nervously, sensing a sudden dark turn of events.

"I need to pick up more groceries. We're almost out of everything… How do you like the pasta? I think I put a little too much cream in the sauce."

"…Good…" Robert said.

Joanna brightened. "So when can I see the cottage? You keep saying any day now."

He spoke at a low whisper. "It's not finished."

The sea was loud, covering up his soft mumble.

Her alert face waited. "…I didn't hear you."

"I said, it's not finished!" he said, sharply. "It's too much work for one person. I'll never finish the damn thing."

Joanna lowered her head and ate in silence, unwilling to ask what brought on the mood. She didn't want to know. It would pass. Everyone gets in a mood now and then.

That same night, Robert left the bed right after love-making, disappearing into the dark. He'd been particularly quiet and tender, bringing her to ecstasy and peace. Concerned when he didn't return, Joanna slid into her robe and went downstairs. She found him in a chair on the back deck, in his undershorts, staring blankly.

She lingered in the doorway, the light off, as warm wind brushed the wind chimes.

"What's the matter, Robert?"

He was motionless.

She concealed her anxiety. "Something has happened. You haven't been yourself all night."

He folded his hands. "Did I ever tell you about my mother?"

"No…"

"She came from wealth. Her family was loaded. Old money. Her two brothers were both losers: one an alcoholic, who managed to become a doctor, although a pretty poor one, and the other was a womanizer and a gambler. He was actually killed in a duel, if you can believe it. In France, about 10 years ago. Fighting over a woman, of course.

"Anyway, my mother is a good and honorable woman. The money didn't destroy her, as it does most people. She has the gentleness and the good heart of a saint. She raised my sister and me to be honorable; to be responsible people. She used to say 'Do your best during the day. Do what your good conscience tells you to do at all times, so that you can sleep well at night; so that you can be proud of your life. Then no matter what comes, you'll have your own inner integrity to keep you strong."

Joanna shut her eyes. Her hands formed fists. She turned from him. "Robert…I can't talk about goodbyes right now. I'm not ready for it."

He twisted toward her. He stood. "Goodbyes? Joanna, I want to stay here with you."

Joanna's throat tightened. Her eyes opened, wet. The word nearly stuck in her throat. "Stay…?"

He went to her. "Of course. Don't you understand? Don't you get it? I love you. That's the truth. That's what I want."

She faced him, frightened and vulnerable. "Robert, we both know that you can't hide here forever. We're living a fantasy. You have to go back to the world. The real world."

"Of course…I know that. I know I have to go back, but I know what I want now. I want you. I want us. That's what I'm going to tell them."

Joanna searched his eyes for signs of hope.

He nodded, widening his eyes, bending toward her. "Yes, I know what you're thinking. When? When will I go? Well, you know what? We have all the time in the world. We can go as slow or as fast as we want, Joanna, because nobody out there knows about us."

When he kissed her, Joanna shivered. She knew the planetary transits, those catalysts of change that her father had spoken about, were on the move. She didn't have to look at her own chart to know that time was running out. She felt it in her heart of hearts. Some event was about to be triggered by Mars, the planet of action. Time was running out.

Chapter 10

Two days later Robert led Joanna to the cottage blindfolded. He'd chopped the weeds, uprooted the stones and smoothed the path. It was an easy walk now, past a quiescent stream, through the balmy morning air that held the fading scent of honeysuckle.

When they arrived, Robert gently lifted the blindfold. They stood shining in the full blaze of sun, dressed in ball caps, shorts and T-shirts. Joanna looked in rapt wonder. Robert with a face full of a parent's pride.

"Well," he said, indicating toward the cottage. "What do you think? It still needs a lot of work, but it's getting there."

The rickety and sad little clapboard house had been resurrected, radiating cheerfulness and life. It was egg-shell white, with blue trim and lilac shutters. There was a screened-in porch and an old rocker that provided a spectacular view of the sea. There was a wild flower garden on one side of the stairs leading to the porch, and on the other, a wheelbarrow filled with glimmering stones and seashells.

"It's beautiful," Joanna said, beaming. "Absolutely beautiful!"

"Wait till you look inside. Now you've got to use a little imagination. It's not finished. Just remember that when you see it. It still needs a lot of work."

Robert took her hand as they entered, their eyes slowly adjusting to the shadows. Robert watched intently as Joanna drifted through the study with pine paneled walls, checked out the little stone fireplace, and ran her hand across the brown Formica countertop in the kitchenette, awed and excited.

He rocked on his heals with pleasure, when she paused in the bedroom, smiling. She saw a lopsided double bed, and a big brown teddy bear Robert had found in the basement.

Joanna's soft footsteps creaked along the bare wooden floors as she passed, eager and excited, from the bedroom to the narrow bathroom.

"I'm going to put a salmon colored porcelain sink in the bathroom. And we're going to have to do something with the water pressure in the shower. We'll have to get a real plumber in here to fix that."

Her presence in the cottage—after so many days of solitary work—lifted his spirits. Joanna turned to him, fully opening her warm, rich eyes. "I love it, Robert."

Outside, as Joanna sat on the porch, rocking, and Robert stood staring out to sea, Joanna removed her sunglasses. "I have a surprise for you."

Robert turned to her. "Good. I love surprises."

"Well, you gave me this wonderful surprise so I want to return one."

"Okay…"

"We're going sailing today."

"Sailing?"

"Yep."

"Do you sail?" he asked.

"Nope. Don't know anything about it and don't know how."

"Okay…How are we going sailing then?"

"Friends."

He lifted his head. "Friends!?"

"Yes."

Robert stiffened. "Is that a good idea? I mean, can you trust these people?"

Joanna stopped rocking. "Yes… of course I can trust them."

Robert took a short little thoughtful walk toward the cliffs, before returning. "I don't know, Joanna. What if somebody sees me?"

Joanna stood. "They won't. We'll just shoot over to the Sound, pick up the boat, and sail away. You'll slump low in the seat and keep your cap pulled down over your face."

Robert wiped his forehead with the back of his hand.

Joanna went to him. "We've been alone for so long—so isolated. I'm getting stressed or something. I keep hearing those damn planes flying over…and every time the phone rings I jump. I just think it would be good for both of us to get out of here and be with some other people. Put our minds on something else for awhile."

Robert placed his hands on his hips, thinking. "You're absolutely sure you can trust these people?"

"Yes, of course."

Robert managed a tight smile. "Okay…if you want to."

As Joanna drew up next to him, he felt a sudden heaviness, as if the wind had shifted and a grand season was about to end.

They traveled Route 27 in light traffic, searching for the turnoff to the marina, adjusting their sunglasses nervously. Robert was crouched in the seat, like a thief, the cap pulled low. Joanna was hatless, radiant and breezy. They took a hard right turn, and raced along a narrow asphalt road to its conclusion: Doc's Marina. They found a parking place with a good view of the 20 slips, the pilings, boardwalks and railings. There were fishing boats, sailboats and cabin cruisers, gently rocking in a snappy wind.

They left the car, grabbed a canvas bag and a cooler, and walked rapidly across the dirt parking lot. They stepped onto the narrow boardwalk that led to the slips, passing sailboats and a cabin cruiser with tinted windows and a modern sleek design that smelled of big money.

Robert shuffled along the ramp, gawking, until Joanna aimed him toward a blue and white sailboat with the name *Resolute*. It was an elegant 42 footer, rising impressively out of the water. They viewed the rigid stainless bimini over the cockpit, and the lightweight fiberglass top where the radar dome and antennas were mounted. Shading his eyes, Robert admired the clean design and fiberglass hull.

Becky and Gerry Corcoran appeared on deck, waiting. Robert tugged the bill of the cap lower over his shifting, suspicious eyes. Becky jumped down to meet them. She was in her early 30s with short, dyed red hair and large silver hoop earrings. Despite the tough earthy body, Becky had a friendly toothy smile, freckles that made her young, and an easy manner. She extended her hand and shook Robert's. He took it reluctantly. She gave Joanna a peck on the cheek.

Gerry was hanging easily on a line. He was thin, muscular and shirtless, wearing electric red and yellow swimming trunks. He was 35ish, with militaristically short brown hair and a tanned-weathered triangular face. A large tattoo of a pitchfork was on his upper right arm and a little red tattooed rose adorned his navel. He stared back with deep-set serious eyes that suggested defensiveness and suspicion.

Gerry slipped on his sunglasses, said his hellos with an Irish accent, and helped the passengers aboard. Robert mumbled a hello and kept his tense body at a distance.

"Beer, wine or champagne?" Gerry asked. "I run a happy boat, here." He faced Joanna. "It's good to see you again, Joanna. Ain't seen you for weeks. How's the stargazing business?"

"No complaints. By the way, have you come into a little money lately?"

He looked up surprised, scratching his head. "Now there you go with that stuff again. Yeah…my uncle died a month ago in Ireland. He left me a little over 10 thousand bucks. Nobody even knew he had that much. The cheeky bastard kept it all in the basement of his house."

Joanna smiled, with self-satisfaction. "I thought so. Your 8th house was active. It rules death and legacies."

Gerry winked at her, impressed. "You are scary there, Joanna."

Gerry turned to Robert. "You better be careful with Joanna, here, Robert. She knows things about yourself that you don't even know."

Robert nodded uncomfortably. "Yeah, I've experienced that a couple of times."

"They'd burn her as a witch in the old days," Gerry said, grinning darkly, working his way to the cockpit.

Becky threw her hands to her hips, shaking her disapproving head at him. "He has a friggin' weird sense of humor, doesn't he Joanna?"

"Oh, yeah… That's the afflicted Scorpio in him."

"You ever sail, Robert?"

Robert lowered his head. "I owned a boat a while back..."

Gerry and Becky went to work preparing the boat. Gerry removed the sail cover, as Becky pulled on her gloves and began untying the lines.

Joanna and Robert stepped down through the small doorway into the lower cabin, ducking their heads as they descended below.

They paused, taking in the surroundings. The spectacular interior was finished in a glistening varnished cherry. The folded-out main cabin table had a silver tray of finger sandwiches. Another held various cheeses: Brie, Cheddar and Swiss. There was an artistic arrangement of crackers, sliced apples and pears covered in plastic wrap. Joanna touched the damp white tablecloth that held the trays.

"They won't slide as we glide," she said, grinning at her own joke.

A wine rack was richly stocked with red and white wine and crystal glasses. In the sink was a silver champagne cooler with a chilled bottle of Dom Perignon.

"Impressive," Robert said.

"We certainly won't get thirsty or hungry," she said.

"What does Gerry do for a living?"

"He repairs boats. Makes a good living."

Robert inspected the double berths, drawers and lockers. He ran his hands along the smooth cherry finish. "Quite a home," Robert said. "Beautifully done."

"I love the sea, but I don't think I could live on it for long periods like Gerry and Becky," Joanna said, as she sat down at the chart table.

"How did you meet them?"

"I did their charts about two years ago when I first moved here. I suggested that they were very compatible and should get married. They did. I went to the wedding and they seem to be living happily ever after."

They heard the engine kick over and thrum.

"Are you hungry?" Joanna asked.

"No. I think I'd rather go up top and watch."

"Me too."

On deck, they joined Gerry in the cockpit. They sat across from him. Becky was forward, readying the sails.

"We're going to motor out a little ways." Gerry said, looking around, checking either side as they left the slip. "Then we're going to kick some serious wind ass."

They motored out of the inlet between two stone jetties, passing fishing boats, watching gulls drift and screech over a patio seafood restaurant on shore.

Gerry turned the boat downwind and shut off the engine. Under spinnaker and mainsail, and carried by the current, they left the land and drifted toward open sea. They met the first ocean swells, feeling the deck rise under their feet.

Resolute leapt eagerly into the waves, as wind whistled through the rigging and the bow spray reached the cockpit. The sails rumpled and the mast swirled hypnotically, dancing through clouds and the blue sky. The sea slid by, steadily away from the shore. Joanna relaxed and glimpsed the lumps of hazy green land far behind, as she watched Robert lean back on his elbows staring up into the sky.

The boat gathered speed, progressing into deeper water. Gerry held the wheel lightly, almost perfectly still. He called out to Becky. "We're looking good, Baby!"

Becky continued checking the lines, adjusting them as the wind shifted, grabbing the side rails as she moved about the boat with great skill and alacrity.

"We belong on the water," Gerry said, as if talking to the winds. "98% water we're made of… and that's sea water."

"Where are we headed?" Robert asked.

Gerry pointed toward the horizon. "Out there, Robert. Way out there. Maybe we'll take a little turn out to the lighthouse."

There was a lull in the conversation. The horizon expanded into an infinite hot blue line and the quiet dialogue of the sea and the glittering sun mellowed them into silence and private thoughts.

Finally, Robert turned to Gerry.

"Do you mind if I steer for awhile?"

Gerry didn't flinch. "Hell no. Take it."

Gerry stepped aside and let Robert take the wheel. Robert adjusted his balance with the motion of the boat, glancing up at the sails and steadying the wheel.

"The wind isn't shifting that much now," Robert said.

Gerry looked about. "Yeah…we're probably only doing about 4 knots."

Gerry removed his sunglasses and squinted a bright eye toward Robert. "So, how does it feel to be a hunted man, with a price on his head, hiding out with a beautiful girl, Robert?"

Robert bristled.

"Gerry!! Shut up!" Becky called.

Joanna looked on, stunned.

"Hey, I was just makin' a joke. I didn't mean nothin."

"It's not funny, Gerry," Becky called, approaching.

Gerry spread his hands. "It was just a joke."

Becky frowned. "Let's go down and get some lunch, Gerry."

"I'm not hungry," Gerry said.

"Yes you are. Let's go."

Becky worked her way back to the cockpit. "Cheers, you two. Can I bring you anything?"

"No thanks, Becky," Joanna said.

Becky seized Gerry's arm and pulled him below.

Joanna studied Robert. "Sorry about that."

Robert was noticeably disturbed. "I can tell you right now, you can't trust them. I'll bet anything he tells on us."

"He won't, Robert. I know he won't."

"What the hell did he mean, price on my head."

"Nothing. That's just his sense of humor."

Robert's face darkened. "We shouldn't have done this, Joanna."

"I had to get away from that house, Robert. I was feeling like a prisoner. Like the whole world had us by the throat."

"We are prisoners. We both knew it when we started this. We're prisoners and we'll keep on being prisoners until…ah the hell with it."

Joanna leaned toward him. "Robert, Gerry won't tell."

Robert shook his head. "I've seen too many crooks, Joanna. I've seen their eyes. That guy's a crook."

"You're over-reacting. I gave them some money."

"It won't be enough. They'll want more."

"I know them. They won't."

"Okay, okay, let's just drop it."

Joanna sat in an uneasy silence as she watched Robert at the helm. Minutes later, the sun and sea softened his face. He adjusted the wheel and Joanna felt the boat respond, gliding on updrafts, sails rippling. She contemplated his quiet determination and self-assuredness, as he seemed to understand the sea and embrace the boat. A gust of breeze, cool and salty, washed across her face, and she presented her face to it, fully, eyes fully open.

Robert removed his sunglasses for a moment. He looked at her and she saw something ignite in his eyes. "I'm sorry, Joanna. I just don't want all this to end. I don't want us to end."

Joanna watched, absently, as he set the compass on the autopilot. He released the wheel and eased down next to her. They sat in silence, feeling their bodies sway with the rolling seas, hearing Gerry and Becky's muffled conversation in the cabin below.

Robert crossed his arms looking first at the sails, and then at the position of the boat. His eyes finally rested on her.

He made a fist, and then opened his hand, staring down at it. "I'm seeing that damn egg fall again. It's so silly. I mean, what the hell does it mean?"

Joanna looked him over, in a slow thoughtful silence. Her eyes were as clear as a child's. "Robert…the next time you see that egg falling, I want you to do something. I want you to picture yourself standing under the tree, cupping your hands and catching it."

He relaxed a little, studying her with admiration. "Alright, doctor. I'll try it." After a short pause he wrapped his arm around her shoulder. "Joanna… I want you to make my horoscope or whatever the right name for it is. Let's just see what the future holds. Hell, why not?"

Her eyes fell softly on him. "Okay, if you really want me to."

He leaned over and kissed her. After they disengaged, Joanna gave a little audible sigh.

"What was that for?"

"...I was just thinking.... When I was a little girl, all the boys used to make fun of me because I was crippled. I hated them. I never cried in front of them and never let them know how much it hurt. I wasn't going to give them the satisfaction. But at home I cried my eyes out."

Robert took her hand. "Kids are cruel as hell."

"They're confused and scared by anything that's different. Just like adults. They're just more honest about it."

"And what did your father and mother say to you during those times? Did they comfort you?"

"My father would say something philosophical and my mother would say that God had some special purpose for me. I hated that and one day, just before I went out on a big date, I told her to shut up about it."

"And what was this big date like?" Robert asked.

"His name was Hal Blake and he was on the football team. I was a junior in high school."

"Didn't you hate him, like you did all boys?"

"Well, not exactly. He was very handsome. He'd gone out with me on a bet."

"A bet?"

"Yes. He'd made a bet with some of the guys that he could screw me on the first date. I had a somewhat questionable reputation at the time, from something that had happened a year back, and they all figured that I was desperate for a boyfriend and so I'd do anything—especially with a football star."

"You knew this and you went out with him anyway?"

"I didn't know about the bet when he asked me out. Hal told me, while we were eating pizza later on that night."

"He told you? I don't understand."

"Hal and I really hit if off. We just sort of liked each other and felt comfortable right away. He told me how ashamed he was and of course I fell in love with him."

Joanna stopped, looking skyward.

"And what happened to Hal?" Robert asked.

"We stayed friends, but he never asked me out again. Broke my heart, but I knew why. He didn't want to be seen with a crippled girlfriend, when he could be with a blond beauty with two big boobs and two good feet. But that was okay. Thanks to Hal, I felt a little better about myself."

Robert narrowed his eyes. "Joanna, you're about to say something thoughtful. I've learned a little how your mind works."

She squeezed his hand, staring intently into his eyes. "Robert, tell me the truth. Does my…foot, my limp bother you?"

"What the hell kind of question is that?"

"An honest one and you can give me an honest answer. It has bothered men in the past. Most men talk about it at some point. You never have."

He looked at her frankly. "Joanna, I don't give a damn about what anybody thinks about anything. I do give a damn about you—and your foot. I love you and I love your foot. Both of your feet."

Joanna persisted. "I walk with a limp, Robert. Sometimes my ankle swells up. Sometimes I can barely walk on it. When I get older, I'll probably have to walk with a crutch or a cane. Sometimes…"

Robert placed his hand over her mouth to quiet her. "I don't care! When it swells, we'll soak it. When it hurts, you prop it up and I'll kiss it. When you need a crutch, you'll have me. Okay?"

Joanna swallowed away emotion. Her eyes glistened and she wiped them. "Okay…"

Robert retracted his hand, leaned and kissed her.

Minutes later, they sat close, contented and warm in the sparkling sun.

Joanna ran her hand through his hair, feeling the wind on her face. "Robert, they're all going to want to know where you've been all this time. Have you thought about what you're going to say?"

"I'm going to tell the truth. I crashed my plane in a storm and you saved my life. We fell in love. Happy ending. End of story."

Joanna slumped a little. "Robert… you'll have to go back…soon. We can't move forward until you go back."

Robert stood, returning to the wheel, troubled. "Yes… I know. I'll have to go back soon. But not today."

The early afternoon was spent eating and talking about sailing, astrology and Gerry's hometown in Ireland. At 5 o'clock, the winds became shifty and gusting, pinwheeling *Resolute* around in all angles. Dark clouds and gusts between 15 and 25 knots blew in and Becky, Gerry and Robert flew into motion, tacking, jibing and sheeting, in and out. Joanna struggled below, cleaning up and fighting seasickness.

The boat returned to the marina just as the winds had died away and the red sun was setting across a pink tinted sky.

Joanna remained on the boat because Becky had asked her to. They stood, talking softly, in private tones, barely moving. Robert and Gerry strolled the marina, reviewing the boats, discussing sailing and stopping occasionally to take in the crimson sun as it slowly slipped into the sea.

Robert spoke in short phrases, distracted by "the girls'" secret conversation. Becky's solemn expression was unmistakable. When she'd asked Joanna to stay behind, her eyes had held a warning.

While Gerry rambled on about their recent trip to the Bahamas, Robert stole a glance toward the boat. He saw Joanna's body slacken. Her head dropped into her chest. Gerry's conversation turned to politics, but only snatches of it reached Robert's ears. His uneasy attention drifted frequently from Gerry to Joanna.

In the car on the way home, Joanna seemed oppressed. Robert asked if anything was wrong. He asked if Becky had said something that upset her.

"No…no…nothing. You know, just female talk."

Back at the house, they both showered and met on the deck. Joanna poured two glasses of wine and they toasted a wonderful day and took in the swirl of stars and the sliver of moon. It was obvious to Robert that amidst the lively sounds of singing insects, the high pounding surf and the music of the windchimes, Joanna's spirit had flagged. He couldn't draw her out of her dark mood. She was remote and tentative and when he touched and kissed her neck, she pulled away, fragile and trembling.

"Joanna, something has happened. Why won't you tell me?"

Joanna finally turned to face him. Her eyes had changed. The seconds became heavy and unimaginable as he waited. She opened her mouth to speak, and then stopped.

She tried again, in a voice strangely serene. "Becky…Becky told me something. She didn't know if she should or not. It wasn't easy for her."

Robert leaned sideways against the railing. The yellow deck light cast a shadow across his face. Joanna took a sip of wine and sat down, facing the sea. She avoided his eyes.

"Robert…your mother is ill. Very ill. It was in the news, along with a story about you…about your death." She swallowed. "Robert, she's dying."

Robert began to wilt. His jaw sagged in sorrow; his shoulders dropped. He turned away in a sudden guilty agony. "Oh…my God."

Chapter 11

They slept in the cottage, although neither had slept much. Joanna now lay in bed alone, staring into the humid darkness, confused and haunted by feelings of betrayal and compassion; her mind filled with a virulent strain of anger. She felt betrayed by a capricious world that promenades romance and love across the movie screens and the pages of steamy novels, with the false promise of fulfillment and happiness. In magazines, pop songs and TV ads, the young, with sassy attitudes and adolescent insouciance, gyrate and pose, licking their fat sensual lips in an invitation to fall under the sinister spell of Neptune, the planet of illusion.

She knew all this. She'd written about it in her book, using the symbols and signs of astrology. She had even used fairy tales as an example: Cinderella and Snow White. She had warned her readers about these not so innocent Neptunian stories and had just stopped short of writing that the naked reality of love often lies somewhere between deplorable hope and childish despair.

Joanna rolled to her side and stared out the window in an effort of self-control. The first gray light of dawn began chasing away shadows. Her compassion for Robert grew as the aching minutes passed. He had left a few minutes before and was surely roaming the beach, haggard and conflicted, as he had been most of the night.

The sun would rise shortly and the unraveling, indefinite day would begin. The painful process of separation would begin. Their perfect lifetime together was coming to an end and she was entirely unprepared for it, despite all of her astrological "wisdom" and counseling experience. She had conveniently shut out the possibility that Robert would ever leave. Over the past weeks, she had completely ignored the inevitable and the obvious: Robert had another life and he would have to go back to it. She was, after all, the "other" woman.

Joanna had no illusions. Regardless of whether Robert returned to her or not, their life together would never be the same. Their transparent innocence had finally been seen for what it was: a chimera, a little fairy tale that would have lasted forever, except that there was an epilogue. A disclaimer: "Dear Reader, all of the previous pages were written under the influence of self-delusion."

Morning came with a wet silver light, a brisk wind and a gentle mist. Joanna dressed in jeans, a sweatshirt and a jacket, and left the cottage for the house. She paused near the edge of the cliff and searched for Robert. The beach was empty. The surf restless.

Back at the house, she called for him, but there was no answer. Her voice fell into a flat echo. She made coffee and drifted outside, warm mug in cold hands, and stood, feeling lost. Her eyes were sandy from lack of sleep. She smoked a cigarette, the first in two weeks, and waited. She waited for him, and finished the coffee.

She left the deck and returned to the damp cliffs, peering down as the wind began to shred the fog. Then she saw him. Robert was facing the sea, standing stiffly, hands stuffed deeply into his pockets. She refused to cry. But a dull ache scraped away at her insides and she found it hard to breathe.

When he returned, she was sitting at the kitchen counter, chin propped in her hand, staring bleakly. Robert's jacket was beaded with water, his hair damp, his face set in a dreary resignation. He poured a mug of coffee and sat down next to her. He was hoarse from lack of sleep.

"I'll leave today. This morning. I'll call home from a pay phone in town. I don't want anyone to know about you yet. About us. When the truth does get out, it could get pretty messy for you."

Joanna nodded. "I don't care about that. I'll be fine."

"It could take a week or so, until I can get back. Obviously, a lot depends on what mother's condition is. Anyway, I'll call you when I know."

"I hope she's okay," Joanna said.

He nodded. "I'm not going to take anything with me. I'll feel better if I know I'm coming back to everything. It will give me the strength I need to tell Connie and my father… to make the necessary plans."

Joanna straightened. "Robert, maybe you should wait to tell Connie. Maybe wait to tell…everything, with your mother being so sick. Maybe it's best to wait." It hurt to say the words, and she prayed he wouldn't wait.

"No…I've thought about it. The sooner I tell the truth the better. The better it will be for everyone. We can keep mother from knowing. No one will tell her."

Then the silence became excruciating.

Robert stood, waiting, hands clasped. "Well…okay. I should go." His wounded eyes shifted.

Joanna stood. They kissed, softly, as if the distance was already between them.

Robert carried nothing: no suitcase, no bag. Joanna stood on the deck and watched him move toward the cliff. She watched him turn and wave as he descended the stairs and disappeared from sight. She wasn't going to watch him leave—walk away on the beach—but a painful urgency pushed her forward. She leapt from the last step of the deck, stumbled and then hurried toward the cliffs. Gray clouds were low over the ocean and moving eastward. A light rain fell, gently tapping her bare head. At the top of the stairs she watched him draw away from her.

She loved his walk, sure and graceful. She loved the sight of him.

He would swing around the house and leave through the distant beach paths that led to an obscure part of the road. From there he would walk into town, make the call and then leave. Leave her.

The moment held too much emotion for her to manage. She turned away and made a small sound of grief.

Chapter 12

Bix Halloran, Joanna's father, would arrive in a couple of hours. She had cleaned the house thoroughly and packed Robert's clothes in boxes and stored them in the basement next to some old dusty boxes of books and winter clothes. Her father was a snoop, who was often stung into alertness by the smallest signs of odd behavior or intrigue. She didn't want to have to answer any sensitive questions. She was in a brittle, precarious state, barely managing to keep her emotions locked up and guarded. Robert had been gone for over two weeks and she hadn't heard from him.

On Labor Day, the sunlight was broiling. The day after, it was as though God had thrown the "Autumn Switch." It turned unseasonably cold and raw. Ominous fat clouds hung over a heavy gray sea and the beach was deserted. The tourists and vacationers were gone. The wind blew in desolate, hollow moans, slinging sand and rippling dune grass.

Joanna had thrown herself into work, slamming the doors on the hypothetical scenarios of "What is Robert doing now? Has he already forgotten about me? Why hasn't he called? Did his mother die? Is that why he hasn't called? Maybe, he decided to marry Connie. Maybe the price of severing his old life was too much to pay. "

Her history of door slamming was renowned. She had become an expert. She'd practiced this slamming and locking for years—ever since childhood—when her father and mother had argued over religion, money, how to cook a roast or why he wasn't more conventional. They sparred over why her mother couldn't see that "the narrow path to God" didn't mean "being closed and narrow-minded." And, finally, the one colossal argument that ran repeatedly and tragically, like a first-run film, went as follows:

Her father: "Your son's a queer or gay or whatever you want to call it, because that's the way God made him!"

Her mother: "God didn't make him that way. Timmy made himself that way! He stopped praying, stopped believing that he could be healed. And you've always encouraged him. Just like you encouraged Joni to take up the devil's work like you did! The next thing you know she's running around with some low-life who got her pregnant. And then you allowed her to go get that abortion! You took her! You took my precious baby away from me because you were jealous of our closeness. God forgive me for hating you!"

"She was only 16, Aggie. For God's sake! Did you want her whole life ruined?! She was so sick and scared; so down on herself already because of her lame foot. She tried to kill herself. And that 'boy', as you call him, was the goddamned preacher at your church, who was thrown out of that church a month later when he went after another young girl!"

"He was not the father of that child and you know it! It was that drugged up trumpet player that you brought into our house! How dare you blaspheme in this house! How dare you! You have made both of my blessed children into instruments for evil and I will never, ever forgive you for that!"

So Joanna slammed the doors. Joanna locked the doors. Joanna threw away the keys. But as she matured and sought therapy, she also knew that behind those locked doors were the starving prisoners—the innocents—who wanted freedom. She was also aware, after two weeks of not hearing from Robert, that the innocents and the frightened were pounding on those doors with heavy fists, frantic to get out.

She resisted turning on the TV, afraid of the news—terrified she'd hear a devastating truth. She didn't play the radio. She didn't leave the house. She had everything delivered.

Her tight resolve was weakening. After her father had called, telling her he was on his way, she began searching for some of those keys. The key to how she'd get through the next couple of days without cracking—without spilling out everything to a man who already considered her a little off balance and fragile.

Bix Halloran entered his daughter's house with the bravado and authority of a man who had recently discovered a brave new world, carved out a national monument or broken new ground in the fight against some rare disease. His tall, thin, wiry body worked a space with busy hands and eyes. His steel gray flattop added a stern touch, his crisp goatee was white, his voice deep and resonant, the envy of many preachers who'd had the unfortunate experience of meeting him when they'd come to the house to minister to his wife.

"Do you believe in God?" they sometimes asked.

"Hell yes," he replied.

"Then why don't you come to church with your wife?"

"Because you people talk a lot about goodness, charity and loving your neighbor as yourself, but do very little about it. You all dwell in these little insidious camps where you snipe and criticize, believing that yours is the way—the only way—and that everyone else is going to hell. Camp Methodist. Camp Baptist. Camp Presbyterian. Camp Catholic! I don't like camps and I don't like hypocrites!"

They had seldom asked him to church a second time.

Joanna greeted him at the door, a mass of tangled nerves. She wore a heavy brown sweater, jeans and red sneakers. Bix wore a red and black flannel shirt and brown corduroys. He dropped his suitcase and bear-hugged his daughter. Then he held her at arm's length, his bright green eyes exploring her face and figure.

"Yep, just what I thought."

"Thought what?"

"Something's up."

"Nothing's up."

"Yep."

"Don't start with me, Dad. Nothing's up. I've been working a lot."

"On the new book?"

"Yes…and other things."

Joanna kept moving her eyes away from him.

"You've gained weight, which is good. You've got good color and your hair is gleaming. Very interesting."

Joanna stepped backwards, away from the force of his scrutiny. She snatched his suitcase, yanked it up and started for the guest bedroom—Robert's room. Her father followed, appraising the rooms.

"Hasn't changed since I was last here."

She dropped the suitcase beside the bed, and he wandered in, sniffing about.

"You heard from your brother?" Bix asked.

"He called from St. Thomas. He's working on another cruise ship. For Cunard, I think. The Cunard Countess. He's going to all the Caribbean islands."

"Well I'm glad those piano lessons didn't go to waste. He doesn't call me much anymore. Hasn't been by to see me in 2 years. Pisces and Aquarius. That's a strange combination. Aquarius makes him eccentric and Pisces makes him want to hide it."

"Well, I'm sure you want to rest," Joanna said, hoping it was true.

"Yeah, I'm bone-tired. I left the house at seven. I'll just nap for a little while. Then we'll catch up."

Joanna winced at the thought, and left the room.

Joanna went into her office and shut the door. She tried to work but couldn't. She felt heavy and defeated. As she yawned and lay her head on the desk, one of the locked doors opened. Why hadn't Robert called?

She sought distraction. She slipped a tape into her tape recorder. It was Miles Davis. Joanna had received her love of jazz from her father. His father had named him Bix, after the legendary trumpeter Bix Biederbecke. A celebrated guitarist, Eddie Conden, once said that Bix's horn sounded like a girl saying yes. Her father loved that, and he often told the story of Biederbecke's brief life and tragic death, embellishing and revising it each time, depending on his audience, making sure to include himself in some way. "I play the trumpet, you know. I played professionally for a while. My son plays piano, and I insisted he take lessons. My wife plays the organ and I bought her the best organ on the market. Everybody in the family plays something, except Joanna. She just loves to play around."

After dinner, Joanna deflected her father's jabbing questions with the skill of a Samurai warrior.

"Why don't you tell me who you met?"

"Because I haven't met anyone."

"Why have you gained weight?"

"I'm getting older. I haven't been exercising."

"Why haven't you changed anything around here?"

"I have. I remodeled the cottage."

After dinner, they walked the silent, manicured path to the cottage. There was no criticism on his face, just genuine wonder. "This is really nice."

"It increases the property value, you know, Dad."

"Are you thinking about selling?" he asked, lifting an eyebrow.

"No, no…just thought I should do it."

They explored exterior and interior, finishing the tour outside as the day relaxed into evening.

To her surprise, he approved. "Who did this?"

She shrugged. "Just, you know… some guys in town."

"Damn good work. Damned good. A lot of nice touches. Hell, whoever did it really put some hard work in it. Really put themselves in it."

Joanna shivered in the chilly wind. She folded her arms across her chest, feeling a disconsolate loneliness. "Yes…they did."

On the second day of his visit, Bix sat Joanna down on the deck, handed her a mug of coffee and leaned back in his chair, looking oddly serene as he glimpsed the sea and wide dome of blue sky. The morning air crackled with a cool refreshing wind.

"Joni…Joanna, the reason I came by, other than wanting to see you, is that I have updated my will and have made you the executor. I've done this because I have some rather nasty aspects coming up in the next year."

Joanna felt a chill. "What aspects?"

"Doesn't matter. Let's just say that I'm updating my insurance after I return from England. In short, my darling girl, I'm going to die, probably in June of next year."

"Come on, Dad. You know how difficult it is to predict death in a horoscope. Death doesn't always mean physical death in a chart; it can be the end of something: a new job, a shift of some kind."

"I know, Joni, I taught you, remember?"

"Dad… you…"

He waved her away with his hand. "It doesn't matter, Joanna, we're all going to die. It's okay. It's just that I want to see you, well, taken care of. I want to know that you're going to be all right."

"I'm fine, Dad, really. I'm good."

"You're not. Some damn thing has happened and for the life of me, I don't understand why you don't tell me what it is."

Her mouth trembled a little. "Stop worrying. I'm fine. My work is going well. I have more clients than I can handle, I've already received an advance for the book I'm working on and I've got some speaking engagements coming up that I've finally decided to take because it will be good for me to get out and away from here once in awhile."

He stared at her, looking uncomfortable. "I'm worried about Tim, too. He lives a reckless, dissolute life, Joni.

He has no Saturn to steady him or caution him. He has all those planets in Pisces squaring Uranus. He's so damn unstable. Do you talk to him more than I…is he okay? I mean, really okay?"

Her voice took on a confidential tone. "Dad…he's just, I don't know, looking for something. He seems real confused. He had a boyfriend for a while but then after they broke up, he's just been…" Her voice fell away.

Bix lowered his head. "…Yeah, I know. God, you want the best for your kids. You want their happiness more than you want breath in your body." He looked at her lovingly. "I hope someday you'll experience that, Joni. I'm so damn sorry your marriage didn't work out."

"Let's not get into that again, Dad. We both know of my afflictions to the Seventh House of marriage."

"Now don't sell yourself short. You've also got some good supporting aspects, Joni. You've got a good horoscope. You'll find the right guy someday. I'm sure of it."

Joanna took a sip of coffee. When she spoke, it was in the tone of reverie. "Dad…do you ever think about Mom?"

After a glum silence, he wiped his mouth and sat back. "Yes, Joanna, I do. I think about her everyday and I chastise myself everyday and I reproach myself everyday for not being the husband I wanted to be. The truth is, Joanna, I fell short. In the end, I think I left your mother feeling isolated and unhappy."

He struggled to make his voice sound impartial and just. "God, it can be an awful thing to be in love with a woman who thinks the very opposite of yourself. Who seems to breathe different breaths; who seems to walk the ground of an entirely different planet. But I tried to find her, Joanna, I tried to find her and please her as best I could.

"When we were first married we had such a hell of a good time. Then after about five years, she met this crazy woman who took her to church and that was that. Your mother got all fired on trying to make everybody perfect and good and right. Hell, all I could say to her was that human beings are innately flawed and that's the way the good Lord made them—if you can call the good Lord 'good.' I personally think that the good Lord is a mischievous little instigator."

After some consideration, he nodded a little. "But you know what, Joanna, I loved your mother dearly. I surely did."

At dinner that evening Bix told her of the seminar he was going to give in London. He took her there with his excitement and his roaring melodramatic voice, spinning tales of past trips, describing the characters, the questions and the spunky women who had thrown themselves at him.

"I feel like a rock star sometimes, Joni. A damned rock star."

As they were eating chocolate ice cream, Bix became uncustomarily quiet. From experience, Joanna knew he was working on a thought; shifting, measuring and weighing the approach of his inevitable communication. Finally, with the quiet confident voice of a scholar, he cleared his throat and spoke. "I just happened to stumble upon a chart that was lying on your desk today. You had gone walking on the beach."

Joanna stopped eating. A swift anger arose. "Just happened to stumble…"

"Yes…I was just passing by. Just curious. All very innocent."

"Dad, that's my private office and you know it!"

"Of course it is, but the door was open. Anyway, I saw a chart. A very interesting chart. And you know how I'm irresistibly drawn to charts."

"It's none of your business!"

He ignored her indignation. "It was the chart of a man: one Robert Zachary Harrison."

Joanna's eyes hardened. "You had no right to go in there and you know it!"

"A strong chart. A powerful chart. I found it endlessly fascinating. This man could make a very big noise in the world someday, if he plays his cards right."

Joanna slammed down her spoon.

Bix lowered his eyes on his food, like a little boy about to be scolded. His voice dropped into a causal innocence. "And from your rather violent response and choice of words, I can see that this gentleman is more than just a client."

"He is a client! Nothing more! He called, asked for a consultation and I'm giving him one. Whether you ignore me or not, you know very well that you invaded my private space. You still haven't learned there are certain boundaries that you don't cross. That's one of the things about you that drove mother crazy."

Joanna wanted to hurt him, but he grinned, instead, aware of her tactic. "I also saw you had the chart of the United States of America next to it. I glanced at both. I saw your notes. If you're comparing the two charts, then I'd imagine that this person, Robert, might be interested in politics? Why? Because he could be the son of Senator Harrison, from the great state of Connecticut. It's just a guess, of course. But then, I think he crashed his plane into the ocean over a month ago, not too far from here, if memory serves. Yes, and my memory serves. It always serves. Everyone had given him up for dead."

Joanna shoved her chair back from the table and shot up. With burning eyes she stormed out of the kitchen to the deck, slamming the door.

Minutes later Bix drifted out, wine glass in hand. Joanna stood bolt erect, with her back to him, staring blindly at the sea.

"Joanna…you're over-reacting," he said with a consoling, wise tone. "You always did over-react to things."

Enraged, she whirled to face him. "This is my home! And in my home you respect my privacy or get out!"

He held up a hand. "Okay, okay, Joanna. Okay. Just calm down. It was all very innocent."

"Nothing you do is innocent, father. It's always calculated."

"Now that's unfair."

"Don't play hurt with me! Don't play the victim!"

"Okay, Joanna then who is the victim? You? Don't get mad at me because of the truth. Because Robert Harrison left you. Because he's not coming back."

Sobering from her anger, she glared at him, the energy draining from her body. "What are you talking about? What do you know about it?"

"Joanna, I watch TV. Do you?"

Joanna stared in a frightened wonder… "No…"

Bix spoke with caution. "Joanna…look, I don't know what happened, but I'm not a stupid man. I know, some how or the other, you two met. From the look on your face and your strong reactions, I'd say you fell in love with the man. That much I'm sure of. I know that from your chart and from your response."

Joanna was still, afraid she'd shatter if she moved a muscle. "What about the TV? What did they say?"

"You must know the story. He must have called you."

"Just tell me, dammit!"

"It was all over the papers and TV for a week. Johnny Carson even had a joke about it in his monologue the other night. Anyway, the papers had headlines like: 'Man Resurrected from the Sea.' 'Senator's Son Loses Plane and Memory.'"

"Robert said he crashed into the sea and was rescued by two people on a sail boat: Becky and Gerry Day. They've become quite famous, too. Anyway, Robert said he'd lost his memory and couldn't remember who he was or where he'd come from. He said that the couple unselfishly nursed him back to health."

Joanna felt a sharp knifing pain in her chest. Her shoulders slumped.

"There were some holes in the story: like why didn't they call the authorities sooner, and why didn't he visit a doctor after such a dramatic accident, but, all of those questions just add to the mystery. And with his family name and money, everyone just assumes they cover up whatever is unpleasant and potentially damaging. That is the way of the rich and powerful or so some of the commentators say. The mysteries help to sell newspapers. And the TV folks are just loving it."

Joanna spoke weakly. "And what about his family?"

"There was a big fat photograph of Robert and his very attractive fiancée. The caption read: Reunited at Last. The story that followed read something like: It was a bittersweet reunion. Four days after Robert Harrison mysteriously returned to his family, his loving mother died. As one newspaper put it, 'There was great happiness mixed with great loss in the Harrison family.'"

Joanna turned from him. Her tears came softly and slowly.

Bix advanced toward her, and then stopped. "Joanna, I'll stay a couple more days if you want me to."

She shook her head. "No…I want you to go. In the morning."

"Joanna, I am very sorry. I didn't know…well, I didn't know you felt so strongly."

"…Please…Just leave…in the morning."

"Joanna…" His hands became nervous. "These are powerful people…I hate to be the one to say it, but you're probably going to get a visit. I'm surprised they've waited this long. You're a loose end that they can't afford to stay loose. Some representative of the family will surely come by to talk to you."

Beaten and humble, Joanna gave a futile shrug of her shoulders. "I don't care."

"Joanna… I really…"

She cut him off in a meek voice. "Please…."

She descended the stairs and hurried off toward the path to the cottage.

Bix watched her disappear into the darkness, feeling a bitter self-disparagement. He slammed his wine glass down and it shattered. "Damn you, Bix Halloran! Damn you and your boastful tongue!"

Chapter 13

Joanna sat in a rocker on the screened-in cottage porch, wrapped in a woolen blanket. Her swollen eyes wandered with the gray morning shadows. The agony in her chest had robbed her of sleep. She'd awaited the coming dawn with reluctance and restlessness. She'd lain in bed feeling the empty spaces in the rooms and in her heart.

It was under her pillow that she found the envelope. She drew it out and gripped it, as if it held the secret to her life. In careful script, it read "JOANNA". She finally got up and wandered to the porch, taking it with her, unopened.

The sky was layered with gray broken clouds, pushed westward by a chilly erratic autumn wind. The song birds sang shrilly and the fog was high in the trees. She watched a boat, under full white sail, appear like a cloud on the silver slate sea, drift across her line of vision and then fade like a ghost into mist.

She slowly opened the envelope and drew out the folded page. With care she peeled open the panels and read:

Dearest Joanna:

I am not a poet or a writer of sonnets. I'm a practical man who has had his foundation shaken to the core. If there were truths I once held as true, they are now questioned. If there were absolutes, they have been shattered. If life held promise and clear pathways to success and achievement, they have been obscured and lost.

My darling, I have simply fallen in love with you. It is frightening and wonderful. I sometimes think that when God created heaven and earth that love was the one thing that he kept a secret, deep within the hearts of the blessed and the deserving. I think he probably placed the diamond of it in very few hearts. But he placed it in yours, Joanna, and I have benefited from your prodigious intelligence and astounding beauty.

I will come back to you, Joanna. I have to. I have no other choice. Wait for me, my darling. Wait for me. We have many wonderful years together.

With deepest love,

I, Robert Zachary Harrison, vow to return to you.

Joanna wiped away an agony of tears. At 7:30, she started for the house. She hoped her father would be gone. To her delight and surprise, he was. The dishes from the night before had been washed and put away. He'd left her a note on the kitchen counter.

Dear Daughter:

Please forgive your old man. He is often insufferable and insensitive when he should be a good listener and a friend. I am not blessed with the compassion of a Pisces nor the nurturing kindness of a Cancer. My Leo Moon and Mars in Aries in the 3rd house have gotten me into many scrapes.

Despite my many shortcomings, I do love you and I implore you to please call me in London and let me know how you are. The hotel and number are below. I leave you with a quote by Jane Austen. I often use it in seminars whenever I talk about that wonderfully mysterious planet Neptune that seems to be plaguing you of late.

> *'Seldom, very seldom does complete truth belong to any human disclosure; seldom can it happen that something is not a little disguised, or a little mistaken.'*

Perhaps the truth of what has recently happened to you is disguised or a little mistaken, Joanna. Perhaps, in time, it will all be revealed. I hope so.

My dear daughter, my love for you may seem remote, but I assure you it is alive and rich and it only wants the best for you.

Your gruff old man,

Bix

After she forced herself to eat a bowl of oatmeal, Joanna finally fell into a deep sleep. She lay tucked away in her L-shaped swallow-you-up living room couch, when the doorbell rang. It took a second round of rings before she snapped awake.

"Hello," she called out, thinking it was the telephone. It had been part of a shattered dream. "Hello!!"

She pushed up, rubbed her sleepy eyes and padded off barefoot to the door, her vision fuzzy, her mouth funky, her hair a mess. She opened the door and shaded her hand from the glare of bright autumn sunlight.

A woman carrying a briefcase, dressed smartly in a pinstriped business suit, stood staring back, caught between seriousness and the casual.

"Ms. Halloran?"

Joanna squinted at her. "Yes?"

"I'm Emma Pierson. I wonder if I might speak to you."

Joanna looked her over. Emma was an attractive woman of about 40. Her jet-black hair was short and stylish, her cheekbones high, her deep blue eyes focused and clear. Her smile was uncomfortable and forced, and despite her effort to appear informal, Joanna's impression was that Emma had quickly buffed her personality to make it appear shinier than it actually was.

"Speak to me about what?"

"A rather personal matter."

Joanna blinked, closed her eyes, reopened them and focused. She inhaled slowly, in recognition.

"Ah…yes…a personal matter," she said, remembering her father's words about loose ends. "And who sent you on this personal matter?" she asked in a scratchy voice.

"May I come in so we can discuss it?"

"Only if you tell me who sent you."

"Alright, Ms. Halloran. I'm here as a representative of the Harrison family."

"I see," Joanna said. She looked past Emma, letting her wait for an answer. She made her wait a long time.

"Ms. Halloran?"

"Yes?" Joanna asked, innocently.

"May I come in?"

Joanna backed away. "Oh, of course."

Emma crossed the threshold and Joanna closed the door, leaning back against it. She made no effort to move.

Emma fumbled with her purse that was swung over her shoulder. "May we sit?"

"Of course we may," Joanna said, ready to start a fight. She suddenly saw this "representative" as an ice cream truck, pulling into a school yard, its tinny speakers playing "Mary had a Little Lamb."

Emma sat on the recliner, but did not recline; Joanna eased down on the couch. Joanna made no attempt to fix her frizzy hair or smooth out her wrinkled blue fleece sweatshirt. Her black running pants had a spot of dried oatmeal that Joanna hadn't bothered to wash off.

Emma laid the briefcase on her lap and folded her hands on it. Her posture was ruler straight, her features relaxed, her voice sonorous and smooth.

"As I said, Ms. Halloran, I am here…"

"Joanna!" she said, curtly. "Call me Joanna."

Emma swallowed and began again. She blinked quickly and cleared her throat. Joanna saw a slight crack in her presentation. Emma started from the beginning as if reading from a script. "As I said, Joanna, I am here as a representative of the Harrison family and…"

Joanna interrupted. "…The entire Harrison family or just one or two members of the Harrison family?"

"I am here as a …I represent the entire Harrison family."

"Every single one of the Harrisons? All the kids and grandchildren. The pets?"

Emma hesitated, regrouped and tried again. Her voice grew softer, but Joanna saw sparks of irritation in her eyes. "Joanna, I am here because the Harrison family is aware of your very sensitive relationship with Robert, and they want to express their profound gratitude for everything you've done."

"What have I done?"

"You saved his life."

"He would have survived with or without me."

"Nonetheless, the family is grateful and they would like to express their gratitude."

"I accept their gratitude."

Emma looked down at her briefcase. "They want to express their gratitude in monetary means."

"Hummm...monetary means."

Emma's eyes lifted from the briefcase. Her voice gained strength. "They're prepared to offer you money for your kindness."

"Ah, money. Now we're getting someplace. How much money are they offering for my kindness?"

Emma went back to the script. "In addition to their gratitude for your unselfishness, with regard to Robert's recovery and return, their gratitude includes and extends to the fact that you have not made public the full truth of the relationship."

"Yeah, and I've been wondering what took you so long to stop by. The Harrison family must be very trusting of me to have waited this long."

Joanna sensed that Emma had the answer and wanted to express it, but she wasn't about to. "As I said, the Harrison family is grateful and they want to compensate you."

"In other words, I'm being compensated for not having gone to the press with the fact that Robert and I were lovers. For the fact that Robert said he'd call me within a week. For the fact that he said he'd tell his fiancée that he loved me. It's such an old, old sordid story, isn't it? Is that what you mean, Emma?"

Emma licked her lower lip. "They are grateful to you, Joanna. Profoundly grateful."

Joanna reached for a pack of cigarettes. She shook one out, snatched up a book of matches, plucked one from the stack and struck it. She watched it flare, and then lit the cigarette. She blew the smoke toward the ceiling. "Emma, you have got one helluva job. I hope they're paying you well."

Emma didn't respond.

"How much?" Joanna asked.

Emma blinked and cleared her throat. "The family is prepared to offer you five hundred thousand dollars."

Joanna lifted an eyebrow. "I see…to be honest, Emma, I'd expected more. I could make much more if I went to the press. Went on TV. If I wrote a book. Look, Emma, we both know that 'the family' is prepared to offer more than that. Let's not play games here, what is the highest offer you've been approved to make?"

Emma gave Joanna a significant look. "One million five hundred thousand dollars."

"A million and a half. That's about what I expected. Not bad. Not bad at all. And if I accept, what do I have to do?"

"Sign a contract that you will never disclose to any commercial media, be it print, film or television, or to your friends or any members of your family, the sum and substance of your relationship with Robert Harrison."

Joanna took a long drag on the cigarette. "I see. And what if I take the money and then go to the media anyway. What will you do, kill me?"

"We will sue you for breach of contract. We will take the necessary steps to protect the family."

"In other words, you'll try to discredit me, hound my family and friends and try to take everything I own."

"We will protect the family."

"By the way, did Robert authorize this?"

"I'm not at liberty to say."

"Oh, not at liberty..." Joanna said, sarcastically. "And I guess you or some other representative stopped by to see Becky and Gerry Day and Dr. Ned Palmer?"

"I cannot say."

"No, of course not. They obviously accepted the offer. I hope they held out for the big bucks."

Emma waited stoically.

Joanna concentrated on her. "Emma...would you accept the offer? Would you sell out?"

Emma was gently startled by the question. "I...it...a. Ms. Hallo... Joanna, it's not for me to say. I can say, in all honesty, that the Harrison family is truly grateful to you. I can say that."

"Yeah, yeah, yeah, blah, blah, blah."

"Do you need time to think about it?" Emma asked.

"No, Emma, I don't need any time at all. I don't want the money."

"I beg your pardon?"

"I don't want the money. None of it. Not one dollar of it."

Emma's eyes searched the walls for an answer. "Joanna, I'm sure I can get approval for a little more."

"I don't want more."

"Are you telling me that you intend to go the press?"

"No, I'm not."

"Then I'm afraid I don't understand. What is it that you want?"

Joanna dabbed the cigarette out in the ashtray and pulled her legs up so that she sat cross-legged, leaning slightly forward, her eyes fixed and hard.

"This is what I want, Emma. I want you to draw up another contract. In that contract I want you to include, with the necessary and appropriate legal language, the following words: I, Robert Harrison, do agree to release all present and future custody as the biological father of Joanna Halloran's child. Neither I, nor any member of my family, will ever attempt to contact Joanna or her child as long as any of us live.

"I want the contract signed by the legal representative of the Harrison family; and, by the way, I will have my attorney look it over to make sure there are no loopholes of any kind. If Robert or any member of the Harrison family declines to sign the contract, I will go to the press with the entire story and I will milk it for all it's worth. I will do my very best to destroy Robert's career and disgrace the Harrison family. Is all of that very clear, Ms. Pierson?"

Emma sat rigid. She gave Joanna a frosty stare. "I see. You realize, I'm sure, Joanna, that before we can sign such a contract, we will require a doctor of our choosing to examine you. We will need proof that the child is Mr. Harrison's."

Joanna grinned, darkly. "Emma, you graduated from law school, didn't you? You probably went to Harvard or Yale. You are not a stupid woman, are you? I am not going to submit to one goddamn examination by your doctor or by anyone else's doctor. I have been to my doctor and I can assure you I am pregnant and that Robert is the father. Do you understand?"

Emma glared, but didn't speak.

Joanna continued. "Emma, I want that contract signed and delivered to me within five days—that is, by next Monday—or I will write the most sensational tell-all book you have ever read. Do I make myself clear?"

Emma grabbed hold of her briefcase and shot up. Her voice took on an edge. "Yes, Ms. Halloran. You've made yourself perfectly clear. I'll see myself out."

She whirled in offense, and walked heavily to the front door. She jerked it open and left, shutting it firmly.

After Emma left, Joanna didn't move from the couch. She sat there for hours, drunk with depression and fatigue. She stared at nothing with half-dead eyes. As evening approached, she went to the kitchen and reached for a bottle of wine. She was about to uncork it, when a thought struck: the baby. That's what Dr. Hanover, her OBGYN had said only two days before. They had sat in his little claustrophobic office, with photos of fishing expeditions from the Midwest to Montauk, and stared at each other for a time. He was a big tree of a man in his early 30's, and handsome, with long brown hair, a strong chin and lucid brown eyes. She stared into the emerald carpet, holding a paper cup of half drunk water. He sat behind his desk, white coat on, stethoscope looped around his neck.

"They're all positive, Joanna. You're definitely pregnant," he'd said in a small apologetic voice, not lifting his eyes from the desktop. "What are you going to do?"

"I'm going to have it," she'd said.

"And the father has left you?"

She'd stood abruptly. Her voice fell into bland artificiality. "Thank you, Dr. Hanover. Thanks for everything."

He pushed up. "Joanna, call me if you need anything. Anything at all."

Joanna sat in the kitchen, drinking a soda, listening to the driving rain strike the windows. She turned on the radio—the first time in weeks—and found a jazz station out of Riverhead, Long Island. They played Ella Fitzgerald and Art Tatum, before cutting away to the weather report.

Lightning and wind are gusting at nearly 40 miles per hour in some places, knocking down powerlines and causing havoc with the electrical systems across the region.

Worst hit is Long Island, with a power failure already affecting more than 60,000 households, mostly on the eastern tip of Long Island. More than 6000 lightning strikes have already been detected on Long Island during the storm that began soon after four p.m.

More than 25,000 people have reported losing power in Brooklyn, Westchester, Staten Island and the Bronx as well as 32,000 in Connecticut and 11,000 in New Jersey.

When darkness descended in gray eerie shadows, Joanna stood and made her way, tortuously, toward the back door, as if death itself were calling. She reached for her raincoat and then paused, staring as if it were unfamiliar and unnecessary. She replaced it on the hook, and moved toward the door, opening it slowly. A sudden burst of wet wind pushed her backwards. She switched on the porch light and peered out. In the last light of day, she saw rain falling hard; great sliding doors of it were drenching the world. It drummed on the deck and pocked the ground, forming puddles, streams and rivulets. Thunder rolled heavily, rattling the windows; the ugly sky was stabbed by strobes of lightning.

Joanna stepped outside, bending into the storm. The cold pelting arrows didn't stop her. She marched down the stairs and angled left, toward the far jagged cliffs, where piles of fallen rock absorbed the full impact of the angry sea.

She strode rapidly, as if beckoned. Water streamed down her hair and face. Her fleece sweatshirt grew heavy, so she tugged it off and flung it away into the sharp wind. She kicked off her sandals.

She lifted her head to the black moving sky, silently raging at God, at any kind of God. She cursed him. She advanced steadily toward the edge of the cliff, looking about hopelessly, lost in a vicious sorrow.

As she approached the rim, lightning violently struck the cliffs, just missing her. She didn't flinch, she didn't move.

She stepped forward, her toes gripping the very soft edge of the cliff. Rocks ticked away, falling 70 feet below. Her feet ached from the cold. She wiped soaking strands of hair from her eyes and peered down at the towering waves smashing against the rocks. Tears streamed down her face.

How easy it would be, she thought. Then, it would all be over. The raging storm in her chest would stop and she'd be at peace. She'd be away from them all: her father, Robert, the Harrison family. Herself!

But the baby. The baby!

Slowly, reluctantly, she backed away, in acceptance of the catastrophe of her life: a lonely, foolish woman who'd allowed herself to become trapped. A prisoner of her own stupidity.

She doubled over in pain and fell to her knees, grabbing her stomach, weeping, her body a spasm of anguish.

She tilted her head back to let the rain beat her face in a ritualistic punishment and purification. Wash it all away, she thought. Wash away all the memories and all the joys and all the pain. Make me clean and new so that my baby will never have to feel the hurt and treachery of the world! Make my baby perfect, pure and wise. Make my baby strong, resilient and vengeful!

Part 2
The Tides of Time

Chapter 1
25 Years Later

Paula Powers Live was only minutes away from 8 o'clock air time on CNN. Paula was petit, pretty and perky. Her innocent dark eyes were perceptive, her smile easy, her manner relaxed and natural. She was Senator Bob Harrison's preferred alternative to the superd-up, high octane interviewers that many candidates had to face as they worked their way through the election process from New Hampshire to Iowa.

Paula had shot to fame in only three years, traveling the route that many recent entertainment celebrities had traveled: her father knew the right people in the entertainment world, being a rather stalwart executive with a major international corporation that was connected to entertainment.

Paula finished her degree in broadcasting at NYU and was swiftly ushered into television, beginning on the TV Guide Channel. After several interviews with the wicked and famous, her wholesome face, conservative ideas and conservative dress had struck a stark contrast to the trendy, wild and careless guests that were always carefully screened.

Her questions were simple and non-threatening. She was unassuming and funny. The camera loved her round, appealing face. When she began a relationship with an Italian billionaire—20 years older than she—her publicity and career sky-rocketed. Women of every age followed her in the tabloids, the gossip columns and the entertainment shows. Her ratings soared.

Her father's pride and joy had joined CNN when she was 26 years old. Her timing couldn't have been better. She instantly captured, and held, the much sought-after, elusive and envied television audience: the 16 to 35 year olds.

Paula left her dressing room, walking aggressively down the red carpeted corridor toward the burgundy and blue set, her high heels adding over two inches to her 5 feet 1 inch height. She was dressed casually in black slacks, a blue silk blouse and simple pearl earrings. Her hair was pulled back off her forehead and tied with a tangerine silk scarf. She smiled indulgently as she walked, passing ubiquitous TV monitors, waving at production staff and security.

As usual, the news room was bright with energy, lights and information. Regular news anchors passed and wished her luck. Famous commentators and consultants, coming or going from other shows, looked on raptly. Paula had already spoken to her boyfriend, who'd sent flowers and congrat's. Her father had called from Madrid to say he'd be watching.

She'd won the prized interview with Senator Bob Harrison, when many seasoned interviewers and news anchors had failed. Senator Harrison needed a boost in the polls and he was hoping a family interview on her show would do the trick. He'd insisted that all of his immediate family be present. He did not discuss format or send a list of preferred questions. He said he'd leave all that up to her, feeling confident that her causal friendly style wouldn't challenge him or his family dramatically.

Paula made a sharp right turn toward the set and nearly ran into her producer, Ralph Winter. His skinny, busy body often seemed to be going in 3 directions at once. His 30's something worry lines were deeper than normal. His purple and blue tie was loose at the neck and his hands were in motion, as if he were doing a Woody Allen impression.

"Okay, Paula, so they're on the set and waiting. Mrs. Harrison refused makeup, but that's okay. She looks good with her own. Senator Harrison seems cool, but I haven't been able to talk to him for more than a minute. His damned cell phone never stops ringing and the Secret Service are like, everywhere. His campaign manager reminds me of a 45-year-old Harry Potter, and I haven't eaten all day. I don't mind saying that I'm nervous as hell."

"I hope you turned down the usual cappuccino," she said, examining his bulging shifting eyes.

"Funny. The Senator and his wife don't seem nervous at all. The sons…are…"

She interrupted. "…I know, Ralph, good looking. I wouldn't kick either one of them out of bed."

"That's why I like you, Paula, you're so wholesome."

She gave him an exaggerated grin. "No, that's why you <u>love</u> me."

Paula stepped over a thick cable and paused, folding her arms. She craned her neck and sized up the famous family she was about to interview. They were seated in soft burgundy chairs, arranged in a little friendly semi-circle. Senator Harrison and his wife sat next to each other; the sons on either side; Robert Jr. next to his father and Matt next to his mother.

The background was robin-egg blue with the unobtrusive name of the show attached midway: PAULA POWERS LIVE. There would be red and yellow roses arranged tastefully behind them. That was it. Simple. Elegant. There was no live studio audience.

The three cameras would have easy access for close and long shots. Paula's empty chair faced them. Senator Harrison and his wife, Connie, were speaking quietly as a tall skinny technician attached microphones to their lapels.

The Senator was dressed in a dark suit, white shirt and powder-blue tie. His salt and pepper hair added distinction to his strong handsome face and Paula felt he was more attractive in person than on television. His expression was of calm assurance and friendliness.

His wife, Connie, wore a pale gray suit and white blouse. Her black hair with silver highlights added a glow of wisdom, and at 57 years old, she appeared vital and confident.

Their biological son, 24 year-old Robert Jr., sat restlessly. His short black hair, tight face and busy eyes revealed impatience and impulse. He was staring up into the rows of lights as if counting them. As the cameras rolled in, preparing for work, Robert Jr. adjusted his dark blue pinstriped coat and burgundy tie, looking annoyed, as if he had more important things to do.

"Probably has a couple of starlets waiting," Paula thought. *People Magazine* had rated him as one of the top 5 most handsome and eligible bachelors of the year. He had the classic rakish charm, with a slight snarling lip and piercing dark eyes.

Matt Harrison, the Harrisons' adopted son, sat quietly in a simple pride, staring at nothing in particular. His sandy hair was well over the ears and combed straight back, revealing a smooth forehead and the strong chiseled features of an athlete. She watched him as he quietly spoke to his mother. His easy manner and steady eyes inspired trust. Paula sensed that, even at 23 years old, he was someone you could lean into and trust with your deepest secrets, and it was obvious that his mother was reassured by him.

Paula sensed an integrity in Matt that she'd seldom experienced in her superficial world. She congratulated herself on her keen impressions, as she allowed her eyes to linger on Matt; on his light brown suit and open yellow shirt. His perfect jawline and broad shoulders kept drawing her eyes and, despite the rise of nerves as she glanced at the clock, Paula found herself strangely aroused by him.

"You nervous?" Ralph asked.

Paula shrugged. "A little. These aren't rock stars or actors, you know. Not the usual bubble brains I talk to. I've never interviewed a politician before. Certainly not a candidate for President. I'm not even sure I'm smart enough."

"You're smart enough or at least smart-assed enough."

"Ha, ha! Aren't we funny tonight. But you know what, Ralphy, I am gonna be more smart-assed than usual."

"Don't even joke about it."

"I'm gonna ask Mrs. Harrison about her alcoholism," Paula said.

Ralph frowned. "Paula, stop it, okay. We've been through this. The polls show that the public doesn't like it. They all like her."

"I've been getting tons of e-mails and tweets, Ralphy, and my friends are texting me constantly about this. I guarantee my listeners will blitz me if I don't ask her. They'll call me everything from a wimpy whore to a chicken shit."

"Paula!" Ralph scolded. "I'm asking you not to. The Senator is known to be very touchy about it."

"Good. Let him get touchy. It's time I got a little edgy. I've been getting blasted because I'm so sugary nice. David Letterman even makes fun of me."

"Paula!"

"You're the one who brings me those e-mails, Ralphy. You know what they say. 'How did that little slut get on TV? Her questions are so juvenile. It's obvious that her IQ doesn't rise above room temperature.'"

"This is not the night!" Ralph said, forcefully. "Not with these people. Now we went over this a hundred times, Paula. Come on!"

"There is nothing wrong about asking these people about their past, Ralphy. People expect that. Like this whole thing about the Senator's plane crash and how he lost his memory for almost 3 weeks and nobody knew where he was."

"Dammit, Paula. Are you listening to me?! Don't bring that up! That's old shit. Okay. Old! It'll just look like a cheap shot!"

She touched his nose with the tip of her index finger. "Not coming from me, Ralphy boy." She canted her head sideways, giving him a coquettish little grin. "I'll just pretend I don't know anything about it, poor little me. I'm so young and naïve. Could you please enlighten me, Senator Sir? I've heard so many conflicting stories."

Ralph threw up his hands. "No, Paula. We talked about this…over and over. He agreed to do this because he doesn't want an attack dog."

"Bullshit, Ralph!" she said, sharply. "He agreed to it because he's 10 points behind President Taylor and he needs the young vote. You know that! Like my father says, think of it as just another interview. Tomorrow morning, we'll barely remember who was on."

Ralph narrowed his serious eyes on her. "That is a family over there, Paula—a very important and influential family, who may be walking into the White House in a little over 6 months. When you ask him questions, you're asking the family questions. If you make him look bad, you look bad and you make the entire American family look bad, because tonight, Senator Harrison knows that his family represents *The* American family. You got that?! Do you understand that?!"

Paula's face reddened. Her eyes burned. "Don't patronize me, Ralph! Don't you ever patronize me!"

Ralph wiped his damp forehead, softening, but firm. "Paula… This is a very fickle business. You may be too young to know it, because you've had nothing but success. But I can tell you, because I have failed and I know the fucking bitter taste of it, that it only takes one or two bad nights for your 'loyal' fans to run off to a reality show or to *America's Funniest Home Videos.* All I'm saying is don't change your style tonight. You're easy. You're friendly. You're funny. Don't come off as a bitch! This guy will have a lot of his own loyal base watching tonight. People who never watch your show. So, be careful.

You've been prepped and you know what you need to do. So, just follow the format and do it!"

Paula heaved out a breath and grabbed him by his tie, trying to lighten the mood. "Don't worry. I'll make nice with them, Ralphy boy. Especially Matt. I could eat him up. Maybe I will after the show."

Ralph rolled his eyes and hurried away to the set to prepare for show time.

Senator Bob Harrison sat comfortably and waited, while the crew arranged the porcelain vases of peach and yellow roses on a table behind them.

Connie was silent, but her expression was pleasant. Robert Jr. drummed his fingers on his leg and Matt turned to see Paula coming toward them with a dazzling smile, her small, delicate, snow-white hand outstretched.

The Harrison family stood and greeted her, and she thanked each one for coming, allowing her hand to linger in Matt's before drawing it back slowly to her side. She felt Robert Jr.'s hungry eyes probing her body and, from the corner of her eye, she saw his father's disapproving stare.

Paula sat and allowed Makeup to add the finishing touches to her face, brushing her cheeks, examining their work through a TV monitor. The technician attached her ear mic, nodded and moved away. A nervous production assistant handed her a clipboard with typed notes attached, and then slipped away behind the camera.

"We're on in 1 minute," the red-headed female director said.

Bob Harrison waited in a detached silence.

The overhead spots burst to life, flooding the set in heat and brilliant light. The director held up five fingers, counting down to one. The red lights atop the cameras blinked on. Twenty million people, worldwide, were suddenly watching.

Paula felt a tightness in her throat. Her hands were clammy. Her heart raced. She looked directly into the camera, flashing her game smile.

"Good evening and welcome to *Paula Powers Live*. Tonight I have the pleasure of welcoming a great American family to my show. Tonight, Senator Bob Harrison, the leading Republican candidate for the President of the United States, his wife, Connie, and their two sons are here, and I couldn't be more pleased."

The cameras floated around them, taking a group shot of the Harrison family and then focusing tight shots on each of their faces. Ralph was directing the cameras from the control booth.

Paula hitched one leg over the other, to show she was causal and relaxed and leaned toward Connie.

"I have so many things I'd like to discuss in the next fifteen minutes, but if it's alright with you, Senator, I'd like to begin with you wife, Mrs. Harrison."

He nodded, looking at her adoringly. "I think that's a great idea."

"May I call you Connie?" Paula asked.

Connie smiled warmly. "Please do."

"Connie, you have been active in so many charities and programs for the needy over the years: one, The Stamp Out Child Poverty Now, has been perhaps the most celebrated. You actually lived in Appalachia for a time and worked with health care workers, educators and local businesses to help raise the standard of living for children and poor families. But you have also championed education and helped to develop programs for underprivileged women, and you have spoken before Congress on at least two occasions about the need for more training and education for women left behind.

"You have also been active establishing new libraries and working to expand hours shortened by budget cuts. Of all of these, and there are more that I haven't listed, which is the dearest to your heart?"

Connie folded her hands comfortably in her lap. "That is a very good question, Paula. My life has been greatly enriched by so many people whose names you will never hear. These people dedicate themselves day in and day out to uplifting others; they give of their time and their hearts freely and generously. I have had the wonderful privilege to work with so many of them, in small ways really, to try to improve the minds, bodies and souls of people who struggle from day to day just trying to put food on the table for their kids.

"You know, Paula, when we speak of the underprivileged, we sometimes forget that these bright and wonderful folks have so much to offer to this country if they are given even the slightest opportunity. I have seen miracles happen in a family when a hungry child eats regularly. To see that happy face, the natural play, the easy way that the child sleeps at night as a result, is a stirring miracle. It uplifts the entire family and it enriches all Americans.

"So, in answer to your question, it is the people I have met, worked with and continue to work with, who are the dearest to my heart, because they have greatly expanded and enriched my life."

Paula looked up into the lights as if pondering her next question. Then, slowly, somewhat dramatically, she looked directly into Connie's face.

"Connie, you wrote a book some years ago and in it you included a chapter about a very difficult time in your life."

Paula noticed that the Senator's right hand clinched into a fist, then quickly relaxed. The cameras went close on his face. His eyes didn't move from his wife's face. His face was expressionless.

Paula pictured Ralph in the control room, slapping himself in the forehead with the palm of his hand, shouting "You stupid bitch!"

Connie nodded, her expression placid. "Yes."

"It was a chapter about your struggle with alcoholism, was it not?"

"Yes."

Paula struggled for the right words, suddenly lost, regretting the decision to ask the question. In her ear mic, she heard a voice, "What did you learn from that experience?"

Paula swallowed. "Connie, what did you learn from that experience?"

"Well, first of all, alcoholism is a disease. A very serious disease and it needs the appropriate professional treatment. For me, it was a long battle I fought for many years and," she said, taking her husband's hand, "I would not have succeeded as well as I did without Bob's heroic support. Without my children's support.

"As to what I learned, I'd say that once again, it was the doctors and nurses, the many patients I met, who inspired me and gave me the courage and insight to overcome my addiction. I call them my family of support and love, because they did become like family to me. I'm still in touch with many of them and they continue to inspire and support me as I try to support them."

Connie left a small silence. "But, in the end, after many months of reflection, I included that chapter in the book because I wanted to offer my experience to others, with the hope of prevention or to provide a kind of road map to recovery. I simply wanted to give something back for all that I had been given. I wanted to say to others, who are battling addictions of any kind, that there is hope and there is strength in friends, community and family. Sometimes, we need to summon the courage to reach out and accept our addiction and then ask for help. And help and opportunity for recovery and support are there. That's mainly what I wanted to say in that chapter: that we are not alone. I have walked down that path and there is help and hope and success."

The cameras lingered on Connie, briefly, and through the monitors, her honesty and authenticity were memorable and inspiring. Paula looked on in admiration.

As they went to a commercial, Paula relaxed her tight shoulders and closed her eyes briefly, as Makeup rushed in.

Chapter 2

After the commercial break, Paula turned her attention to Robert Jr. On camera, he surprised her with his charm and intelligence.

"Robert Jr., you are currently an Assistant District Attorney in New York and you have said in recent interviews that you are interested in a career in politics. You seem to be following in your father's footsteps."

"Well, they're big footsteps to follow, but it is a worthy goal."

"I hear that, like your father, you're also a pilot and that your father taught you to fly."

"Well, he gave me a few lessons. The important lessons, like, keep the darn thing up there in the sky."

Paula giggled. "So what do you think about the magazines voting you as one of the five most handsome and eligible bachelors in the country?"

He crossed his legs. "Well, you know, Paula, I have to say that I have been in love with you for two years. Me and thousands of other guys."

"Where were you all when I was in high school," Paula said. "Did you know that I didn't have a date for the junior prom?"

"I would have called you," Robert Jr. said, quickly. "But you would have probably turned me down."

"No way," Paula said. "But, seriously, no one called me. I spent prom night eating pizza and crying while I watched old reruns of *I Love Lucy.*"

"I bet the guys were afraid of you. You're so pretty."

"Aren't you the charmer?"

"I get it from my father."

Paula seized the opportunity. "So tell me about your father. One thing that really stands out in your mind about him."

He didn't hesitate. He'd prepared. "My father loves baseball. So one summer when I was about 9 or 10 he became the assistant manager of our little league team. He was like the first base coach and somehow, with his crazy schedule, he made it to all but 1 or 2 games.

"So, anyway, it was our last game of the summer and my father was there. Before the game, he'd sat us down and reviewed all of the signs with us—you know like, the silent hand movements that coaches and managers use to help direct the game. Things like don't swing at the next pitch, or definitely swing at the pitch, or bunt or whatever.

"So the game starts and the other team starts racking up the hits and runs. We come to our last inning to score and it's my turn to bat. So I wander up to the plate standing tall, and look to my dad for the sign. Now, you've got to understand that the bases are loaded, there are 2 outs, and we're down 3 runs. And the team we're playing is our arch rival: we're like the New York Yankees and the Boston Red Socks.

"Okay, so the pitcher on the opposite team has already walked two runs in, so it's a given that I should take the pitch; you know, not swing at anything so I can walk to first base too. I mean this guy is not even throwing the ball anywhere near the plate.

"Well, my father flashes the sign: he slaps his knee a couple of times and then pats his face. Something like that. The only problem is, I don't remember the signs, so I don't know what the heck he's telling me to do.

"So I look at my dad again, straining to remember, as he repeats the sign. I still don't know what he's saying, but I'm too scared to let him know, because, well he's like this big guy who works with the President in Washington and everybody's watching me.

"So I really start sweating. I step to the plate and get into position. The pitcher eyes me darkly, trying to intimidate me. The infielders are thwacking their gloves, taunting me. The outfielders are loose and nervous, anxious for action.

"The pitcher winds, kicks up his leg and throws. I see the release and the ball coming toward me—like it's in slow motion—and it's right down the middle of the plate. I mean it is just asking me to swing at it. So I do. I swing with everything I've got. I swing for the fences and hit the ball so hard that it sails high and far, way over the left fielder's head. I know it's a home run.

"Stunned, I drop the bat and tear off for first base. As I race toward first, I see that my father has steam coming out of his ears. I mean, he's really upset. He yells, 'I told you to take the pitch! I told you to take the pitch!' So, I slow down, confused. Then he freaks out and starts waving me on, shouting, ' Run, Robert! Run! Run! Go, son! Go!' So I charge off again, and as I touch first and advance toward second, I look back over my shoulder and he's shouting at me again. "I told you to take the pitch! I told you to take the darn pitch!"

Paula laughs, slapping her knee. The boys and Connie laugh.

Senator Harrison lowered his face, grinning sheepishly, shaking his head at his son. "That's the one story I told you not to tell," he said, jokingly. "And may I add that from that day on, Robert Jr. has never taken any of my advice."

They laughed again and cut to a commercial.

Back on the air, Connie leveled her lovely eyes on Matt. She batted them flirtatiously, although she wasn't aware of it. Ralph would tell her later and he would show her the clip. She would be mortified.

"Is it Matt, or should I call you Matthew?"

"Matt is good," he said, in a light baritone.

"There are people who don't know that you were adopted by the Harrisons when you were an infant."

"Yes, they adopted me right after birth. At the time, Mom was involved with a charity that placed newborns with adoptive parents. I guess she saw me and said something like 'that poor little guy definitely needs a home.'"

Connie spoke up. "Actually, I didn't say anything. I just fell in love with Matt at first sight. I called Robert and said, honey, you've got another son."

Paula swung her attention to Robert. "And what did you say, Senator?"

"Something like, I thought those things took a few months…something like that."

They all laughed. Paula returned her sweet, flirtatious gaze to Matt. "Matt, if you are uncomfortable in discussing this, I'll understand. It's just that I have received hundreds of e-mails from listeners who are interested in your background. And, just so you know, most of them are from women."

"I'm not uncomfortable at all."

"Have you ever contacted your birth mother?"

"No, she died a few years after my birth."

"And your biological father?"

"Unknown. According to the records, my mother refused to say who he was. We tried to find him a couple of times, but were never successful."

"I see..." Paula shifted in her chair, feeling the fatigue of stress. "So, Matt, you seem to be the environmentalist in the family."

"Well, not the only one. Dad has been working for the environment for years. He's even taken a lot of criticism from many conservatives for his views and for the bills he's supported. He was a supporter of the Kyoto Treaty and he took a lot of heat because of it. But he believed it was a good first step and that it was important that America sign on and even lead, because we are the biggest polluters in the world."

Paula leaned her head slightly to the left, aware that men often found her attractive in that particular pose. "Matt…what do you think?"

"About?"

"The environment."

He rolled his shoulders. "Wow. That's a big question. I think a lot of young people are upset that the present administration hasn't done more to protect the environment. And, frankly, I don't think the media has done enough to separate truth from spin. If the news media doesn't bring things to light and say, this is important to the American people and to the world, then it becomes really difficult for politicians to do so.

"I mean, what has happened to all of the funding for research and testing of alternative fuels? Why are we still driving around in cars with gasoline engines that were invented nearly 100 years ago, dependent on foreign governments to supply us with our daily fix? Are we so unmotivated, uncreative and myopic that we can't come up with a car that doesn't destroy the very air we breathe? I don't think so. I think we're smarter than that."

Paula straightened. "So you are obviously very passionate…about the environment."

"Of course. It's called Survival 101. If you pollute the ground water, pollute the air, poison the food and chop down all the forests in the name of progress, then what are we progressing to? What are we leaving behind for the next generations?"

"But you got your college degree in history, not environmental science."

"That's right. I love history—especially American History."

"And you're not interested in politics like your father and brother?"

"Yes, I am very interested in politics, but I'm not interested in a political career. I want to write books about history, and teach."

"And you're currently working on your Masters Degree in American History at Columbia?"

"Yes, that's right."

"Do you feel that your father has done enough about the environment while he's been a Senator?"

"My father has done a fantastic job in raising awareness that we, as a nation, must lead by taking the active practical steps to change our present disastrous environmental course. Dad is a great leader. He's proven that many times: as a combat pilot in Vietnam, as a husband and father, as a district attorney fighting organized crime and white collar crime, and as a United States Senator for 10 years. I believe that, given the chance, he will be a great President and I urge all young people and all concerned Americans to support his presidency. At this time, more than ever, we need good, strong leadership."

Paula's eyes widened. "You seem to be his biggest fan and supporter."

"Yes, I am. I am proud to be his son. Very proud. I am very proud of both of my parents."

Connie beamed when he looked at her.

Paula clasped her hands together and faced the Senator. "So that is a perfect segue over to you, Senator. I'd like to ask you some of the questions that have been recently e-mailed in by our listeners, who were excited that you were going to be on my show."

"As I said earlier, Paula, my family and I are grateful to you for giving us so much time."

Paula stared into the middle distance, searching for the right words. "Senator, your career has been both distinguished and controversial. From your colleagues on both sides of the aisle, you've been called, and I quote..." Paula glanced down at her notes. "Brilliant, reckless, visionary, misguided, honest, dangerous, candid and splendid."

The Senator gave a gentle laugh. "Well, I'm sure they've said a few other words that didn't show up on your list."

"Oh, I get a lot of those, too," Paula threw in, chuckling. "You should read my e-mails…on the other hand, maybe you shouldn't. But seriously, Senator, what are you most proud of when you reflect back on your amazing career? And what do you believe you can bring to the Presidency that would improve our country at this very challenging and difficult time?"

The Senator considered her question with a little smile. "Paula, in the year or so since I announced my candidacy for President, I have traveled to many American small towns and cities. I've met so many people and I have learned so much from these people. I have learned that—without exception—they all want the same things: they want good jobs with a fair living wage to provide for their families; they want affordable healthcare; they want good educational opportunities for their kids; they want to feel safe in a world where terrorism is a constant threat, and they want clean air and water and a good environmental legacy to leave their kids and grandkids.

"In many town meetings we've held, people ask me: why can't we have these? What is preventing us from having the basics—because these things that I've listed are the basics. Good job, affordable healthcare, a good clean environment. Safety.

"I say to them, we don't have them today because it takes leadership, and the current administration is not providing good leadership. I tell them that it takes a leader who is willing to stick his chin out there every day and risk someone taking a swing at it. It takes a courageous, compassionate leader who defines the goals, creates a plan of action and then follows through, challenging the lobbies, the corporate interests and the lazy, we're-doing-fine-as-we-are people, who don't have what it takes to get us back on track so that we can have the basics. We're always told it's so difficult and hard.

"Well I have the goals, a plan and the experience to put all of these goals into action so that we can have a balanced budget; so that we can have affordable healthcare for all Americans; so that we can have educational opportunities for our young people. We can defeat the terrorists and we can have respect and support from people all over the world while we work with them to achieve it. We can achieve all of this, with the right leader. And I believe that I am that leader. If anyone watching would like more information about our campaign or if they would like to make a donation to the Bob Harrison campaign, they can log on to the internet and go to www.BobHarrison.com."

He paused, changing the pitch of his voice. He became softer and reflective. "Paula, many people know that when my father retired from the Senate I was elected to fill his seat: a very daunting challenge. He was a great Senator for the State of Connecticut, a wonderful father and a great man. My father was also a lover of the theatre and one of his favorite plays was Thorton Wilder's *Our Town.*

"It's a rich play—I believe an uplifting play—about a small town in America at a time when things seemed simpler. In some ways they were and in other ways they were just as challenging.

"But what I would like to see in America today is for all of us to stop all the bickering, the partisan politics, the red state and blue state politics. I'd like us to pause a little and reach back with one hand and grab hold of some of the things that made us the great country that we have become: things like a positive can-do attitude and innovating spirit.

"Then with our other hand I'd like us to reach out into the future and grab hold of all the possibilities and opportunities that await us." The Senator demonstrated with his hands, slowly bringing them together. "And then we slowly bring our hands together into one single unit of achievement, peace and prosperity. We make all this complicated big talk, big deficits and big problems small, because we are working together again like we did when things were just a little bit slower and simpler.

"We are, after all, Americans, living in small towns and big cities. We can begin returning to the basics by reaching across the dinner table, across the neighbor's yard; across the aisle of the church, synagogue and mosque; across the small town to big city and big city to small town. We are a big country with a small town can-do American spirit. This is Our Town America, and we can solve any problem together. We can achieve anything together. This is what I believe we can do and, with God's help, what we will do."

Paula nodded, thoughtfully. "Senator, what are you most proud of?"

"I am most proud of my wife, my kids and this great country. I am proud that every day of my life, I have done the best possible job that I could do, no matter what it has been: husband and father, combat pilot, district attorney and United States Senator.

"And if I'm elected the next President, that's what I'll continue to do for the American people. I will go out there every day and do my very best to give us all back the basics of peace, pride and prosperity."

During the commercial break, Paula decided not to ask the Senator about the 25 year-old plane crash and the subsequent mystery. But in the seconds before they were live, she'd changed her mind, not wanting the show to end on a strong political note. It was a dull ending. She could already imagine what the comments from the cascading e-mails would be: "Boring, Boring, Boring! Weak little airhead interviewing bimbo."

And the Senator had used most of the remaining time to make a speech, leaving her little time for additional questions. It irked her.

"Senator Harrison," Paula said, when they were back on the air. "Recently, an old story has been appearing on the internet: the story of your plane crash 25 years ago, your memory lapse and the rather large gap of time before you contacted your family and the authorities."

The Senator's forehead lifted a little. "Yes, such a long time ago."

"We've received e-mails that still ask why it took you and your rescuers so long before you contacted the authorities."

"As I have said many times over the years, I was very lucky to have even survived the crash. The storm was a fierce one and I swam around in the ocean for what seemed like hours before Gerry and Becky Day spotted me."

"They were in a sailboat in the storm?"

"The storm had subsided by then. They were not under sail at the time and it was just luck that they happened to come along when they did. Gerry was tying down his mainsail when he spotted this orange object. It was me, wearing a life jacket. I had somehow managed to slip it on after the crash.

"At any rate, they pulled me inside, wrapped me in blankets and took me below. I immediately passed out."

"You would think they'd be on the radio instantly, though, calling for help," Paula said.

"Gerry was an illegal immigrant at the time and scared that he'd be deported. He was going to call for help, anyway, but Becky stopped him. She was a nurse; after she'd examined me, she felt certain I had no life-threatening injuries."

"But in fact, you did have an injury."

"Yes. Temporary amnesia, which is why I'd lost my memory for a time and didn't know who I was or where I was."

"So you stayed with them on board for over two weeks?"

"Yes, they lived on the boat. It was their home."

"And they never read newspapers or watched the news so that they would have known who you were? I mean, they could have collected a substantial reward, couldn't they?"

"They didn't own a TV. As for the radio, they seldom listened and never heard the news about me. With respect to the reward, I think it's pretty clear they had nothing to hide. My family was very grateful for their help, and it's no secret that my family did offer them a reward for saving my life, which they used to pay for Gerry's legal fees to help him become an American citizen. So it was certainly a happy ending for him and for me."

Paula twisted her face up, as if trying to understand. "But Senator, why didn't you want to be found? Why didn't you want to know who you were and where you came from?"

"Well, of course, that's a good question. Paula, you have to understand that I was injured and frightened. After an accident of that magnitude, one doesn't always think rationally. I was actually scared to find out who I was at first. And then, after a time, when I wanted to regain my memory, I felt that if I didn't stress myself too much, if I just relaxed and rested, it would come back. And, of course, it did."

Paula knew time was running out and that Ralphy boy was fuming away in the control booth. She stared earnestly. "There were reports, Senator, that Gerry and Becky were actually married at the time, so the issue of his being an illegal immigrant was irrelevant. Some reports said that Becky and Gerry were in fact smuggling drugs and that's why everything was so hush-hush. That's why they didn't call the police."

"Yes, I've heard of those, but I have no knowledge of it."

"So when you got your memory back, you immediately called your family?"

"That's right."

"And that was nearly three weeks after the crash?" Paula asked.

"Yes, as I recall."

"What did you do all that time on the boat?"

"Read. Sailed…struggled to remember who I was."

Paula looked down at her clipboard, then lifted her curious eyes and spoke in a confidential voice. "Recently, Senator, there was a story on the internet about another story—an entirely different story."

"Oh, I'm sure," the Senator said, blithely. "I've heard there are many now."

"Some people are even suggesting that the story was put there by your opponents. It essentially says that you weren't rescued by Gerry and Becky Day at all. The story says that you were rescued by a beautiful woman and that you stayed with her, isolated and alone, for that time. It says that you fell in love with this woman and that you actually wanted to stay with her and not return to your family. It also says that you had a baby daughter with her."

The Senator nodded, grinning affably, with an expression of absurd humor. "Oh yes, the mermaid rescue story and the cover-up conspiracy theory," he said, dismissively. "Well, whoever invented that fairy tale has a very romantic imagination. They should be writing romance novels, not wasting their time fabricating stories on the internet.

"I can assure you that crashing your airplane into the sea, barely surviving, losing your memory and struggling every day for weeks to recall even the smallest details of 33 years is not very romantic: it's terrifying."

"Do you stay in touch with Gerry and Becky Day?"

"I will always be grateful to Gerry and Becky for saving my life. Gerry died about five years ago. Becky and I exchange Christmas cards and speak on the phone occasionally. She has remarried and is very happy."

Paula pulled a little breath, closing her hands in conclusion. "Thank you all for appearing on my show. I have enjoyed this so much."

The Senator said, "Thank you, Paula."

Connie said, "It's been delightful."

The two boys nodded and waited for the red lights on the cameras to blink off. Senator Harrison and Connie exchanged enigmatic glances as they rose, ignoring Paula's indulgent smile.

Chapter 3

Bob Harrison was at his home in West Town, Connecticut, sitting alone in the library, at his antique mahogany desk. The electric green desk lamp framed him warmly, but cast a lonely glow upon the floor-to-ceiling cherry wood book shelves towering behind him. A light rain fell and tapped at the windows.

He'd left his home at 7:30 that morning, traveling through five different states. He'd spoken to leaders of the African-American community in Philadelphia, sung *Country Roads* with the Governor and supporters in West Virginia, given interviews with NPR and Piers Morgan, and made two TV commercials to be aired in the Midwest the following week. His day concluded with the *Paula Powers* show. He had shaken so many hands that his arm hurt and his right hand was swollen. He had met thousands of joyful, enthusiastic people.

He was stooped at his desk, adding the finishing touches to a speech he was to give to a veterans group in Atlanta at ten in the morning. Fatigue blurred his vision and set his mouth into a frown. His tieless white shirt was loose at the neck and he wore the same suit pants he'd worn at the interview with Paula Powers earlier in the evening. The little gold "Big Ben" desk clock, a gift from a British diplomat, ticked obtrusively, and said it was 1:26 in the morning.

He was glad to be alone and away from his campaign staff: his speech writers, his Chief of Staff, the pollsters, the consultants, the attorneys, and the Secret Service, although two were in the house and two were positioned outside, hidden away somewhere. It was the first time in days that he'd had seclusion and he was savoring it.

He'd fly to Atlanta in the morning for the speech and breakfast, then to Orlando for a luncheon, then drop into West Palm Beach in late afternoon for a rally, and conclude the day in Miami with a dinner and fund raiser. There'd be interviews on the plane and quick visits to old friends of his father's in West Palm and Miami. It would be a full day—an exhausting day—and Bob knew he'd need a sleeping pill if he was to sleep at all. His snagged nerves and strained back muscles would not relinquish their grip without help from a miracle pill. His wakeup call was scheduled for 6 am.

He sipped a cup of the now cold peppermint tea that his housekeeper, Carla, had brought to him over an hour ago. He'd sent her to bed. Connie had retired soon after they'd arrived home from the New York City studios, leaving him with a kiss and a weak smile. They'd said little as they traveled home by helicopter.

"You were wonderful, as usual," Bob had said.

She was silent for a time before saying, "I would have much preferred an interview with Charlie Rose. I found that young lady a bit silly and pretentious."

"Yes, well, the boys were a hit, I think," Bob said.

"Yes, if the boys were running for President, they would have ticked up a point or two in the polls. But then, of course, we both know that young girls don't vote—at least not for Presidents. They vote for the most eligible bachelor of the week on their cell phones and laptops. This generation confuses me. They seem so vacuous and short-sighted. It's unsettling."

Bob stared out into the darkness, lost in thought, his face constrained and impassive. He glanced down occasionally at the Connecticut landscape, viewing the patterns of lights floating beneath them, like old memories. He listened to the steady thumping of the helicopter blades, still feeling a little thrill at being airborne.

"Don't all 'mature' people think the young are too young and much too vacuous?" he finally asked.

Connie shrugged. "Perhaps…"

"And then there's Matt. He's a young person you definitely wouldn't call vacuous."

"No, thank God," Connie said. "But I think he comes on too strong. He scares people off sometimes. Robert Jr. is much more accessible."

"They're a good contrast. Matt's intense, that's for sure, but I believe people see that he has a good, genuine heart."

Bob looked at his wife, apprehensively. "So, do you think we'll tick up in the polls tomorrow?"

Connie stared out the window. He saw her gloomy reflection in the glass. "I think more people will go to the story of you and the mermaid, than will go to BobHarrison.com."

The fingers of Bob's right hand tapped the desktop. His left hand supported his chin. He felt the swell of anxiety and an inexplicable feeling of loneliness. He was still a month away from the late August Republican convention and already his weary body was begging for a vacation. He was hoarse. The backaches were growing progressively worse, the result of the airplane crash 25 years ago. By 9pm every night, he had a headache and his digestive problems persisted, despite the medication his nephew had prescribed.

For months, Bob had been bolstered by enthusiastic support and the white heat of publicity and triumph. He'd distinguished himself from the other three Republican candidates early, right after New Hampshire, and led the pack in campaign contributions after the Super Tuesday primaries in March. He'd struck a chord with moderate Republicans and Democrats with his "let's be wise, strong and ready" speeches on defense. His war record and years as a relentless prosecutor of white collar crime added stature. The bold initiatives on reestablishing ties with Vietnam and his backing of the Kyoto Agreement as Senator had isolated many conservatives, but brought the support of women and moderates.

Bob knew that the conservatives would have to come on board, eventually, and he'd have to deal with their relentless demands after he was in the White House.

It also didn't hurt that he'd been called handsome and personable. His cheerful broad smile and deep confident speaking voice added charm. He'd topped the major polls as the most likeable Republican candidate, as well as the candidate that most people trusted in the event of a terrorist attack or serious crisis.

But President Taylor, who hailed from Kentucky, was leading by at least 8 points. In some polls, as much as 12. The President's strategy of labeling Bob a wishy-washy Republican who "dances to the left and dances to the right and does the hokey pokey with anybody in between, but doesn't have one good idea of his own," was working.

Bob reached for his TV remote and switched on the TV. It was set to CSPAN, and from the schedule on his desk, Bob knew that a rerun of President Taylor's speech was beginning. The President had given the speech at a labor union dinner in Columbus, Ohio, at the same time Bob was on the *Paula Powers* show.

Bob eased back in his black leather desk chair, laced his hands behind his back and watched, his eyes burning and dry.

There he was, President Howard Taylor, standing behind a podium bearing the Presidential Seal. Behind him was a blue and white backdrop that had the phrase: BETTER JOBS FOR A STRONGER AMERICA. His sky-blue shirt was open at the neck and he was emoting and shouting like a country preacher high on power and glory. He was an iron little man, with steel gray hair, a pugnacious jaw, playful eyes and a no- nonsense tight little mouth. Many had compared his political style to Harry Truman's, a comparison that pleased the President. President Taylor was fond of saying "That sharp little man had more guts than a host of tight-fisted, shiny-faced Republicans who talk a good game, but don't want anybody else in the game except their own kind!"

Bob turned up the volume just in time to hear the President, in his dramatically broadened Kentucky accent, speak about Bob's "Our Town America."

"Bob calls his vision for America, Our Town America. Now when I think about a town, I think about the town I come from. Most of you know that I hail from the great State of Kentucky…"

There were whistles and cheers.

"…From the wonderful little town called London. London, Kentucky. Now, when I lived there, I used to have an old hound dog named Jasper. Now Jasper could hunt like nobody's business, his big old nose to the ground smellin' and his floppy ears listenin'. Well we hunted together for, oh, I'd say 8 or 9 years and then old

Jasper just got old, rolled over and died. I gave him an honorable, deserving burial, high atop a hill, under quiet trees. That was fitting. That was right."

The President's voice expanded with volume and intensity. "Now, my fellow Americans, that was a long time ago. It's in the past. Good for its time, but gone. That old hound dog hunted and sniffed, did his duty, and, God love him, he's gone to his maker!

"Now my point here, folks, is that Bob Harrison wants us to reach back into the past, with this hand." He extended his right hand and then held it aloft. "Yes, this very hand, and then do what with it? He wants us to reach back. Yes, my friends. He wants us to go backwards!! Yeah, can you imagine? At a time when our country needs the best education *now*, the best military *now*, the best jobs now, the best solution to Social Security *now*; because my friends we ain't gonna solve that one by going back into time. No sir. No ma'am.

"Okay so we reach back—way back—and then what? Where are the solutions for today and tomorrow!? Not way back there, Bob Harrison! No, my fellow Americans. Let old Bob Harrison go huntin' with his old hound dog called Been there and done that! That old hound dog called, MY HOUND AMERICA!"

The crowd, seated at round tables and chairs, rose to their feet in applause.

"What we don't need right now is Bob Harrison's old hound dog, My Hound America, sniffin' and huntin' around the White House, looking for old and tired solutions! We need brand new ideas and exciting bold solutions to today's problems!"

The rousing applause eclipsed the President's voice.

"We need an experienced leader who can take on today's problems while creating tomorrow's opportunities!"

The applause crescendoed steadily, while the President sipped water. He waited, allowing the coughs and murmuring to fade.

"And now Bob Harrison wants us to reach across the aisle and hold hands." The President twisted up his mouth, as if perplexed, nodding rapidly. "Yep, that's right. Let's all sit around, reminisce about the past and hold hands. Can you imagine, my friends? Didn't we do that way back in the 1960's?"

The President waited for the scattered laughter to cease.

"Well I say, good, Bob. It's about time! It's about time you reached across the aisle and took my hand. But may I ask you, why didn't you take some of your own advice in the last four years and reach across the Senate aisle to help pass my environmental bill, my education bill, my healthcare bill, my jobs bill? My friends, not only did Bob Harrison not reach across the aisle, but for many of these very timely and important decisions, he wasn't even anywhere near the aisle, because he wasn't even in the Senate chamber or in Washington! No, my friends, he was out campaigning—out tellin' everybody else to reach across some table or some yard, when he himself wasn't even doin' the job that his folks back in Connecticut had elected him to do."

Bob snapped upright in his chair, shouting at the TV screen. "I *was* in town for the crucial votes, you moron, and I voted against them because they were filled with pork—gifts to your friends who'd kissed your ass in the last election. How about the high school football stadium in Lawrence, Kansas that would have cost the tax payers four hundred thousand dollars, or the new laboratory for some university in Oklahoma for research on flatworms, at a price of six hundred thousand dollars!?"

The President had paused, briefly, taking another drink of water, waiting for the thunderous applause to subside.

"No, my fellow Americans, Bob Harrison was out of town, during crucial moments and crucial decisions that affect all Americans. Now I say that, not only is Bob Harrison way, way out of touch, but I also say that he is way, way out of town and not even close to living in the real Our Town America!"

The room exploded into applause and shouts of "FOUR MORE YEARS! FOUR MORE YEARS!"

Bob snatched the remote and shut the TV off. He closed his eyes, massaging them. He wasn't aware that the door had opened and Connie stood quietly on the threshold, staring with sleepy eyes, wearing a long silky bath robe.

"You should be in bed," Connie said, her voice low and scratchy.

Startled, Bob jumped. His eyes opened. "What are you doing up?"

Connie shut the door and started toward him. "Robert, you have got to get some rest. It's almost two o'clock."

"Yeah, I know. It's just…"

She stood before the desk. "Have you taken the sleeping pill?"

"No, not yet."

"Take it. You can't keep this up, night after night. You're going to burn out."

"I get cat naps on the plane."

"That's not enough."

"They worked for John Kennedy."

"He was a Democrat and he was younger."

Robert laughed a little. "You always could make me laugh."

"And you always could surprise me."

Robert stared, trying to decipher her statement.

"Robert…don't look at me that way. You know…", she said, shaking her head a little.

Robert looked down at the desk, folding his hands. "It's going to come out, isn't it?"

"It's out. It's on the internet. The real question is, can we contain it?"

Robert heaved out a sigh. "I don't know. She's not the type to go public. She's reclusive and private." Robert looked up to gauge his wife's reaction. He saw the old contempt and it silenced him.

"What if it isn't her?" Connie asked. "What about her daughter?"

"I don't know," Robert said. "I don't think so. And it can't be that doctor—what's his name…?"

"Ned Palmer," Connie said, distastefully.

"Yes…he's been dead for almost 8 years. I mean the damn story came out just after it was clear I was the front runner and going to get the nomination."

"One of the lawyers?" Connie added. "There were many. Maybe Becky?"

"It isn't Becky. I talked to her a few days ago. She's got kids. She doesn't want them to know… She wants the whole thing over with. She's got reporters tailing her, the tabloids, book publishers. She's moving to France in a week or so to get away from them."

Connie folded her arms. "Well, you know what? It doesn't matter. There's absolutely nothing we can do right now. The fact that whoever it is hasn't gone public by now, probably means that they're not going to. It's just a cowardly political technique that somebody is trying to use to damage your campaign and it won't work. Does Carlton know about any of this?"

Robert coughed out a laugh. "Carlton. He's an idealistic campaign manager, who believed me when I told him the story was false. But then, I need a true believer and there are no others around."

Connie's face fell, and it took Bob only seconds to realize he'd said the wrong thing. The air became contaminated, toxic with old memories and betrayals. He tried to recover.

"Connie… we knew this was going to come out at some point. We never discussed it, but we knew it."

Connie relaxed her arms, speaking as if she hadn't heard him. It was Connie's usual tactic: focus her personal anger onto a political strategy.

"How's the fund-raising going?"

"Okay, not like Super Tuesday, but not bad. We're having the usual big fundraisers and fishing for the big checks."

"And the internet…of course. The kids love the internet."

"Yes, without the internet…Well, it's paying off."

Connie chuckled, darkly. "Yes, that damned…internet."

Bob let the acidity of her words fade into the white noise of falling rain.

"…We've spent 38 million on commercials since May," he said.

"Less than the President's?"

"Yes, he's spent about 75 million. We're still adding paid staff and on-the-ground organizers in swing states and that's going to pay off down the line."

"Still thinking about John Cahill for Vice President?"

"Yes…he's a good man, don't you think?"

She nodded. "He comes off a little angry sometimes."

"That's okay. I'm good cop, he's bad cop."

"I'm just concerned about the polls," Connie said. "That damned story hasn't helped us any."

"We've got a lot of fundraisers scheduled; Carlton's on it."

"You're going to have to attack Taylor with greater force," Connie said, "He's hammering you. He's a poor excuse for a President but he is an excellent campaigner. You've got to start attacking him with everything you've got!"

"Connie..."

"I know Carlton doesn't want us to peak too soon, but we've got to start gaining on him before it's too late or we'll never peak at all. There are so many issues to call him on: the ballooning deficits, his disastrous foreign policy record, his joke of an education bill that throws money to the four winds without solving the basics...and..."

"Connie... please... I only meant..."

Connie's back stiffened. "I know what you meant!" she said, sharply. "I know! Don't you think I know after nearly 30 years!?"

Robert stood. "Connie..." Words failed him and Connie looked on, with dark hostile eyes, enjoying his struggle. He started again. "Connie, I've tried to make up for it. I've done everything I could to...make it right for you...for us. You know I have."

Connie's countenance held no compassion or forgiveness. "You will make a great president, Robert, and I will do everything in my power to put us into the White House. Robert Jr. and I are traveling to Indianapolis tomorrow morning to open a new library and then we're going to Cincinnati, Ohio, where I'm going to tell that crowd of supporters that you, and only you, have the talent, the skill and experience to pull us out of this mess our country's in right now, because I firmly believe it.

Because I believe in you. I'm also going because a Bob Harrison presidency is what we have been working for, for almost 30 years.

"As the President and First Lady of this country, there will be no better. We will shine! We will make things happen and we will work together to make this country great again. I'm convinced of that."

She let a little gap of silence intrude. "But, as husband and wife…well…Robert, we lost that campaign a long, long time ago and we both know it. We're good pretenders, you and I, but when that mermaid internet story appeared, it just brought it all back again, didn't it. It finished us. Your presidency is all we have left and so we've got to win or we will surely tear each other to pieces one way or the other."

Robert snaked his hands into his pockets, lowering his chin to his chest.

Connie continued. "Now, I'm going to bed and suggest you do the same. We've got a long, hard three months ahead of us. And a wonderful eight years to follow."

Connie turned and started for the door.

Bob lifted his heavy chin. "Connie?"

She paused at the door, but didn't turn to face him.

"I'll win it for you. I promise."

She reached for the golden doorknob, twisted and opened it. "I know you will, Robert. I've never doubted that you would. I'm also a true believer."

After the door closed him into a ringing, stifling silence, Robert switched off the desk lamp and lowered himself down into the chair with a heavy sigh. The darkness seemed to expand, engulfing him in a pulsing sorrow.

Chapter 4

Carlton Emery, Bob Harrison's campaign manager, had the studious, placid look of a professor, the clear, shifting eyes of a general under fire and the lean body of a long distance runner. He was proud of his pop-bottle glasses, shaggy dog haircut and black Ked's tennis shoes that he wore to nearly every political function. He was proud that he came from a working class family from Racine, Wisconsin and proud that he had "scholarshiped" his way through college without having to take any money from his family and very little from the banks.

He loved politics, tennis and peanut butter Balance Power Bars, in that order. Women were a distraction, although he dated Harriet Cronin occasionally, but only if she refused to criticize his tennis shoes, and if she sent her "yapping" Boston Terrier to her neighbors whenever he spent the night.

Carlton graduated Magna Cum Laude from Princeton in History and Political Science and received an MBA from Harvard. While there, he'd met several like-minded political minds and through these meetings, he was introduced to, and soon went to work for, Robert's father, Senator Raymond Harrison, during his final campaign, when Carlton was only 27. Bob Harrison met him while both worked on Raymond's campaign and they struck up an amiable friendship, finding common ground on such things as sports, wines from the Loire Valley in France and, of course, politics, with a goal to get to the White House. Carlton himself did not crave the spotlight and he was not interested in holding political office. He loved maneuvering behind the scenes. He loved the direct thrill of indirect power, and the under-the-radar whispers of his name in power circles. His formal ego was never more happily inflated than when some young hot-shot reporter didn't know his name but was able to spot him in a crowd from his signature tennis shoes and Harry Potter glasses.

Carlton joined the consulting firm of Wilson, Evans and Stevenson, where he sharpened his political craft, while working for several Senatorial elections over a 10-year period, as well as becoming Bob Harrison's campaign manager during the Senator's last election.

Carlton also taught history and Poly Sci at two colleges in Wisconsin, where he, with his sharp youthful eye, searched for future political talent. He became good friends with Lee Collins, the Chairman of the Republican National Committee, and was eagerly shepherded along by powerful arms and commanding hands, and recognized as "a brilliant statistician, who could help shape the hearts and minds of the nation someday."

When Bob Harrison called him, Carlton had simply said, "Bob, let's go win this thing."

Carlton's long purposeful stride moved across the parking lot, through a light West Palm Beach rain. He held no umbrella. His head was low as he passed under blowing palms, eventually ducking under the shelter of the awning entranceway of a low red-bricked community center. He barely noticed the police cars and black Lincoln Towne cars, lined up like barricades. He looked past the curious and the thin line of protesters 30 yards away, huddled under umbrellas.

In the inside pocket of his suit jacket, his cell phone vibrated and rang. He didn't reach for it. Bob Harrison was inside the community center, rallying the faithful: a group of six-to-seven hundred loyal and enthusiastic supporters. Carlton heard the cheers. He heard Bob Harrison's enthusiastic voice swell and then break from overuse, riding over the applause. "…This Our Town America is ours and we're going to take it back! Are you with me?!!"

Carlton stood staring, blankly, oblivious to his wet tennis shoes, his dripping hair and clinging clothes. After he had received the call, he'd left the building, intentionally stepping out into the then heavy downpour. His usual steady mind pendulumed clumsily, as it struggled to reason and strategize. Its watch-like precision suddenly lost time and he actually shook his head, violently, a couple of times, as if to get it ticking again. He placed both hands on his head and, for the first time that he could recall, he wanted to scream.

He was astonished to suddenly remember words written by Marcus Aurelius, a Roman Emperor and philosopher he'd studied in high school.

The art of living is more like wrestling than dancing, in that we stand watchful and rooted to meet whatever comes from unexpected directions.

His cell phone rang on as he watched the rain. It fell like steel arrows—without mercy—flooding the parking lot, lashing at the leaning palms. He felt the mounting pressure of fulfilling a job he simply wasn't prepared to do. So he waited until the rain had nearly stopped and the sun broke through. He waited until Bob Harrison was about to conclude. Carlton knew the speech verbatim.

He waited until a driving rock beat and pounding bassline stirred him into action. He found the ranking Secret Service agent, named Rollins, near the rear entrance. He was tall, beefy and stoic. Carlton pulled him aside and delivered his information in little whispers. Rollins listened without reaction. When Carlton had finished, Rollins nodded and went into action.

Carlton spun on his heels and started for the back door, past two formidable looking Secret Service Agents, pulled open the heavy steel door and entered. The celebratory force of cheers and noise, hit him like a gust of wind. He angled left down a polished corridor, his sneakers squeaking, past more Secret Service agents, and ducked into the stage door. Music and chanting were in full riot. He ignored everyone: Ron Cassidy, the Chief of Staff, Molly Stivers, the Press Secretary, Paul Groves, the head speech writer; two glossy-faced adoring women volunteers who were literally jumping up and down, clapping and shouting "Bobby! Bobby! Bobby!!"

Carlton crept to the right wing of the stage, to the edge of the curtain and peaked out. He saw Bob's profile. His arms were stretched toward the ceiling, his face, glossy from sweat, ecstatic.

"We can do it together," he yelled. "Will you give me your support?!"

The crowd hollered back "Yes!!! YES!!!"

Carlton waited, feeling detached and uncharacteristically ill at ease. His cell phone rang again. This time he reached for it and shut it off.

He took a piece of paper from his suit pocket and a pen. He scribbled the words

I have to talk to you now. Urgent!
–Carlton

Carlton folded it and waved for Molly, a tall woman with short black hair and alert eyes. She came over. He handed her the note. "Take this to Bob. Now!"

"But…"

"Do it!" Carlton said, crisply.

Molly arranged herself, lifted her head and crossed the stage to the podium. She gently touched Bob's right shoulder. He took the note and skimmed it as she exited. Before she'd entered the wing, Bob's head snapped toward Carlton. Carlton nodded, firmly.

Bob stuffed the note in his pocket and waved his grateful goodbyes. The tireless crowd surged forward as the music swelled. Bob made a broad gesture of goodbye, with a flashing smile, clinching his hands together triumphantly high above his head as he made his dramatic exit. A chorus of cheers persisted.

Offstage, Bob approached Carlton. "What's up?"

Carlton averted his eyes. "There's a room down the hall. It's private."

Carlton started off. Bob, wiping his damp face with a handkerchief, followed. They exited the stage door, walked briskly down the hallway, made a left and continued across a freshly waxed floor, stopping before a closed door. Carlton opened it and allowed Bob to enter ahead of him. He closed the door behind them, shutting out the sharp cries and heavy music. Anxiety filled the stillness.

Bob lifted his hands. "So shoot."

They stood in a classroom with neatly arranged rows of desks and chairs. Carlton walked to the teacher's desk, folded his hands and took off his glasses.

"Carlton?" Bob ask. "This is very dramatic for you. What is it?"

Carlton took a breath. "Bob…there's been an accident."

"Yes…?"

"Connie…and a …" he faltered.

"Carlton. What?! Come out with it."

"Connie's and Robert Jr.'s plane went down."

Bob stiffened. His eyes filled with alarm. "When? Where?"

"About 15 miles from Cincinnati—actually in northern Kentucky. I got the first call about 20 minutes ago."

"Twenty minutes!! Why didn't you…"

Carlton interrupted. "…They didn't know much then. More calls came a few minutes later."

"How bad is it?" Bob said, blinking fast, hands clenched.

"The plane went down in a wooded area near a private home about 15 miles east of the airport. It crashed and…a…" Carlton wiped the beads of sweat from his upper lip. "…It crashed and then burst into flames."

Bob sank a little, his eyes moving and wide. He felt the rise of a searing agony.

"The Ohio Highway Patrol was quick to get to the crash site. The controllers said the last contact with the plane was at 2:20 p.m. EST when it was about 20 miles from the airport. There had been some violent storms, high wind and rain. Rescue teams have just arrived."

Bob went to a desk chair, pulled it from the desk and dropped heavily into it. "And how are my wife and son!?"

Carlton lowered his voice to a painful whisper. "I don't know, Bob." And then in a dying cadence of despair, Carlton added, "First reports…aren't very positive."

Bob closed his eyes and lowered his head, as if to shut the door on the terrible reality.

"A National Transportation Safety Board team is on its way. President Taylor called minutes ago. You have expedited clearance to Cincinnati. He said to call him with any request."

Bob pounded the desktop violently. "God in heaven!" he said, his voice cracking, in horror and anger. "God in heaven!!"

Carlton waited in the turning point of an unbearable stillness.

Finally, Bob stood abruptly, as if spurred. "They may have survived, Carlton! They may have. They were in a good airplane: a King Air twin-engine turboprop. Marty Compton and Biff Shaw were flying that plane. They're some of the best. Nobody flies better than Marty. He has thousands of miles with that plane."

Bob started for the door, buoyed by the thought "Let's go. Let's get up there."

Bob walked assertively. Carlton hurried to keep up.

"Media know?" Bob asked, falling back into an official take-charge tone.

"No, not yet. But soon. I have to brief Molly and the others."

"Do it, now, and keep the damn press off of me."

"I've asked for more Secret Service. They'll be in Cincinnati and at your Connecticut home."

"Good. Does Matt know?"

"No… I thought maybe you…"

"Of course. I'll call him in the car on the way to the airport. Hold all calls and cancel everything."

"Of course."

Bob left the community center via the back door, oblivious to sight or sound. His black sedan was waiting and he slid inside the backseat, sealing himself away from the world. Sirens wailed as the procession, led by a black SUV, bounced out of the parking lot and rolled swiftly through light traffic toward the airport.

Bob sat alone in the first class section of the leased 757 on route to the Cincinnati/Northern Kentucky International Airport. Bob had called Matt, who was in New York. He'd heard the news in a Starbucks on the upper West Side of Manhattan and had just tried to call his father. When Bob heard his son's voice break in quiet grief, it brought him to tears. Matt was on his way to Cincinnati, under heavy escort from the Secret Service. Bob then called the rest of the family.

Bob had also spoken to President Taylor, who had pledged "the full support of this office in the rescue and recovery of your family." He said he wouldn't issue any statement until Bob gave him the okay to do so. Bob could call him at any time—day or night—and the White House Operator would put him through to the President's direct and secure line.

Bob was updated by cell phone promptly by Carlton who was still in West Palm Beach. Molly had given her first press conference, just as CNN went live from the crash area. The community center erupted into a frenzied chaos, with supporters, reporters and photographers rushing the little stage, anxious for news. A woman fainted, a fist fight broke out, TV crews surged forward shouting, faces red and frantic. Extra police were called in to maintain order and, finally, the Secret Service called off the conference and whisked Molly away, as she begged for "civility" for the sake of the Harrison family and the country.

Bob stared out the window, chin in hand. Thick white clouds drifted by like icebergs as the plane climbed to 30,000 feet.

Above him, on the sides of the luggage compartments, were newspaper clippings, photos and postcards, scotched-taped on by journalists. One particular clipping showed Bob and Connie holding hands and waving to supporters after their big win on Super Tuesday.

A young female aide, who hadn't slept at home for over six months, checked on him frequently, as did the distressed flight attendants. At the stand-up bar, a few aides, the flight attendants, the bartender and the chef stared numbly at the little TV screen, their faces slack, bodies hunched in a profound reaction of sorrow and disbelief.

Only a few hours ago, the plane had seemed to bulge with campaign staff, reporters and volunteers, all bantering ideas, telling jokes, playing poker, filing deadlines and conducting interviews. Years of education, experience and ripe ambition had gathered to promote, extol and scrutinize the man who could become the most powerful leader in the world. One reporter had said, "When I'm on this plane, I feel like a drunk man spinning from one high to another, trying to keep my damn balance."

And the energy of many trips still hung in the air: the dizzying scenes of celebration and promise, especially whenever Bob and Connie were together working the press and joking with the staff, as the fulfillment of vast ambition seemed close and touchable.

Another reporter had written:

As Bob Harrison tears across this country, gathering support, giving town meetings and winning primaries, one feels a natural hope arise, and a kind of prevailing eternal sunshine spreads richly.

Bob sat low in his seat, in a fragility of helplessness, like a man who had come to the end of thought. He'd just received a call from Carlton. It was final. Terrible. Crushing.

"Bob…there were no survivors."

Chapter 5

Bob and Matt retreated to their Georgian Connecticut home, while funeral arrangements were underway. It was decided that Connie and Robert Jr. would be buried side by side on the same day. It was to be a private ceremony. Bob believed that's what Connie would have wanted and it was what he wanted.

The country had jolted to a near stop as shock and grief filled homes, offices, restaurants and bars. People hovered near computer screens, TVs and radios with downcast faces and low spirits. As requested by President Taylor, flags were flown at half mast. Many churches opened and remained opened through the night, for prayer vigils. Bells tolled. Thousands of flower arrangements were sent to the crash site and TV stations were jammed with calls requesting the addresses and phone numbers of the charities that Connie had actively supported. Cable stations reran a biography of Connie's life, while others hastily programmed old interviews of her with the Senator. Her last interview, with Paula Powers, seemed to repeat every hour.

Robert Jr.'s brief life was recapitulated and analyzed. That he would have been a gifted politician, most commentators left no doubt. Others simply stated his strong charisma and prodigious intellect. Women left their office computers in tears. Men puzzled about how such a crash could have happened and speculated as to whether it was a terrorist act. High school girls gathered in the hallways and wept. Schools cancelled classes for the remainder of the day.

From leaders and statesmen all over the world, came an outpouring of support and condolences, and President Taylor appeared on prime time television to express "My deep and profound grief over this unfortunate and awful tragedy. Helen and I, along with all Americans, send the Harrison family our most heartfelt prayers of healing and comfort."

Before Senator Harrison left his house the morning of his wife's and son's funeral services, he noted that the stock market was rising, another suicide terrorist had killed 43 people in Iraq, the temperature was 82 and the Red Socks had beat the Yankees the following evening by a score of 4 to 2.

The world had moved on unapologetically and relentlessly, its engine fueled by the ambitions of the powerful, the seekers, the greedy and the lost. So the business of the day would continue, and the weatherman had said that there had been more rain than usual so far that year. A pollution alert was in effect in Los Angeles. Obesity had become an epidemic.

An attractive female news anchor said, "We have been told by Molly Stivers, Senator Harrison's press secretary, that he will hold a press conference sometime after his wife and son are laid to rest. When asked if Senator Harrison planned to continue his bid for the presidency, she said that he would address the question at that time.

The anchor woman faced the camera with an earnest expression. "It has been speculated that Senator Harrison will renounce his bid for the presidency. Behind the scenes, many within his party, as well as the Democratic Party, are scrambling to adjust the messages and tone of the campaign, in light of the recent tragedy.

"President Taylor has cancelled all his campaign appearances, including fundraisers, stating that 'This is not the time for political campaigning. This is the time to honor six great Americans (Connie Harrison, Robert Jr., the two pilots and the two Secret Service agents) and offer our prayers and support to Senator Harrison and his family, and indeed to all the families who lost loved ones, in this, their heavy hour of heartbreak and loss.'"

Senator Harrison switched off the television. He paused at the full length hall mirror and pulled a heavy breath. He adjusted his gray tie and dark suit and shut his eyes, buffeted by memory and guilt. When Matt descended the stairs, they left the house for the awaiting limo.

It was a clear warm July day, with low humidity and an easy wind. The limo crept silently through the back streets, with a full escort of Secret Service. Neither Bob nor Matt spoke, their vitality being low, their faces blank and private.

The service was brief but elegant, another request Connie had made in her will. It was held at the old stone Presbyterian Church, with its towering spire—the one that Connie had attended as a child, and attended until her death. It lay at the base of a long low, mossy hill, surrounded by stately oaks and elms.

Secret Service agents had occupied the area for three days. Snipers hid in and among the great oaks and towering elm trees. The duck pond nearby was deceptively quiet. Snipers were concealed on its grassy banks, watching the ducks glide on the placid water. The air was patrolled by helicopters that hovered over the woods and distant hills, and guarded the airspace over the two-laned highway that was barricaded on approach and return for a mile.

President Taylor and his wife, Helen, arrived early, followed by the British Prime minister, and his wife, both friends of the Harrisons. Other dignitaries included the Secretary of State, two senators and their wives, three congressmen, the celebrated author and poet Willaby Ryder, who'd composed a poem for the occasion, and close friends and family.

Because the church could only seat about 400, there was the inevitable disappointed friend, colleague and disgruntled family member who had not received an invitation and had communicated their displeasure to the Senator's staff. What they didn't realize was that the Senator had worked closely with his willing and tireless staff, assiduously, seeing to every detail, including who was invited and who was not.

The guests arrived, remote and voiceless, wearing variations of black. The closed caskets were adorned with pink and white lilies; the altar with red and white roses. In the 18th century candleholders, candles burned in the stillness, their flames unperturbed by a demure breeze. As the President and the First Lady were seated in the second row, along with the British Prime Minister, the rattling helicopters drifted away, leaving the church in a reverent silence.

The Senator and Matt entered and were sat in the first row. Bob sat closed and rigid, as if every muscle and every emotion had been beaten into a tenuous submission. Matt, who had been silent for days, sat dejected and still. As he had stepped into the church and viewed the coffins, he felt as though he'd entered an open wound.

The Reverend William D. Townsend, a tall, gray stately man of 63, spoke warmly of Connie, in his soothing bass voice. He recalled their friendship of 35 years. He spoke of her generosity of spirit, of her courage, of her love for her husband and sons, of her profound love of country, "and not the least, I can assure you," Reverend Townsend said, with a soft smile, "Constance, Connie, possessed an incorruptible faith and love of God.

"In a conversation we had only last week, after we had discussed plans to build a summer camp for kids in New Jersey and Connecticut, Connie said to me 'Bill, I have been so blessed. I have had the best of lives and God knows that I am grateful.'"

After a moment of recovery, as tears flowed, Matt rose and ascended the two carpeted stairs to the pulpit. He was still, his eyes downcast. When he spoke, he did not lift his head.

"Robert Jr. was a competitive brother. He played hard. He liked to win. He was smart and he worked persistently and skillfully at whatever he did. When we were kids, he taught me how to play baseball and football and then when we played with some of the other guys at school or in the neighborhood, if I screwed up—and I did—he inevitably got into a fight to defend me. Then he'd take me back home and show me what I did wrong and we'd work on it until I got it right.

"As a teenager, he explained girls to me. He said, girls are the greatest, man, but you can't let them know that or they'll rule you. He chose my first date and we doubled. He insisted on paying for everything—and Dad made us both work hard for our allowance. There were no giveaways. So Robert Jr. spent all of his hard-earned money on all four of us. Of course, he told the girls that I had paid for everything. He was a perfect gentleman and extremely entertaining. Needless to say, both of our dates fell in love with him.

"My brother was a generous man. Honest and straightforward. He once told me that it was actually easier to be honest than dishonest. 'Let people know where you stand, right up front' he said. 'It's so much easier in the long run.'"

Matt paused. He scratched his head. "The other night, before he left, he told me we've got to do something good with our lives, Matt. We've been given so much."

Matt lifted his head for the first time. "Robert Jr. gave me so many good memories. So many good things to remember. So many things to think about and reflect on. I was given so much by him and I will always honor that and I will always honor his memory."

Matt lowered his head and returned to his seat.

Willaby Ryder came slowly to his feet and approached the pulpit. He was thin and elderly, with frosty hair and watery eyes that seemed fixed on a distant planet. He wore a black suit and white shirt, buttoned at the neck, tieless. He retrieved a folded piece of paper from his inside jacket pocket, smoothed it out with the flat of his shaky hand and then reached for his wire-framed spectacles. Taking a prayerful moment, he slipped them on and began to read in a thin reedy tenor voice.

If we search for answers where none exist
We run the risk
Of searching the highs and lows of heaven
And of losing the heaven that sent us searching.

If we sit with her for heavenly hours
worshiping the time
With pleasure and love
...and question the heart,
There'll be no learning this side of heaven.

If Connie opened the hearts of things
And placed her jewel inside
And she did, with love, Oh yes, with love,
Then who's to question the heart of things,
When such a woman with sterling gifts
Was proof of heaven and earth.

And of love, my friends, she was no doubt
Of this, she was the proof of love.

After the poet had returned to his chair, Connie's favorite opera singer Charlotte Lamb, a thin, regal woman of 40, rose from the balcony choir stall and sang, acappella, "Amazing Grace." She sang the hymn so tenderly, and with such purity of tone and color, that most eyes dampened and heads were hung low.

When the service concluded, the soundless gathering filed past the caskets and left the church. Outside, in good sunlight, the Senator and Matt acknowledged friends and family with gentle nods and handshakes. To the President, who told Matt he prayed for them everyday, Matt simply nodded, shook his hand weakly and then turned and started for the waiting limo. To Senator Harrison, the President said, "Bob, God bless you."

Bob and Matt sat silently in the limo, as they passed through West Town, on the way to the cemetery. Supporters and mourners lined both sides of the streets, quiet and reverent, some in tears, some waving, some with signs raised that read "We're Praying For You." "We Love You." "God Bless You."

The limo followed the meandering cemetery road that quietly rose to a crest beside a band of private trees, with a glorious view of soft rolling hills and the distant church spire of the Presbyterian Church. Only the immediate family proceeded from the limos to attend the solemn burial. They gathered around the caskets, poised for final burial, with folded hands, helpless hands, or hands that held handkerchiefs for weeping.

Connie had requested burial. She loved the Earth and wanted to return to it. "All God's creatures are equal here," she once said.

"All God's creatures buried in this hollowed ground will rise with spring and be sanctified anew," Reverend Townsend said, before he read a verse from the Bible: one of Connie's favorites.

> *No eye has seen no ear has heard*
> *no mind has conceived*
> *what God has prepared for those who love him.*

Constance Marion Dowd Harrison was laid to rest on Tuesday afternoon, along with her son, Robert Zachary Harrison, Junior. There was an abundance of birds, flicking about the trees, sailing the pleasantly scented currents. Clouds covered the hot sun for a time and long blue shadows cooled the burial spot. Bob Harrison stood tall, refusing a chair, and Matt stood ramrod straight beside him.

After everyone else had left the gravesite, including Matt, Bob wept, his big shoulders rolling in spasm, his still handsome face contorted in agony. Finally, he did sit, placing his face in his hands.

His treasonous act of 25 years ago had returned with a savage retribution. The blatant, unmistakable irony was clear: killed in a plane crash that should have killed him so many years ago; killed near Cincinnati, the home of Joanna's birth and childhood. Truth was indeed stranger than any fiction.

Bob had never been particularly religious, but as he peeled his tear-stained hands from his face, staring up into endless blue sky, he began worshiping the religion of bitterness; the religion of regret; the religion of self-loathing.

Chapter 6

Two days later, on Thursday morning, Senator Harrison appeared at the front of the house, with Matt at his side. They strolled easily across the vivid green lawn and trimmed hedges toward the far end, where a sea of national and international television crews waited, cameras perched and rolling, recorders jutted forward and held aloft; anchors waiting, high on anticipation. All the networks had preempted regular programming and were live; all the cable news stations were live; public radio was also live.

The United States, as well as most of the world, had paused to tune in. The business of America had stopped.

At 10:30, it was already hot and humid, with large frothy clouds and the lazy circling of two crows, one making sounds like an Indian war cry.

Bob was dressed casually in white cotton trousers, a blue and white striped shirt and blue blazer. Matt wore brown Khakis and a light blue polo shirt. As they advanced toward the mass, Bob put the estimate at several hundred. As they left the house, Matt told him "I'd give anything not to have to do this."

Bob responded, "It's our duty, Matt."

The Senator drew up to the awaiting podium, with a commanding presence and soft eyes. Matt stood obediently at his side, chin up, hands still. Cameras exploded to life as reporters waited, spellbound.

Bob gathered a furtive breath, scanning the crowd courageously. When he spoke, his voice was steady, warm and resonant.

"My fellow Americans. My family and I want to thank you for the many kindnesses that you have given us during these very difficult and challenging days. We thank you for your generous hearts, for your many letters of encouragement and for your compassion. We thank you for your heartfelt prayers and good wishes. We thank you for your fond remembrances of Connie and Robert Jr.

"I cannot express to you just how much all of these have touched our hearts and supported us through these long days and nights. We are truly grateful and humbled.

"To President Taylor and First Lady, Helen Taylor, I am deeply grateful for their thoughtfulness, goodwill and generosity, which I will never forget, nor will my family. They have shown us all—by shining example—just how good and kind our country is and how strong and charitable our leaders are. I thank God for their kindnesses and pray that he continue to richly bless them.

"My dear Americans, I also want to thank you for your patience. Our country is in the midst of a presidential campaign, and we are all keenly aware that our beloved country faces some of the most difficult problems that it has ever faced. It will soon be time for us to exercise our right as true American citizens to go to the ballot box to vote.

"My dear friends, I am deeply thankful that I have had the opportunity to visit the great towns and cities of this wonderful and blessed country, and to shake the hands of many of you, break bread in your homes, restaurants and diners, and talk about the issues that are most important to you and your families. It has truly been a privilege."

Bob waited, scanning the crowd. "I love and cherish this country with all my heart. It is, as it has always been, a beacon of hope, light and opportunity for people all over the world, and it must remain so."

Bob paused to sip water. Beads of sweat popped out on his forehead. He leaned forward, narrowing his eyes, his mouth firm, gaze clear.

"Therefore, after many discussions with Matt and with the rest of my family, as well as discussions with my dedicated staff, and after personal reflection, I have decided that our campaign must go on. Our work must go on. Connie was not a quitter and she would not want me to be. She believed in our cause and she would have wanted us to continue. Connie was a practical dreamer and I will honor her and my son's great lives and spirits by continuing on with our campaign."

Bob saw the mass of reporters boil into action. Cameras flashed, reporters shoved forward, cell phones were raised.

"Therefore, this coming Monday, August 2nd, I will once again be criss-crossing this great nation, meeting as many of you as possible, spreading our message of hope, and looking toward the future with renewed strength and optimism."

Bob took a pause, smiling modestly. "I am honored and proud to be a candidate for President of the United States and I can promise you that, if you elect me as your next President, I will never let you down. Thank you all again. May God bless you and may God bless America!"

Bob gave a final wave, turned, wrapped an arm around Matt's shoulder and started back toward the house.

Chapter 7

Matt Harrison had watched his father pace the spacious rooms of the house for many hours, head down, hands locked behind his back. He'd watched him pour several glasses of single malt scotch and then drift, inevitably, toward the black lacquered grand piano to gaze at Connie's and Robert Jr.'s gilded framed photos. Connie had played the piano well: Bach, Beethoven and show tunes. She'd delighted many a foreign diplomat and head of state. It was said that Vice President Richard Plumb had a crush on her, born on the night she gave a 15 minute concert before dinner.

At times Bob, still dressed in his pajamas and house slippers, stared for long minutes at the oil painting of Connie that hung in the living room above the generous oak mantelled stone fireplace. It had been painted when she was 36. She was resplendently dressed in a royal blue gown, with a long golden necklace and matching earrings, seated in a garden adorned by pink and white roses. Her dark eyes were appealing, drawing the eyes of the beholder to her earthy beauty. Her full ruby lips added sensuality, her high cheek bones gave a touch of the classic. The overall impression was one of intelligence and warm invitation. Bob would stare, lower his head in covert thoughts, and then stare again.

Despite their housekeeper, Carla's, protestations, Bob ate little and it was obvious that he was losing weight. The day he addressed the nation to say he was continuing the campaign, he ate nothing. Immediately following the address, he'd locked himself away in his library, refusing all calls except from Carlton, Molly and President Taylor, who had congratulated him on his decision to stay in the race.

Matt and his father had said little to one another for days, and despite what the Senator had told the press, their discussion about continuing the campaign went as follows:

"I'm going to keep going," his father had said. "I mean, I'm going to continue the campaign."

Matt shrugged.

End of conversation.

Matt had not told his father that he had dropped out of school. His professors understood perfectly and told him he could pick up where he left off whenever he wished.

Matt also paced the house and the gardens and refused calls from his friends, many of whom had called to flatter their own egos and to spread the word at parties and to girlfriends that they knew Matt Harrison.

When girls called—girls Matt had never met but who professed to be friends of friends offering sympathy and their company—Matt trashed his cell phone and asked the Secret Service to change his private home number.

To Matt's surprise, his former girlfriend didn't call. She'd sent a letter; a very sensitive, articulate letter, offering an ear, pizza and her bed, if he was so inclined. He wasn't. The relationship was over, but he'd e-mailed her a thank you note, wishing her well.

Matt had been offered tranquilizers and therapy by a good friend of the family, Dr. James Highland, a prominent psychiatrist, but Matt had refused, although Bob had received the doctor at their home and spent a couple of hours with him. Matt didn't know what was discussed. But he did know that his father was taking some kind of mild tranquilizer and sleeping pills.

On Saturday morning, the weekend before his father was to restart his campaign, Matt had walked the six-acre grounds, threading the elms and maples, struggling to decipher his feverish tangled emotions. It had turned unseasonably cool; there was a light mist falling. He wore jeans and a hooded blue sweatshirt that had Columbia printed across the chest in bold white letters. His red sneakers kicked at the ground as if searching beneath things: twigs, damp leaves, rich earth. Matt had the sense that his life was in retrograde, as if he had lost all forward movement and was drifting irrevocably. It had become apparent that he had neglected to exercise certain emotional muscles and, at the first test of their strength, they had faltered; the object they were instructed to lift and hold had crashed to the ground. He felt he couldn't continue his life until he isolated those muscles and strengthened them.

He had wept a number of times after the plane crash, but only in private, and he'd gotten good and drunk only once, oddly enjoying the hangover the next morning, as it had briefly distracted his troubled mind.

Matt had wandered into his brother's old room often, picking through his closet, exploring boxes of baseballs and gloves, an old basketball and a couple of trophies

Robert Jr. had won for wrestling and swimming in high school and college.

Matt too, had stared at his mother's portrait and felt the need for a swift deliverance from pain and anger. Why? How could it have happened? He'd awakened at night—in a cold sweat—believing that it had all been a terrible dream, but at the first light of morning, the hammer of reality would strike and he'd rise and stare and pace.

By mid-morning on Friday, fog clung to the tops of trees. Mist cooled Matt's face and glazed the world in wet silver tones. An uneasy bubble of a thought kept rising to the surface of Matt's mind and he kept blowing it away, until, finally, every other thought became devitalized and dull. At last he seized it, like the swift hand-grab of a mosquito. He opened the hand of his mind, feeling his breathing change, and he looked at it, as if it were an artifact.

Was the mermaid story true? If not, who invented it and why? "Just politics" his father had always said. His mother had been more mum. If fact, as the thought worked Matt over, like little slaps to the face, he recalled that his mother had always grown silent whenever the subject had been raised, retreating from any explanation or hint of deflection. Once, she'd even risen from the dinner table and left the room.

His father had lifted a helpless hand and said, "It's the dirty side of politics that upsets her so."

But Matt kept picking at the thread of emotion—patiently analyzing and unraveling it. The word "betrayal" kept repeating and rattling about in his head. Not only had he lost his birth mother, but he'd lost his "real" mother—the one person he loved more than anyone else.

Betrayal. Betrayed by fate, by God or by whomever or whatever; betrayed at birth by a natural father who had never been found; betrayed by his birth mother for never telling anyone his father's true identity. Matt's father had no face. He had no name. There was no internet search available to find a ghost. No detective had ever found more than a thin trail that had led to a broken down trailer park in Pine Bluff, Arkansas. But it was a false trail. Why hadn't his mother revealed his identity? Embarrassment? Perhaps his father was famous or married or a convict. Perhaps she had been betrayed?

What if the mermaid story were true? What if his Dad, Senator Bob Harrison, had fathered "the mermaid's child"? Then he had betrayed every one of them, and everything he had ever said, and everything he had ever told the American people, was tainted with his lies and betrayal.

But Matt would have a sister! Though not connected in blood, she would be family. Matt had always burned with a new pride every time he thought of himself as being a part of a family; as having a family. The sudden realization revitalized him. He turned toward the two-chimney Georgian house and an intrepid thought struck: ask your father for the truth! Demand to know the truth, once and for all!

Matt walked purposefully toward the back door. Inside, he shed his shoes and sweatshirt, leaving only his jeans and T-shirt. Without speaking to Carla, he crossed the house, padding across rich oriental rugs, stopping at the library door. He heard his father's muffled voice from inside; he was talking on the phone. Matt drew a breath and knocked.

"Yes…" his father called.

"It's Matt."

"I'm on the phone with Carlton."

"It's important. I need to talk to you."

Matt heard silence.

"Okay, Matt. Come in."

Matt opened the door and entered. His father was seated behind his impressive oak desk, his reading glasses perched on the end of his nose. He waved Matt forward, while continuing his conversation with Carlton.

"I know, Carl…Yes, of course, but I don't want or need to come on too strong. The convention tone should be one of easy reconciliation…Yes… well, okay…Look, I have to go. Let's go over this later on. Yes, come tomorrow for dinner. And bring Molly. I miss and need her input. Okay, bye."

Matt sat in the black leather easy chair before his father's desk.

Bob removed his glasses, tossed them on his desk and squeezed his tired eyes shut. He took a long stretch and yawned. Matt noticed the dark circles that weren't there a few days ago.

"You should try and get some sleep," Matt said, as his father opened his eyes.

"I slept some last night. The damn sleeping pill woke me up after 4 hours and I couldn't get back to sleep."

"How's it going?" Matt asked.

"Oh…it's going."

"All the polls are showing that you're two-to-three points ahead of President Taylor."

The words seemed to hurt him. He shook his head. "…Inevitable, I guess. I don't know….I just…" his quiet voice fell off. He lifted his eyes and seemed to focus on his son for the first time. "How are you, Matt? I mean…you left school didn't you?"

"Yes, I'm taking some time off."

Bob nodded. "Well, that's probably a good idea. Why don't you go up to Maine, hang out at the cabin until the convention. That'll give you three weeks to rest."

"I thought about it, but I don't think I will. Not yet anyway."

Bob shuffled some papers about and waited for Matt to speak. When he didn't, Bob did. "So what did you want to talk about?" Bob asked.

Matt shifted his weight. "Dad…I know we're both kind of struggling…"

"Matthew," Bob said, warmly, "I'm sorry I haven't been there for you like I should. I've just been…To tell you the truth, I'm carrying on with this business because I'm afraid I'll go crazy if I don't. It consumes me 24 and 7 and that's what I need. We haven't really had a good talk since…"

"I don't need to talk about it. I just need to get over it."

Bob nodded, running his hands through his hair. "So, then…Matt, what's up?"

Matt shifted again, his eyes focused on the plush blue carpet. "Dad…is it true?"

Bob folded his hands on the desktop, leaning forward. "Is what true?"

Matt paused, apprehensive. "The woman…25 years ago?"

It took a total committed effort for Bob not to react in a defensive outburst. He hardly moved.

Matt saw his father's jaw tighten.

The silenced lengthened into a miserable tension.

"How could you?" Bob asked.

Matt felt his father's withering gaze. He didn't answer.

"After all we've been through. How could you?"

Matt summoned strength. "I'd just like to hear it from you. Once and for all. Then I promise, I'll never mention it again."

Bob pounded the desk and shot up. "Dammit! Matt! Dammit!!" His breathing quickened, his tired angry face aged him five years. "How many times do I have to answer that damned question!?"

Matt waited, a technique he had learned from his Dad.

Bob threw his hands to his hips, fuming. "Of course it's not true! Of course they're dirty political lies! How many times do I have to say it! To them!?" he raged, pointing to the window. "To you and to everybody else in this god forsaken world! It is a fucking lie! Okay! Okay!! Now get out of my sight! Get out!!"

Matt pushed himself up and left.

Outside in the hallway, Matt leaned back against the closed library door. His heart raced. He was certain now. He'd seen the raw, agonizing fear in his father's eyes. Before Matt could move on with his life, he would have to know the truth. He set off up the stairs to begin his quest.

Matt sat at his computer with martial eyes, searching internet sites for stories and links to "the mermaid" stories. Many were identical repeats of the same story, without deviation, while others embellished and theorized. Others were Bob Harrison bash sites that ridiculed his Senate record and his stance on stem cell research. They called him a phony and a liar. And there were others—excruciatingly painful to read—who claimed that he had had his wife and son killed just so he could win the election; an election he'd had no hope of winning.

The bloggers wrote for and against him. Some were diatribes, ungrammatical and profane, while the majority supported him and the family, although there was speculation that if "the mermaid" was out there—and she probably was—it was she who had spread the story as an act of revenge. Many went on to support the Senator anyway. It had all happened long ago, they read, and his actions—right or wrong—should be forgotten, especially in light of the recent family tragedy. The spreading story was undoubtedly a rotten political act.

But after hours of searching and reading, Matt landed on a website that drew his full interest. The website was entitled "The Talk of the Net." At the top left panel, he read the link and caption "The Mermaid's Daughter." Matt reacted by nosing forward to his laptop screen and clicking on it. He began to read.

"Why hasn't the mermaid been found after so much press—so much searching and speculation? Simple. She either doesn't exist or she's dead. But let's just say for the sake of it that she did exist and that she did have a daughter, as has been conjectured. Well now, isn't that interesting, folks? This is what really interests me and turns me on! Maybe this is the revengeful little bitch who's trying to bring down, to another fiery crash, her old man, because he abandoned her so many years ago. Hell, maybe she was responsible for crashing his wife's and son's plane. Oh juicy, juicy gossip, I love you! I say, it's the girl, Holmes. It's the girl!"

Angry, Matt logged off and went for a walk.

At three o'clock in the morning, Matt awoke and returned to his father's library. The house seemed secluded from the world, draped in a ringing silence. He switched on the desk lamp and searched his father's drawers. Fortunately, they were unlocked. Careful not to disturb the neat piles and folders, Matt examined manila folders, notebooks and stacks of letters from colleagues, supporters and old friends. He read some of the letters to see if there was a clue or hint or an outright admission of his affair. But after an hour, he found nothing.

Matt recalled that his father had a safe, hidden somewhere in the library, but he'd never bothered to ask where it was—it hadn't been important. He searched for a while, scanning the generous shelves for a key to its location. Suddenly, his attention was drawn to a book high on a top bookshelf. It seemed uncharacteristically out of place with the others. Matt stretched his neck, squinting in the thin light. It was in the biography section, next to a biography of Washington and Lord Wellington. It was a thin paperback. Matt was well aware of his father's fastidiousness when it came to the arrangement and care of his books. It seemed to Matt that this little book had been placed there by design.

Matt climbed the double step oak stool, reached and plucked the little pink book from the rack, blew off a little top dust and read the title:

Astrology Looking for Love
by
Joanna Halloran

The book was stiff, the pages yellow. It looked as though it had never been opened. Matt flipped to the copyright page: 1978. The first printing was 1978. The Second 1980. The Third 1982. The Fourth 1984.

Matt turned the page. The dedication read:

To my father, Bix, a bright star in a dark sky.

Matt leafed through the pages. It seemed like cheap astrological pop wisdom on how to meet your dream man or woman, based on your astrological sign. Definitely not the kind of book his father would ever read. It seemed obvious that it was a campaign gift he'd never thrown away. He'd received hundreds over the years. He'd tossed most. This one had somehow survived.

Matt replaced it, climbed down and went back to the desk. Just before dawn, Matt searched his father's old Rolodex. The Senator had never grown especially found of computers, feeling them impersonal and "frighteningly unpredictable."

Matt scanned the cards with haste, unclear what he was looking for. When he saw the name BECKY MEYER, he stopped. It was a California address and phone number. Matt knew that this was the former Becky Day of Gerry and Becky Day, the couple who'd saved his father's life 25 years ago. Matt paused, massaging his strained eyes. When he opened them, he snatched a pen and paper and jotted down the cell and home numbers.

Just as he'd switched the light off, he heard a sound outside the door. He froze. There was a light rap on the door. Matt waited.

"Senator?" a male voice asked.

Matt crept forward toward the door.

"Senator, is that you?"

Matt recognized the voice. It was Don, one of the two Secret Service agents who patrolled the house. Matt opened the door, smiling.

"Hey, Don. Just me. Couldn't sleep. Decided to read."

Don, tall, beefy and all business, simply nodded, turned and disappeared into the house like a quiet ghost.

Matt sighed. With stealthy footfalls, he returned to his room and to bed. He'd call Becky in the morning. Surely, the recent tragedy would elicit her sympathy and she'd tell him the truth. The challenge would be to persuade her never to reveal their conversation to his father.

Chapter 8

On Saturday morning, Matt called Becky Meyer on her cellphone. Her home number had been disconnected.

"I'd like to speak with Becky Meyer, please," he said.

Matt had called her cell number.

There was a long silence. "Who's calling?" a low suspicious female voice asked.

"This is Matt Harrison. Senator Harrison's son."

"Oh, really," she answered, harshly.

"Yes…"

She hung up.

Undaunted, Matt redialed and waited. It rang with no answer and then went to voicemail. He didn't leave a message.

Matt waited a half hour and tried again.

"Hello," the same voice answered.

"Don't hang up. I *am* Matt Harrison. Please, I really need to talk to you."

She hung up.

Frustrated, Matt slapped his cell phone shut. He sat on the edge of his bed, fuming.

He and his father ate at separate times. The Senator remained locked in his library for most of the day, refusing lunch and drinking several scotches.

By evening, Matt returned to his room and tried again. He dialed Becky's number.

"Yes?"

"Mrs. Meyer, please, don't hang up."

"What do you want!?" she snapped.

"Please…please, just don't hang up."

"Look, whoever you are, I don't know how you got this number but if you call me one more time, I'll have you thrown into jail. Okay!?"

Before Matt could respond, she was gone.

After a solitary dinner of salmon, rice and salad, Matt stepped outside into darkness. The humidity had returned; a hazy moon appeared; cicadas scratched at the night. He walked the grounds, dejected but determined.

He returned to his room around 11 and logged onto the internet. He engaged in another round of searches and clicks, probing every link, article and blog. When he did a Google search for the words "Mermaid Bob Harrison", 367,434 sites and related links appeared.

By 2:20 in the morning, he was exhausted. He fell into bed fully clothed. As he lay on the edge of sleep, his tireless mind reran a portion of a chat room conversation he'd read earlier.

…President Reagan and his wife Nancy went to astrologers. That's why his security was beefed up, because this astrologer told him that he was coming to a dangerous time. It was probably what saved his life when he was shot. Any less security that day and he would have been dead.

So here's my point. I heard that Bob Harrison went to an astrologer for a while, back in the 1980's. I think that the rescue at sea with those two people in the sailboat is total bullshit. I also think that the whole mermaid story is also just a cover-up. I think he was seeing this woman astrologer—probably sleeping with her—and the family didn't want it to get out. Maybe the whole plane crash was made up too. I could never vote for that sleazebag.

Matt shot up out of bed and rushed downstairs to the library. He entered, found the light and crossed to the bookshelf, peering up, feeling an expectant rush of adrenaline. He mounted the step stool, reached and retracted the paperback.

Back at his father's desk, he read the name of the author, slowly, feeling a perfect pitch of excitement and discovery. JOANNA HALLORAN.

With the light out, book in hand, he fled the library, scaled the stairs and burst into his room with renewed energy.

The computer came to life. The internet appeared. He typed in the name JOANNA HALLORAN. 9,173 references!

Many were book references: she'd written five, in addition to the one that lay beside him. Most of the links were how and where to buy her books. Some were articles she'd written and others were written about her.

Matt typed in "Joanna Halloran bio."

After the screen refreshed, he clicked on the first link and read.

She was born in Cincinnati and went to school there. She took a degree in psychology. Her father was a famous astrologer, Bix Halloran. She'd moved to New York and worked with battered women before beginning a full-time astrology business. She'd written several popular astrology books. She did astrological counseling, but it took months to get an appointment because of her popularity. She rarely lectured or traveled. She'd never been married, but had one daughter, named Maya. Joanna lived in Montauk, New York.

Matt stared, numbly. Montauk… near where his father had crashed. A daughter named Maya. Never been married. The woman, an astrologer. The astrology book, found in his father's library. The same woman.

An inner tension tightened Matt's chest, constricted his breathing. As he reread the bio, and the obvious, authentic truth struck him in the heart with the force of a stabbing sword, his face closed and he lost his posture. He lowered his head in defeat. The air seemed to resonate with the word "betrayal."

At 9:30 on Sunday morning, Matt and his father ate together at the large mahogany dinner table, though at opposite ends. They seemed small and narrow, as if not wishing to intrude on the empty spaces around them. Both faces held fatigue. Both wore old T-shirts and jeans.

Mildred Combs, the family's full-time cook for the past five years, brought eggs, bacon, toast, juice and coffee. Though both had refused anything but coffee and toast, her stubborn attitude and thick, folded arms across her abundant bosom delivered the appropriate message and they attempted to please her. After she'd left the room, Bob pushed his plate away and reached for his cup of coffee.

"Look…Matt, I'm sorry about what I said the other day. I was out of line. It was a complete over-reaction to a simple question."

Matt didn't speak. He nibbled on his toast.

Bob continued. "…You sure you don't want to spend some time up at the cabin? Bring some friends if you want to. It will do you good."

Matt kept his tone respectful. "Actually, I think I will go up for awhile."

"Good…good."

Silence gathered around them like a haunting of regret and old memories, filling the corners, amplifying the tick of the 200 year-old grandfather's clock. Silence merged with sunlight, breaking glaringly through yellow linen curtains, paneling the parquet floors. Silence fell into the crevices of deteriorating trust, leaving doubt and suspicion. "I know it's not your thing—all this campaigning—but I was hoping you could join me the last week before the convention," Bob said.

The thought sickened Matt. "Yeah…sure."

Bob stared into his cup. "Tell you the truth, son, I could use the support. I'm feeling kind of wobbly." He looked at Matt, concerned. "Are you okay?"

Matt nodded. "Yeah, sure."

Bob searched for the precise words. "Son…you know Dr. Highland is there if you need him. He's very good."

"I'm fine. Really," Matt muttered. "I'm leaving for Maine today. I've already packed. A couple of weeks up there and I'll be good."

Bob cradled the coffee cup in his hand. "Are you still seeing Lauren?"

"No…we broke up."

"Too bad. I liked her. She's classy. Comes from a good family. Davis is her last name, isn't it?"

"Yeah…Davis. She sent a letter. A nice letter."

"That was thoughtful."

Bob tried not to press him. "So, did she break it off?"

"She wanted to get married."

"Oh… I see. Well, she has good taste," Bob said, trying to brighten the mood.

Matt drained the glass of orange juice, still and silent.

"You're not ready for marriage?" Bob asked, softly.

"No. Not with her."

"You can say it's none of my business, Matt, but she's a very intelligent and attractive girl. A very pretty girl."

Matt shrugged. "She thinks I should go to law school."

"Okay…Nothing wrong with that."

"Except I don't want to. She's so damned ambitious for her and for me."

"Ambition is good."

"Is it?"

"There's nothing wrong with wanting to make something of yourself, Matt."

Matt bristled. "I have made something of myself! I'm not Robert Jr. I don't want a career in politics!"

Bob held up his hand. "Let me clarify. Of course you have made something of yourself and I couldn't be prouder of you. You want to teach, and that's as noble a profession as there is. And nowadays, God knows we need good teachers in this country. I mean, look at the Japanese auto companies that are moving to Canada because our workers don't have the education to handle basic technology. Look at the kids today who don't even know what years the revolution was fought or when the Civil War was or who the President was at the time! No, teaching is a wonderful profession, Matt."

Bob drank his coffee and set the cup down. "But, you can do many things with a law degree. It doesn't hurt to have it."

Matt's tone hardened. "I don't want to. I don't just want to teach. I want to write books—books on history—biographies, I want to find new ways of fleshing out the people who made this country; lesser known people who had a major impact on this country."

Bob looked away toward the sunlight. "Okay. That is fine, Matt. Admirable goals."

Matt crumbled his napkin and dropped it next to his unfinished breakfast. "I think Lauren would be happier with somebody more like you than me. She loves politics. She thought Mom *was* the greatest…" his voice trailed off in sudden misery.

The words seemed to echo with throbbing importance.

"Your mother was the greatest, Matt," Bob said, in a soft guilty tone.

Matt looked down and away. "My point is that Lauren wants a political life."

"And you don't."

"We shouldn't go there, Dad."

"We've been there before."

"And we both know I don't admire politicians."

"Yes, son, I know that. But, as I have said, many times, there are those of us who truly, truly want the best for this country and for the American people. We try very hard to be honorable and truthful."

Matt heaved himself from his chair, eyes cold. "Yeah. Right! Well, I've got to go. Good luck with it all."

Matt burned out of the dining room and his father watched, troubled and perplexed.

Matt had formulated a plan. He would cut his hair short and dye it blond. He'd wear sunglasses and a baseball cap most of the time. He'd call himself Kurt Davis. Kurt was his best friend at Columbia and Davis was Lauren's last name. His Dad always called Matt's cell phone so his calling wouldn't pose a problem when Matt wasn't at the cabin in Maine.

Two Secret Service agents were assigned to him and would stick to him like glue, so he'd have to explain to them that he was in love and that they were to be as unobtrusive and discrete as possible. He'd requested Don and Allen. Don didn't talk much and Allen was more laid back and "loved" the girls. They would eventually report to their superiors where they were and that, in turn, would get back to his father. But by then, Senator Harrison would be so busy riding the tail of the campaign dragon, he wouldn't have the time to do more than rant and shout.

At a little after 11a.m. on Sunday, Matt stopped by his father's library and said goodbye. Bob was on the phone, locked in a policy moment with Carlton. He waved goodbye.

Moments later Matt piled into his red convertible Mustang and drove away. A black Ford sedan, holding Allen and Don, followed.

TV crews would be waiting at the security gate. Matt would drive to the West Town airport, hire a plane and escape. He would falsely declare that he was flying off to Maine for rest and relaxation. That would throw the reporters off for a time.

But Matt was on his way to Montauk, Long Island, to find Joanna and Maya.

Part 3

The Lover Returns

Chapter 1

Early Sunday morning, Maya Halloran drove through Amagansett, Long Island. She passed its chic shops and stately white-columned homes, with their manicured lawns and broad shady oaks. She paused near the shaded Farmers Market near the center of town. Should she get pastry, corn, flowers? She was in the high mood to browse and buy. And so she parked her blue Toyota Corolla and strolled the market, coffee to-go cup in one hand and a freshly baked gooey cinnamon roll in the other.

The morning air had the color and effervescence of freshly poured champagne. Leaves glittered like green ice in the sun. Flowers dazzled. People seemed to hover a few inches above the ground as they roamed the rows of bright fruit and vegetables. Red apples stood at attention, arranged in West Point perfection. Lilies, snap dragons, petunias and daisies reached from bushel baskets and overflowed shelves. Corn was piled high in wicker baskets and smelled of freshly turned earth.

Maya wore white Capri pants, one inch heels and a turquoise halter top. Shining black hair spilled out from beneath a wide-brimmed hat, and her long silver earrings made delicate music when she walked. Her neck was regal, her shoulders thin and proud, her breasts modest but firm. She had a dark mole just below her left lower lip. Men noticed her alert hazelnut eyes, the soft lines of her lovely face and the little diamond stud embedded in the side of her slightly up-turned nose. Her naturally pursed lips offered both a pensive quality and the air of well-bred intelligence. She was tall and moved with a proud femininity.

At 24, she had already broken several hearts, one being an English Lit professor at Brown University where she'd received her undergraduate degree in English. She was 21 and he 42. He had begged her to marry him and she had begged him to stop asking her. She loved his knowledge of the classics, but hated his "lack of knowledge of the world."

"You've lived in books your whole life," she'd told him. "You lived with your mother until you were 35."

"She was a good and decent woman," he said, defensively, in an Irish brogue. He was originally from Dublin. "I brought her from Ireland and I was responsible for her."

"I'm sure you were, Patrick," Maya said, "but the world is more than a classroom, your adoring mother, and shelves filled with books."

"And who are you to be so wise at the young age of 21, Maya, Goddess of Illusion?"

"Don't be a smart ass!" Maya said.

"Then don't get all supercilious on me, Maya. What is your grand vision of the world?"

"I don't see in visions, Patrick. I leave that to you and my crazy mother! I see the world for what it is."

"And what is that, pray tell, Maya, the all wise?"

Maya's eyes fired up. "It's a world that never is what anyone tells you it is. It's fickle. It double-crosses. It leaves you cold when you should be hot. It makes you believe in the folly of dreams and then slaps you hard across the face for believing in those dreams. It seldom ever delivers what it promises."

Patrick shook his head in pity. "Maya, girl, someone has really put the curse of the cynic on you. What has the living of your short life and the reading of my books done to you?"

"They've made me wise, Patrick. Living in the real world and reading your books has made me wise. I see the world for what it is. Not the world as I'd like it to be."

Maya's last lover was a man younger than she, by two years. He was a bartender and a long distance runner. Their passion was quick and intense—and had burned itself out when he lost the New York Marathon.

Maya scowled whenever she thought of him. He'd barely finished the Marathon, and had limped around and whined about his loss for days. He was a dreamer of the worst kind: a blathering "big baby," who decided that he was going to India to find a Guru because "running had disappointed him." Good looking? Yes. Stupid? Yes.

Maya loaded a bag filled with native corn, lush red tomatoes, sunflowers and fresh scallions into her back seat. She finished the coffee and toted the grease-spotted little paper bag, holding the last quarter of her beloved cinnamon roll, to the front seat. She buckled up and drove away toward Montauk, the last town on the tip of Long Island. She'd be home in about 15 minutes.

Her spirits lifted when a sprawling resort hotel and scrub pine gave way to undulating dunes and elegant shoots of scattering dune grass. She felt a shift of consciousness from pleasant mediocrity to the thrilling helplessness of a first love. The ocean was near!

Navigating the two-lane road with care, she took the rolling curves and hills on Old Montauk Highway, cruising past neatly trimmed hedges, oval gravel driveways and the quaint bed and breakfast homes tucked under shady trees. She crested a hill and took in the breathtaking view of the sliver of scintillating ocean, where white waves were rushing to shore, and she sighed into the euphoric breeze rushing in through open windows.

She passed bikers, pedaling leisurely, saw joggers on the little asphalt path that skirted the road. She saw kites decorating the skyline, rippling above the beach. Gulls drifted in lazy patterns. All of this flowed into her worshiping soul and healed and relaxed the inner turmoil of the last few months.

She'd have three days alone before her mother arrived from Chicago. She was giving one of her rare seminars on "Astrology and the Modern Woman." The money must have been astronomical to get her away from her beloved beach house, Maya thought.

Maya's plans were simple: she had the entire month of August free and she intended to relax on the beach, get a tan, read novels and prepare her mind for September, when she'd begin her new job, working at a preschool on the upper West Side of Manhattan, with children who had autism.

She'd just completed her course work and clinical internships, finally completing a degree in Speech-Language Pathology, after two and a half years of continuous work. She was exhausted.

She drove through the Village of Montauk. All the diners were full, the shops were busy and there was a book fair, in full swing, on the broad village green surrounding the Gazebo. The crowds surprised her. Montauk had grown more popular in the last few years.

She continued on another mile, found the turn off and took it, advancing along a quiet narrow road, angling left up a hill and making a right turn. The top floor of the house came into view, all windows and decking. The rest was concealed by robust hedges and tall trees. A clearly visible sign read:

PRIVATE PROPERTY. PATROLED BY SECURITY

Maya entered the gravel drive and pulled up to the imposing security gate. She got out, leaving her car door open, and punched in the security code. It buzzed and swung open. She drove through, stopping again on the other side, returning to the gate to close and secure it.

As she struggled with her new key to open the front door, straining to hold the bags of groceries, her cell phone rang. She cursed, lowered the bags, unzipped her purse and answered.

"Hello!"

"Maya!"

"Mom…"

"What's the matter?"

"Nothing. I just got to the house. The damn key's not working."

"Well I checked it and it works. Don't be so impatient."

"And don't be so impatient with me."

"Maya…" Joanna said, more gently.

"What?!"

"I'm so glad you're there."

Maya sighed. "Yeah…I am too. I'm bushed. How's it going out there?"

"Oh God, Maya. There are 548 people at this seminar. It's overflowing. There are over a hundred men."

"It just shows how popular you are."

"It shows why I don't do these things very often. I just get all tongue tied. It was so easy for my father. He loved it. I just feel bizarre and think I say stupid things."

"Mom. The only stupid things you say are to me," she said, teasing.

"Be careful, Maya," Joanna said, in a mock serious tone. "Just because you've graduated doesn't mean you can insult your mother."

"Mom, hang on a minute. I'm going to try the key again."

Maya inserted the key, twisted and wiggled. No success. "Dammit!"

"Maya, pull back on the door when you turn it. You're making it more difficult than it is."

"It's that tone of voice that drives me up a wall, Mother!"

"Just try it, Maya!"

Maya yanked on the door and jiggled the lock. It caught. Maya put her shoulder against the door and nudged it. It swung open. "Thank God."

"I assume a miracle has happened."

"I'm in!" Maya exclaimed.

"The prodigal daughter has turned the magic key and returned home."

"Oh, you are a riot, Mother," Maya said, hunching up her left shoulder and anchoring the phone against her ear. She grabbed her bags and crossed the threshold, kicking the door closed with her right foot. She quickly took in the place, as she lowered her bags and removed her hat and sunglasses.

"Oh my God, it's so hot and stuffy in here."

"Open the windows, dear. Turn on the ceiling fans."

"You changed the curtains. They're dune grass green," she said gathering up the groceries again and crossing the tan living room carpet, as she headed for the kitchen. "And the walls are light yellow. Wow. I like it."

"Yes. Oh and you haven't seen the new mahogany decks. They're gorgeous. I also bought a stainless steel grill, just in case we wanted to grill out."

"Awesome! I bought a bunch of vegetables. We can do zucchini, eggplant and red peppers. You can grill the fish. I always over-cook it."

Maya entered the kitchen, with its modern island, and a wall filled with hanging pots and pans. She lowered the groceries on the sandy colored Formica countertop. "New dishwasher?"

"Yes. The other one went kaput."

Maya lifted the kitchen window and gazed out, viewing the panoramic view of the ocean. "God, it is a stunningly beautiful day, Mother. I can't wait to get down to the beach. Oh! I love the yellow linen curtains in here."

"You've seen them."

"Don't remember," Maya said, kicking off her heels and padding into the living room.

"I also added that other bathroom," Joanna said.

"I've seen it," Maya said, raising windows, feeling the first breath of a cool breeze. She found the switch and turned on the ceiling fans.

"It wasn't finished," Joanna said.

"Mother…it has a skylight, it's blue; there's a little powder room, sink and shower."

"And smoky blue tiles that you picked out last time you were here, which was at Christmas."

"I've been busy, Mother," Maya said, returning to the kitchen.

"I know…I'm so glad you're home, Maya. I can't wait to see you."

"I don't understand why you're staying there until Wednesday. I thought it was over today."

"It was, originally, but because the turnout was so large, they added two days."

"It amazes me that so many people believe in that stuff."

Joanna's voice deepened in reprimand. "Maya, we know there are some subjects we don't discuss, okay?"

"Yes, Mother…I didn't mean that I'm not happy for you. I am. I'm thrilled that people appreciate what you do. I'm also thrilled that you finally got out of this house—as beautiful as it is—and actually went somewhere."

"…Some subjects, Maya…Maybe now it's many subjects, we shouldn't discuss."

"Okay. Okay…" Maya said, surrendering.

"I bought you some cereal and soy milk. Also, there's plenty of Breyers Ice Cream. I couldn't get you other things because I thought they'd spoil."

"I'll do some grocery shopping."

"Okay, honey, I've got to go. There are so many people asking me who I think the next president will be. They're driving me crazy."

Maya began placing things in the frig, switching the phone to her other ear. "So, what do you tell them?"

"I don't. I tell them we're here to talk about the modern woman."

"So who do you think will be the next President?"

"I have no idea."

"I think Harrison's got it. He's rising in the polls and if Taylor criticizes him for anything he looks like an insensitive jerk."

Maya closed the refrigerator door.

"It was a horrible tragedy," Joanna said. "I can't imagine what he must be going through."

Maya unwrapped the flowers and began cutting the stems and placing them in vases. "I heard this morning on the radio that the investigators think that Robert Jr. was sitting in the co-pilot's seat when the plane crashed."

"Oh my God," Joanna said, in a small sorrowful voice. "They should have waited a while before letting that out."

"I don't see how President Taylor is going to get reelected," Maya said, arranging the daisies. "There is so much sympathy for Harrison."

"He'll make a good President," Joanna said.

"You're a democrat, Mother!"

"Who has a right to her opinion."

Maya stopped working, her interest caught by the sound of a single engine airplane passing over. "Has anyone at the seminar asked you about the mermaid story?"

Joanna was silent.

"Mother?"

"…Yes… a few have asked."

"In what context?"

"In the context that they want to know what I think about it. They want to know if, astrologically, it's true."

"And what do you say?"

"I say…we're here to talk about the modern woman, not about some woman who may or may not have existed 25 years ago."

Maya was silent.

"Maya…are you there?"

"Yes. Do you know what I think, Mother?"

"Maya, I have a feeling we should add this subject to our 'do not discuss' list."

Maya continued. "I think the mermaid story is true. And, if the truth ever got out, I think he would lose, even if he's leading in the polls right now."

Joanna's voice turned remote. "You're entitled to your opinion. I've got to go."

"See you Wednesday," Maya said.

"Have fun and relax," Joanna said.

Maya went back outside, collected her suitcase and bags and dragged them into the back first floor bedroom. She unpacked her canary yellow bikini, a few books, and her iPod.

She stripped and moved to the bathroom. She found sunscreen and smoothed it on. Minutes later, she was in her bikini, pastel colored beach bag swung over her shoulder, packed with bottled water, a towel, two books and the iPod. She grabbed her wide brimmed hat, sunglasses and a blue beach umbrella near the door to the back deck, and journeyed off. She passed through the locked security gate, shaking her head at her mother's paranoia about intruders, and ventured toward the newly built wood staircase.

As she descended the steep stairs down to the beach, she noticed the brand new hard plastic sign, chained to the railing. In bold red letters it said:

NO TRESPASSING. PRIVATE PROPERTY.
VIOLATORS WILL BE PROSECUTED.

She paused to inhale, opening to the infinite sky and wide sparkling sea. Sail boats roamed the skyline—white sails like praying hands. The glistening sand shimmered and beckoned.

A quarter mile on either side of her, crowds had gathered. But her mother's relatively private spot of beach had largely remained private, except for the occasional beachcomber or hiker on the way to the cliffs or Ditch Plains, the surfer's beach.

She spread out her turquoise towel, planted the umbrella and settled in, sitting cross-legged for a time, eyes closed, soaking up the pure sun, blessed air and sounds of the sea.

For a time, she wandered barefoot along the edge of the tide, wiggling her toes into the rushing surf, jumping back at the shock of the cold. Gathering courage, she ran and plunged head-first into a curling wave and swam luxuriously for 10 minutes.

Contented, she lay on her stomach, facing the sea, not wanting to listen to music, not wanting words or any stimulation other than the sea, sky and beach.

It was late in the afternoon when she noticed a lone figure approach. She frowned at the intrusion. She adjusted her hat and sunglasses and ignored the invader until he took a more definite interesting shape. He wore a ball cap, sunglasses and orange swim trunks. He had a nice body. Good shoulders, trim waist and long legs. His broad chest was hairless.

Maya pushed up on her elbows, eyeing him carefully. She took off her hat and shook out her shoulder-length hair, fully aware that the sun would strike its midnight tones richly.

He couldn't have been more than middle-to-late 20's, she thought. His legs were muscular, his gait assured.

He wandered by, frequently glancing her way. She allowed her eyes to hold him and then follow him, while he proceeded on toward the cliffs. There was a familiarity about him, but it was overruled by a swift and suspicious attraction. Following behind, were two men, one larger than the other. They wore dark trunks, T-shirts, sneakers and dark glasses. They seemed out of place and uncomfortable.

When they had faded from view, Maya left the beach.

After a shower, Maya grilled a hamburger, ate an ear of fresh corn and drank a beer, while listening to Diana Krall, Bob Dylan and Steely Dan. Long after the sun set, she sat outside on the deck, talking to friends on her cell phone and reading *Resistance*, a novel by Anita Shreve, one of her favorite authors.

At a little after ten o'clock, she wandered into her mother's study. It was crowded with bookshelves, an old armoire, and a worn white couch that her mother napped on between conference calls.

Maya went to the file cabinet and gave the top drawer a little tug. It was locked. Of course. It was always locked. Her mother was a lock freak. Maya grabbed the foot stool, stood, reached and felt the dusty top closet shelf until she found the key, where she'd found it last Christmas, when her mother had gone out Christmas shopping.

Back at the file cabinet, she opened it. She pulled out the lower drawer and searched for the file that was labeled PERSONAL. Maya snaked her hand into the file and drew out an old yellow envelope that had JOANNA written on it in very skillful script.

She extracted the yellow creased letter, shook it open and read it again, just as she had done several times the previous Christmas. The handwriting was clear, the letters carefully formed.

Dearest Joanna:

I am not a poet or a writer of sonnets. I'm a practical man who has had his foundation shaken to the core. If there were truths I once held as true, they are now questioned. If there were absolutes, they have been shattered. If life held promise and clear pathways to success and achievement, they have been obscured and lost.

My darling, I have simply fallen in love with you. It is frightening and wonderful. I sometimes think that when God created heaven and earth—if he did—that love was the one thing that he kept a secret, deep within the hearts of the blessed and the deserving. I think he probably placed the diamond of it in very few hearts. But he placed it in yours, Joanna, and I have benefited from your prodigious intelligence and your astounding beauty.

I will come back to you, Joanna. I have to. I have no other choice. Wait for me, my darling. Wait for me. We have many wonderful years together.

With deepest love,

—I, Robert Zachary Harrison, vow to return to you.

Maya carefully replaced the letter into the envelope and returned it to the file. She stared at nothing, her eyes unfocused and filled with gloomy thoughts. As she gently lowered herself into her mother's brown leather desk chair, it came to her that perhaps it was all for the best. It was best that he wouldn't be disgraced and her mother exposed and humiliated. It was best that her own photograph wouldn't appear on the cover of magazines and newspapers all of the world, as being the one—his daughter—who had anonymously leaked the story to a blogger and a newspaper reporter, some months ago.

But Maya couldn't help feeling pity, anger and disappointment. She had wanted him to pay for his sins.

She'd wanted him to pay dearly for his lies! But Bob Harrison would go free and never have to pay the piper. He would become the next president of the United States and nothing could stop him.

Maya locked the cabinet, returned the key and started off to bed.

As she was drifting off to sleep, with the sound of sea already insinuating itself into a dream, she wept. Surely, he was suffering. Surely, he had suffered enough.

Chapter 2

Monday morning was overcast and cool. Maya dressed in jeans and a white sweatshirt with MONTAUK stitched on it in blue letters. She'd brushed her hair back off her face and tied it into a little pony tail. As she unpacked, she banished all the demon thoughts of the night before. It was a new day and she was soon to begin a new life. Despite feeling a touch lonely, she listened to some jazz and willed herself into a jolly mood.

She ate breakfast, called friends and made a list of needed grocery items. Around 11:30 she drove to the IGA. She caught the rhythm and fell into the dance of shopping, wheeling her cart through the excessively wide aisles, at least by New York City standards, feeling a return of innocence she hadn't felt since last December, when she'd first discovered the letter.

During that time, her need for retribution had acted like a drug, heating her blood, heightening her senses and driving her pulse to that of a hungry animal on the hunt. Now, as she mended, she was aware there would be the occasional slips of rage as she went through withdrawal, but the pain and insidious desire for revenge had already subsided. As her mother would say, "You have begun the peace process of forgetting and forgiving."

After checkout, Maya rolled the loaded cart outside to the wooden barriers. She'd have to carry the bags to her car that was parked on the other side of the lot.

Out of the corner of her eye she saw him. The same guy she'd seen on the beach the day before. He wore the same ball cap and sunglasses. He wore jeans and a blue polo shirt. He stood 10 feet away, eyeing her.

"Can I help you with those?" he asked, his hands in his pockets.

She shook her head. "I can manage."

She hooked five full plastic bags over her left arm. With her free hand, she griped two plastic gallons of spring water and started off. With effort, she opened the back door and loaded her items, feeling his eyes on her. She drove away, searching for him in her rearview mirror.

By afternoon, the sun appeared and the sky turned to a fine blue silk. Maya returned to the beach, this time wearing a red bikini. She read for a time, swam and surreptitiously searched for the man. By 5:30, it grew cool again and she was about to leave when she saw him, wandering lazily along the water's edge. She was gathering her things. She stopped, promptly re-spread the towel and sat on it cross-legged. She returned to her book and read absolutely nothing. She waited, her heart racing.

Over the top of the book, she watched him approach, dressed in the ball cap, sunglasses, yellow trunks and a white tank top. He was full of presence, shining with strength and allure. She nosed toward the pages. He stopped a few feet away.

"Excuse me…"

She condescended to peel her eyes from the book and look at him. "Yes?"

"Does Joanna Halloran live around here?"

"Yes."

"Do you know where?"

"Maybe."

He put his hands on his hips and lowered his head to his chest. She had difficulty glimpsing his face. Her cool expression hid her excitement. His smooth skin and athletic body dominated her thoughts.

"I hear she's an astrologer," he said.

Maya didn't speak.

"I want to see her. Get a reading or whatever it's called."

"She doesn't do consultations in person. Only over the phone and only after she's taken down your credit card information."

"Do you have her number?"

"No."

"It's unlisted."

"Try the internet. Joanna Halloran.com. It's posted there and anything else you want to know about her."

"Are you her daughter?"

"Maybe."

"Do you think she could talk to me soon?"

"No. She's booked up for about two months."

"I see...Well...okay then. Sorry to bother you."

He was formal, respectful. That touched her. He wasn't overt or flirtatious. That disappointed her.

"No bother," she said.

She let him go. She could have held on to him by uttering a word or two. She watched him amble away and she sank a little. Moments later, the same two men as before followed behind. Her mind went to work.

It wasn't until she was in the shower that a thought struck. She left wet footprints across the glossy wood floors as she searched for her cell phone, naked. Standing under a ceiling fan, shivering, she called her girl friend, Stacy, who was in West Hampton.

"Can you come over tonight?" Maya asked.

"No way."

"Come on, Stacy. I want to go out tonight and I don't want to be alone."

"I've got a date tonight, Maya."

"That was fast."

"A lawyer."

Maya hurried back to the bathroom, snatched a towel and wrapped herself. "Another lawyer? Every other guy you meet's a lawyer."

"That's because every other guy is a lawyer."

"All right. What about tomorrow. My mother will be home but I can make an excuse."

"I can't. He's already invited me to this party."

"All right, all right, forget it."

"Why don't you come here? There are tons of good lookin' guys, Maya. Mike has a friend. An investment banker."

"No thanks. I'll call you later."

"Maya, there is nothing going on in Montauk. Drive down tomorrow and spend the night. There are so many parties and guys around."

"I don't think so, Stacy. Maybe in a week or two."

While Maya ate fettuccini with marinara sauce at the kitchen island, perched on a high-backed wooden stool, she began piecing together fragments of thoughts and images.

She fidgeted with her yellow sun dress and sipped white wine, as the low light of evening fell. She twirled the last of the pasta, sprinkling flakes of freshly grated Parmesan cheese. She sucked it down, grateful to be alone, to make any disgusting sound that pleased her, chewing with her mouth slightly open, feeling a full range of emotions brought on by the wine, the letter and thoughts of the guy on the beach.

By the time she'd dropped her dishes into the dishwasher, she'd formed a plan for the evening. She called her mother, but got her voicemail, so she left a message, saying she was going out and she'd call in the morning.

In her bedroom, under sharp lamplight, Maya sat before her mirror, applying makeup and bright red lipstick. She plucked her eyebrows and examined her red fingernails, recently manicured in the City before she'd left. She combed her hair until it fell into a lush thick sheen and then adjusted and readjusted her light blue eye shadow.

She dressed in tight designer jeans, two inch black heels and a black silk low-cut blouse, with spaghetti straps, that showed cleavage. Her gold necklace, with its tear drop diamond, accentuated and pointed to that cleavage. Before she left the room, she dabbed on Angel by Thierry Muglar.

Driving into town she grew progressively tense. If she'd finally managed to complete her little puzzle, and if all of the pieces had fit together to form a clear picture, and if that picture was correct, then she was in big trouble. She rolled her window down for fresh air. The wind blew her hair abruptly. She'd never thought she'd be found out. It had never occurred to her. She'd been cleverly careful. She had made sure that there were no clear signs—no bold arrows—pointing back to her.

But after dinner, while she'd stared at herself in the mirror, all the dots had suddenly connected. The sky of her mind had opened and cleared. An undercurrent of anxiety swept through her like a blast of summer heat. The man on the beach, with the poor half-hearted disguise; the two men tailing him; his questions; the timing; her recognition of the face when sunlight struck it. There was no question: It was Matt Harrison!

Maya drove into the crowded parking lot of the Oyster Bay Restaurant and Bar. She parked, waited, gathered herself and then pushed out, closing the door softly. She stole glances, looking for him, heard the murmur of guests inside and the distant pound of the surf.

She walked hesitantly toward the front door, spine erect, with an expression of detached boredom. Inside she was met by a young hostess, with spiked blond hair and hoop earrings. Maya indicated toward the horseshoe bar and moved toward it. She angled to the less occupied side, pulled up a wooden stool and sat. Two TVs played baseball: one the Yankees and the Chicago White Sox. The other, the Mets and St. Louis. Mostly men sat hunched over beers, half watching. The dining room, on the other side of a wooden trestle, hummed with conversation.

Seated across from Maya, a young couple seemed to be arguing. A middle-aged man, obviously alone, wearing a green cotton Izod sweater, had zeroed in on Maya the second she'd entered. He had the healthy eye of a thoroughbred race horse and the confidence of a championship golfer. As soon as Maya sat, she knew it would only be seconds before he'd make a bee-line toward her.

The chunky female bartender, with a warm smile and a 1920's bobbed haircut, came over.

Maya spoke loud enough for the thoroughbred to hear. "Two Coronas and two glasses. My boyfriend will be here in a minute."

The bartender went to work. From the corner of her eye, Maya saw the swift disappointment spread across

Izod's face. His unhappy attention went back to the Yankee's game.

Once the beers were delivered and Maya's was poured, she retrieved her cell phone from her purse and idly scanned it for messages. There were none. She took the opportunity to explore menu options, feeling anxious and foolish.

Fifteen minutes later, Maya's beer glass was nearly drained. The beer and glass next to her loomed large and lonely. The bar was mostly full and Izod's attention had returned to her. He reminded her of a hound dog with a long lazy tongue, panting out his desire for a good dinner.

The music from a corner juke box played The Eagles. Maya had just reached into her purse for her wallet to pay for the beers, when she noticed the two men from the beach—the men who had followed Matt—enter the bar, their bodies tight, eyes suspicious and roaming. They separated, one moving toward her side of the bar, the other opposite, near Izod.

Both men's eyes averted hers. They ordered draft beer, paid and waited. The room had changed. There was a celebratory atmosphere about the place, brought on by the thickening crowd, the music, and the fact that both the Yankees and the Mets were leading in late innings.

Maya waited, uncomfortably, anxiety producing perspiration. She took a tissue from her purse and discretely blotted her forehead and upper lip. She drank the last of her warm beer, trying to find a comfortable position on the hard stool.

When Matt entered, silent and guarded, the impossibility of his presence—of who he was and of all the history and meaning he brought with him—unsettled her. Suddenly cold with anticipation, she shivered a little. He was dressed in the ball cap, the sunglasses. He wore jeans and a lime green cotton sweater, rolled at the sleeves. It only took seconds until he spotted her, just as a loud roar rose up from the crowd when Derek Jeter doubled in two runs.

Matt started toward her, with an athletic swing of his shoulders, head down, hands shoved deep into his pockets.

This would be a moment Maya would remember for the rest of her life. She knew that. Its poignancy came in cool ripples of emotion, as her immediate attraction to him abducted her reason and trepidation.

He stopped, looking questioningly at the empty stool beside her; at the untouched beer.

"It's for you," Maya said.

He took off his glasses and eyed her warily.

Maya turned left, to an empty table that abutted the knotty pine wall. "Maybe we should sit over there."

He nodded. He waited while she ordered another beer. Together they drifted from the bar and sat at the table. Izod watched with renewed interest.

For a moment, Maya kept her eyes resolutely away from Matt's. He poured his beer into the glass and watched it foam.

"It's not a great disguise," Maya finally said, still not looking at him.

"When did you know?"

"This afternoon. I should have known sooner."

"No one else has spotted me. Of course I haven't been out of my room all that much."

Maya finally looked up, sinking deeper into the reality of him and her sudden desire. "Where are you staying?"

"A little room on old Montauk highway."

"And your two friends?"

"Close by, as always."

"Did you follow me, or did one of them?"

"One of them. Then he called me."

Maya lowered her voice. "Does…your father know you're here?"

"No."

Maya slid her beer aside, opening her warm oval eyes on him. "Why are you here?"

He ran his forefinger across his lips, studying her, considering his answer. "I came to see you…and your mother."

"How did you find us? How did you know?"

"The internet… A book your mother wrote that was in my father's library."

"Which book?"

"*Astrology Looking for Love.* The copyright date. Your mother's bio. The place and time."

"It seems flimsy…Not so much to go on," Maya said.

"I put it together. It made sense to me. And then I knew."

"What are you going to tell my mother?"

He shrugged. "I don't know."

"You must have some idea."

"Some."

"What do you want to tell me?"

He grinned a little. "You're not what I thought you'd be."

Maya lifted her chin, intrigued. "Really? What did you expect?"

"Oh, I don't know. Someone younger."

"I'm twenty four."

"Yeah, I know, but…"

Maya lifted an eyebrow. "But?"

"Your name is Maya?" he asked, quickly changing the subject.

"Yes."

"I like it."

"I used to hate it. It sounds so New Age or something."

"What does it mean?"

Maya looked at him daringly. "The enchantress of illusion."

Matt's forehead lifted. "That's a heck of a name."

She widened her eyes. "And so is yours. All I'd have to do is stand up, repeat your name once, rather loudly, and the entire room would get quiet and turn to you."

"But you won't do that…"

"Probably not."

Maya grabbed the neck of her beer and took a drink. "You're sure your father didn't send you?"

"Of course I'm sure."

"What will you say to my mother when you meet her?"

"I don't know. I suppose, I just wanted to see what she was like. I guess I want to know the truth about everything."

Maya took another drink from the bottle. "The truth…" she said, flatly. "Are you sure you really want to know the truth?"

He nodded.

Maya gave him a sour look. "The truth is, your father promised my mother he'd come back to her 25 years ago and he didn't. He got her pregnant—hence yours truly—and then he abandoned her. That's the truth."

Matt folded his hands. "It was you, wasn't it, who started the mermaid story?"

He stared with a solemn expectancy.

Her gaze was clear and frank. "Yes."

He lowered his head. "I thought so."

"Aren't you the smart one?"

"Not really. It just made sense, after I found the book. My father would never buy a book like that and he'd never put it where he'd put it. I know him. He put it there because he knew no one else would ever think to look up there."

"You did."

"By accident. I was looking for a safe. I thought I might found some old letters or diaries or something about his past."

"So you suspected the mermaid rescue was true?" Maya asked.

"Yes..." he said, leaning in closer to her. His voice grew soft and strained.

"How did you find out? Did your mother tell you?"

Maya leaned back, folding her arms across her chest. "No. My mother lied to me. She told me my father died just after I was born. She said he was a fisherman. I found the letter your father..." She paused, speaking with disdain. "...Our father wrote to my mother when he left her. I found it last December, when I was searching the personal file in her desk. As she would say, I have a lot of the snoop in me that my grandfather had. Anyway, I found the letter. I've never told her about it or confronted her.

"I decided I'd go after him instead. Destroy his career. Embarrass him and his family. Embarrass all of you, because I figured you all knew the truth and you were covering up for him, while you laughed at us.

"I was going to make him a joke to the entire world. I pictured his face on the front page of the tabloids, and all over the internet. I knew all the TV news shows would discuss it: bring in experts and commentators. All of the late night comedians would tell jokes about him. The cartoonists would spoof him.

"I was going to release the letter to the media a couple of weeks before the election. I spent hours thinking about it, planning it and waiting. That would finish him and his political career. I also figured it would finish his marriage and might damage his relationship to his sons… I certainly hoped so."

Matt's wounded eyes had watched her lips as she spoke. His eyes had narrowed and widened with certain words and emphasis, and then they finally lowered in defeat, coming to rest on the scratched and tarnished brown enameled table top.

Both were quiet—an uncomfortable silence—when all around them the boisterous crowd cheered as the Mets scored another run.

A long moment later, Matt slowly pushed to his feet, avoiding her eyes. "I need some air. I feel a little sick. Goodbye."

He turned and left the room.

Maya's shoulders slackened. Her breath became labored. A slow cold disgust arose as she stared blankly at the far wall. She'd been so willing to tell him—anxious really. She'd been delighted to sling all the dirt at him. To hurt him and revel in seeing that hurt spread across his strong but gentle face.

In that interval of self-recrimination, she felt desperately alone. She saw the two Secret Service agents start for the door. What if she never saw Matt again? The thought seemed both absurd and terrifying.

Where was the feeling of elation, when after unburdening the wicked truth on an enemy, you were entitled to feel victorious and liberated? She'd waited so long for the sweet taste of revenge. She deserved to feel that she had vanquished her opponent. Instead, she felt sick and pathetic.

Maya suddenly realized she was swaying—just a little. Swaying as if she were in mourning. She felt the start of tears. She turned toward the wall so no one would see. Her chest convulsed, tears stung her eyes. She squeezed them shut, taking deep breaths. She couldn't stop them.

And then she saw her life in a series of old agonizing memories: a shining little girl of four, playing with her mother alone on the beach, watching men stride by. She remembered birthday parties, party hats, balloons and fathers who snapped photographs.

At the Wilfred Academy, in Massachusetts, where she'd gone to high school, she recalled parents wandering the shady walkways on parents' day. She saw fathers walking the private wooded paths, hand in hand with their daughters, discussing school, vacations and boys. More tears were pumped from her eyes.

She remembered vacations, prom dresses and dates, first jobs, first days at college—all fatherless, and all achingly incomplete. She recalled graduations, concerts and dinner parties; she heard her high anxious voice reciting the tired old phrase, "You don't really miss what you never had. "

It was easy to remember the endless string of Father's Days, when she'd wept and pondered the empty chairs in the house, wondering if he'd ever sat in any and read or smoked or if—by chance—he'd somehow survived the storm and would come bursting into the house one day, gather her up in his muscular arms and claim her finally and lovingly as his own.

But then she'd learned the truth—she'd read the letter—his confession of love and the proof of his selfish and cowardly abandonment. He was no longer a mystery.

He was no longer a phantom. He existed, and the very thought terrified her. He was alive, and had been alive for her entire life!

But he had never wanted her. He would never claim her and so she would remain fatherless. She would remain stunted, bitter and incomplete.

Maya had so many memories—but not one of her father. Not one single photo that she could treasure or admire. Not one single photo of them together. She had not spent one precious moment with her big and important father, who had advised presidents, kings and prime ministers; had written important legislation on education reform and women's rights, and yet not once had he ever advised or counseled her.

Not once had he ever reviewed her school work or heard her practice the piano. He did not attend her high school graduation or hear her salutatorian speech. Never had he seen her off to college or sworn to strangle the first boy who tried to have sex with her, as her friend Amanda's father had done.

No. He had never been there for her. Never. But soon he would be the most powerful man in the world and he would be there for everyone—everyone in the entire country.

She cursed him, burning with rage, burning with guilt, burning with desperation to run after Matt and beg him to forgive her.

Chapter 3

Maya dried her eyes, paid for the beers and left the restaurant, avoiding the eyes of curious faces. She found Matt alone on the quiet asphalt road that skirted the rolling dunes and beach. He stood thirty feet away, in silhouette, staring up at the stars.

She watched him for a time, allowing her emotion to dissipate. Fearing her eyes were puffy from the tears, she wiped them with a tissue and hesitated before starting toward him. A cool freshening breeze from the sea brought goose pimples to her arms.

Matt turned, gently startled, when he heard her heels scratching across the pavement, moving toward him. He waited, listening to the sea, turning an ear as if he were hearing the melody of her, an exotic tune that stirred him to respond and advance toward her.

Maya felt exposed and vulnerable, having just revealed her most intimate feelings to a perfect stranger. She also felt strangely sexual, lingering, not wanting to be alone in that large beach house.

"Would you like some company?" he asked, meekly.

She looked back toward her car, standing awkwardly. "...Okay."

They strolled away from the lights, down the dark private road, not speaking. both moving cautiously, as if each had a new injury, unsure of what movement could cause a sudden spasm of pain. They listened to the insects, examined the swirl of stars and drifted closer, but were careful not to touch.

Maya pointed to a narrow path that led to the beach and they took it. She pulled off her heels and followed Matt past rose hip bushes, up the incline and down the other side. She thrilled to feel the damp sand under her feet, as they sauntered toward the moving purple sea, flecked by moonlight. They faced the ocean, nearly touching, feeling its power.

Maya folded her arms against the chill.

"Are you cold?" Matt asked.

"A little."

He pulled off his sweater, exposing his white T-shirt, and wrapped her shoulders with it. They spotted the glow of a campfire up the beach, and, at the same time, they nodded and started toward it. When they drew near the family of four, roasting marshmallows, Maya left Matt to ask them for matches.

Then they continued on across the silver sand until they found a secluded spot. They gathered wood, dug a pit and lit a fire. Afterwards, Maya sat with her knees drawn up to her chest and her arms embracing them. Matt sat cross-legged, staring into the flames.

"I'm sorry for what I said," Maya said.

"Don't be. I asked you for it."

Maya rubbed her hands close to the fire. "I could have used some tact."

He shrugged.

Maya changed the pitch of her voice. It softened, cello-like. "Ever since December, when I first read that damned letter, I've been obsessed by it. It never occurred to me that I was just a whining, self-pitying bitch."

"Don't be so hard on yourself."

He grabbed a handful of sand, held it in his hand for a moment and then slung it away. He looked directly into her face. "But what about your mother? Didn't you think about what would happen to her if you released that letter? The press would eat her alive."

"I was angry at her too, for lying to me all these years. I had a right to know who my father was. I had the right to know the truth!"

"What made you look for the letter? How did you know there even was a letter?"

"I wasn't really looking for it. I was looking for something—anything. For years I knew that things just didn't add up. There were no pictures of my father. Nobody knew him. He had no family. There were no letters. Just my mother's feeble little story about how he went out fishing one morning and didn't come back. I mean, come on. I'm not stupid. And then, every time Bob Harrison was on TV, my mother would either get up abruptly or quickly switch the channel.

"Sometimes, she'd go to her room and I'd hear her crying. She'd always make some excuse, like she was missing my drowned father, or she was missing her father, who died when I was 6 years old. God how I loved him—because he was the only father I'd ever known. I had an uncle, too, but he died of AIDS when I was about seven. I remember him as being so kind and playful. My mother talks about him all the time."

Matt sat rigid, gazing into the dancing firelight. Maya angled a look at his handsome face, caught by the pleasure of it.

"It all seems kind of fantastic, doesn't it?" Matt said, making a definite gesture at the sky. "And then…here we are."

His words stirred her. Aroused her. She suddenly felt an odd sense of belonging—to him and to the intimate night; feeling as though even at this distance she was unnaturally too far away from him.

If she had been damaged by life, by her lack of fathering, by her inability to surmount and grow from the experience, then perhaps her confession to Matt and the release of imprisoned emotion signified that the healing process had begun.

Maya moved imperceptibly closer to him. He didn't seem to notice.

"Ah…damn. I wanted to get back at him, too. That's why I'm here. I wanted him to pay for betraying us all; my mother; Robert Jr. and me. For lying to the whole damned country over and over again. For not having the courage to stand up and say, yes, I had an affair with a woman 25 years ago, I have a daughter, but I chose not to go back to them because I was engaged. At least I could respect that. I mean, I wouldn't be happy about it or condone what he did, but at least I could respect him for his honesty."

Maya adjusted the sweater around her shoulders.

"Still cold?" Matt asked.

"No…I'm getting warm."

Matt's voice dropped. "Are you going to release the letter?"

The wind scattered her hair. She swept it from her face. "After the plane crash, I couldn't do it. When I saw you both on television and I saw the devastation on your faces…" She lifted a hand. "No, Matt. To tell you the truth, I think I'm going to burn the damned thing."

Matt allowed his bold eyes to linger on her breasts and then slowly ascend to her face, as if he'd just noticed how attractive she was.

Maya's lips gently parted. His fame was attractive—he had been on the cover of magazines and on television—but his quiet energy, lean face and full mouth were what provoked her flirtatious glance.

He grew self-conscious.

Maya enjoyed her sense of power, before she pulled her eyes from him and looked about. "Those two guys…are they always around?"

"Oh yeah. You won't see them, but they're around."

"Really?"

"I'm their job."

"Do you like that?"

"Yes and no. When you need them, you like it. Right now, I don't like it."

"I don't think I could ever get used to that. Not having privacy."

"It goes with the territory. You get used to it."

"Maybe because my mother is such a private person."

Matt took a beat, enjoying their intimacy. "What was it like growing up out here?"

Maya smiled, reflectively. "I loved it. My mother and I have almost nothing in common except that we both love the ocean and the beach. All of our happy photographs were taken on the beach. Summer, winter, icy cold, burning heat, we love it. We love the winter snows and summer squalls. The town fills up with tourists in the summer and is quiet as death in winter. There are no stop lights, no chain stores and no ugly condos or hotels on the beach. There's plenty of fresh fish, fresh air and eccentric people. So, I loved it here and hated it when my mother shipped me off to a boarding school in Massachusetts."

Matt unwrapped his legs, grabbed a stick and agitated the fire with it. "Why?

"She thought I'd get a better education. I don't think I forgave her for that until I went into therapy three years ago. We still argue about it, so I guess I'm still not over it. It's just that it made me feel like an orphan…" The word stuck in her throat. She sat stricken. "Oh… Matt, I'm sorry… I didn't…"

He lowered the stick and sat up on his knees. "Don't be. I didn't feel like an orphan. I had a family. And they were wonderful…Robert Jr. and I didn't always get along, but we cared for each other. He loved playing big brother and I didn't really mind his bullying me around sometimes. I think he felt that Dad was a lot harder on him than he was on me. He was probably right. I always felt like Mom was closer to him than me. They were a lot alike: really ambitious and driven. Mom would have made a great president and I heard Dad tell her so a few times. He relied on her a lot for policy issues and advice."

Maya straightened her legs and tied the arms of the sweater around her neck. "Were they close?"

"That's a tough one. They were great actors. When it came to politics and ambition, yes, they were a formidable team. They were amazing to watch too; their collective focused energy was astounding. They fed off each other. They would electrify any room they entered. They would dazzle a crowd. It always amazed me."

Matt picked up the stick again and poked thoughtfully at the fire. "Privately, they often seemed like strangers. Sometimes at dinner, after the political talk, they wouldn't say a word to each other. They slept in separate bedrooms and I seldom—if ever—saw them touch or laugh…It was almost as if they were great political partners, but not very good friends, and certainly not lovers."

His sad words lingered in the air for a time, and then slowly faded into the rise and fall of the tide. The moon had risen higher in the sky and turned white. A few stringy clouds swam across it.

Maya finally spoke. "Do you think that your father…and my mother really loved each other?"

Matt ran his hand along the side of his face, as he considered her question. "I don't know… I mean, how can we know?"

He turned from her, presenting his face to the open bowl of the sky. "Look at all those stars. So old. We're seeing the light from them that took millions of years to get to Earth." He looked at her again. "So do you believe in Astrology? Do you believe that the planets direct our lives and make us dance like puppets on a string?"

Maya sighed a little. "The whole thing seems irrelevant to me."

"Irrelevant?"

"Yes," Maya said, straightening her spine. "I mean, we're here on this planet. We need to just face what we are, for better or for worse. We face our problems and we do the best we can. What's it matter whether we have the Sun in Capricorn or in Pisces? That's who we are and we're probably not going to change that much. We all just do the best we can."

"You sound forgiving of human nature. It seems contradictory to what you said earlier."

"No, no. Not at all. Let's take my mother and...." She swallowed hard as if having difficulty speaking the words, "…our father. Let's say 25 years ago they fell in love or fell in lust or, whatever, and after a night of Ooo-la-la, they made me. Now that was stupid."

Caught between keen interest and amusement, Matt directed his full attention toward her. "Why stupid?"

"That's a no-brainer. He just shouldn't have done it. He was engaged to marry another woman. And he knew he wasn't going to stay with my mother. I mean, come on, he was from a prominent New England political family and she was a nobody weird astrologer with a limp."

"A limp?" Matt asked, surprised.

"Yes, she's limped since birth. She had another operation about 5 years ago and it's less obvious now, but she still limps some."

"...I didn't know."

"But she's an attractive woman and she was a knockout when she was younger... At least I think so."

Matt shut his eyes for a moment, digesting her words. "Maybe he did care about her. I mean, he kept her book all these years."

Maya shook away the thought. "The one thing I'm sure of is that my mother knew what was going on astrologically, because she always knows what's going on, and she went ahead with the relationship anyway. So what good is astrology?"

"If they hadn't met, you wouldn't be here."

"That's beside the point."

"Maybe that is precisely the point."

"Meaning?" Maya asked.

"Meaning, somebody is pulling the strings and you were meant to be and nothing in heaven or earth could have stopped it."

"Then there's no free will?" Maya asked.

"There's the perception of free will. But, in the final analysis, it's all just smoke and mirrors. An illusion."

She shook her head vigorously. "I can't believe that. I refuse to believe that I don't have any free will. Let's take us, for instance. We've just met. We have an incredible history that ties us together and there's nothing we can do about that. But we can choose where we want to go from here."

"And where is that? Where do we want to go from here?" Matt asked, his attention acute.

The half-play half-serious nature of the conversation made her emotionally confused. The wind picked up and Maya moved closer to the fire. Matt lay on his side with his hand propping up his head.

"I shouldn't have said that," Maya said, avoiding his persistent gaze.

"Why?"

"Because everything is all screwed up and I don't know what to think about anything. And we've just met."

Matt's gaze grew bold, as he studied her pursed lips and shimmering hair. "Does that mean I shouldn't ask you out?"

Maya shot him a startled glance and then stared into the fire. She leaned toward it, feeling the lure of him. "No…it doesn't mean that."

"Can I see you tomorrow?"

With her forefinger, Maya drew a circle in the sand. She waited a long time to answer. She whispered. "Yes…"

Desire moved in around them, insulating them from the outer world. They dwelled in it for awhile, silent, staring at the sea and the moon—and into the jagged flames.

Chapter 4

They left the beach and returned to the quiet road, strolling leisurely, silent and meditative. Maya felt a new pulsing life force, sanctified and warm. She grew in stature as she drew closer to Matt.

He was fixed on a thought, seeking grace notes to explain his sudden attraction to her. He pondered realities and consequences, occasionally picking up scents of her perfume. He reveled in the abundance of rising sensation, allowing his wayward thoughts to grapple with what it would be like to make love to her.

"What do you do?" Matt asked.

"Speech-language pathologist. I just graduated. I'm starting my first job in the fall."

"Working with kids?"

"Yes, at a preschool. I'll be working with autistic kids, on socialization and relating."

"Sounds admirable."

She shrugged her left shoulder. "And you're going to be a history teacher and write books," Maya stated. "I've read two articles about you and I saw you on the Paula Powers show."

Matt stuffed his hands into his pants and shook his head. "It all seems so…I don't know, fuzzy and far away right now: the future, the past."

"…And the present?"

Matt looked at her. She kept herself in profile to his glance.

"I like the present."

They passed the restaurant and kept walking, feeling the intensity of their attraction ripen all around them in the soft wind, the quivering shadows and the moonlight on the road before them. The scent of honeysuckle; the lazy drone of an airplane motor overhead; the sound of their footsteps scratching across the pavement; all gradually lulled them into silence; into more serious currents of thought.

"Mom will be back in a day and a half," Maya said, quietly.

Matt nodded. "And in three weeks I have to go to New York for the convention."

To Maya, his words meant that their relationship had begun. She controlled a breathy exhilaration.

Moments later, they started back to Maya's car. Matt opened the door for her. She stood looking at him, in an expression of wonder. He did not offer a kiss.

"Can you come for breakfast?" she asked.

"Yes… and after breakfast, how about we go sailing?" Matt asked.

"Is it safe…I mean, what if you're recognized renting the boat or something?"

"I'll have Don, the Secret Service guy, arrange it. He won't want to, but he will."

She waited, absorbing him. "See you at eight, then?"

Matt nodded and closed the door.

As she drove back to the house, with a nervous desire, Maya checked her phone messages. She had three: two from girlfriends and one from her mother.

"Where are you?" her mother asked. "Why didn't you leave your phone on? Well, anyway, if you get this before eleven, call me."

It was after twelve.

Later that night, Maya sat on the back deck until almost two, drinking a glass of Sauvignon Blanc. She'd fought the urge to call her girlfriends to tell them who she'd just met. Of course she couldn't tell them. She couldn't tell anyone. It irked her. Confused her. There were so many perilous emotions inside that needed categorizing, analysis and scrutiny that she didn't know where to begin. She felt rebellious, frightened, sexy, and ecstatic. Her vision of the world had shifted. In one single night, everything had changed. Inside the house of her soul, windows had been flung open, light and wind had rushed in, rooms had been found and would have to be cleaned out, explored and expanded. The world would have to be redefined in terms of Matt and the future.

Matt Harrison had entered her, just as surely as if they had made love back on the beach. She felt him even now. The youthful power of him gently rocked her. She shifted several times in the cushioned brown wicker chair, her eyes glazed with pleasure.

She thought of his strong tanned neck, his clear eyes and firm hands. She drank more wine and fantasized, grinning mischievously, as her thoughts grew playfully prurient and inventive.

Maya fell asleep in the chair, awaking sometime after three, cold and achy. She staggered off to bed and, fully clothed, collapsed into sleep.

When the doorbell rang at 8 a.m., Maya had just sliced strawberries and bananas and was reaching for the eggs in the frig. She hurried through the house, pausing to check her makeup and hair in the hall mirror, and winced at her still-puffy eyes.

She took an uneasy breath before opening the door. Matt stood tall and anxious, with a touch of morning shyness about him, as if they had done something taboo the night before.

"Good morning," he said, with a broad smile. "I smell bacon."

Maya nearly sighed with desire. Every cell in her body, asleep only moments before and complaining of a slight hangover, awoke blissfully. "Good morning…"

He was hatless, with sunglasses perched on his head. His short, blond hair lightly moussed. He wore khakis, deck shoes and a burgundy T-shirt, with a little blue fish on the chest. She wore white cotton pants and a blue and white striped cotton T-shirt. Her hair was tied in the back with a scrunchy.

Matt explored the house while Maya scooped and patted the bacon dry, and whipped, poured and scrambled the eggs. Matt helped carry the plates to the deck and poured coffee and orange juice.

They sat on the deck under a muted sky and a heavy rolling fog. The humid air whistled. They talked about the house, and the cliffs and the weather, and for a time, the fog obliterated all views from the house.

"You sleep good?" Matt asked.

"Yeah. Good," she lied. "You?"

"Yeah, went right to sleep," he lied. He'd pace his little room, watched his father's sound bites on the news and finally fell asleep on the over-soft couch at 4 in the morning. He awoke with a stiff neck and a backache.

Matt glanced around, taking drinks of his orange juice. "It's so private up here. What a great place."

"Yeah. Mom's been offered millions for it."

"I'll bet."

"Compared to some of the homes out here, it's very modest."

Matt peered through the stringy fog and saw a little structure, ghostlike, appearing and vanishing. "What is that? A little house?"

"It's a cottage, or at least it used to be. Mom's let it go and it's falling apart. I used to play in it when I was a little girl, until it became too unsafe."

"Why didn't she fix it up?"

"I don't know. I used to tell her she could rent it out for the summer and make a fortune, but she refused. She wouldn't even discuss it. Still won't. She's just slowly letting it rot."

They sat in an eager silence for a time, finishing the fruit and the eggs and the bacon.

"Do you still want to go sailing?" Matt asked.

Maya leaned her head, questioningly. "I was thinking…The weather report said we could get thunderstorms this afternoon. And mom will be back tomorrow. Maybe we should just stay here. Go to the beach, swim. I could make us a picnic. We wouldn't have to worry about crowds or…you know."

Matt chewed thoughtfully. Maya slipped on her sunglasses and angled her chair so that she faced the sea. "What are we going to do about all this, Matthew?"

He knew what she was referring to. "Go out with me tomorrow."

"And after that? What about that great big world out there? What about you and me having the same father?"

"He's not my birth father, Maya. I was adopted."

Maya closed her eyes for a moment, straining with her thoughts. "I don't know, Matt. I mean, how long can we keep all this—us—away from them?"

He gave her a brief smile. "Us?"

Maya took off her glasses and looked at him pointedly. "Yes…us."

He frowned a little. "I don't know, Maya. Let's just take it one day at a time."

Maya distanced herself from his words. She didn't like the sound of them. They weren't as appealing as his words the night before, when he was much more expansive.

Matt brightened. "Do you surf?"

"Yeah. But not in a while."

"Do you have a board?"

"In the basement. I haven't used it in four or five years."

After a quick kitchen clean-up, they rummaged through the basement, locating the 6-foot, pale-yellow board propped against the back wall near stacks of boxes. Gripping either side, Matt lifted, wiggling it free. They climbed the stairs to the backyard, excited and eager. Matt washed the board down while Maya packed towels, sunscreen, sunglasses and her cell phone. She stepped into her canary yellow bikini and purposely ignored the sunscreen. She'd ask Matt to do the honors. She smiled at the little genius of the scheme. And then she'd reciprocate.

When Maya appeared on the deck, a shining beauty, Matt turned, his eyes gleaming. She first saw desire, then vulnerability, finally, uncertainty.

"I'm ready," she said, and she clearly intended a double meaning. She put on her sunglasses.

They launched toward the beach just as the fog began to flee. The dunes changed color under the sun; the long dune grass rippled in lavish waves; the sea and sky expanded into a shimmering glory.

Matt walked proudly, with the fiberglass board tucked under his arm. Maya maneuvered close to him, walking briskly, lifted from the torso, hand planted on the crown of her wide brimmed hat. She was excruciatingly happy, and, for the first time in her life, she felt completed.

They descended the stairs laughing.

"We may have to develop some accents," Matt said.

"Accents?"

"Yeah, to confuse people as to who we are."

"I have a good French accent," Maya said and then she demonstrated. "Oh, Mon Cheri," Maya said, batting her eyes adoringly at him. "You are making me zo deeZee, Monsieur." She stopped, looking him over. "Perhaps a leetal beret on zee' ed would add a touch of zee continental. No?"

"Wee, Mademoiselle. Je crois que oui."

Matt pointed to the sea. "Ach, himmel! Vee are going to schvim like zee little fishes out dair in dat beeig vahsir!"

Maya said. "Ya…and I'm glad dat all dat beeig smoky schtuff foggy has gone away."

They laughed and hurried off to the beach. Maya spread the colorful towels, while Matt judged water and wind. "It's not so rough."

"Good. I haven't done this in a long time. I used to be pretty good."

Matt shed his T-shirt and dropped his pants, displaying orange and yellow swim trunks. "Do you ever fish out here?"

"Not much anymore. When I was a girl, my grandfather took me a few times. We caught an 18 pound striped bass once."

"That's big!" Matt exclaimed.

"It's my big fish story."

Maya held the sunscreen aloft. "Can you do me?" she asked, with the hint of a grin.

Matt strolled over. He explored her vague, dreamy eyes and tanned shoulders. "Sure, if you'll do me."

She gave him a flirtatious wink. "Of course."

He took the lotion and squeezed a worm of it into his hand. Maya turned, presenting her back, standing erect, anticipating his touch with half-hooded eyes. At the first caress of his hand on her cool right shoulder, she trembled a little, feeling growing inner fires.

His gentle strength weakened the unpleasant pesky questions that had been bantering about in her head for hours: Will this relationship last? What will happen when her mother returns? Is he using her in some way? Has he been lying to her? Did his father really send him to keep her occupied, to keep her quiet until after the election?

"Maya…"

"Yes…"

"We're going to have to be careful."

She kept her eyes closed. "Careful?"

"Yes. You can't tell anyone about us."

"I know. I haven't. I won't."

"If any of this gets out…"

"I know, Matt. I won't tell anyone."

"It's just that…My father would lose the election."

When he stopped for a moment, Maya opened her eyes. She didn't face him. "I know, Matt." She waited a moment. "My mother would freak out, to say the least. I won't say anything."

She heard him squeeze more sunscreen into his hand. He applied it from the nape of her neck, slowly down her spine, pausing to tenderly massage her thin shoulders. He became lost in the motion, standing formally, as if denying his sudden arousal. Maya was lost in sensation and she moved back against him, feeling his hardness.

"You're beautiful, Maya."

"And you have great hands. …ummm, that feels so good."

She tilted her head back, in relaxation, as his hands went deeper into the tightness in her neck.

"Too hard…?" he asked.

"No…not at all."

He felt the response of her skin to his touch. He began to swell with desire. "We'll have to keep everything a secret," Matt said.

Maya's voice dropped an octave. The word "secret" aroused her even more. "We will."

He paused. "It's just that…I didn't plan this to happen...never even gave it a thought."

She turned abruptly, searching his eyes. He dropped his hands to his sides.

"…Everything's crazy," he continued. "Everything's changed so fast. I don't know what the hell is happening. I don't know who I am anymore. I keep thinking about my mother—I mean my birth mother. I've been having all of these screwy dreams about her and about my brother."

Maya reached for his hand, softening her voice. "It will take time, Matt. A lot of time to get over something like that. I can't even imagine what you must be going through."

"I really loved her, Maya, I mean my adopted mother. She was a great mother. I was so lucky to have her…and my father."

"She must have adored you."

Matt withdrew his hand. "Maya, I didn't come here for this. For us, I mean. I didn't plan this."

"How do you plan something like this, Matthew? You don't. We both know that."

Maya took his hand again and squeezed it. "I get such an irresistible urge to call you Matthew some times. Is that okay?"

"…Say it all you want."

"Matthew, Matthew, Matthew…you are one handsome guy."

He lowered his hungry eyes on her. "And you…" he stopped, feeling heat rise to his face.

With two fingers, Maya explored his finely shaped jaw and full mouth. "Yes…?"

"Ever since I first saw you…"

"Yes…?" Maya said, bringing her breasts close to his chest.

Maya stared soberly. His eyes held passion.

A carnival of emotions erupted within them. Maya stood for a moment in a frozen expectation, feeling wonderfully sexy and reckless, wanting Matt with every inspired and bawdy thought. She wanted him with every profane and sacred breath. She wanted to ease every hurt she'd ever felt, giving him her ripe sexy body to mold and to affirm that they would be the best of lovers.

They were alone on the beach, tense and charged, resplendent in new sunshine. Their eyes became warm and fierce, as morning waves rushed the beach. Their attraction seized, stirred and awaked. Matt reached for her, gripping her shoulders, drawing her in. Her eyes willed him on, and as their lips brushed, opened and explored, she pressed into him, electrified.

Through currents of heat and cold they circled in the sand, bodies tightly wedded, their kisses breathless, bodies aching for touch and fulfillment.

Maya dropped her sunglasses and flung away her hat. It sailed and bounced playfully across the sand. A yellow butterfly skimmed the breeze in a chaotic flight across the dunes, fleeing the scene.

Matt tugged her bikini top from her shoulders, exposing her fine milky white breasts and large brown nipples. In a trance, he crushed them against his chest as her eager fingers found the ridges and hard muscles of his back.

They were exposed to the world. Their sharp passion made them oblivious and deliciously frantic. They whispered private words, coaxing action, stripping off their suits and lowering themselves onto the warm beach towel. Their youth and strength drove them impatiently to action.

Matt quickly scanned the empty beach, in an excited madness, as Maya reached for him, drawing him down on top of her. Viewing his magnificent nakedness, she opened her legs wide and lifted her hips, hot with expectation. He entered her with a long, slow quiver. She called his name, feeling the first hot rain of sensation. Matt began unhurriedly. She rose to meet him in a series of easy arching rhythms and little cries of pleasure. More words were whispered, but the sea swallowed them.

In a mounting desperation, their lovemaking gathered force and power. Maya opened to take all of his persistence, feeling his taut body falter in delight, then drive hard and fast, his muscles bulging, his face tight.

She'd been waiting for this since their first meeting. From their first conversation, she'd been waiting for the solid power of him, riding her through the currents of the brilliant sun-soaked day.

This was the first time—the first time in her life she felt a loosening of resistance. Could she trust? Could she trust her own ferocious appetite for him as she inched closer to frightening bliss? She'd have to let go completely—give up her anger and pain; release the old hurts and fears; the easy nagging cynicism about love and all its silly sweet words.

A startling ecstasy boiled up her spine, searing her face. Her hands tightened into fists as she fought it. It was an unknown and thrilling rapture that swept through her like a heat storm. Matt found new rhythms. Maya pushed him on with her hips, her breathing rapid and her eyes wild, as the first climax approached. It began in her feet, crawled up her legs and thighs, and spread into her breasts and neck like an electric current. As Matt drove on, she shattered into fitful cries and helpless sobs of joy.

She shivered, falling limp and helpless, startled by the enduring, forceful waves of passion. As she struggled to recover, Matt plunged deeper and then stopped, sensing she was overwhelmed. He rested. She felt his breath hot and labored. She stroked his damp hair and wide shoulders and called to him, asking for more.

He kissed her face and eyes worshipfully. He licked her steamy lips and neck, caressed her breasts and squeezed her hard nipples.

She felt his bold pulsing size, throbbing inside. Shivering with rapture, she squeezed his firmness, gently, in little twisting hip maneuvers—gripping and releasing him possessively, feeling her power as he moaned.

He moved her again, possessed her again, with force and rhythm. She called to him, helpless, falling and rising.

He crescendoed, bringing the rise of her next climax. It engulfed her in sensational spasms.

Emotion and passion collided. Matt galloped on as if possessed, driving her buttocks into the sand. She met his thrusts full and fast. He rocked her, wildly, as his potent, youthful strength focused on stupendous fulfillment. He felt her full resistance finally give way. It galvanized him. She cried out, low and hard.

Seconds later, he felt the approaching climax—swelling him—an unbearable expectation. He ramped on, wanting to devour her, own her, unite with her and make a new world. He wanted a child. Their child. Their own world. He wanted his own family, and he wanted it all with Maya.

When he was struck, and all of his life force poured into Maya, he called her name, loudly, profoundly, lovingly. Her legs locked around his back, and tightened, forcing one last final thrust. They convulsed, stunned by climax.

Gradually, they reawakened to a bright blue sky, lazy clouds, and a gentle raspy surf. They lay blessed and golden in the sunlight.

Gulls drifted quietly over them, but they didn't notice.

But someone did. She had been watching their love making from the cliff atop the stairs, through a pair of binoculars.

Joanna Halloran had arrived home early to be with her daughter.

Chapter 5

Matt and Maya were surprised and contented. They lay close, touching, valuing the timeless minutes from the fresh perspective of gifted lovers. They were sated, their nakedness covered by towels. The sand on their backs was itchy and cool. A quarter of a mile away, people had gathered. They pitched candy-colored umbrellas and splashed in the fortunate day and calm sea. A couple approached from 80 yards away, walking erratically, exploring shells and debris that had washed ashore.

Matt's cell phone rang, shattering the peace. He winced, and with effort, using the towel for cover, he grabbed his pants, snaked a hand into the pocket and withdrew the phone. He slung it open and checked the LCD display.

"Damn! It's my father."

He sat cross-legged, hesitating before answering.

Maya pushed up on her elbows, keenly interested.

"Hey, Dad…" he said in forced enthusiasm. "…A Yeah… Doing good. You? Yeah, I know…It's going to take time…"

Matt nodded, looking back at Maya, winking. "They're giving you a lot of air time… Good, good.

Well, you know Maine. It's always cooler than you think… Have to wear a sweatshirt or sweater at night."

Maya's face suddenly darkened. She gathered up her suit, slipped on the bottoms, then wiggled into the top. She stood. Matt noticed her change of expression and shrugged her a question. She ignored him and started toward the sea. As the waves washed ashore, she tested the temperature with her right foot. It was warm for Montauk: maybe 68 or 70 degrees. Locking her hands behind her back, she strolled, squinting into the sky, kicking along the edge of the water, feeling the sun baking her face and shoulders. She watched sandpipers skitter across wet sand.

When Matt finally joined her, asking if she was alright, she didn't face him or speak. He said something else but the crashing waves muffled it.

He raised his voice. "I'm sorry, Maya. I had to talk to him. If I don't answer he'll get nervous and call certain people to find out where I am."

Her shoulders rose a little to indicate it was alright. They strolled in a long subdued silence.

"What's he like?" she asked, almost at a whisper.

They passed below the craggy 70 foot cliffs, weathered by old storms and punishing winds.

"He's honest, Maya. At least as honest as any politician can be. He plays the game—compromises here and there and sometimes relaxes his true convictions to make a deal or gain some votes."

"No, I mean, as a father. As a person, without all the political bullshit?"

Matt stopped, reaching for her hand. He turned her to face him, staring quietly, lovingly. "I'm sorry… Of course you want to know what he's like. He's your father, too." And then with greater emphasis, narrowing his eyes. "He is your father."

Maya's face darkened. "I want to hate him. I've tried to hate him for months. Dammit, I do hate him, the selfish, weak, son of a bitch!"

"You have a right to hate him! Every right in the world, but he's a good man, Maya. He's always been there for me. He's compassionate and sensitive; strong-willed and stubborn as hell, yes, but I have to believe that he tries hard to be a good man."

Maya's eyes filled with tears. She spun away from him, snatching her hand free of his. She started back toward their beach spot. He let her go, watching helplessly.

He returned to her fifteen minutes later. She lay on her stomach on the bright blue and green beach towel, her regal head turned aside, eyes closed. He sat beside her, drawing his knees up to his chest and embracing them. He watched her.

Minutes later, he fell asleep beside her, wrapping a gentle arm around her waist.

They awoke a half hour later, refreshed, and Maya's dark mood had past. They charged the beach, surfboard poised under Matt's arm, and hit the water, splashing, kicking and shouting.

Matt held the board at arm's length, with one hand on each rail. He jumped over the rushing waves as he waded further out. Beside him, Maya twisted through the churning foam, splashing water on her face and arms.

In deeper water, Matt leaped, belly first, onto the surface of the board and paddled with both arms, heading for the swells where the waves were forming, before breaking toward shore. Maya dived forward, swimming energetically after him.

In the nirvana of pure morning light and infinite sea, they reached the ideal depth, bobbing in cool undulating water. Matt gingerly passed the board to a nervous Maya. She angled the board at her side, with her nose facing the beach, just as her first boyfriend, a surfer, had taught her to do when she was 16. She studied the waves, measuring wave, height and distances, feeling her heart pumping wildly.

"Here comes a good one, Maya!" Matt yelled. "Go for it!"

Maya pushed the board toward the brown line of beach, seeing the cliffs and the distant top floor of her house and the glare of the sun off the windows. She felt the first thrilling rise of an approaching wave. With clumsy effort, she heaved herself up onto the board, and lay flat, not too close to the nose so she wouldn't plunge straight underwater. She paddled vigorously, with both arms, her breathing coming fast, as the wave swelled and lifted her. She took a final courageous breath, judged her balance, pushed up to her knees, felt the immense power of the sea heaving her forward, and she leaped, triumphantly, to her feet.

With a furious concentration, she danced across the board seeking balance, her body taut, her arms outstretched. The wind burst across her face, scattering her hair. The sea lurched and sparkled as she gathered speed.

With bent knees and a perfection of balance and form, the board dipped, lurched, and glided across the wave's crest, the water hissing, wind whistling across Maya's ears. She felt drunk and euphoric, shooting off toward the beach.

Matt clapped, screamed and cheered her on, bouncing and sinking. He could not understand how so much happiness could fill him up so completely, after the deepest lesions of sadness had nearly destroyed him. It was at that moment that he realized he wanted to marry Maya.

After an hour of surfing, they collapsed on the beach, winded and spent. They took a quick nap, then awoke hungry. Maya left for the house, to get food and bring it back to the beach. Matt stayed behind, working on an idea he wanted to discuss with Maya when she returned.

Matt called Betty, the housekeeper in Maine. He told her to prepare the house. He and a "friend" were coming to stay for a while. Next he called Don and relayed the information.

Don hesitated, and then said, in a grave, deep voice. "No problem."

As soon as Maya entered the house, she knew something was wrong. A wisp of her mother's perfume lingered in the kitchen. The binoculars lay on the kitchen table. Maya froze, calculating what she would say and do. She swallowed away nerves.

"Mother…" Her voice fell flat, dying in the silence. She inched her way through the kitchen, peeking into the living room. "Mother…"

She heard footsteps above on bare floors.

"Dammit!" Maya said, in a loud whisper.

Maya straightened, yanked at the bikini top, adjusted the straps so that her breasts weren't so exposed, and then started up the stairs. She treaded quietly across the wooden floors, past the walls that held a local artist's seascapes, toward her mother's bright room, where the door was wide open. Maya paused at the threshold. Under a skylight that flooded Joanna with morning sun, Maya stared at her mother's back. She wore jeans, a blue T-shirt and blue sneakers. Joanna stood at the side of the bed, lifting folded clothes from her suitcase and placing them in neat little stacks beside her. She was the neatest packer Maya had ever known. A psycho for a neat suitcase, where there was absolutely no excuse for anything to shift or adjust during travel.

"Hello, Mother…" Maya said, softly.

Joanna didn't flinch or turn to face her daughter. "Hello…" Her voice rose barely above a whisper.

Maya rolled her eyes, grasping for patience. "How long have you been here?"

"A while."

Maya went to her, standing a foot from her mother's back. "Do I get a hug?"

Joanna stopped. Maya saw her mother's shoulders rise as she took a long suffering breath and exhaled. She trembled a little before turning. Their eyes met: Joanna's held first despair, then disappointment, and finally a slow creeping pleasure. Maya's were filled with apprehension and concern as she took in her mother's smooth youthful face and short spiked hair. Though her mother had gained a little weight around the hips, she still possessed the attractive body of a woman in her early 40's.

They embraced. Within the physical warmth and the sudden hush of the room, there arose an old tenderness, an old camaraderie; two battle-scared veterans, who had survived difficult days and lonely nights, were reunited. They held the embrace longer than normal, because they both realized that the exchange to come would be distressing and hurtful. It was the truce before certain battle. Joanna kissed her daughter's wet hair and as they disengaged, she kissed her cool cheek.

They faced off. Their expressions immediately lost their softness. Joanna's gaze was harsh. Maya crossed her arms stiffly across her chest, staring at the floor.

"Who is he?" Joanna said.

"You don't waste any time do you, Mother? You get home and you grab your damn binoculars and you're out there scanning the beach for any scandal you can find."

"I was looking for you. I came home a day early to be with you! I called you three times and you never called me back. I was worried sick. Scared to death! So I rush home and you're not here. I'm looking everywhere, ready to call the police, and then I grab my binoculars to look down on the beach and I see some guy humping you! For God's sake, Maya! Right there on the beach where anybody could walk by or where old man Scott could look down from his upper deck and see you!"

"He can't see that far or make it up to the upper deck anymore."

"You are bold lovers, with nothing to hide," Joanna said, building in agitation. "I'll give you that!"

Maya nearly laughed at the irony.

"Who is he, Maya?"

Maya spoke in a defensive, nervous voice. "A guy I met."

"Oh, really. And I suppose you've known him longer than a day or two."

Maya's eyelids fluttered. "Of course…" she stuttered. "I…I've known him for a long time."

"What's his name?"

Maya faltered, as an urgent thought eclipsed the cross-examination. If she delayed much longer, Matt would surely come looking for her.

"Maya, what is his name? Where did you meet him? I'm assuming you didn't just meet him yesterday, fall head over heels in something called love and decide to have sex with him right out on the beach where the whole world could see."

Maya pulled out her maturity speech. "Mother, I'm 24 years old! I am old enough to make decisions about my own life, just like you did when you were my age. I didn't know you were coming or Ma…" she quickly corrected herself, "…he wouldn't have been here. I did listen to your calls and I did call you back and leave a message. You are overacting the way you always over-react, because you don't trust me and you have never trusted me!"

"Don't try and turn this thing around so that it's suddenly all my fault, Maya!"

"It's nobody's fault, Mother! I made love to a man on the beach, okay!"

Joanna withdrew her eyes from her daughter, finding the subject distasteful. "Love…" she said, indignantly.

"I had sex! Okay?! So shoot me. I care about this man. He likes me. It just happened. It happened so fast that I didn't even think about who was watching or who might come by."

Joanna spun around and snatched a mound of panties from her suitcase. She held them for an irritable moment and then tossed them carelessly on to the bed. "Okay fine. I hope you protect yourself, Maya. That's all I've got to say about it. If you're going to do that kind of thing whenever and wherever it strikes you, with whomever, I just hope you have the sense to protect yourself."

Maya shook her head, hopelessly.

She pivoted and started out of the room. She stopped and turned. "I like your hair," she said, peevishly.

Maya left the room, scrambled down the stairs and hurried off toward the beach.

Matt was anxiously waiting, pacing along the tide. When he saw her descend the stairs, he jogged toward her. They met and kissed.

Maya caught her breath. "My mother's here."

Matt stiffened in alarm. "What?!"

"She came home early and she saw us."

"Saw us! You mean…"

Maya nodded.

"Does she know…I mean about…?"

Maya interrupted. "No, but you've got to get out of here." She grabbed his shoulders and whirled him toward the sea. "She may be looking at us right now through her damn binoculars."

Matt threw his hands to his hips, shutting his eyes to think. "Okay, look…" He gave her a sideways glance. "I want you to come to Maine."

"Maine?"

"Yes. We have a cabin up there. My father thinks I'm there. It'll be perfect. It's secluded."

"What about your father?"

"He's so busy doing 5 or 7 states a day he won't be anywhere around. We'll have two weeks before I have to join him for the convention."

Maya eyes moved restlessly. "…Matt, I have to spend some time with my mother."

"Okay, fine. Stay here a few days and then come up."

"A few days. I don't want to be away from you a few hours."

She kissed him.

"Then meet me up there tonight or tomorrow. You'll love it. It's on the coast."

Maya kissed his neck from left to right. "Did I tell you that I fell in love with you when I saw you on the *Paula Powers* show…"

Matt shrank a little with surprise.

"I did, Matt. I thought you were the sexiest thing I'd ever seen."

"Thing?" Matt asked, touched and amused.

She lowered her voice to a sexy little growl. "You know what I mean, baby."

He kissed her deeply.

"Come to Maine, Maya, as fast as you can," he said.

They exchanged phone numbers and e-mail addresses and fell into an intoxicating kiss that left them both warm and aroused.

Her heart sank when she saw him grab his clothes and jog off across the sand toward the public beach.

Chapter 6

Joanna and Maya avoided each other until dinner. Maya had secretly re-packed her suitcase, with a week's worth of clothes, obsessing over every article, viewing it through Matt's eyes, and tossing it aside if it didn't prove sexy or provocative.

She'd called friends and told them, in a high excitable voice, about "this incredible sexy guy I met, who is, like, so famous you wouldn't believe it!" She ached to blurt out the truth, and under her friends' intense and unrelenting questioning, it took all her restraint not to do so. But she knew her entire future depended on keeping her big mouth shut. So she did.

Under strong protest, Maya insisted on taking her mother out to dinner that night. It was both an act of generosity and self-protection. Maya knew that her mother would be less obsessive and scolding about what she'd witnessed on the beach, and less inclined to "come unglued" in public when she heard the news that Maya was going to Maine.

In Maya's car, in route to the Surfside Restaurant, Credence Clearwater Revival's *Bad Moon Rising* was pounding out through the speakers. Maya's driving was erratic, and Joanna called her on it.

"You're not even watching the road, Maya! And turn the music down! Please!"

"Relax, Mother, I saw the car pull out and I missed it. And anyway, I've driven this road so many times that I don't need to look at it."

Joanna barked an incredulous laugh. "God help us."

Maya switched off the music. She was riding the crest of high energy and a feverish expectation about her trip to Maine, and she drove as if she were fleeing town.

"Slow down, Maya!" Joanna said. "You're going to kill us!"

"I'm driving the speed limit."

"You are not! I'm driving next time."

"Do you know how controlling that sounds?"

"Controlling to stay alive. I hope you don't tell people that I taught you to drive."

"Don't worry. I always say it was my surfer boyfriend, Tucker."

"Oh, God, Tucker. What an airhead he was."

"Hellova driver though," Maya said, laughing.

Joanna rolled her eyes.

The Surfside Inn and Restaurant was a Country Inn, housed in a broad, quaint, two-story white house. On the second floor, rooms were rented out by the week. The main room downstairs was used for the restaurant and bar. Its generous porch ran the length of the place and was wide enough to accommodate tables for dining. With an easy turn of the head, you had a commanding view of the sea and sky, and though you faced east at sunset, the sky would often blaze crimson before melting into pastel wisps of clouds and long purple shadows. Christmas lights were strung in the eves and through the hedges. Hanging plants swung leisurely, scenting the sea breezes.

A tall, gangly host, seated Maya and Joanna on the porch, and presented them with menus. Through the open windows, they heard the rattle of dishes and the murmur of conversation, while a guitarist strummed and wailed Neil Young tunes in a high lilting tenor. Maya sipped her water, observing a black cat prowl the gravel parking lot, entranced by movement in a rosehip bush near the road. Joanna took out a pair of reading glasses and slipped them on.

"I'm getting the lobster," Maya said, without glancing at the menu.

"You always make your mind up so fast," Joanna said, assiduously perusing the menu.

"Just like my father."

Joanna peeked over the menu, with gentle surprise. "Your father?"

"Yes. You once said that I make up my mind fast, just like my father did."

With uncertainty, Joanna's eyes fell back onto the menu. "Oh…yes…well, that's true."

"You also said that I have his rebellious streak."

"I never said that," Joanna said, defensively.

"You did, several times."

"Well I don't remember ever saying that."

"Did I get it from you, then?"

"I never thought of myself as being particularly rebellious."

"From granddaddy, then."

"Yes," Joanna said, with a firm nod, but not looking up from the menu. "He was definitely rebellious."

Maya placed her elbows on the table, folded her hands and rested her chin on them. She stared at her mother intently. She felt feisty and impetuous. "Did you meet any men in Chicago?"

"A few."

"Any come on to you?"

"A couple. One very old. One very young."

Maya brightened. "How old was the young one?"

"I'd say early 30's."

"Really?"

"What did he say to you?"

"It was silly."

"I love silly."

"I know you do."

"So?"

"So, I think I'll have the striped bass."

"Mother!? Details. Give me details."

Joanna closed her menu and took off her glasses. She feigned indifference. "Well now, let's see. He's from L.A. He's a screenwriter..."

Maya sat up straight, eyes widening. "A real one or just one of those guys who writes and waits on tables?"

"He's written *Three Towns in Texas* and *Chances Are*."

Maya dropped her hands, slapping them on the table with enough force to shake their water glasses. "Colin Selfe!"

"I think that was his name," Joanna said, mildly, reaching for the bread basket and extracting a warm brown roll. "Yes, that's his name."

"He's like huge, Mother! Big time. Those were top grossing movies. He's writing and directing his next movie!"

"That's what they said. Some of the people at the seminar."

"Did he ask you out?"

"We did lunch. I think that's the expression."

"Lunch…"

"Yes. He's an amateur astrologer and he's read all my books."

"Oh…My… God! What did you talk about?"

Joanna spread butter on her roll. "Astrology. He wants to do a horror movie and use astrology in some way."

"So did he come on to you?"

Joanna considered the question. "Let me put it this way. He wanted us to get together after lunch, discuss the possibility of my being the consultant for the movie, and then, and I quote, 'really get up close and personal.'"

Maya lowered her chin, fastening her hungry-for-more eyes on her mother. "…And?"

"I told him I hated horror movies and that he'd be disappointed when he saw me up close and personal."

Maya closed her eyes, wagging her head in disbelief. "You didn't. Please tell me you didn't say that?"

Joanna sunk her teeth into the roll and ripped off a piece. She nodded. "Yes, I did."

A sturdy waitress arrived—flushed and distracted. She raised her pencil, like a baton, and in a hectic overture of stumbles, mumbles and fumbles, she commenced the specials in a booming brassy voice. Joanna gently touched her hand and stopped her before the finale.

"We know what we want…You must be very busy."

Grateful, the waitress relaxed a bit, forming a little smile. "Oh, yes. Everything at once."

Maya and Joanna ordered a bottle of local white wine, along with their entrées. The waitress fled, as if snatched by a giant hook.

After a moment of curious silence, while Maya watched her mother saturate the roll with butter and then devour it with relish and pleasure, Maya inclined toward her with a low confessional voice.

"Mom...we should probably have a heart-to-heart."

Joanna stopped chewing. Her furrowed brow and anxious eyes blended to form a perfect storm of dread. "Oh God, no. Not that, Maya."

"Mother, I'm not always going to be around."

Joanna swallowed. "May I remind you that you haven't been around for over six months and you live under a hundred miles away."

"I don't want to get into that right now," Maya said. "And anyway, who was it who sent me off to school in Massachusetts when she pleaded with you to stay here?"

"Maya...please. Let's not bring all this up again. Every time we have our little 'heart-to-heart' you bring that up."

"I would have received just as good an education here as I got in Massachusetts."

"Don't be ridiculous!"

"It's true."

"Maya, I wanted you to have a variety of experiences and to meet interesting people. I wanted you to see more of the world than just Long Island, not that there is anything at all the matter with Long Island. Do you think I wanted you to leave me? Do you know how hard it was to see you go off to school for those four years? It broke my heart, not to mention my check book." Joanna sat up rigid. "But I'd do it again."

"And I will never send my kids away from me—especially my only daughter—who didn't have a father."

Joanna grew crimson with irritation. "Maya, how many times...I mean how many times do you want me to say I'm sorry? How many? For God's sake, I'm sorry your father died just before you were born. I can't tell you how sorry I am, but I can't raise him up from the dead and I can't keep beating myself up over it. What do you want from me?"

"I want the truth, Mother! For once in my life I don't want lies and pretty little stories. I want the goddamn truth! And I know there's a lot more than you've told me!"

Maya had blurted out the words without thinking—without editing them. Once freed from the driving force of her tongue, they charged the air with contempt and rancor. Maya sat trembling, suddenly fragile, as if she were guilty for the act of indiscretion that had brought her into the world.

Joanna was appalled and enfeebled by her daughter's outburst. The violence of the tone wounded her. She couldn't speak.

Neither spoke until the food was delivered—a good 10 minutes later. Meanwhile, they sipped wine; let their eyes stray toward the sea, up to the soft pink horizon, and out toward nothing.

When their food arrived, they stared into their plates, straining to understand the new language that had suddenly been created between them, rendering them mute and confused.

Maya was scared, fighting an emotional pandemonium that was tearing her apart. She knew her mother was supremely sensitive, intelligent and incisive and that she was calculating words and possibilities, seeking answers and reasons as to her daughter's outburst. She'd probably created some damned astrological chart, in her head, and was delineating the aspects at that very moment.

If she learned of Matt's identity—if she learned that Maya had read the letter and knew the truth about Bob Harrison, there was no telling what she'd do.

As a little girl, Maya had seen her mother's mood swings; heard the emotional outbursts as her mother struggled through therapy to exorcise the "demons of the night" as she had called them. Maya was fairly certain that these were the reasons she'd been sent away to school: her mother had nearly shattered into shards of black angry pieces several times before Maya was 14 years old.

Maya loved her mother deeply. She did not want to return to those awful raging years. She did not want to lose her mother again and she did not want to lose Matt's trust.

Matt had awakened Maya from the sleep of relationship complacency and cynicism, where men were either good for conversation, good for sex or good to condemn as hopelessly male. With Matt she felt newly created—reshaped and extraordinary. He'd cracked open the hard shell of her fear and pain and embraced them. He'd lit the fire of her secret passions and sent her rioting. Even now she felt the subtle currents of desire for him, remembering their perfect fit; their perfect caress; their perfect sighs.

It was after Joanna took the first bite of the striped bass that she lifted her eyes and spoke to her daughter. Her voice had changed and so had her eyes. There was a hopeless resignation in them. "Something happened six months ago, Maya. Something has changed you."

Maya tied on her lobster bib. "I didn't mean what I said. Just forget it," Maya said. She lifted her roasted corn on the cob and chewed.

Joanna ate absently. "I sent you away to school because I didn't want you to be like me…I didn't want you to become a recluse, retreating from the world. I didn't want you living with a crazy eccentric woman, that your classmates and teachers made jokes about."

"They didn't..."

"Yes, they did, Maya. I knew that. From the time you started school. I heard all about it."

"I didn't care."

"You would have. You would have grown to hate them, me and school. I couldn't let that happen. Well, anyway, those were the main reasons I sent you away. Not because I didn't love you or want you with me. God knows it almost killed me to send you off like that," she concluded in an unsteady voice.

The conversation distressed Maya. She sought to steer it into another direction. "Mother...it's just that I worry about you. I wish you'd get out more and meet someone."

"I don't need someone," Joanna said testily.

"Okay, a friend then. I mean why did you turn that writer down in Chicago? It might have been fun."

"Don't be ridiculous, Maya!" she exclaimed in an excited tone. "The thought of that kind of empty, selfish, vulgar relationship sickens me. Up close and personal," she repeated with disdain. "Now you can think I'm an old prude if you want to. I don't care. But at least give me some credit for 56 years of living in this world. I've learned a few things about life." Joanna's voice grew in conviction and strength. "And I can tell you that having sex with some near-stranger on the beach is a good way to throw your whole life away. It cheapens you. Demeans you."

"Mother, you don't know anything about it."

"Oh God, yes, I do!"

"You don't know him."

"And I don't want to. I'd probably want to kill him."

Maya flung herself back in her chair. "Do you hear yourself? Do you hear what you just said? You don't know one damned thing about it!"

Joanna's disapproving eyes turned away. She slammed down her fork. Her voice turned bitter. "I'm so disappointed in you, Maya."

Maya had not even cracked one claw of her lobster. She stared numbly at her mother, feeling the slow rise of a turbulent raging insolence. She wanted to retaliate—blast her mother at point blank range with the damning proof of her old crime and the unconscionable cover-up.

But Maya reigned in her burning emotions. She had a better plan—a better response than lashing out in revenge—as sweet as it would be. But it wasn't worth the risk of losing Matt. She had a better, stunning weapon that would cut her mother to the heart.

Maya reached for the claw cracker. She placed a shiny red claw between the steel clamp, and with an ugly grimace and grunting sound, she squeezed hard. Juice squirted out. "Oh, by the way, Mother, I'm leaving for Maine in the morning."

Maya's voice was oddly serene, controlled and sweetly pleasant, as if it lay in the eye of a raging hurricane. "I going to be staying with the man I had sex with on the beach."

It was a stunning victory and an agonizing defeat.

Both mother and daughter wilted by degrees: head, neck and shoulders, until, in the low drowsy evening, they sat hunched and still, consuming regret.

Chapter 7

Matt met Maya in the Portland, Maine Airport parking lot. They'd discussed the details the night before, agreeing he'd wait for her in his red Mustang, in case he was recognized. But when Matt saw her, he emerged from the car, and she went to him in a rush. They kissed long and tender, as if they were the first and only lovers in the world.

Maya was melting and affectionate as they drove north, past fields of Queen Ann's Lace, white and gray shingled New England homes and towering 19th century church spires. Matt was radiant with excitement. He stroked her neck with his magnetic hand—kissed her at stop lights and a railroad crossing, as red and yellow cars lumbered by, rattling and squeaking.

As they edged along the coast, Maya took in the rocky shoreline, the stacks of lobster pots on boat docks, and the distant lighthouses at sea emerging from a scrim of mist.

They stopped at a local ice cream shop and ordered a chocolate sundae and a banana split. Moving through birch and pine, they rolled down their windows to allow the cool wind to wash and caress them. They laughed, kissed and listened to driving rock music. They danced in their seats and felt the reckoning power of privileged youth, as if, for the first time in their lives, it all added up and made sense: love was truly the answer to a confusing and difficult existence.

By late afternoon, they arrived at the secluded luxury cabin. The sky had clouded over and a rising humidity glossed their faces as they pulled the suitcases from the trunk and started down the gravel path toward the front entrance.

Maya viewed the "cabin." It was actually a sprawling modern home, with ample windows, a peaked roof and a generous porch. Inside, she took in the pine interior, high ceilings and second floor balcony. There was a large masonry fireplace, a spacious living room and den with brown leather couches and chairs. Wide picture windows had breathtaking views of the woods and Silver Lake. Matt played tour guide and ushered her through the house, presenting the luxurious master bedroom suite; the four private bedrooms with queen-sized beds; the "little" spa, with its sunken Jacuzzi and steam room; and the game room with a pool table, wide plasma screen TV, L-shape couch, and a card table.

Maya was impressed. "Well it's not exactly what I pictured when you said, 'the cabin.'"

"It used to be smaller, but Dad kept adding on to it. Mom never came up here much. She preferred the beach house in Nantucket."

Matt stored Maya's suitcases in the room next to his. While they unpacked, they pulled privacy around them, detaching themselves from the world. They were wedded, moment to moment, by thoughts of lovemaking, anticipating a rich future, their lives an unopened gift.

Matt came to her before she had completely unpacked. She saw herself absorbed in his eyes, saw his bulging desire. Her temperature and passion rose. They made love on the bed and finished on the floor. Afterwards, they scampered naked down to the Jacuzzi, wrapped in cozy terry cloth robes. They languished there until their bodies grew slack and hot.

Donna, the housekeeper, had supplied the refrigerator and cupboards with food, so Matt prepared a quick feast: omelets and whole wheat toast. They ate voraciously, drinking a bottle of Pinot Noir that Matt found in his father's wine cellar. They were high and playful.

In the game room they watched *Key Largo* on DVD and made love once more before passing out on the couch, tangled, blissful and spent.

Many days passed effortlessly. They hiked, went whitewater rafting, canoed on Silver Lake and fished without goal or skill. Whenever Bob called his son, Matt's cheerful tone lifted Bob's spirits.

Feeling guilty and vaguely ashamed for leaving her, Maya called her mother every night. At first, their conversations were crisp and cold, but by the second week, they had thawed into a guarded civility.

"Are you going to spend any time with me before you start your job?" Joanna had asked.

"Yes, I'm coming the last week of August."

Joanna was silent and Maya knew her mother well enough to know that her eyes had probably filled with tears. More guilt invaded Maya's heart.

"Mother…" she searched for difficult words. "I…love him."

"I look forward to seeing you," Joanna said, flatly, before hanging up.

On Thursday evening, the third week of August, Matt and Maya lay arm and arm on the leather couch in the living room, watching the orange moon rise lazily over the lake. They drank a romantic Rosé from Languedoc, France and listened to a Louis Armstrong and Ella Fitzgerald CD. They'd just finished a full day of biking the countryside and swimming Silver Lake. Matt's cell phone rang. It was his father.

"You sound better every time I talk to you, son. I knew it would do you good to spend time there."

"I see you're still gaining in the polls," Matt said.

"Yes…But the money we're spending, Matt, is unholy. This month alone the campaign has spent nearly $11,000 just for event photographers. We've spent over $200,000 for hats and T-shirts and buttons, and almost $8,000 for parking."

"It's the nature of the beast, Dad."

"I still don't like it."

"How do you feel, Dad?"

"Tired, but good. I'm going to win this, Matt. I'm going to win this for your mother and for Robert. This old fighter pilot will never give up."

"I'm proud of you, Dad."

"After the convention, we'll tick up in the polls even more. That's only a week away, you know."

Matt sat up, gently startled. Maya stared, concerned.

"Next week?"

"Yes. You need to be in New York this Tuesday."

Matt stuttered. "Tuesday?"

"Yes, I'm giving my acceptance speech on Thursday. You'll precede me."

"I didn't realize it was so close."

"Have you worked on your speech?"

"Umm, yeah sure."

"Good, good. When you're done, e-mail it off to Paul and Molly. They'll shape the content and tone, and they'll coach you to make it sound natural."

"Yeah…sure," Matt said, uncomfortably.

"I love you, son, take care now."

After the call, Matt paced the room while Maya sat perched on the edge of the couch.

"Every time I try and put two words together for this thing, it sounds cloying and insincere."

"Think of things about your father that you like most—simple things. Start with that."

Matt stopped, planting himself before the window, staring at the moon. "The truth is, Maya, I'm still angry at him. The thought of going to that convention and standing up there in front of millions of people makes me sick."

Maya went to him. She wrapped his shoulder with her arm. "I'm going to go downstairs so you can work on this alone."

"No, stay with me. Work on it with me."

"No. You need to do this alone," she said, and then planted a kiss on his lips.

Matt lifted his hands, helplessly. "I thought we said we'd never do anything alone again."

Maya winked at him. "This, my darling, you have to do alone. But I won't be far away, just in case you need physical inspiration."

On Monday night, the day before they were to leave the house—the day they would separate for five days—they made love after dinner and fell asleep. It was the day they had been dreading for nearly two weeks and, although they had celebrated with champagne and a delicious dinner they'd prepared together, their soaring spirits had dipped as the dinner progressed and the golden dining room clock had tick-tocked relentlessly.

Maya arose from a light sleep a little after 8 o'clock and left Matt dreaming, his eyes twitching. She pulled on his extra-large gray T-shirt, passing him a loving smile as she exited the room. She traversed the hall and descended the stairs to the living room. In the murky evening light, she realized the air-conditioner was off and she felt the warm, humid breath of the night wafting in from open windows. Sheer curtains billowed, puffed and flapped. She heard the chatter of cicadas. She heard honking geese passing over the house, beating toward the lake.

Barefoot, she moved fluidly across the sticky wooden floor en route to the kitchen for a can of soda. When she heard the metallic sound of the lock turn—when she saw the front door open—she froze. Bob Harrison stood tall, framed in porch light.

Chapter 8

Bob caught sight of Maya standing poised with surprise, scantily dressed, her hair teased from love making. He looked sideways, embarrassed.

Maya felt an instant hysteria—a raw, burning panic. She stared at him, dumbly. She wanted to run—not from her near nakedness—but from the naked emotion hammering in her chest—but her feet felt nailed to the floor.

Bob felt like an intruder, arriving at the worst possible moment.

Neither of them could find words.

"Well," he finally said. "I…a… should go and a…"

Maya somehow found her voice. "No! I'm…a…Matt is a…well I should go get dressed."

She had just ducked her head and was in the midst of a pivot, when Matt appeared, sleepy-faced. The stark scene awoke him. His eyes bulged with surprise. "Dad!?"

Maya fled.

Bob quietly closed the door behind him. Seeing that Maya was gone, Bob found the light switch. Matt shaded his eyes, squinting.

"I guess I should have called," Bob said.

Matt wore Bermuda shorts, but was shirtless. He hunted for words.

"I thought I'd surprise you. I thought we could travel down to New York together."

Matt's eyes dropped to the floor.

"We held a rally in Portland…it came up rather suddenly, so I thought that…" He lifted his arm, and then let it fall to his side. "Well, I thought it would be a nice surprise."

"This isn't what you think…" Matt said.

"I'm afraid it is, Matt."

"No, it isn't."

Matt noticed his father's hands began to tremble. He looked back toward the door. "I would leave, but it's a little too late now."

"Of course you'll stay," Matt said, placing his hands on his hips. "She'll be gone first thing in the morning."

Bob lifted his bags and started past his son. "So will I."

Matt's voice stopped him. "Dad…I was going to tell you. I was going to tell you everything about her…about us."

Bob remained motionless. He moved on and Matt heard his heavy footsteps as he climbed the stairs.

Matt found Maya in her room, sitting dejectedly on the side of her bed. "Are you okay?"

She didn't look up. "No… I'm not. It's not exactly how I had pictured meeting him."

Matt sat beside her. "I'm sorry…"

"It's nobody's fault, Matt… What did you tell him?"

"Nothing really. I don't think he wanted to hear it."

"Don't you think you should tell him?"

He clasped his hands together. "I don't know. No…not now."

"When?"

"I don't know, Maya. Are you ready to face him with it?"

Maya slackened. "God, we probably should have waited."

"Why?"

She closed her eyes. "I don't know. I'm just so damn confused."

Matt took her hand. "Do you regret it?"

Her eyes opened and found him. "Of course not. You know that. I just feel odd, meeting him after all these years; after all the fantasies of what it would be like; what he would be like. I don't know… and now he's just down the hall." She faced Matt with a new conviction. "You've got to tell him."

"Let's sleep on it. Let's see how we feel in the morning."

"I won't be able to face him in the morning," Maya said.

"Then we'll tell him later."

"Are you scared of him?" she asked.

"No! I'm not scared of him, but he's had a lot to deal with lately. And he looks so tired. Let's just give it a little time. We should probably wait until after the convention."

She withdrew her eyes from him. "I hate it that he thinks I'm just some slut who's shacking up with you."

"He doesn't think that."

"He does, Matt, and you know it!"

"Okay, well, we know different. Maya, I'll tell him. We'll tell him everything, soon."

Maya got up and went to the window. "Damn! I feel trapped. I hate feeling this way."

Matt went to her; took her by the shoulders. "Maya…just relax. You're not trapped. You're as free as you want to be. You know that."

She turned slowly, lifting her face toward his. "God, Matt…what's he going to think when we tell him I'm his daughter."

"Everything will be fine, Maya. We'll work it out. You're so tense."

"With him sleeping down the hall, I guess that means we'll sleep in our own rooms tonight," Maya said, sadly.

Matt grabbed a handful of her hair, pulled her close and kissed her. "No, Maya. That's not what it means."

Deep into the night, Maya awoke, startled and anxious. She gently slipped away from Matt's arms, wrapped herself in a robe and stood there, wondering if it would be too dangerous to go downstairs for something to drink. Bob Harrison was down the hall—her father was down the hall. The thought of seeing him terrified and attracted her. She tantalized herself with things she'd say when they met again; with scenarios of accusation; with clever words and phrases that might impress him. Finally, she moved carefully to the door, opened it and ventured a glance down the dark hall. All was quiet.

She crept downstairs to the kitchen, found some seltzer water and poured a glass. Lingering for a while in thought, she eventually wandered to the living room, found a night light and sat on the couch, staring out into the smooth silk of night.

She felt strange and surprised, as if she'd just awakened from a long sleep in a dark lonely room. Her instincts, which had always been sure, wavered in confusion; her dignified emotions now seemed reckless and peculiar. Was it her new love for Matt that had made her madly vulnerable and on the edge of tears? Was it the power of their love-making that, with each joining, seemed to loosen the taut strings of tension and bitterness that had held her captive for so long?

Had she been living a half-awake existence—a sleepwalking silly girl—dreaming so much of her life away in pretense and artifice, playing hide-go-seek with the inevitable truth that her father would never appear and therefore he would never be an issue in her life? "So shut the windows of that room, Maya; pull down the shades, retreat and lock the door. Go ahead, Maya, fall asleep and pretend that you are whole and well and wise."

When she had seen him—her father—he had roused her, troubled and frightened her; made her want to scream out curses and praises. Standing there before her, he had pried open the door, lifted the shades and flung open the windows. She was wide awake now, in the deepest part of the night, and she was scared to death to look into the light.

She leaned her head back, sighed and heard quiet footsteps on the stairs. Sure it was Matt, she rolled her head to the side and glimpsed him in the quiet gray light. It was her father! She snapped erect, twisting her body awkwardly toward him.

Bob paused at the foot of the stairs, taking her in, his eyes doleful and unsure. He tied the belt of his midnight blue silk robe securely. "I'm sorry, I didn't know anyone was up."

She started a word, but faltered.

"I'm just going to pour a scotch," he said pointing toward the liquor cabinet. Maya watched him move, rapt, feeling the moment by moment anxiety of the approaching encounter.

He poured with unsteady hands—neat—no ice. He replaced the bottle and took his time to turn and level his eyes on her. "May I join you?"

She swallowed, hard. "…Yes…"

As he drew near, she saw the resemblance: the dark hair, the cheekbones, the proud countenance. He reached for the light switch.

"You don't mind the light, do you?"

Maya gave a half-hearted shake of her head and the light bathed them in a hard, honest light.

As Robert lowered himself down on the opposite side of the couch, Maya took a fast shallow breath.

He sipped scotch. She sipped her water, but wished for scotch.

"This place is one of the few spots on earth where I relax. Whenever I have a big piece of legislation to consider, an important speech to write or a family problem to solve, I come here and, within a few hours, my head clears and I see things much more clearly… I think Matt feels the same way. He always loved coming up here, even when he was a kid."

"It's very quiet up here," Maya said, filling in the sudden gap of silence.

"Have you known Matt long?" Bob asked.

"No…"

The unsteady silence lengthened. It rang.

"When Matt was a boy, he used to have nightmares. It was nearly always the same dream. An old woman, frail and green, would come and threaten to steal him away from us. She had a long staff and she'd pound the base on the floor several times and screech at him to get out of bed and follow her into the closet. She told him that unless he followed, she'd snag him with the end of her staff, jerk him out of bed and beat him to death. He even had a name for her: she was Mrs. Squishal."

Maya stared with interest, gripping the glass tightly. "How long…I mean, how old was he when they stopped?"

"About seven, I think. He would cry out and Connie would rush into his bedroom and calm him down with little kisses and soft words. Sometimes she'd even spend the rest of the night with him. A few times, I went in, but I think he preferred his mother."

Maya waited for the conclusion—for the point of the story.

"Matt was a very sensitive boy and continues to be a complex and sensitive man."

Maya blinked slowly. "Yes…he is."

"He's been through a very difficult time. I know he's confused and searching…probably angry. I'm very worried about him."

Maya set her glass on the coffee table. "We've talked some about it."

Bob narrowed his questioning eyes. "Did you?"

"Yes… Matt and I talk a lot."

"How did you find him?"

Maya was confused by the question. "Find him?"

Bob took a long indulgent drink, purposefully avoiding her eyes. "Yes…"

Maya grew hot and shaky. She wanted to avoid details. "We…sort of found each other."

"I see…"

Maya sensed disapproval.

Bob's face was suddenly expressionless. "Your name is Maya, isn't it?"

Hearing him say it—saying her name—shocked her. Pleased her. Angered her. "Yes. It's Maya."

"It's a pretty name."

"Unusual. When I was a girl I wanted my mother to change it to Jennifer or Amber."

Bob took a long, calculated pause. "And where is your mother?"

Maya reached for her glass and took a drink, considering her answer. "She lives on the east coast."

"Is that where you and Matt first met?"

"Yes…"

"Are you going with Matt to New York?"

"No…We're going to meet afterwards."

"And then?"

"And then, we'll…we'll be together."

Bob played with a sudden twisting frown. He drained the last of the scotch. Her face changed. His voice deepened. "What do you want, Maya?"

Feeling vaguely challenged and confused, Maya adjusted herself. "Want?"

"Yes."

She grew guarded. "Matt and I care for each other."

"I'm sure you do," he said, weakly. "Did you go looking for Matt?"

"Looking?"

"You must have."

Maya felt the easy pull of confrontation. On the hot surface of her skin, an oily perspiration oozed. Her heart pumped alarm as she began to apprehend his questions. "Actually, he found me."

Bob was gently surprised. "Found you?"

"Yes…"

His mind went to work. "I don't understand."

Maya grew increasingly uncomfortable, feeling as though she was being probed and pressed. He knew more than he was revealing and she'd already said too much. "It doesn't matter," she said, placing her half-drunk glass on the coffee table.

"But it does matter. How could he have found you?"

"What are we talking about?" Maya said, provoked.

Bob blinked her question away. "I think we both know what I'm talking about."

Her eyes opened fully on her father, in awe, affection and disorder. "I'm afraid I don't…"

"Come on, Maya, neither of us is stupid."

Maya's arms were cradled against her, her elbows in her palms. Her stomach soured at an obvious awful thought. "You knew all about us, didn't you?"

He stared coldly.

"You weren't surprised when you walked in here. You planned it and …" She stopped, feeling the full impact of the truth.

Bob shot up and went for more scotch. He poured liberally and then held the glass to his lips. He swirled the brown liquid, hesitant and conflicted. He drank a little, keeping his back to her.

Maya tried to break through the shell of pounding emotion and confusion. "Why did you come?"

He turned. "We keep asking each other the same questions, don't we, Maya?"

Maya stood, and as she did, in mid-movement, it occurred to her that he knew absolutely everything. It blunted her thoughts and emotions. Her mouth worked a little against the possibility.

He saw it on her face. He straightened. "I'll fight you, Maya, and I'll win. Do you think I'm going to let you destroy my son and ruin my political career? Of course I knew you were here. I found out about you two days ago. Let me tell you this. I'll fight you with everything I've got and I will win!"

Maya's eyes moved at intervals around the room, seeking some place of understanding. "Fight me…" she said, almost breathless.

"If you want to destroy me, fine! I can handle it, but leave Matt out of it for God's sake! He's been through enough."

"I love Matt!"

"I doubt it!"

A wildness had been set free in the room. An inferno of emotion. For Maya, hope, fright, love and hate all converged in a call to arms.

"You doubt it?" Maya repeated, incredulous.

"I know what you're doing and I'm going to stop you."

"Did your people report our every move? Did they give you all the sexy details?"

"Pretty close," Bob said, squaring his wide shoulders. "I intend to stop this, Maya; stop this ridiculous thing before the press gets ahold of it."

In a surging agony, Maya summoned strength, spitting out words harshly, as if striking him with them. "And I sure you doubt me…doubt that I'm your daughter?"

He was motionless, wounded a little, pondering his response. "No, Maya. I don't doubt that. I know you're my daughter. I've known it ever since you were born."

Shaken, Maya struggled for composure, her face a dismal expression of pain.

"I have pictures of you on your first birthday. I have video clips of you taking your first steps. I have photos of you skateboarding with two tough looking boys down the streets of Montauk, and surfing with a handsome boy—your first love—who broke your heart when he moved to California.

"I visited your school in Massachusetts, when you were 16 years old, and I saw you standing in the hallway with your girlfriends; but you didn't look at me. I was just another politician roaming the halls, studying educational reform. I even managed to get a copy of your salutatorian speech when you graduated from high school and I read it several times sitting" he pointed, "right out there on the back porch."

Maya's eyes filled with unwanted tears. Her legs weakened.

Bob stared into his drink. "I stopped keeping up with you after high school and began again, only recently, when the mermaid story surfaced. I knew—or was nearly positive—that you were behind it. I knew your mother would never have…" He left the thought in the air. "I suppose I expected something like this would happen someday. I knew you'd find me and I'd have to face you…face the truth."

"You bastard…" Maya said, angry and hurt. "You pathetic, fucking coward!"

He looked at her, his expression grave. "Go after me if you want, Maya. I understand that you hate me and I don't blame you for it. But leave Matt alone. I'm warning you. Don't get him involved in all this."

From atop the staircase, Matt gazed down. "It's too late for that, Dad. I'm already involved."

Maya and Bob shot him surprised glances. He stood tall and resolute; his hair mussed, his eyes sleepy.

The room gathered into an icy hush. "Dad… Maya and I slipped away from the Secret Service yesterday. They didn't find us until later. Until after we left the church."

Bob's face tightened.

"Dad, Maya and I are married."

Bob took in the disturbing words, and then began to melt into a slow despair.

"We were married at the little Methodist Church down the road."

Bob shook his head in disbelief. He sat his glass down, looking at his son with bewilderment. "Why, Matt? Why did you do this!?"

"Because I fell in love."

Bob's uncomprehending eyes slid toward the dark windows. "…Love?" he asked, hoarsely. "You have ruined me, Matt. You have let her destroy us both."

Matt started down the stairs. "No, Dad! It's not what you think. We love each other. We didn't plan it, it just happened."

Bob refused to look at Maya, who stood submerged in dejection and fury. She wanted to lash out at him; she wanted to apologize and explain; she wanted to run away.

Matt's face was desperate and beseeching. "No one will know, Dad. No one knows that Maya and I are married but the minister, his wife and the gardener: the witnesses. I paid them—extra—to keep quiet. They said they would. And we won't tell anyone until after the election. We have it all worked out. We're going to stay out of sight and hide."

Bob looked at him pitifully. "Matt…surely you're not so naïve. Those people will spread the story all over that little town. By morning, it will be all over the media and internet. And when they learn who Maya is—and they will—my campaign, my political career, will be finished."

Bob shifted his hard, accusing gaze to Maya. "God forgive you, Maya, if you have done this to hurt my son. God forgive you!"

Maya's shoulders sank.

Chapter 9

On Thursday afternoon, Maya strolled the Montauk beach, hearing the chop of the waves, viewing the sun, a white blister burning through a thin blanket of gray clouds. It was unseasonably cool, with a snappy breeze and a rising mist. She was dressed in jeans, red flip flops and a peach sweatshirt; she wore a New York Yankees baseball cap. She rambled along the tide and lingered by the cliffs, holding a gleaming shell up to the sky, wishing for the talent of a painter so as to capture the quiet religion of color, sand and sky. She sought escape from her aching, disobedient heart.

In the months after she'd found her father's letter to her mother—that 25 year old cursed relic—it had been her primary assumption that someday he would pay for his treachery. She'd planned and prepared for it, and the righteous truth of payment would be justifiably handed down by her own wringing hand, for the good of her mother and for the greater good of the world. She'd anticipated a delicious revenge—a swift retribution. But when it finally came, in that painful, fumbling night in Maine, she was left confused, and fragile.

She kicked along the beach, pondering the nature of relationships, love and family. She pondered her father's final look, as he had turned from her, beaten and diminutive. He shambled off toward the recreation room to finish his drink, alone and defeated, like a wounded animal gone off to die.

He didn't know how much she loved him in that moment; how much she wanted to rush to him, apologize and explain the process of her thoughts and actions; explain the vicious emotions that begged for resolution; explain the raging confusion of a lifetime of living without a father and the vibrant and infinite love she felt for Matt. She wanted to communicate to him the quiet fantasies of a little girl whose father held her close, whispered forgiving comfort and approval.

But as he turned to leave—in that silent, terrible interval—her ragged emotions bewildered her; the words tangled and strained, and never rose to her trembling lips.

He'd shut the door, the latch was thrown, the metallic sound echoed, and the quiescent house seemed to breathe Maya's own breaths of disappointment and loss. She and Matt stared blankly, ashamed and wanting.

She did not know that a heart—her heart—could throb with such a stabbing pain. She had never experienced a breaking heart.

Still on the beach, Maya stared into the quilted sky. She felt feverish. She felt low. She felt dreadful.

On Tuesday morning, Matt had dropped her off at the Southhampton Jitney bus stop, and then he drove back to New York to the Republican Convention. She returned to Montauk and caught a cold. She lay in bed for two days, while her mother brought her tea, soup and homemade chocolate chip cookies. She wept and cursed and lied to her mother about who Matt was and what they had done. She'd lied a hundred different ways, perjuring her soul for years or perhaps lifetimes. She exuded gloom and misfortune. She sniffed away her mother's encouragement and happy moods.

Bob Harrison had been right about the media, although he was a day off. On Wednesday morning, Matt's photo and the sensational story of his marriage to a mystery woman named "Marjorie," at a little country church in Maine, appeared on the internet, the news shows and the newspapers. Fortunately, she and Matt had left the Maine house at 5 o'clock on Tuesday morning and Bob had left at seven. On Wednesday morning, a knot of news vans, cars and reporters descended on the little Methodist Church and the minister and his wife and the gardener fled town, frightened and repentant.

In the two days that followed, reporters had yet to learn who the mystery wife was, and Bob and Matt deflected the barrage of questions about the new wife, with convention hyperbole and election fever.

Maya tossed shells into the sea, keenly aware that it was only a matter of time before she was discovered and the whole truth would come crashing down around her. Her mother would suffer. Her father, already shouldering heavy personal losses, would lose everything: a lifetime of work and ambition and the impetus to continue. And when the onslaught of accusation and contemptuous questioning crescendoed and persisted, she and Matt and their new green sprig of a struggling marriage, could easily wither into the dust before it ever had a chance to grow.

Maya pulled a tissue from her pocket and wiped her sore, tender nose. "Congratulations," she said aloud. "You did it. You won."

On Thursday evening, Maya sat in the living room watching the Republican Convention. She was highly nervous, aware of her mother's all-pervading presence sliding in and out of the room, passing suspicious glances back and forth, from the TV screen to her daughter.

"Why are you watching that?" Joanna asked, irritated and distracted, as she idly dusted surfaces, missing whole patches.

"It's part of being a good citizen, Mother; an informed citizen."

"Oh, pahleeeze. It's so pathetically staged and phony."

Maya blew her nose and sneezed.

"And you should be in bed."

"I have a backache from being in bed. I'm just going to watch a little of this, okay?"

"Whatever," Joanna said, leaving the room.

Maya saw the boiling enthusiastic crowds, half-listened to the bantering commentators and speakers and sniffed repeatedly as she nosed toward the screen, hoping to catch a glimpse of Matt. She missed him terribly. She'd spoken to him earlier on the beach, by cell phone, and he'd sounded edgy and distant.

"You don't sound like yourself, Matt. Is everything alright?"

"Yeah, yeah, I'll just be glad when this whole speech thing is over with."

"I miss you," she said, with a little sniff.

"Yeah, me too… I mean, I miss you, too. You sound like you have a cold."

"I do. I told you."

"Oh, yeah…right. Sorry. Feeling better?"

"No… I miss you. I feel like hell without you."

"Just a couple more days."

"Matt, I was thinking about where we're going to live. We can't live in New York…not with all this going on."

"I know, Maya, I know. You keep saying that. I keep telling you that we're just going to have to go back to Maine and lay low for awhile."

"But what about my new job and your school and…?"

"I don't know, Maya. I just can't think about it all now. Maybe once we're in Maine and away from everything we can come up with some solutions."

"But I thought you said your father…" she stopped, confused about what to call her father. "…I thought you said he didn't want us in Maine."

"I'll talk to him. I've already talked to him. He'll be okay with it."

"How is he?" she asked, softly.

"He's amazing. I don't know where he gets the energy. I'm exhausted and he acts like he's on top of the world. He's like a 20-year-old around these people. They love him! …Okay, look, I've got to go. They're calling me."

An hour later, Senator Langston Homer of Ohio, along with four of Bob's old fighter pilot buddies and Matt, strode enthusiastically across the broad red, white and blue stage, under a blaze of light, planting themselves firmly against the backdrop. Driving rock music exploded, and the crowd jumped to its feet, cheering, whistling and yelling, waving BOB HARRISON FOR PRESIDENT signs and banners.

Maya edged forward on the couch, biting her nails, eyes holding pride as she followed Matt's footsteps. Senator Homer offered a controlled and inspirational introduction of Matt Harrison, stating that he had heard from Bob Harrison, personally, that Matt had been a beacon for him during the last difficult weeks. He said "'I couldn't be more proud and thankful for my son.'"

After ringing applause, Senator Homer turned toward Matt, with a wide open arm. "Please welcome, Matt Harrison!"

The room jumped to its feet and expanded with lively appreciation.

Maya's entranced eyes widened in pleasure and encouragement as she leaned toward the TV screen—watching intently—as if her husband were standing before her, looking to her for support. Matt took the riotous welcome with an easy humility, uncomfortable roving eyes and an affable smile.

Joanna had re-entered the room and eased down into a chair. Maya whirled to her, alert and radiant, wanting to shout out the whole thrilling truth: "That's my husband, Mother! Isn't he gorgeous?!" The words reverberated in her head, but never left her parted, frustrated lips.

Matt began softly, and, as the audience grew silent and still, he expressed gratitude for their support during difficult days and nights. He used simple words and phrases, reading from the teleprompter awkwardly, lending authenticity and appeal to his overall presentation. He wore a dark blue sport jacket, gray pants, white shirt and golden tie.

"As he has done throughout my life, my father has been there for me during the last few weeks, despite his hectic schedule. If I faltered, he supported me. If I was confused, he brought a calm clarity. If I had questions—and I had many—we tried to find the answers together. This is what we have done for years, as a family.

"Dad often reminded me of what my mother had believed in and tried her best to be: a person of character and conviction; a woman who wanted to make a difference for her country and for the world.

"I heard my brother, Robert Jr., often say that he wanted to be a politician, mainly because Dad was such a good example of what a true politician should be: honest, hardworking and inspirational. He's an excellent problem solver and a man who fights for what he believes in for the greater good of all, no matter what the consequences will be."

Matt paused, taking a sip of water. "Many of you know Dad's great sense of humor. You know of his inspirational strength in adversity and great personal loss; you know of his leadership skills and experience through a lifetime of example. You know about his persistence and boundless enthusiasm.

"But perhaps a lot of you do not know the man who searches his heart every day, striving for honesty and dignity, working tirelessly to ensure that he is doing the best he can, to live up to the principals that he believes in, as he represents the people and the country he feels so fortunate to serve."

Matt paused. "But should you think that I have only good things to say about my father, I want to tell you certain little secrets that should be known, just to clear the air and to give you a more balanced understanding of him: first, he snores like a bullhorn, second, he's a terrible singer, especially when he tries to sound like Tony Bennett, and, finally, if you ask him a question or try to carry on a conversation with him during any baseball game, he will not see you, he will not hear you and he will not answer you."

Matt waited for the laughter to subside. Matt grazed the audience with his sincere eyes. "But seriously, for me, personally, my Dad is not only a wonderful father and a good best friend who has never let me down, but he has been the best example anyone could have of how to live a good, purposeful life, filled with service to his family and to his country. I know, without any doubt, that he will never let this country down when he is elected the next President of the United States."

As Matt strolled away, the convention center exploded to life with music, drums, shouts and applause.

After Bob's fighter pilot buddies delivered their short talks, describing his courage under fire, his contagious optimism and winning sense of humor, Senator Homer returned to the podium.

In a towering voice, swelling with passion, a stately, silver-haired Senator Homer claimed the podium, calmed and welcomed the crowd, and then began his dramatic introduction of the five minute video composite of Bob Harrison's life.

On a wide overhead screen, images of Bob as a young fighter pilot, a prosecutor, a family man and Senator, all rolled across it, in close-ups and easy smiles; in professional concern in an oak-paneled courtroom; in a bowed head of tragic humility near an old stone church where Connie's funeral had been held; in expressions of unbounded hope and enthusiasm, as he walked the small towns, the rippling green fields and towering cities of America, shaking hands and flashing his winning smile.

Joanna sat still, feeling her rapid pulse, eyes focused on the TV's movement, drifting in and out of memory.

Maya stole an occasional glance and, once, she thought her mother's eyes had filled with tears.

The stirring images continued, accompanied by inspirational strings, soaring French horns and trumpets, narrated by an assuring baritone voice that repeated "Bob Harrison" with frequent, resonant emphasis.

When the last image of Bob Harrison's proud and courageous face froze on the screen, fixed on the horizon of the future, as an American flag snapped and rippled behind him, the music crescendoed, romantically, fading into a pastoral hymn-like recapitulation and cadence.

Senator Homer leaned close to the microphone and exclaimed. "Please welcome the next President of the United States, Bob Harrison!"

Bob Harrison burst from behind the red, white and blue background, stepping lively across the stage, arms raised, smile broad, eyes beaming. He met his son with an embrace, as a cacophony of celebration rattled the place.

He broke from his son, pumping the arms of his fighter pilot buddies, and of senators and congressmen, dignitaries and his choice for Vice President, Texas Governor John Cahill. As the room thundered, he approached the podium and waited, smiling, both arms raised in triumph, acknowledging the surging waves of delegates, swinging signs, banners, hats and arms. His face was stretched in joy and wonder, as the summit of achievement and grace descended upon him, making him exalted, undamaged and pure.

No one who watched or listened felt Bob's deep fatigue or witnessed the clanging emotions of self-doubt, self-loathing and grief. No one could pierce the magnificent gleaming bubble of his illusion to see a grim reality of old sins and new misdemeanors lurking like antagonists, anxious and ready to take the stage and bring the third act to a tragic end. For Bob knew that within a very short time, a lifetime of hard work, high achievement and the best intentions would soon be a confederacy of insignificance and infamy.

As Bob waved grandly, smiled richly and took in the storm of volatile adulation, he suddenly felt compelled to listen for his own inner true voice—the voice of a true lover; the voice of a husband and a true friend; the voice of a true politician. He was desperate to hear it, as if some mystical being were nudging him in the ribs, insisting that unless his own genuine words were released, there would be no true hope of victory.

Bob lifted his hands, forming the victory sign. His speech would soon roll across the teleprompter—words that he'd created, sanctioned and rehearsed. The speech of a lifetime. But to his sudden surprise, he knew that those words were not true. He realized—more at that moment than at any other time in his entire life—that the true words that lived and rang with freedom and justice for all, had only been released from the dark regions of his heart but once—only once in a lifetime.

As he accepted his party's official nomination and began his acceptance speech, he heard his strong voice delivering the words and phrases, rhythmically and forcefully, with a practiced ease that sounded natural and inspired. He modulated his voice for style and effect and paused often for cheers and for rousing applause.

But as he proceeded, feeling power and a support emanating from the energized room, he recalled the beach on Montauk, 25 years ago, with a high blue sky and gentle surf, when his own true voice had emerged—broken through—the hard layers of conditioning, family requirements and public perception, and had blessed and healed him. He recalled Joanna Halloran, and he felt an old stirring of feeling and a longing, and he wondered if she was watching.

At an unnoticed moment, Maya studied her mother, now fully engaged in the spectacle on the screen, as Bob Harrison moved adroitly through his speech. Soft lamplight revealed a nakedness of expression on her mother's radiant and handsome face; something Maya had rarely seen. To her surprise, it was a face that embraced the moment fully, honestly, with expressions of dark mood, uneasy pleasure and thoughtful tilts of her head. Her eyes enlarged, narrowed; her eyebrows lifted and, when a gentle secret smile crossed her lips, Maya felt intrusive. She looked away.

When Bob finished, a frenzy of unbridled glee and celebration seemed to shake the TV set. Joanna stood, without expression, and moved off toward the kitchen. Maya continued watching the bouncing assembly, until Matt left the stage. She heaved out a sigh, feeling relieved and, when she glanced toward the kitchen, she knotted up with tension.

Was it time to tell her mother the truth?

Chapter 10

"Mother, I need to talk to you."

Joanna looked at her daughter, searchingly. "Yes, I suppose you do."

They were outside on the deck. They had just cleaned up after having a late dinner, where their conversation had been fragmented and mundane.

It was cool and still and they both wore jeans, sweat-shirts and jackets.

"What does that mean?" Maya asked, finally lowering herself in a wicker chair opposite her mother.

Joanna angled her head left and stared out into the chilly darkness. "I guess it means that I've been waiting for you to tell me how far along it is."

"How far along what is?"

"Your relationship."

Maya dug her hands deep into her jacket pockets, wordless, gazing at her mother apprehensively.

"It already feels like autumn," Joanna said. "You shouldn't stay out here too long. You'll catch a chill and get sick all over again."

"Don't change the subject, Mother."

"Okay…I'm waiting."

"I hate it when you're smug like this," Maya said, tossing her head back. "As if you already know everything."

"I don't know everything, but I do know that you're keeping secrets from me. I suppose that's the Scorpio in you."

"Oh, God, Mother, let's not talk about astrology."

"You have the Sun and Mars in Scorpio, Maya. You're strong-willed, secretive, magnetic and passionate."

"I know, Mother…"

"Your Venus in Cancer makes you emotional, with a strong need to seek security in relationships and your Leo Moon makes you dramatic and …"

"…Mother, please. I know my chart. We've been over it hundreds of times and I don't want to go there, okay?"

Joanna ignored her. "Maya, astrology is my second language. I know it and I know you. You're involved in something that…" Joanna looked skyward. "You're over your head in something."

"I care about him, Mother, okay! I love him! That's what I want to talk about."

"I'm sure," Joanna said, evenly. "Your chart is very active right now: transits and progressions. I've seen these aspects many times and in many variations over the years." She looked directly at her daughter. "Shall I make it easy for you…for us both? You are either seriously considering marrying this boy or you've already married him."

Astonished, Maya's jaw tightened and, in a reflex response, she jerked her head away from her mother's scrutiny.

"Maya… I know your chart as well as I know my own. This relationship you're in…I saw it coming a year ago. I knew it would be sudden, intense and far-reaching. I also knew that it will have serious consequences. I don't know what those consequences are, but I know they're there."

Maya stood abruptly. She wandered to the edge of the deck, head pounding. "I still don't feel very well."

"Are you pregnant?" Joanna asked.

Maya whirled. "No!"

"Are you married?"

Maya swallowed. She eased down on the top step and hunched her shoulders. She spoke in a delicate whisper. "Yes… I'm married."

Joanna shuttered, breathing in the aching truth. "Yes…I figured."

Maya began to brood.

"But there's more, isn't there, Maya?"

Maya didn't stir. Finally, she lowered her head, and then raised it. "Mother, I didn't want to hurt you."

"I wish you'd have told me, Maya, that's all. I wish you would have at least introduced him to me."

"I couldn't…and then it happened so fast."

Joanna's voice grew emotional. "I would have liked to have come to the wedding. You're my only daughter, Maya. You're all I have."

Maya turned. "I couldn't, Mother."

Joanna strained to understand. "Couldn't?"

Maya trembled. There was tenderness beneath her anxiety. "I didn't know how to tell you. I still don't."

"Tell me what?"

"You said there was more to it. There is. A lot more."

"Then tell me, Maya. Tell me. I am so sick of you shutting me out. Do you know how painful it is to be shut out?"

"For God's sake, Mother, you shut yourself out! You always have." Maya shot up, regretful. "No, I don't mean that. I mean…"

"Just tell me the truth, Maya," Joanna said, on the cusp of anger and tears.

"Dammit! It all just happened so fast. I fell in love and…"

"Just tell me, Maya!"

Maya's words struck the air in a stammering misery. "It …it was the letter."

"…What letter?"

"His letter. The letter he wrote to you 25 years ago!"

Joanna grew cold. She slowly awakened to something terrifying.

"I found it in your filing cabinet last January. I read it. When I realized that he was my father…when I realized that you had lied to me all those years and I realized that Bob Harrison was my father, I went a little crazy. I decided to destroy him." Maya folded her arms across her chest, bracing herself. "I put the mermaid story out on the internet. I knew it would catch on. I knew it would reopen the old stories about him."

Joanna stiffened at the impossibility of the truth.

"I was going to post the letter on the internet, just after the Republican convention. I was going to destroy him, his family and his career. Pay him back for leaving you—for abandoning you after you were pregnant. I had it all worked out. But then after his wife and son were killed, I changed my mind… He'd suffered enough. It wasn't long after that, that Matt came looking for us."

Joanna sat rigid, eyes lowered.

"…He found us through one of your books…a book he found in his father's library. He put it all together and..." Maya took a long breath and blew it out toward the sky. "I fell in love with him."

Joanna didn't look up.

"Mother...Matt Harrison is my husband."

The silence grew unbearable.

"Mother... I met him. Bob Harrison. I met my father."

Joanna slowly pushed up to her feet, avoiding her daughter's pleading eyes.

"Mother...? I didn't mean to hurt you."

Joanna walked past Maya, pulled open the door and disappeared inside, into the quiet darkness.

Chapter 11

Joanna stayed locked away in her office all of Friday morning. Maya knocked several times but her mother wouldn't open the door.

"Mom, please, we need to talk about all this."

"I can't talk today, Maya. Maybe tonight."

"Mom, don't punish me like this."

"I need to be alone, Maya…and I have a lot of work to do."

"I'm not leaving tomorrow…Do you hear me? Mom? I'm staying with you. I'm staying until we work all this out."

Maya pressed her ear to the door, but heard nothing.

Maya slumped through the soundless house feeling guilty and low, busying herself with packing and cleaning. In the early afternoon, she drove into town, bought fresh flowers, a funny card and fresh fruit and vegetables.

After she'd returned, finding her mother still locked away, she had arranged the flowers and was seated at the kitchen table writing her mother a note of love and apology, when her cell phone rang. It was Matt!

"Matt! Why haven't you called? I've called you three times this morning and left messages."

"Maya..." his voice was deep and serious. "Look...I've...a..."

"Matt, what is it?"

"I got your message about your mother...about telling her everything."

"Yes...I told her last night."

"How is she?"

"She won't talk to me."

"Are you okay?"

"Yes. But I'm really worried about her. Matt, I can't leave her right now. I've got to stay here until she's better—until we're all better."

"God, what a mess," Matt said.

"How are you?"

"Fine, I think. It's been crazy. It's all a blur. People, politicians, the damn press climbing all over me wanting to know who my wife is—who you are. I almost slugged a guy who stuck a camera and microphone in my face."

"How's your father?"

"I don't know. He's acting strange. I was going to ask you if I could stay with him awhile. I thought maybe I'd even campaign with him."

"For how long?"

"I don't know. I was thinking that maybe we should plan a honeymoon in a couple of weeks and just get the hell away from all this."

"Can we get away from all this, Matt?"

"I don't know. It's out of control."

"Is your father okay?"

"I don't know. I can't put my finger on it exactly. He just doesn't seem like himself. Maybe he's just exhausted. His doctor gave him something to calm him down. Maybe that's all it is. I don't think anyone else notices anything—maybe Carlton, his campaign manager. Everybody else is so blissed out right now. Dad is soaring in the polls."

"Have you talked to him, you know, about the other night?" Maya asked, hopefully.

"No. I haven't had the chance. Look, Maya, I know this is going to sound crazy, but he wants to call your mother."

Maya froze. "What?! No way. I mean, that's not a good idea."

"I don't think it is either, but he's insisting."

"She won't talk to him, Matt, I know it. And, anyway, isn't it too chancy right now?"

"Yes… I don't know. I tried to talk him out of it, but he keeps insisting. He keeps pulling me aside, asking me to call you to arrange it. He's waiting for me up in his hotel suite right now. I'm standing in a stairwell."

"She won't even talk to me, Matt. No way she's going to talk to him."

"Please ask her."

"Now?"

"Yes. He wants you to tell her that he'll call her at 5 o'clock."

"She won't talk to him, Matt. I know it."

"Please, Maya, just ask her."

Maya looked apprehensively in the direction of Joanna's office. Her thoughts came to an agonizing standstill. "Okay. God help me. Hang on."

Maya left the kitchen and eased along the hallway until she came to the closed door of her mother's office. "Mom… Mom, I have to talk to you. It's urgent."

No answer.

She knocked. "Mother…"

She heard the lock release. The door slowly swung open. Joanna stood before her in her burgundy bathrobe and silly-looking tangled hair. Her eyes were red rimmed with fatigue, her posture was slack, her skin pallid. Maya smelled wine on her stale breath. "Yes…?" Joanna asked, enlarging her slitted eyes.

Taken aback, Maya swallowed away a dry throat and cupped her hand over the telephone receiver. "You look terrible."

"Thank you."

"No, Mother…Look," Maya said, frustrated. "Are you alright?"

"Yes. What's so urgent?"

Maya decided to say it all in one breath. "Bob Harrison wants to call you today at 5 o'clock. He wants to know if you'll take the call."

Without a pause, Joanna said, "Yes. I'll take his call."

She closed the door and locked it.

The sun reappeared around 3 o'clock, then fled behind gray rolling clouds a little before four. At four-thirty, wind drove a thin rain sideways, lashing at the windows.

At exactly at 5 o'clock, the telephone rang. Maya was seated in the living room, thumbing through a fashion magazine. She shot up, as if electrified. Three rings later, the phone went silent. Rain drummed on the skylights.

Maya lay the magazine aside and waited. Unable to quash her curiosity, she crept to her mother's office door and inclined an ear toward the keyhole. All she heard was her mother's infrequent mumble. No recognizable words or phrases. Minutes later, all was quiet, except for rain and distant thunder.

Maya made coffee and called Matt. His father had told him nothing about the call and had left the hotel for a fundraising dinner.

The rain stopped around seven, when Maya returned to her mother's door and told her she was cooking supper: baked chicken, mashed potatoes and broccoli.

"It will be ready in a half hour. Please come and eat with me."

Maya heard her mother leave her office around 7:15. She heard the shower kick on in the upstairs bathroom. She heard her mother's hair dryer. She heard her mother's radio playing jazz.

At a quarter to eight, Joanna made an appearance in the kitchen, wearing white cotton pants, a royal blue sweat shirt and white sneakers. Her hair was still damp and combed smoothly back from her forehead. Since she'd applied makeup, she was apple-cheeked, but her eyes still held weariness.

The table was set, the white wine poured and two long-tapered red candles flickered in the easy draft of wind which came from the open kitchen door.

"Well, isn't this nice," Joanna said. "It smells good."

They ate sequestered in expectation and private thought. Maya wanted details about the phone call, and for her mother to be happy again. She wanted approval, the affectionate glance that reassured. She wanted all her confusion and all her baffled emotions to find a resting place in the familiar: in her mother's forgiving, lovely brown eyes.

Joanna wanted what had never been: a normal home. Even now, she didn't possess the ability to define that word. But she pondered it, and the accompanying emotions, as she tasted the mashed potatoes. Perhaps it was a yearning for the serenity of predictability in a grossly unpredictable world, or the soul's own primordial desire for a musical theme in one's life, that persists when everything seems to fall apart—a personal melody that inspires, without the need for words. Perhaps it was the stark realization that, in a twinkling of an eye, her daughter was grown and it was time to accept the pleasure and the heartache of the inevitable.

"It's not too dry, is it?" Maya finally asked.

"No. It's good. Tender. The potatoes are creamy."

"Butter and milk."

Joanna smiled. "I taught you well."

"So you did," Maya said, watching her mother eat and drawing pleasure from it. "Are you feeling better?"

"Yes."

"Did you sleep at all last night?" Maya asked.

"Not much," Joanna said, with her wine glass halfway to her mouth.

"Did you sleep today?"

"Some."

Joanna drank, canting her head to study her daughter. "Don't feel guilty, Maya. It isn't your fault."

"I shouldn't have read that damned letter."

"I should have thrown it away 25 years ago. I started to so many times but…"

Maya tried to sound casual. "What did he want?"

Joanna cut into a piece of white meat. She ate and drank and looked out the window at nothing. "We're going to meet."

Maya laid her fork aside, gently alarmed. "When?"

"On Wednesday night."

"Where?"

"He's coming here."

"Here!? Is that a good idea?"

"No… But he said it was important. He said he had things to say."

Maya shoved her plate away, mind spinning. "Does he want me to be here?"

"No, Maya. It will just be the two of us."

"How do you feel about it?"

"Scared... nervous. Wishing I'd said no."

"Why didn't you?"

"Because I have things to say, too. Because you're married to his son. Because you are our daughter."

Maya's expression turned profound with wonder. "God, will I ever get used to that?"

"In time."

"Mother…what do you think? What do you…" She tried again. "Did you love him back then?"

Joanna smiled. "Oh, yes. I loved him very much. And he loved me."

"But you must have hated him for what he did?"

"I hated the situation…maybe I hated him for a time." Joanna looked pointedly at her daughter. "How could I hate him when I see so much of him in you? How could I hate him for very long when he gave me you? And, Maya, surely you know that I love you. I don't know what I would have done without you. I don't think I would have made it."

Maya's eyes welled up. She wiped tears and then pushed her chair back from the table. "Sitting here, away from everything, it all seems like a dream…Everything."

"Yes, that's the problem with this place. It seems like such a safe little island, away from the sound and the fury of the world."

"Matt seems so far away."

"You should go to him. He's your husband."

"I'm staying with you for awhile, until I know you're okay."

"Guilt?"

"No, because I want to."

Joanna's eyes warmed. "Stay until Wednesday then."

Wax had pooled at the base of the candleholder. Maya pressed her forefinger into it, feeling its mushy warmth. "Matt and I will have to go hide somewhere—probably Maine—until after the election."

"The truth will come out long before the election, Maya. I'm sure that's what Robert wants to discuss."

Maya got up and turned off the overhead light. In tremulous candlelight, she wandered to the back door, staring out into the darkness. "We shouldn't have done it. Matt and I should have waited to get married. I pushed him… He wanted to marry me, but he thought we should wait until after the election. But I thought we shouldn't wait. I was scared I'd lose him. Scared something would break us up."

Maya crossed her arms, lifting her chin toward the gentle rushing breeze. "But it was more than that, too. I knew that if we were married, my father would have to notice me. He'd never be able to ignore me again. Mother… forgive me, but I wanted to hurt him. I think a big part of me wanted to pay him back for what he did to us and I knew that the marriage would finish him politically."

She faced her mother with downcast eyes. "What do you think about that?"

Joanna did not speak. She didn't move.

Maya turned back to the darkness. "What will happen to him, Mother? What will happen to all of us all when the truth comes out?"

Chapter 12

At the Montauk Airport, Bob Harrison climbed out of the six-seat Beech Baron 58 airplane and stepped down onto the tarmac. Two Secret Service agents followed, scanning the area with narrowed eyes. All was quiet. It was dark, after 10 pm, and cool for September 2nd. Bob unbuttoned his dark blue suit coat and glanced back at the plane as if it were an enemy. It had not been a smooth ride from Syracuse and his lower back ached. It was the old injury from the airplane crash of 25 years ago that had never fully healed, despite the chiropractors, the massages and the acupuncture. Some injuries never heal.

The pilot emerged from the plane, handing Bob his briefcase with a respectful nod. Bob mumbled his thanks and, tucking his chin into his chest, and flanked by the agents, he walked briskly toward the black Lincoln Town Car that was waiting for him. The driver approached, greeted him and opened the rear door. Bob quickly slipped inside. The two agents followed, one in back and one in front.

Once the car was underway, and the driver was given his instructions neatly typed on a folded sheet of 8½ x 11 paper, Bob shut his tired eyes and began massaging the nape of his neck. It had been a long day: Madison, Wisconsin, Chicago, Cleveland, Buffalo and Syracuse. The crowds were robust, the faces a blur, the speeches spirited. Tomorrow would be the same, as would the days and weeks that followed, until November 7th, Election Day.

His throat felt raw. He was hoarse. His head throbbed. His body sagged heavily into the soft leather seat. A reluctant Carlton had planned this little detour and, as usual when it came to anything that Carlton handled personally, all was progressing swimmingly. Bob's staff believed he had retired early and was sleeping soundly in his Syracuse hotel room. He wouldn't be awakened until 6:30 a.m. and, by then, he'd be in his bed, in that hotel room.

Bob's mind was swirling with bits of conversation, images and ideas of the day. He longed for a scotch; he longed for sleep. He was cautiously excited about seeing Joanna again, but he had not indulged in thoughts of her or their meeting all day. He hadn't had the time or the excess mental energy. Frankly, he'd fought it.

His visit would not be a purging of old demons; it would not be a purification, but a condemnation; a resurrection of old murdered desires and buried regrets, seeking compensation and retribution. Once again and forever, he'd have to face the inquisition of his own mind and consent to any verdict it handed down. And every verdict could only be "guilty as charged," just as it had always been, whenever he'd thought about that brief affair so many years ago. Guilty as charged, for a promise made, an old promise kept and a promise broken.

Suddenly, his head rolled to the side, and he fell asleep.

Bob awoke with a start when the driver opened the rear door and bent forward. "Senator, we're here."

The agents had exited and were securing the area. Bob rubbed his eyes, righted himself and peered toward the house. He saw a single lit window. Joanna was waiting.

Joanna had spent Wednesday in a perpetual restlessness. She and Maya had cleaned, done laundry, argued politics and taken a long walk on the beach.

By late afternoon, Maya was packed and ready to go. She and her mother embraced and wept and then laughed at themselves for weeping, forcing cheerfulness.

Joanna drove Maya to the center of town, where she was to catch the Hampton Jitney to East Hampton. Matt would meet her there. They would drive to the airport, and take a hired plane to Traverse City, Michigan, where Connie's family kept a summer home. They'd stay there until Bob called with new instructions.

Joanna ate dinner alone on the deck, watching the red sun slip behind the charcoal grainy sea. She gazed at the purple clouds hugging the horizon, with shapes that reminded her of giant cruisers or battleships, and she was surprised by the thought. She knew very little about ships.

She was overflowing with high emotion and anticipation. Would he think that time had dimmed her—aged her beyond attraction? Would she see disappointment in his eyes, when he saw the mature woman of 56 and not the girl of 31, with the once svelte body, now turned curvy in the wrong places? Did she really care? Yes.

She'd washed and styled her hair—curled the front—lightly moussed the top and sides and then toweled it, excessively, to remove the mousse; to give her a more natural look; to project a certain lack of concern or a touch of wildness, depending on the lighting or one's particular perspective.

Dressing was the ultimate challenge.

"Wear something sexy," Maya advised. "Tight slacks and low cut blouse. Your breasts are round and wonderful, Mother. Show them off."

Joanna pursed her lips in disapproval. "I don't think so."

Joanna pulled on jeans—not too tight. After going rounds with her closet, boxing through blouses, cotton tops and silk shirts, she yanked out a yellow and blue cotton blouse that reminded her of spring and youth. She left the top button open. She left the shirt tail out, in a kind of defiance. She opted for dark brown loafers.

Joanna waited in the living room, hands folded in her lap, feeling the beat of her heart in that loud pocket of silence. She was fretful and circumspect, as the last light of day fell from the windows and darkness arose, black and ominous, like a special effect.

Joanna reached and switched on the lamp beside her. She settled back into the couch and heard the sea, and heard her own breath, like rolling waves, and remembered a time when she and Robert had roamed the beach, dusty-gold under a buttery moon.

When she heard the car in the driveway, she snatched a startled breath, feeling as though an explosive gust of wind lifted her up. Standing, she faced the front door, stoical and resolved.

She'd waited a long time for his return. He'd vowed he would return.

Chapter 13

Joanna opened the door, slowly, feeling the cool doorknob, the heaviness of the oak door and the heaviness of the moment.

Robert stood erect and tall, the hint of a shy smile on his tired, handsome face. His eyes held reserve and pleasure at seeing her. Joanna felt the sudden and unexpected hot grease of anger and betrayal. He must have seen it. He instantly lowered his gaze, fixing it on her shoes.

"Hello, Joanna."

For days, Joanna had practiced a benevolent demeanor and a forgiving smile, searching her heart for a charitable welcoming. The sudden heat on her face—the burning in her chest shocked her, making her immovable.

"May I come in?" Robert asked.

Joanna recovered and stood aside. Robert entered and she shut the door behind him. The room swelled and pulsed with vengeance, as if each spiteful year—slung away by Joanna like 25 boomerangs—had suddenly returned, and she caught one and then the other and then, adroitly, she caught them all, with the triumph of an Olympian. She held them, smoldering with dark memory, feeling the power of her revenge pumping through her veins; feeling the just and rightful moment to puncture his hope and shatter any reconciliation. In that rarified unpitying moment, she worshiped her daughter for what she had done.

The old lovers hesitated, while self-consciously lingering in shadow, searching for words to emancipate the paralysis of the moment.

Joanna found her voice, but it held resentment. "Sit down…anywhere." She purposely did not say his name.

Robert ventured into the living room, viewed the place and sat in the cream colored recliner. Joanna clasped her hands behind her back, took a few steps forward and paused. "Can I get you something?"

Joanna noticed that his face was leaner, his body not as robust as on TV. He had aged, but was still handsome and, whether it was calculated or practiced, he did have a sheen of wisdom about him that surprised her.

"I'd love a scotch if you have it."

"I don't. Maybe I have some vodka. I have wine."

"Wine sounds good," Robert said, with a little nod.

She soon returned with two glasses of red. She handed him one, retiring to the couch, taking a first generous drink.

"We have a lot to talk about, Joanna," Robert said.

"We have very little to talk about, but it's got to be said," she said, curtly.

Robert drank and considered her response. "You know about Matt and Maya."

"Yes."

"That's really why I'm here."

Joanna waited, aware that he'd said nothing about how she looked or how she'd changed. But then she hadn't offered the same about him.

"Like you, I knew nothing about their relationship until a few days ago. I didn't know they were married."

"I didn't know anything until Maya told me last Thursday or Friday," Joanna said. "I've lost track of the days."

"I never dreamed they'd marry…at least not so fast," Robert said. "At first, I thought Maya was using Matt to destroy me. Matt has since convinced me otherwise. He says they're in love and so I believe him. Matt is not a liar. But anyway, whatever the reasons and no matter how crazy all of this is, the fact is that they are married and they want to stay married."

"Stay married?" Joanna asked, with a lift of her elegant eyebrow.

"I was going to get it quickly annulled, before the press got wind of it."

Joanna turned away, taking another drink. "Of course."

"Only because I thought it was motivated by revenge. I didn't want my son hurt or broiled in the media. Especially after what he's recently been through. My son is very dear to me."

Joanna grew boldly belligerent. "Your son? What do you think of your daughter? Any thoughts about her?"

"Of course, Joanna."

She hated the feeling of delight that came from him saying her name. She drank the wine and thought about going to get the bottle. "And what do you think about her?" Joanna repeated. "Our daughter?"

He sat back, staring over her. "She's a beauty. She's a wonder."

"And she looks more like you than me."

Robert lowered his eyes on her. "She has your intelligence, your magnetism and your will."

"And yours," Joanna said, softly.

"Your spirit."

"And yours."

"Your impulsiveness," Robert said.

Joanna waited a moment. "And yours."

They stared, surprised by the reconciliatory shift in the air. Robert turned away for a moment. When he set his eyes on her again, it was a warm, significant look. He shook his head. "I don't know, Joanna…I'm caught in the middle of a lot of things here. In one sense, I couldn't be happier that they got married. In another, I don't know what the hell to do or what to think."

Joanna struggled with emotion—suddenly under the spell of him again—as she had been all those years ago. She didn't want him to see it—and he could always read her moods and her eyes. She stared hard at the floor. "It's all beyond understanding."

"I do want them to be happy," Robert said.

Joanna licked her lower lip. "I had all these big dreams about planning Maya's wedding; being the nervous mom, arguing over the guests, her dress, the menu. All those silly things that I never gave a damn about when I got married."

"I wasn't sure Matt would ever get married," Robert said, spreading his hands. "He seemed so uninterested."

Joanna pouted—mad at herself for not holding her rage. She was knocked off balance by the easy flow of their conversation. They had begun to relax—just as they had always done in those magical wonderful days—content to be alone on the beach and talk, sip wine and make love. They had always been easy together.

They were speaking the familiar language of married people, as if Robert had come home from work and they were discussing the events of the day. But what anchored the moment in intimacy was the fact that they were discussing *their* daughter. Joanna found it thrilling and disturbing. She took more generous sips of wine.

Robert pulled a weary breath and leaned toward her, with the wine glass cradled in his hands. "Joanna…I'm going public with the marriage. I'm going to tell the whole story. That's why I came. I wanted to warn you to leave town for awhile."

Joanna stiffened in alarm. "You can't do that!"

"I have to."

"You don't have to! You know what the press will do. They'll destroy Maya. They'll call their marriage perverted. They'll call it incest." She turned away, shaken. "God, Robert, they'll destroy them!"

"Joanna, the media has Maya's photo. They're tracing her as we speak. Then they'll learn that you're her mother. It can't be contained. It's too late."

Joanna shot up. "Dammit! I hate this world sometimes. I hate the whole goddamn human race and all the gossip and bullshit communication!"

Robert, gently startled by her outburst, remained silent, letting the emotion subside. "Joanna, I've got to move fast, before it all comes out. I have to get it out there first."

Joanna raked her fingers through her hair, sighed out an inevitable despair and sat. "When? When are you going public?"

"Tomorrow night. Thursday. I'll be home. It will be carried on prime time."

Joanna swirled around the remainder of the wine. "Are there any other options?"

"No. None. You should leave tomorrow morning."

Joanna looked at him frankly. "What will this do to your campaign?"

"Well, it won't help it, but we've got two months for damage control. It will be a fight, but that's okay. That's what I signed on for. I'm still the best man for the job and I'll keep shouting it and keep trying to get my message out." He shifted his focus. "But enough of that. I really want you to get out of here."

"I'm not leaving."

"Joanna, listen to me. A tidal wave of media will overwhelm this place. You just said it. They'll tear you apart. There'll be helicopters, vans, cameras, reporters from all over the world surrounding this place, day and night. You will be a prisoner. You'll be harassed. They will smother you."

Joanna finished the wine, anchored the glass on the coffee table and stood, her eyes fixed on him, watchful and searching. "Fools rush in where wise men and wise women never go... That's how the song goes, isn't it?"

He shrugged. "I think so." He didn't understand.

She felt emboldened by the wine—a little high and a little sleepy. "It began so quietly, so privately, so personally, didn't it? Our little affair."

Robert blinked fast and didn't speak.

Joanna stepped behind the couch, still eyeing him. "We seemed so far away from the world 25 years ago, alone on our private little love island. So protected and so blessed. And now—all these years later—the world is rushing in to invade us, to ridicule and destroy everything that was good and true and, if I may use the word, sacred." She gripped the top of the couch and glared at him. "What do you think about that, Robert?"

He looked down. He didn't speak.

"Are you sorry?"

He remained silent.

"Are you sorry that you threw me away like that? Threw away our true love? Threw away a lifetime of love and devotion, and tossed away a daughter who would have worshipped and adored you. And despite all her pain and confusion, she still adores you and worships you because you're her father. Are you sorry? Did you ever think about us through the years of achievement and family and happiness? Did we ever figure—in any way—in your thoughts or future plans, or had we just dried up and blown away like old leaves?"

Robert slumped a little, staring blankly. Finally, after a long interval, he stood and drained his glass. He set the glass down and pocketed his hands. "Joanna, I take responsibility for what I did. I take full responsibility for the destruction of my marriage and for hurting Connie. I'll never forgive myself for that and I will have to live with that guilt and pain for the rest of my life. But the fact is, I fell in love with you and wanted you, and wanted Maya.

"When I left you, all those years ago, to return home to be with my dying mother, I fully intended to return. In fact, I told Connie what had happened…I told her the whole truth the day I returned, because when I saw her, I realized I had never truly been in love before. I had sold out. I had agreed to marry her because of some twisted ideal and because my mother and father pushed it. Connie would be the perfect wife for me they said, and so I guess I believed it and went along. They all said I was destined for greatness and Connie would help me get there. And let's face it, I was, and still am, ambitious.

"But it was adolescent and cruel of me to agree to marry Connie when I didn't love her, and it was callous and selfish not to tell her that. When I got back home, I told her the truth: I told her I was in love with you, because I <u>was</u> in love with you. And I was burning with the truth of it. The joy and intoxication of it. So I told her because I thought it was the right thing to do. The honest thing to do. I had found love—an incredible thing to find in this life. A rare thing. I thought it was best for us all if I cleared the air, told the truth, so we could all get on with our lives.

"My mother was very close to death. A very bad stroke. It was Connie who told my mother that I had fallen in love with another woman and that I was leaving her. Leaving the family. Leaving my work. Abdicating the family honor, name and profession. Leaving everything the family had worked for."

Robert drew a long labored breath. "It was my mother's last wish and request that I not do so. That I not leave Connie and the family. She begged me. She wept. She took my hand and begged me not to split up the family. She thought of Connie as family...as a daughter. She wanted us to get married, right away, before her death. She pleaded with me…begged me."

Robert pulled his hands from his pockets, his eyes remembering with a new kind of anguish. "Well…anyway, my mother died the next day. Before she died, I promised her I'd marry Connie. I promised her I'd stay with Connie."

Joanna was motionless, struck dumb by the stalemate of thought and emotion that couldn't sustain itself, so it fell into an awful silence.

"But that's not all of it, Joanna. My father told me that if I left, he'd see to it that I'd never have a political career. He was viciously angry. We had a terrible argument. The truth is…Joanna, I got scared. I was scared of losing everything. Finally, I made the decision not to come back to you. Frankly, I didn't have the courage…and I'm sorry for that. I'm sorry for so many things."

Robert paused, looking down at the floor. "But I can't say, and I won't say, that I regret our love or that it was wrong. We produced Maya and there is certainly nothing wrong with her. I'm sorry for the pain I caused you and I am truly sorry for the life we could have had together but missed."

Robert took out a handkerchief and wiped his damp forehead. "Maya is a treasure to me, despite this whole mess. And despite everything, my love for you remains strong and true, and it always will." He opened his full loving eyes upon her. "My loving you was the truest thing I've ever done. The best thing I've ever done."

Robert walked to the front door, waiting, head bowed.

Joanna approached. "Robert…I'm sorry about your wife and son. I can't imagine what you must be going through."

Robert opened the door. "Joanna, please leave this place—until all this blows over. The storm is coming. Please prepare for it."

She longed to reach for him—to pull him back 25 years into her 31 year-old arms. They would drift beside the tides and return to the fortunate poetry of warm days and cool nights, where love and fulfillment were the only possible consequences.

After he was gone, she stared at the doorknob. She listened as the car drove away; she listened as an immense silence returned, enveloping her in an embrace of loneliness. Robert had returned as he had said he would. Twenty-five years had passed. His visit had lasted only 25 minutes.

A short time later, Joanna sat on the back deck, wrapped in a warm quilt, sipping wine, pondering where to go. Europe? Canada? South America? She hated the thought of leaving her home.

She dragged herself through the crushingly empty house until, by 11 o'clock, she'd completely changed her mind: now she decided it was a good idea to go away. To travel. To retreat for a long time and, perhaps, never return.

Tears came later—much later—after she'd gone to bed and had nearly drifted off to sleep. She sat up as moonlight crept into her window and amplified a poignant isolation.

Chapter 14

Over the following weeks, the headlines raged:

HARRISON STUNS WORLD ADMITTING OLD AFFAIR AND CHILD!

HARRISON ADMITS BIO DAUGHTER MARRIED ADOPTED SON

BOB HARRISON'S SKELETONS RATTLE COUNTRY

HARRISON KEEPS ILLIGIT DAUGHTER IN LEGIT FAMILY

HARRISON HARRASSED AND HECKLED ON CAMPAIGN TRAIL

HARRISON'S NUMBERS PLUMMET

HARRISON'S MERMAID MISTRESS IS OCCULT ASTROLOGER

HARRISON'S MISTRESS ASTROLOGER FLEES COUNTRY

HARRISON'S BIO DAUGHTER AND ADOPTED SON VANISH

BOB HARRISON FIGHTS ON, VOWING VICTORY

PRESIDENT TAYLOR BLASTS HARRISON'S MORALS

PRESIDENT TAYLOR GAINS IN POLLS

ELECTION NIGHT NEARS, HARRISON'S POLL NUMBERS CLIMB

RECORD NUMBER OF VOTERS REGISTERED

NOW IT'S YOUR TURN TO VOTE

Paula Powers Live aired a special election eve program that began with a clip of her summer interview with Bob Harrison: the famous "Mermaid Rescue Story."

"Well, whoever invented that fairy tale has a very romantic imagination," Bob said. "They should be writing romance novels, not wasting their time fabricating stories on the internet.

"I can assure you that crashing your airplane into the sea, barely surviving, loosing your memory and struggling everyday for 6 weeks to recall even the smallest details of 37 years is not very romantic: it's terrifying."

Paula faced her guests earnestly. "Well, there it is. The question tonight is: will this keep Bob Harrison out of the White House?"

Paula wore a red and white suit. Her hair was shorter, curlier, with copper highlights. She projected a practiced authoritative style, fused with a party girl sheen.

Her two guests were political analysts from past administrations: Karen Webber had been President Howard Taylor's first Press Secretary, but had moved on to the private sector. She was a blond in her late 30's, thin and cautiously affable. James L. Staley had been a speech writer for the previous Republican administration. He often made the rounds of the cable news shows and was known for his explosive enthusiasm, combined with a flinty-eyed realism. He was balding, over 40, and spoke with a southern accent.

"Welcome to you both," Paula said, evenly. "So will Senator Harrison's true confession lose him the election, Karen?"

"It could and I think it will. It's hard to forgive a man who has lied to us for 25 years and surely would have continued to lie to us, if his daughter had not married his adopted son, forcing him to finally tell the truth. A very weird truth. It reveals bad judgment, and hardly shows good leadership. It certainly doesn't build any kind of trust."

James Staley screwed up his lips in distaste. "Oh for crying out loud, Karen, it happened 25 years ago. I hope that in the last two months we've finally dropped this whole tabloid feeding-frenzy. We've all had a lot of laughs, a lot of finger pointing, and a lot of outrage. Okay, fine, now let's move on. For 25 years Bob Harrison has been exemplary. I believe the question we should be asking is: has Bob Harrison shown strength and leadership ability throughout his public career, since his wife's and son's tragic deaths and in making the tough decision to go straight to the American people about a mistake he made 25 years ago. I believe, and I believe the polls show, that most Americans forgive him and want to move on to discuss the serious issues facing this country. I believe most Americans respect his experience, leadership and proven ability to get this country back on track with respect to balancing the ballooning budget; taking on health care and education reform; and making real progress on defeating terrorism."

Paula turned to Karen. "Senator Harrison has gained in the polls, Karen. Most of the recent polls show him only 8 or 9 points behind the President. That's amazing, given that only a month ago, after he went public with 'his confession' as it was called, he was 20 points behind. What do you make of that?"

Karen dismissed the question with a cool expression. "Frankly, what has helped the Senator is the very thing that most of us thought would probably be his undoing: his daughter and son. People are fascinated by them. Fascinated by this whole incestuous thing…"

James was outraged. "Give me a damn break, here, Karen. It is not—in any way—incestuous. Matt Harrison was adopted. Maya is Bob Harrison's blood daughter. I'm really sick and tired of hearing about this. You people on the left—of all people—have gone way too far with this whole thing. Blown it way, way, out of proportion."

Paula swung her attention to Karen. "Does he have a point, Karen?"

"Look, Matt and Maya are attractive, obviously in love and, as one reporter described them recently, they have a dreamy intensity toward each other that's contagious. They've become a kind of Hollywood romance team, whose faces keep appearing on the cover of magazines and on the internet. I mean, it's an incredible story. But, whether James likes it or not, a lot of people in this country are very uncomfortable with their relationship. That's just the way it is.

"But, getting away from that whole messy business, I have to say that Senator Harrison has been effective in attacking President Taylor's staggering budget deficit and foreign policy disasters."

Paula leaned pensively forward. "So, Karen, are you saying that Senator Harrison could still win the presidency?"

"I don't think so. He's still got way too much baggage. People don't want that in the White House. I mean, there are people saying that what if, after he's President, he decides to marry his mistress astrologer, who has run off to Europe? The whole story is just too weird for most Americans." She faced James. "You know that, James. The religious right and the conservatives hate this whole dog and pony show. I still hear them say that Bob Harrison would have never gotten the nomination if they'd known all of this before the convention."

James waved her away. "No, look, what the conservatives, the moderates, and the independents all have in common is that they respect Bob Harrison's courage, leadership and experience. Again, all this stuff happened 25 years ago. I dare anybody—who's old enough—to go back 25 years in their own life and remember their own indiscretions. And to the religious right I say, 'He who has not sinned let him throw the first damned stone.'"

Karen said, "James, it may have happened a long time ago but the ramifications are still with us. We still don't know what kind of relationship his daughter, Maya, has with her father. There are reports that they don't even talk."

"That's gossip, Karen. What the hell does that have to do with running the country?"

"Because it shows that Bob Harrison can't even run his private life," she tossed back.

There was a slight tightening of James' neck muscles and an upward twitch of his left eyebrow. "Oh for Pete's sake, give the man a break. Who doesn't have problems with their kids, wives, husbands, cousins and hound dogs? That's life. Look, his daughter supports him; his son supports him and most Americans support him. They know that he has the ability to run this country and get us back to the basics of balancing the budget, creating jobs, and fighting global terrorism the smart way. He will do that and most Americans know it. That's why he's climbing in the polls. How many people do you know could have gone through what Bob Harrison has gone through in the past few months and still be standing, let alone, thriving and battling his way back from the brink of a political disaster. Bob Harrison will be the next President because Americans have seen that when push comes to shove, he's a winner. Americans do not want another four years of bloated do-nothing government, filled with cronyism, corruption and incompetence."

Paula clasped her hands together. "We'll have to leave it there. Thank you both." She presented herself to the camera. "Now, America, it's your turn. We have been told that this election could produce a record turn-out. We hope that you will take advantage of one of our most cherished and envied liberties and go to the polls tomorrow and vote. We will have live coverage of the election, beginning tomorrow morning at 5 am. That's our show. Thank you and good night."

Chapter 15

On Election Day, it was overcast. The clouds were thick and heavy with the promise of rain; the air brisk and chilly. Bob Harrison voted near his Connecticut home at 8 o'clock in the morning, and then returned there to watch the election results. In the evening, he'd be driven to the Sheraton Hotel, only 10 miles away, to join his supporters and prepare for his speech, whether it be victory or concession.

Matt and Maya voted in Manhattan. Matt would join his father at the hotel that evening, but Maya would stay behind with friends, afraid that together, she and Matt would be a detraction.

By afternoon, it rained, gently at first, and then hard and steady. Bob pulled back the curtains and stared at it, feeling vaguely detached from it all, hearing Carlton in the background cursing the weather and fuming as he drank his third cup of coffee in an hour.

Joanna had voted by absentee ballot and had mailed it from Rome, two weeks before the election. On Election Day she was in Paris, where she'd taken a one-bedroom apartment for a month, in a traditional Paris building on the quiet Rue Lacharriere. It was a short walk to the Metro stations of Saint-Ambroise, Saint-Maur or Richard-Lenoir. She could visit the Champs Elysees, the Opera or the Bastille in minutes, if she wanted to, but most days she wandered aimlessly, often ending up at a cafe.

On Tuesday evening, at around 8 o'clock—Election Day in the United States— Joanna sat alone at the La Rotisserie du Beaujolais and ate dinner. It faced the Seine near Notre Dame. Good wine and rotisserie dishes were their specialty. She could see the vertical glass rotisserie in the dining room along the back wall adjacent to the kitchen. She ordered onion soup and the chicken.

As she looked about, she was sure that she was the only American in the place. An attractive salt-and-pepper-haired man with a sharp jaw and dancing blue eyes smiled at her once, and nodded a flirtatious hello a little later. Each time, the attractive woman he was with had either left for the bathroom or was engaged in conversation with her girlfriend. Joanna did not respond to him, but she was flattered and became self-conscious.

For dessert, she ordered tarte tatin. She finished off the dinner with an Armagnac, and a final glance at the Frenchman as he escorted the two women through the dining room and out the front door. He did not look back at her.

Joanna walked the streets, face turned from the gathering wind, raincoat flapping, a white silk scarf knotted at her throat. She missed Maya and, from this vast safe distance, she allowed tender feelings for Robert to warm her and keep her company as she wandered aimlessly—a little high from the wine and Armagnac—a little high from old memories, regrets and old desires.

As she paused to take in the spires of Notre Dame, she wondered if Robert would become the next president—the most powerful man in the world—and she reflected back to the night on her deck when he'd spoken about it and recalled how deeply she'd fallen in love with him.

She wondered if Maya and Matt's marriage would survive the white heat of publicity. She and Maya spoke frequently and Maya said she had grown weary of it; weary of the whole media circus and blizzard of requests for interviews and book deals. She'd said that she and Matt had been arguing about the smallest of things. They were tired of moving and hiding and dodging cameras and reporters. Matt was carrying tremendous guilt about his father and the marriage and hadn't been sleeping well.

Joanna had seen Maya's and Matt's faces in some of the European magazines, along with short blurbs of half truths and speculation. She'd even seen her own photo—a bad one—in an Italian newspaper a few weeks back. The headline read: *L'astrologo - Amante del Candidato* (The Candidate's Lover). A French paper went a little further with the headline *L'Astrologue - Putain du Candidat* (The Candidate's Whore Astrologer).

Joanna ambled on in a light mist. Lovers passed, arms wrapped at the waist and shoulders. They whispered secrets and smiled desire. A soft gleam of recognition opened upon Joanna's face. As they approached, she slowed and watched, until they felt her eyes on them. Embarrassed, Joanna looked down and away and hurriedly crossed the street. But she turned once more to watch their retreating figures fade away from the soft glow of the streetlights, and her face fell into melancholy.

It was time to go home.

Chapter 16

Bob Harrison stood on stage, behind the podium, before the wilted crowds, delivering his concession speech. Standing resolute behind him were Matt and John Cahill. The bloated ballroom of drained supporters stood suspended in disbelief, shock and flowing tears. Reporters and cameras documented the bitter, straining reality.

The glistening chandeliers, the colored balloons, the bold posters that shouted HARRISON FOR PRESIDENT and held Bob's broad, assured smile all bore witness to a bitter truth:

Bob Harrison had lost Florida. He had lost Ohio. He had lost the South and much of the Midwest. He had called President Taylor and congratulated him.

To his downcast supporters, Bob told them they had fought the good fight. They had made a difference and they would continue to make a difference.

"Let us not forget," Bob said, forcefully, "that freedom does not come cheaply. It has to be fought for, challenged, reinvented and worked at every day. And that's what we have done in this campaign and will continue to do in the months and years to come. And tonight, we honor all Americans who voted for us and who also voted for President Taylor."

Bob waited for the boos to subside, and he patted them back with his raised hand.

"We honor the Americans who made the effort to let their voices be heard to keep this great experiment called the United States of America a vibrant, shining example to the rest of the world."

Bob thanked and praised his supporters. He pledged to work with the President as a Senator to get the country back on track.

As Bob approached the end of his speech, he felt his breath change. He felt a precarious shift in his emotions. He felt Connie's presence rebuking him, judging him. He felt Robert Jr.'s disappointed eyes glaring at him. He stumbled over the last words of his speech and forced the brightest of smiles, feeling a malignant disappointment.

Bob glanced out over the worshiping crowd once more and nodded, remembering the good fun and the vanished gaieties of so many days and nights. He was profoundly sorry that he had failed them so completely. He waved, thanked them, finally, and withdrew from the lights, from the thunderous applause and from a political ambition that had begun nearly 30 years ago.

Epilogue

1 Year Later

Fifty-seven-year-old Joanna Halloran stared restlessly out the open bedroom window of her beach house on Montauk. The November sky and sea were a glossy gray, like a new oil painting, still wet and hauntingly moody. An outburst of frenzied snow had come and gone, leaving a moaning, unpredictable wind.

Joanna gripped her cell phone—turned it over in her hand, like an uncomfortable thought incarnate—and searched for herself in the mirror. Still attractive? Yes. She thought so. The new hairstyle helped: short on the sides, longer on top. Blond highlights. She'd had her nails done. She'd lost 10 pounds. Hatha Yoga at the Yoga Center in town had helped tighten her tummy and accent her elegant neck.

Joanna returned her gaze to the expanse of sea, finding courage by inhaling a few deep breaths. She'd stood in the same spot yesterday—with the phone—and the day before and the day before that. She mulled over possibility and conversation.

On the table next to her lay an e-mail with a phone number. She swallowed. She dialed. She waited, pulse throbbing. After the fourth ring, her thumb was poised to disconnect the call. But she heard a voice: his voice.

"This is Robert…"

"…Robert?" she said, weakly.

"Yes…? Who's this?"

"Robert, this is Joanna…Joanna Halloran."

His voice rose a little. "Joanna! What a nice surprise."

Joanna began circling the room. "I hope you don't mind that I called. I got your cell phone number from Matt."

"Of course I don't mind. It's good to hear from you. How are you?"

"I'm good…you know. I'm good. And you? How are you?"

"No complaints, except the usual complaints of a man pushing 60 wishing he were 30 again."

Joanna laughed a little. "Oh, God, yes, I know that feeling." Joanna took a quick breath. "Look…Robert. I…a…well, look, I wanted to offer you—invite you—that is, if you want to… I wanted to invite you over for Thanksgiving."

It was so silent, Joanna heard the sea. "Matt and Maya are coming and I just thought that maybe…maybe you'd like to join us. Believe me, I certainly understand if you don't want to come. Matt said you always go to Wisconsin…"

"…Michigan," he corrected.

"Yes, Michigan. He said you always go there to be with your family on Thanksgiving, but I thought I'd offer."

"…Joanna, I'm very grateful that you asked."

Joanna heard rejection in his voice.

"Do the kids know that you're asking me?"

"Yes… I told them."

"I see. Matt and I haven't seen much of each other since they moved to Colorado. He's so busy being the young professor and, of course, I couldn't be more pleased. I suppose you know that Maya seldom ever talks to me when he calls. Actually, I haven't spoken to her in weeks. And I don't want to make problems for them. They've struggled as it is."

"Yes, they have."

"I don't think Maya would want me to come and spoil the day, Joanna. And I don't want to make it difficult for Matt. Things have finally settled down for them. It's taken a year."

"Robert… Maya is pregnant."

"Pregnant!?"

"Yes, she told me yesterday. Matt was going to call you. I told him I'd like to call and tell you first."

Robert was silent.

"Robert…Maya said she wanted to see you. She said she thought it would be nice if we were all together."

More silence.

"If you want to come…Robert, if you want to come, I'd like to see you."

His voice was unsteady. "Would you?"

"Yes."

Joanna stopped pacing and waited, switching the phone from her left ear to her right.

Joanna heard him sigh gently into the phone. "Then I'd like to come, Joanna. I'd like to come very much."

On Thanksgiving Day, Joanna's house smelled of clove, pumpkin spice and turkey. Matt hauled the kitchen table into the living room, making sure the dunes, the rolling dune fences and the sea were clearly visible from every seat. He covered the table with a white table cloth. Maya created the centerpiece: brown and gold leaves, yellow and green gourds, sea shells and some scattered dried cranberries.

Maya fussed in the kitchen, worried that the apple pie was overdone and that the turkey was going to be too dry. Joanna perspired and fretted; she directed the team with precision and an occasional "Calm down and let's just enjoy ourselves."

At exactly 1 o'clock, the doorbell rang. Joanna jumped, Maya froze and Matt stiffened. Joanna pulled off her apron, smoothed out her chic cranberry-colored dress and started for the door.

She patted her hair, lifted her chin and opened the door, feeling perspiration trickling down her back.

Robert stood awkwardly, a large bouquet of flowers cradled in one arm and two bottles of wine in the other. "Hello," he said, standing awkwardly. "I didn't know what to bring."

"You didn't need to bring anything."

They shuffled between uneasy glances and slim, hopeful smiles.

Inside, Joanna took the flowers and wine as Matt and Maya crept toward them, hesitant and ill at ease. Matt went to his father and Robert bear-hugged him. Maya, with hands twisting behind her back, waited. When her father drew near, she was breathless. He leaned, kissing her softly on her cheek. She closed her eyes and blushed.

"Happy Thanksgiving, Maya," Robert said, in a private whisper.

He straightened, squaring his shoulders, seeking relief from tension. "And congratulations to you both on the baby. What a nice surprise!"

They all stood fidgeting, their eyes moving restlessly.

Robert joined in the preparations. Most conversation began haltingly with wordless smiles and half-finished sentences. They were all careful or effusive with words and expressions, side-stepping any themes of the past. Robert carved the turkey, Matt opened and poured the wine and Joanna and Maya placed the food on the table and lit the long white tapered candles. Maya selected the CDs: James Taylor's *October Road*, *Torch Songs*, by various female singers, and a selection of *Concerti Grossi* by Handel, requested by her mother.

After they were seated, Joanna suggested a moment of thankful silence, mostly to help calm her racing heart. They ate slowly, using few words, except to compliment the food and wine. The weather was discussed. It was cloudy, but surprisingly, for this time of year, not too cold. Matt talked about Colorado State University, where he was teaching history. He said his classes were full and, unfortunately, the questions most his students had asked had nothing to do with history. He left his true meaning hanging in the air, and everyone understood and avoided any retort.

Joanna complimented the French wine and said she'd like to return to France and travel through Provence.

Maya and her father spoke formally; their conversation was stilted and Joanna jumped in whenever a huge gap of silence made everyone reach for their wine or water glasses.

Eventually, the wine helped to ease the tight nerves and soften hard-edged memories. Maya's searching eyes found her father's and when he smiled at her and asked her how she felt being pregnant, she leaned toward him and carefully, procedurally, explained everything she'd learned about babies growing in the womb.

"I did a lot of research on the internet and then Matt brought tons of articles and magazines home."

Joanna watched their faces relax and their conversation grow natural. She grew warm with love for them, feeling a sweetness of heart. Matt noticed and he nodded knowingly at her.

Robert expanded tenderly in Joanna's eyes, his graying hair, the deepening wrinkles; his countenance rounded by triumph, defeat and experience. Joanna watched him lovingly and thought: "Was age so bad after all? Was youth, with its wild hormones, flaming emotion and stifling confusion, really so much better?"

Joanna leaned back in her chair and listened to the three of them talk and discuss and laugh. She cut the apple pie and poured the coffee, while they bantered on, no longer depriving themselves of the pleasure of being in each other's company.

After the cleanup, Joanna suggested a walk. Maya and Matt declined. Robert agreed.

They wore warm coats and red and blue ski caps that Joanna kept on pegs next to the rain slickers and umbrellas. As they left the house, Robert wanted to see the old cottage. Joanna warned him that she'd ignored it for years. Under white and gray stringy clouds, they trudged the old path, snapping old twigs and side-stepping withered shrubs and sharp rocks. Joanna saw the excitement of memory on Robert's face as they advanced in a quickening pace.

When they broke through the brush to the clearing, they stopped. Robert's shoulders slumped a little. The little cottage was crippled and had wilted into ruin.

"Too bad," Robert said, sorrowfully, as he shuffled toward it, hands pushed into his jacket pockets. "I had such fun working on this little place. Such good memories here." He slowly circled it, head down, as if he were involved in his own secret ritual. When he returned to the entrance, he sighed.

"Robert?"

He faced her.

"Remember the old dream you used to have? The one where the egg fell from the nest and was going to shatter?"

"Yes…"

"Did it finally go away?"

"Yes. I took your advice and every time it appeared, I pictured myself beneath the tree ready to catch the egg. It worked. I caught it—every time—and finally, after a few months, it went away and never returned."

Joanna strolled over, appraising the damage. "A little paint here and there might do wonders, you know."

He looked at her doubtfully. "I don't think so, Joanna. It's finished. Have to build an entirely new cottage."

She winked at him. "Yeah…that could be done, too."

He smiled, affectionately. "How's the astrology business?"

"Good. I have another book coming out in a few months."

"I'm glad to hear that. I'm glad you're doing well."

By the time they had descended the staircase and stepped down onto the beach, a new light had changed the day. The sun struck the sea golden and warmed the air. The waves rolled in calm and soothing.

Matt and Maya left the house and walked toward the edge of the staircase. They peered down, watching Joanna and Robert drift away, roaming the edge of the tide.

"What do you think they're talking about?" Maya asked.

"No idea," Matt said. "Maybe he's telling her that he's leaving the Senate and politics for good."

"Is he?"

"Yeah. He said he wants to take it easy for awhile. He said he wants to try and find his own voice. And don't ask me what that means because I have no idea."

"Maybe she's telling him that her books are selling better than her father's ever did," Maya said.

"Maybe they're not talking at all," Matt said, as he wrapped a gentle arm around Maya's shoulders and drew her close. "Sometimes, you don't have to say a thing and you just know…"

Maya's face formed a question as she watched her parents drift and wander, hands stuffed in their jacket pockets. Maya and Matt exchanged a hopeful glance and started back toward the house.

Robert and Joanna meandered on awhile and then stopped. They faced each other and laughed. Not a belly laugh. It was something deliciously covert. Perhaps it was an old memory revisited or, more likely, it was the sudden recognition of a hard-earned humor and contentment that comes with age, after years of struggle, confusion and pain. Maya and Matt wouldn't have understood it, because it is a mysterious island that the young can never inhabit.

After toeing at the sand and examining the beach, Joanna and Robert moved on, under a freshening sky.

The End

Made in the USA
Monee, IL
04 April 2021

64784093R00219